The Guardians

S. Lee Holland

ZAMIZ PRESS

To my son Andrew,
who even from the other side,
inspires me still.

ATTENTION READERS

Not your typical Christian fiction.
This book includes subject matter to provide cautionary
direction against profanity, drugs, sexual
encounters and violence.

Chapter One

Life can be tricky. That's especially true if you're a teenager. It takes strategy, camouflage, inborn navigation skills and a lot of fashion sense if you're hoping to find your way through the maze of high school land mines. And that's just the beginning if you want to end up in the popular group. But I'd done it.

At Pinedale High, I was Cassie Conner, also known as "the girl dating Nathan." And let's face it, that's what actually made me popular. But that was fine with me. Because when you're at the top, people don't look down on you—and it's beneath everything visible, where all the stuff is hidden. Things I didn't want others to see, and truthfully, stuff I didn't want to look at, either.

When I moved to Pinedale, Oregon, over a year earlier, I couldn't imagine why my dad had chosen this god-forsaken town for us. In fact, I'm not sure he even knew. He'd probably seen the trees and the sweet looking house in the real estate ad and imagined it a lovely place for us to live after he'd gone. Because he knew he was going to die. I knew it too, but he was more than my dad; he was my best friend. And so, I refused to look at it; I believed God would save him. You see, before the disease took his life, he'd been a scientist. What made him different from most of his colleagues was he'd also been a deep and true believer in God. And everything my father had been, or done, seemed perfect to me—so, I also chose to believe. Only an innocent child can believe and trust the way I did. But the combination of hero worship and blind faith ended up causing me to stumble. When he died from ALS, I felt as if God had betrayed us all.

Looking back, I realize everyone deals with pain differently. After my dad's death, I found a way to forget— don't ask me how, I still don't understand it—but every single one of my former memories were gone. At the time, it was great. Also, my ability to hide feelings and thoughts from others became an art form. And although I didn't realize it at the time, I was scared, which caused my inner voice to be *pret-ty* hostile. I guess I knew I wasn't completely "right," but honestly, I didn't even know what that meant.

Since my dad's death, my mom had become dependent on pills to relax her, pills to make her sleep, and pills to ease her pain. Her speech was at times incoherent, which went right along with her mind. She was probably trying to be normal, but I could tell she was losing *that* battle. Even though I didn't show it, this totally freaked me out. ...*And then there was my sister Tessa.*

Tessa had such a high IQ, it was almost guaranteed she'd be a nerd. I think I could have lived with that, but her looks were peculiar. I mean, unless you happened to be a fan of short, bushy-haired girls in strange clothing, she was *not* terribly attractive.

Tessa claimed she gave her appearance no thought— however, I had a hard time buying that. She consistently wore outfits of horrific combinations defying even random selection. Still, somehow, she wasn't your typical geek. Nope, she was worse.

Unfortunately for me, Tessa, like my father, was also a Christian. She'd blindly maintained her innocent, misguided faith in God. I did my best to put up with this and for the most part ignore it. But the truth is, even if I were to hold up my old child's faith next to the ridiculous, unquestioning faith of my younger sister, I might as well have called myself a heathen. But that wasn't the worst of it—not by far.

Six months after moving to Pinedale she had a vision. Actually, it was more than that. It was a visitation; it would have been so much easier if it had been a dream, or even a delusion. And it wasn't the comforting kind of visitation one might imagine when thinking of a sweet angelic being, either. No, I'd soon find out that her encounter was a radiant-light-command-from-on-high visit, and not the hallucination I really would have preferred.

When she first came to me with tales of seeing an angel, obviously I thought she was nuts. It also infuriated me. This was just one more proof that the Connor women were a couple sandwiches short of a picnic. Of course, I threw everything I had at her, including ridiculing her mercilessly. At the time, cruelty seemed my last defense against the onslaught of insanity. But when my father placed his finger on the picture in the real estate ad, no one could have guessed that an angel was standing at his shoulder, pointing him to the little home near a circle of trees in the woods, guiding his heart to choose...

∽

It was a fall evening when Tessa tiptoed into my room for a late-night chat—a conversation that seemed, and still does, a foreshadowing of events to come. A squeaky door opening just a crack, an invitation over a threshold.

"Cassie, you awake?"

"Yea, sure." I said, as I propped my head on my arm.

"Whatcha thinkin' about?" Tessa asked, her spiky ringlets frothing around her head like clouds of brown coils, as she climbed onto my bed.

"Just stuff. Nothing much," I answered. She sat silently eyeing me behind her large glasses, and I knew she'd stay until I gave her more. "Oh, you know; like how weird Mom has become," I relented, knowing she'd wait me out. "I thought moving away was supposed to help her," I continued, "but she's had plenty of time. Do you know what I found her doing today? She was sitting in her room with a brown paper bag over her head. I think she's losing it, Tess."

"Yea, I saw that, too. When I asked her about it, she said it helped her concentrate on 'nothing.' Maybe it's like meditation," Tessa added, and I could hear the ridiculous hope in her voice.

"Uh huh, and maybe her brain is hyperventilating. You know she walks around the house most of the night. She's always rustling around with something, but in the morning, everything is exactly the way it was when we went to bed. There aren't even crumbs or dirty dishes anywhere. I can't figure out what she does." But before Tessa could answer, I added, "You realize these are troubling signs."

"Of what?"

"I think our mother is...let's just say she has a very troubled mind."

"I don't know, ...I think she's looking for something."

We sat in silence for several seconds. As I looked at Tessa's small, obscure figure in the semi-dark room, I began feeling the same senseless anger. "Why don't you dress better and do *something* with your hair?" I blurted.

"It's not the way I look that bothers you. It never bothered you before," Tessa answered, turning slightly and looking away.

"You were younger then. So was I. You're older now and in high school it's not easy. But if you start now, you'll have a chance to be somebody...to make the right friends," I'd left out "because of me," but we both knew those unspoken words hung between us. "...And Tessa, you're going to blow it!" I ended.

"I have friends; but thanks, anyway," Tessa said, a little smile curving her mouth.

"Don't be obtuse...you know exactly what I mean," I said.

Tessa's smile grew larger, her small white teeth glowing in the dark.

"What? You don't think I know that word? It means slow-witted. It's only in math you kick my butt so hard." I said defensively.

"Really? Hmm, I kick your '*butt so hard?*'" She asked, cocking her head to the side. "It's kinda funny that you never use all the big words you know when you're with your friends," she added.

"That's because I know how to act... Oh, stay on topic! I'm talking about making *cool* friends, and not your band of geeks. You'll end up on the lowest level of the pecking order." I knew I was being mean, but I also knew if I didn't intervene, she'd be lost.

Tessa took my hands, and in a teasing voice said, "Be honest. What really makes them 'cool'? That they peck-on-people?"

I almost laughed out loud, and I would have if part of me hadn't been so flipping mad. "Grow up!" I pulled my hands away. "There are rules. That's life! If you play by them, you'll get somewhere. You've already been pegged as a nerd for being so smart. Then there's the personal statement you make every day." I held up my fingers in the dark, jabbing them as I continued making my points, "tangled hair, goofy clothes, and zero even *semi*-popular friends. *Zero*." I took the last index finger and made a very round "O" with it and my thumb, as if my math-whiz sister needed help with the math. "I'm telling you; I watch it every day, and I'm warning you Tessa, your life in high school will be a living hell!" I sat looking at her, but I couldn't tell if I was getting through or not.

After a few seconds she sighed and said, "You're purposely being mean, Cassie. And I guess I'd be mad at you, but you're wrong. You don't believe me, but my life isn't hell now, and it won't be then. I know people can be cruel...I know life is hard, but," and then she lowered her voice to a whisper which I could barely hear, "if anyone's in tr..b.l. .ts n.. me."

"What did you say? Do you think I'm the one in trouble!?" I asked, shocked by her statement.

"Never mind," she said, wisely ending that conversation. Then completely out of the blue, as though we'd been talking about some totally boring subject, she said, "I need to tell you something important. I know you don't believe me—and think I'm making it up—but it happened again. He came."

And there it was...*the crazy*. "Crap. You mean, he-who-won't-tell-you-his-name? Well, I don't want to hear about it!" I yelled, unable to control my rising irritation.

Tessa looked at me steadily. "You*'ve* got to listen to me. It concerns you...and a lot of other people. Something important is coming... I don't know what... but he said, '*it's time.*' He said he's going to speak to *you*! In the Pine Circle..."

"Jesus Christ, Tessa! Now isn't this just great? I guess you and Mom can be *roomies* in the nuthouse!"

"*Don't say that!*" Tessa said sternly, looking squarely in my face.

I knew my "nuthouse" remark hadn't bothered Tessa. She was upset because I'd used the Lord's name profanely.

"You know what? You're starting to sound like 'preacher Jack.' *'Cassie, don't take the Lord's name in vain',*" I mimicked. "And *he* is such a *pain*," I said, glaring at her.

I remembered when we'd first moved to Pinedale; it was the beginning of summer. I didn't know a soul my own age, and absolutely nothing looked or felt familiar. Everything even smelled funny, in a frightening, outdoorsy way. Just as I'd given up all hope, new neighbors moved onto the property next to ours.

The first time I'd laid eyes on Jackson Graham, he was unloading their moving truck. Jack looked to be about my age, and I was to discover he was only a year older, just like Nathan. I really didn't know what it was about him, but I found myself staring and unable to look away. Of course, I quickly decided it was the effect of being abandoned in a forest town and bored out of my mind —not his black hair tipped brown in the sun, or his grey eyes, changing from dusky to light, or his masculine kind of attractiveness, the kind with more character than perfect features. No, it had to be my situation. Because before I had a chance to waste too much time mooning over him, I found out Jack had embraced the weird. Jack was a devout Christian. It was a shock, and I'll admit, a disappointment, to find out he was as over-the-edge as my sister.

Jack had *chosen* to be home-schooled. He could quote scripture *and did*. It was downright embarrassing, because, like my sister, he never cared who heard him. Still, I allowed myself to have fun that summer, mainly because no one was around to see us. But I had to admit that something was different about him. He was sincere; he was honestly nice, and he genuinely liked me, even though he had the surprising ability to see behind my mask.

I'd found myself drawn to him but repulsed by his need for God. Then, thankfully, summer came to an end, and I began my junior year at Pinedale High. In my whole life I'd never looked as forward to the beginning of the school year as I did that summer. By escaping to high school, I distanced myself from Jack's undeniable charm... And, more importantly, I met Nathan.

Tessa was looking down at her hands, and I thought for a minute I'd actually succeeded in making her cry. Then she looked up, her eyes dry and flashing even in the darkness.

"I don't believe you've given up on him," she stated matter-of-factly.

"Well, I have. Jack's a loser."

"I'm not talking about Jack. I'm talking about God."

I felt something unexpectedly catch in my chest. Her claim that I still believed in God shouldn't have bothered me, but it had. I managed to keep my face composed. Tapping my chin lightly, I said, "Well, gee, let me think. Have I given up on God? ...God, who supposedly loves us and cares for us? And, oh wait, *He made* us, yet He sits around and doesn't do anything except watch us while we suffer. Hmmm, ya know what? I think the answer would be, *YES, I've given up on Him!* And being a Christian is not only stupid, it's pathetic! I don't see how you, of all people, can believe in Him? Aren't geniuses like you and Dad supposed to be able to deduct simple equations? Why am I the one to figure it out? How come you're being so dense? Don't you see that you couldn't deal with what happened to Dad, and now you can't deal with Mom, so you've gone and invented an angel?" When she sat silently looking at me without so much as blinking, I continued. "Come on, I know you're smart enough to figure out, at least for believability purposes, you could have given your angel a name!"

"I didn't invent him. And I told you, he has a name. It's just too hard for humans to pronounce—"

"Yea, Mi-chael, that's a toughie. And Ga-bri-el. Wow, total tongue twister," I said, mocking her.

"You're afraid to come with me to the Pine Circle and find out." She said, not rising to the bait.

"OK. And if I go, and this 'angel' *doesn't* show, will you renounce God?"

"Of course not."

"Right," I smiled knowingly, "then I'm not going."

"If you do, he *will* come."

"I don't believe you for one second," I said, hoping Tessa couldn't read my strange inner turmoil. Though, she ignored my comment, after a moment she said,

"Jack misses you."

I automatically looked out my window and down the street toward Jack's house. The remark caught me off-guard, and once again, I felt that tightening in my chest. "*Come on, Tessa!* He's homeschooled...how weird is that? He doesn't have any friends, and when he can't figure something out, he hides behind his Bible. I've tried explaining it all, but for some reason you're beyond help. Plus, you know I *have* a boyfriend." At this, Tessa groaned, and this time, *I* ignored her. For some reason she'd never explain to me, Tessa didn't like Nathan.

"I need someone fun, not somebody who's always concerned about doing the *right thing*. Don't you get it? Jack wants me to believe like he does—and I can't—and I don't want to! Why should I believe in something so unreliable? Because if there is a God, then we're just some bizarre experiment gone whacko."

"The only experimenting is on our part ...when we do things our way instead of God's. That's what makes things whacko!" Tessa said, emphatically. "It never works, and you won't ever be OK, Cassie! Everything will just get worse!" The outline of her head against the moonlight made it look like her hair had exploded for effect.

I groaned. "Oh, my Gaw... Things are great! Just go to bed. I don't want to talk anymore," I said, lying back down and rolling over, clearly dismissing her. Tessa sat for a moment longer. Then, sliding off the bed, she walked to the door. I knew her well enough to know she wasn't going to leave me alone without sharing one more brilliant morsel—and I wanted to empty my lungs with a scream. But I was sure I'd bring Pinedale's finest, squalling through town in all four vehicles up to our curb in search of a murder victim.

"Ya know," Tessa said, "No matter what people think, Jack's smarter than Nathan. And Jack can fix just about anything. He's homeschooled because he wants to be. And yes, he reads the Bible a lot, but he stands up for his beliefs too," she continued without a breath, "He may not have a lot of friends, but *you* were his friend this summer...and most important, he was *your* friend when you didn't have anybody else." She ended and was quiet for ten full seconds. I almost thought she'd gone when I heard the door closing and her small voice whisper, "and he's not the only one who misses you."

I lay listening to the house creak in the wind for a very long time. My mom, the confused, aging, beauty queen, Maggie Connor, had begun moving about downstairs, opening drawers, rustling through who-knows-what, and closing them... Searching.

I imagined Tessa in her bed; her hands tucked inward under her chin as she slept, and her words began echoing in my mind, *"he's not the only one who misses you..."* I knew I had changed, but I knew I was better for it. At least I hoped I was better... And then, I couldn't help wondering if maybe I wasn't as happy as I'd thought. For the first time in a very long time, for no reason I could explain, I had to hold back the tears—tears I'd refused to give into since my father's death—until sleep finally came. ...A sleep without comfort.

Chapter Two

The next day, even though it was a glorious fall weekend, and I should have been elsewhere enjoying the beauty of nature—specifically shopping with my friends—I finally finished all my jobs. I'd cleaned my room, vacuumed the floor, mowed the front patch of lawn, and swept the porch. I was hugely tired after all that hard work. But all I had left to do was my laundry. I carried my plastic hamper filled with dirty clothes downstairs and through the kitchen. "Would you put these in the dryer for me when you hear the washing machine beep? I need to go upstairs and take a bath," I called to Tessa as she came through the front door. Her dark hair looked electrified, and her large glasses were slipping down her nose.

"Sure. But why are you taking a bath now?" She asked, coming into the kitchen, opening the refrigerator and pulling out one of the caramel apples she'd made earlier in the day.

"Well, not that it's any of your bee's wax," I quipped, crossing over to the laundry room and loading the clothes into the machine, "but I'm going to spend the night with Jenna and Brittany."

"No, you're not," she answered. I could tell by the quick intake of breath, and the way she clamped her lips together after speaking, that the words had slipped out of her mouth before she could stop herself.

"Excuse me?" I said, stepping into the kitchen and looking at her suspiciously.

"I mean, uh... have y... you a...asked Mom?" she stammered.

"Asked me what?" Mom said, walking into the kitchen carrying groceries. Her shoulder length hair, once dark and glossy, now had gray strands woven through the loose tangles. And despite her beautiful eyes, straight nose and high cheekbones, her beauty looked tired. It was as if though pain had caused her to age beyond her years. I shot Tessa a wilting look, then smiled sweetly at my mother.

"Oh, no big deal. I was just going to ask if I could spend the night at Brittany's house. The three of us are going to a movie tonight," I lied. It was scary how easily these fabrications...uh lies...were beginning to roll off my tongue.

"Why is it, I haven't ever met these girls, Cassie?" Mom asked.

"Because you're rarely feeling well enough to have them over," I replied coolly, knowing it was at least half the truth.

"I'm feeling better today. Why don't they come over here tonight?" she asked, as I headed toward the stairs and blessed escape.

"Mom, it's already set. But thanks. We'll do that next time."

Mom only nodded, then went over to the sink, and taking two pills out of her sweater pocket popped them into her mouth. "Would I like these girls?" she asked, turning to look at me as I headed up the stairs.

"Of course!" I replied, trying not to sound irritated.

"No." Tessa said under her breath. Mom sighed and went to her room to lie down.

"What is with you, anyway?" I hissed, whirling on Tessa.

"I don't think she'd like them, that's all," Tessa said evenly.

"No, *you* don't like them because *they* think you're weird —*which you are*. And just why did you say I wasn't going out with them tonight?" I asked suspiciously.

"Because the angel wants to see you..."

"Holy crap, I rest my case," I said, storming up the stairs. Slamming my door, barely loud enough to make my point, and not nearly hard enough to vent my frustration at having to live in a nuthouse, I went over and turned my stereo on full blast. I walked into my little bathroom and began filling the tub. I poured bubble bath under the pounding spout of hot water, and I couldn't help wondering if any of my friends felt like I did: on the verge of coming unglued. I got undressed and began thinking about the "hypothetical" process of "coming unglued". I decided it would be hard to recognize its start in someone else, since I'd easily become good at covering up my own feelings.

I slid into the water and began pondering this in another way. What if, when bits of a personality started detaching, infinitesimally small molecules began slipping and falling off in hallways, fields, or classrooms? It wasn't something I could prove, but it could just be possible that under stress very, very, tiny, even microscopic pieces of a personality-in-crisis could begin flaking off—over lots of places—until the person was obviously *coming unglued.* Then, calling someone a 'flake,' would actually be a perfect term. Smiling, I wondered what crazy formula my dad would have written up for me. I had plenty of examples, stuck randomly in books, of silly equations he'd written whenever I must have come to him with one of my stupid theories. I shook my head, wondering why I'd recalled that tidbit from my past, and I slid up to my nose in the bubbly water, trying with all my might not to dwell on the possibility of flakiness being a family trait.

My father, Dr. Connor, had been a brilliant and well-known research scientist working for the Lawrence Berkeley National Laboratory in what was known as the Molecular Foundry at the National Center for Electron Microscopy. It had taken me a long time to memorize *that* job description. He was a scientist whose favorite dates were with his beakers in the lab, but according to the stories, from the moment my mom—a past beauty queen courted by a flock of wealthy men—met my dad on a dance floor at a friend's wedding, they'd never spent another day apart. In all fairness, when I say that Mom isn't exactly a rocket scientist, I do it knowing I take after her, and Tessa after my father. And it's not that mom is ...inept; not exactly; but without dad, she'd become confused...and that's putting it mildly.

So, of course, the more I tried to put the idea of genetic shedding out of my mind, the more I thought about it; and when I began to wonder if a paper bag would help, I started getting scared.

Suddenly, images completely out of the blue began pouring into me: early evening...I was maybe six at the time... sitting in the pew of our old church...waiting while my dad spoke with the pastor...a stained-glass window of Jesus' face, simple, beautiful, with light flooding through it. Until this moment I'd forgotten how I'd felt...my little girl heart filling with love.

Just as all this opened up inside me, the memory of a river flowed in behind it—another forgotten time. Was I seven?... Our pastor standing with his hand on my back...*"Cassie, have you given Him your life?"*

...Cold green water washing over me...rising up... breathing in... Dad wrapping me in a towel...My dad...

The images stopped as pain gripped my heart. I hadn't remembered him so clearly in years...and then his ravaged, suffocating body flashed before me...

I pushed myself up and out of the tepid water, shaking my head to clear the terrible image. *What was I doing?* Grabbing my towel, I began scrubbing the sudsy bathwater from my skin, scolding myself the whole time. *What a fool.* Dwelling on the past was something I didn't do, and until now, I hadn't remembered a single thing even when I'd tried! I suddenly realized what a gift I'd given myself by not being able to remember.

So why was this happening? I wasn't *actually* worried about coming unglued, that was ridiculous. All Pinedale High was at my feet...because Nathan was crazy about me. He was what every girl dreamed of, I reminded myself: Handsome, athletic, smart...rich.

The day Nathan Gregory turned around in the quad and looked in my direction without blinking or turning away, I knew something had happened. From that moment on, my ride to the top of Pinedale High royalty was swift and amazing. I must admit, his surprising, actually, *his shocking* interest in me, made me take a new look at myself. I had always been fairly average. Braces in junior high, brown hair and hazel eyes, a crooked smile, and skinny arms and legs. As I reexamined myself, I realized that I'd changed in the few years when nothing mattered but my dad. Looking in the mirror, I recognized that I, Cassandra Connor, (Cassie, for short), had ended up in the pool of my mother's genes. I had her long legs, decent curves, somewhat pretty face, and thank goodness, great hair. I'd been gypped out of my father's brains, but oddly, the one clever gift my dad had left me I'd gotten from his library.

For the seven years my dad was sick, I read to him. I read whatever he asked, beginning with easy reading and ending with great volumes of books. The only downside of my memory loss was that I only had a vague recall of this. The books were still in boxes, but I didn't remember anything I'd read, not their titles or plots—but then, gosh, there were hundreds. When I'd looked in just one of the ten boxes I still had, I found: *The Divine Comedy, In Search of Lost Time, Moby Dick, One Hundred Years of Solitude, Don Quixote,* and even *War and Peace!* And there were also small volumes of poetry by names like Emmerson, Dickenson, Frost, and Pablo Neruda. I wondered if I'd understood any of them, but in truth, I didn't care.

When I asked my mom, she said I *had* understood them, and that my dad loved this time with me and the hours we spent together talking about them. She was particularly sad I'd lost my memories because she told me I'd once had a photographic recall of every single book! All I had to say about losing those memories was, "hallelujah!" I didn't care, and I was glad my brain was broken. I was happy to forget a few books if it meant not remembering the other stuff... But I couldn't help noticing that my body gave an involuntary shudder.

Strangely, my brain had retained some of the words. It was quite a mystery to me how all kinds of big words would filter into my mind on their own. Occasionally, even information about things I had no memory of would slip in unexpectedly. But I figured, it couldn't hurt if once in a while I used words in class that managed to confuse teachers into thinking I was at least of average intelligence. It was just another way I'd learned to disguise myself.

And even though dad hadn't left me a genius IQ, I wasn't so dumb, or so bitter that I'd let the gift from my mom go to waste. I was smart enough to know that Nathan wasn't looking at my brains. In fact, just that week, after months of Nathan's quiet but persistent urging, and the fear of losing him always in the back of my mind, I'd decided it was time to do whatever I needed to...well, to keep him.

Tonight, I was going to show him how much he meant to me. I was finally ready. The little hesitation...fear...I felt, I figured was normal. After all, I was still a virgin...the only "V" in the "A" clique. Perhaps it was mean, I thought, smiling to myself, but I would probably have been the only virgin in *that* group in sixth grade. I tried ignoring the strange sensation that came over me every time I thought about being intimate with a guy. I loved being Nathan's girlfriend, but I couldn't help feeling something was not quite right about all of it. *"You're just a prude, and a goody-two-shoes! Grow up!"* I said out loud, glaring at myself in the mirror.

I barely heard the ring of my phone over the blaring music and my blistering thoughts, but I reached for the volume control on my radio and picked up the call at the same time. It was Brittany, and the news was not good.

"Can't we stay over at Jenna's then?" I responded, knowing the answer before I even asked.

"You know we can't! She's got company, and her mom is telling her she can't even go out tonight. I'm sorry to blow it for you like this; I know you and Nathan had plans up at the lake," Brittany was trying her best to sound sympathetic. In truth, I knew her jealousy made sincerity close to impossible.

Well, this is really great," I continued, "I can't call him because he's at the cabin. He called this morning, and I promised him I'd be there at ten tonight. He was going to sneak out and meet me at the boathouse. And I can't come sneaking back *here* after midnight. My mom would catch me for sure. I guess I'm going to have to drive up there before it gets too late and tell him I can't make it." I complained.

"Oh, his mom will love that. A lone girl showing up at the cabin for a chat with her precious son."

"I know. She hates me. I think she suspects that Nathan and I are going out."

"Good guess, since the entire town knows. Besides, she thinks every girl is trying to get their hooks in him, which, of course, they are... Sorry, Cassie," she said, stifling a giggle.

"Are you sure you can't come with me?"

"Hello? Do you remember why I'm calling you? My Dad...flying in to take me shopping...Portland...is any of this registering in your Nathan addled brain?" Brittany taunted.

"I thought that was in the morning." I said weakly.

"It is, but he'll be here in an hour, and I still have to get ready. Sorry, Cassie, but I'm sure you'll figure something out." Then she tried for a little more sweetness and added, "Good luck."

"Yea, thanks." I said and hung up. *Now what?* I thought angrily.

Refusing to admit defeat yet, I laid out my clothes and dressed carefully, meaning, half my closet was now on the floor. The outfit I ended up wearing was one I'd tried on an hour earlier. As I cleaned up by stuffing things in drawers and throwing them back in my closet, I kept trying to figure out how I was going to deal with the problem of Mrs. Gregory. But, every time I imagined her perfect little self, she was stabbing me with her eyes, and I wanted to throw-up. I began wondering how I could even consider marrying a man with a mother like that. Then, I shook myself. *Think of Nathan,* I said out loud, *not his frightening mother.* But it was useless, so, in order to stop imagining her perfect clothes and frightening glare, I found myself thinking about Tessa and her first encounter with '*the Angel.*'

We'd been in Pinedale a few weeks, and it was Jack who'd first taken us for a picnic to the Pine Circle: a not so clever name for a place in the forest between our houses where the pine trees grow in, well, a circle. And, of course,

Tessa loved it because, according to her, it was like a natural cathedral. With light streaming between the branches and the quiet within, I could almost see how she would come to that. But I also felt it was because she was determined to drive me insane. And it wasn't long after that—just after the start of school—that she first shared what she'd supposedly seen.

"Cassie, I was so scared! I didn't know where the light was coming from! At first, I thought there was a fire, or an explosion, but there wasn't any sound. Then I saw him... He was so big...and I just fell to the ground!" Her small face was fervent, and her eyes, magnified by the large lenses, looked like they might come out of her head.

"Uh huh. And what did he do?" I asked quietly, not wanting to upset her mental balance this early into her story.

"He spoke; he said, *'Don't be afraid.'*" She smiled sweetly, and her eyes shone as she looked away, remembering.

"Uh... OK," and I wondered how far I should let this continue.

"Oh, Cassie, he told me so many things! He only stayed a few seconds, but he told me so much!"

"And does this fella have a name?" I asked. Unfortunately, my tone revealed the end of my patience for all things loony.

"I knew you wouldn't believe me. He said you wouldn't. And yes, he has a name, but I guess it's hard to pronounce... But he said it's not important. He said *he's* not important— only what God has sent him to do."

"I see. And that was to appear to a *FREAKING TWELVE-YEAR-OLD?*" Calming down, I continued, "And did he tell you that you were with child? That there would be another immaculate conception? I swear, if this is something you cooked up after playing doctor with one of Jack's brothers, I'm not buying it now, and I won't nine months from now!" At the time, I remember being surprised by my own words, but something in what Tessa had told me shook me to my very core.

"I knew you wouldn't believe me, but you don't have to be gross," was all Tessa replied. She stood looking at me like *I* was the one who'd lost my mind.

It took me a few seconds, but I finally gained enough control to say, "Look, just don't ever mention this to me again. Or anybody else. I'm very serious. It's not easy to prove insanity, but if you blab about this, people could come, take you away, medicate you and lock you up. Do you understand me?"

"If you come with me, and see him, you won't be afraid." She answered.

"I AM NOT KIDDING!" My face felt like it might explode all over her curly hair.

"All right." She had lowered her head and then turned to leave. Stopping, she looked back at me and dropped the last bomb. "He said, 'God heard you, every prayer'... He wants you to know..."

"Don't ever talk to me about this again, and I'm not kidding," I interrupted, looking her straight in the eye. Tessa sighed and walked out without finishing.

I continued to silently fume. Any half-wit, and my sister wasn't that, would know I'd prayed a million prayers for my dad while I watched him slowly lose control of every muscle function in his body, including his lungs, until he finally died. And she was going to tell me that God *heard them all*. It really made me want to believe in God right away, considering he'd heard a little girl *begging* and did absolutely *nothing* about it.

Luckily, Tessa didn't share much more about her angelic buddy with me, but she'd shared her ridiculous story with Jack. I'd heard them talking outside on the porch while I was supposed to be doing my homework. Evidently, our family hadn't just come to Pinedale willy-nilly—and neither had Jack's. Naturally, Jack was a key player in all this holy baloney. She never made it clear what that was, but then conveniently, neither did his "angel-ship."

Thankfully, it didn't sound like Jack was encouraging her in her story, but I didn't hear him discourage her, either. I'd heard only bits and pieces, but even that was horrifying. In short, I just wanted to ignore it all and hope Tessa would tire of her silly story. At least I knew Jack wouldn't have her committed. It would have been a case of the weirdo calling the whacko cracked. And that got me thinking about Jack again.

I'd already gone over my options. If I went to see Nathan now, his mother was sure to be there. And that was not good. If I waited until 10:00 when he was supposed to meet me, he'd probably convince me to stay too long. Also, I'd have to drive my mom's car without permission, and both of those meant, if caught, I'd be in really BIG trouble. For the most part, my mom was really nice and a bit of an 'airhead.' Quite a bit of an 'airhead.' But just break a curfew rule, and that woman could be without mercy. She would take away privileges for so long I'd begin wondering if she was trying to disprove Newton's law. Everyone knows his third law clearly states that every action has a reaction that's supposed to be equal. And so far, she'd *never* gotten the equal part right.

Just as I was contemplating this in my very thorough way, I saw Jack walking between our two houses. He was headed toward the woods, and I couldn't help noticing he didn't even *glance* up at my window. I would like to say I thought this was interesting, but it was actually troublesome; I wasn't sure when I'd lost my ability to charm him.

Now, I knew I couldn't very well ask him to carry a message for me. He would never do that...but he might go with me... I pulled my window open and yelled down to him. "Hey Jack, wait up!"

I grabbed my lip balm and applied it as I hurried downstairs and out the door. I had to jog to catch up with him. The only way I knew he'd heard me was that he walked a bit slower. And then, glancing back, he kind of smiled, letting me *know* he'd seen me, but didn't stop, which annoyed me no end. The moon was just a sliver, giving off very little light. Then Jack stepped out of the streetlight and into the darkness of the trees, and I lost sight of him.

Chapter Three

As I made my way to the edge of the woods, I realized I should have grabbed a flashlight instead of lip balm. Careful not to trip, I made my way in darkness toward the circle of pines. As I got closer, I heard voices.

"...I don't know what he's planning, but he'll have to knock her down and strike her blind..." The voice sounded like Tessa.

"Jack? Where are you?" I called, standing at the edge of the circle waiting for my eyes to adjust. "We're over here, Cass," Tessa called.

Striding over with more confidence than my night vision allowed, I asked somewhat harshly, "What are you doing here in the dark with Jack, Tessa?"

"We're waiting for you," she answered, calmly. "Why did *you* come here?" I could tell she had to work to keep the smile out of her voice.

I peered at Jack and was grateful I couldn't make out his eyes in the dark. "I...I...followed Jack."

"How come?" Tessa asked, and I could tell she was enjoying my discomfort.

"It's none of your business."

"Well, it's mine. So, how come?" Jack asked, stepping toward me.

"Ah...because I need a favor." I'd planned on asking him using all my charm, not like this. And at that moment, I could have strangled Tessa.

"Yea, it figures. Let me save you the energy of flirting with me. The answer is 'no.' I have a date tonight."

"A date? With Tessa?"

"Not exactly." Jack was now closer, looking down at me. I used all my inner strength to keep my face neutral.

"With who then?" I asked, turning toward Tessa and away from the power of Jack. She didn't answer me immediately. Instead, Tessa turned, and kicking off her shoes, walked forward into the center of the circle. When she knelt down and opened her arms, it was both an answer and a greeting.

The light broke suddenly, showering us with a radiance you could almost feel. I didn't know what knocked me back, its force or my fright. Either way, Jack and I found ourselves pressed painfully into the bark of a pair of pine trees. In a powerful, yet reassuring voice, the angel said, "Don't be afraid." And that phrase finally made sense.

I can't remember moving away from the tree, but when I found myself kneeling next to Tessa, I didn't know whether I did it out of righteous respect, or even choice at all. My legs were soup, and I couldn't have stood up if I'd tried.

The angel began, his voice deep and clear and vibrating throughout my whole body. "There is much to tell you, and the time grows short. I can return but once more. We have received special dispensation for you." I remember the word, "dispensation,"because strangely, at the time, I couldn't recall what it meant, but I knew I didn't like it.

"You must pay close attention..." My mouth was hanging open, and my eyelids felt welded to the top of my eye sockets. I might not have looked terribly bright, but I was definitely at attention.

"Since the Great Fall, the armies of heaven have waged unseen wars for the souls of men in a realm beyond earth's veil. Always Heaven's Laws govern us; but in past hours—which, for you, could be moments, months, or years—the Law has been broken. The enemy, one of Satan's high demons, disobeyed the Law. Without permission, he went where there was no sin in order to discover the location of the *Link*." As the radiant being paused to begin again, I slowly raised my hand. It felt like lead, but he focused his amazing eyes on mine. Suddenly, I forgot my question. "Speak." He commanded.

How quickly I remembered, but my lips moved like glue. "Ah...ah...excuse me. I'm sorry, I don't mean to interrupt, but I sorta missed what you said the devil-guy located," I said stupidly. The look I received from this amazingly-bright-and-giant-angel-being didn't make me feel any smarter, either. It was similar to the look I've gotten from math teachers when I've asked certain, maybe not-so-smart, questions.

He continued as if I hadn't rudely interrupted. "Throughout time, there have been a few humans chosen to become what we refer to as the 'Link.' These are ones to whom a great gift is given—a special ability. They are given power to bring about important change to the world. The *Link* will become a leader. The evil ones know the approximate time this power will be re-assigned. But they do not know where, or who, will become the next *Link*. However, they are on constant watch. They fight a soul-battle to steal this power—or destroy whoever it's bestowed upon before it can be fully assimilated."

His voice rose, "Evil has now discovered *where* this will happen. A force has been mounted, and evil will strike. They will be watching to determine *who* the *Link* is. Although these forces of darkness are very real, they can be defeated— they *must be* defeated—or this light for mankind will be lost to the hands of evil…" He paused for only a second, "These forces of darkness *must be* vanquished in order for the *Link* to survive."

I heard Jack gulp. "Who? Who?" was all he managed to get out, sounding very much like a frightened forest owl. The angel raised his hand, and his light took on a terrible beauty as his voice became stern.

"I have been sent because the outcome of this great battle hangs in the balance. A youth will become the *Link*. However, you, who are called to defend the *Link,* are not alone. For many years, the forces of God have been called by prayer to protect this quadrant of earth by powerful warriors in God's army. They have prepared the gates. Never before have Earth's children been allowed to do battle in our realm… You have been chosen."

"Wha…wha…wha…wha…?" I bravely offered as reply.

"Do not fear. As I said, you will not be alone, and you will receive training. You shall call yourselves the Guardians. Three others shall join you. One, you will recognize by her dreams; she sees things to come. Another has sight that extends beyond the veil. And one comes who seems to offer nothing but offers all.

The forces of darkness do not yet know that you, the Guardians, have been marshaled to fight them. They send an army in preparation for a Destroyer. He is very powerful; you will know him by his rank and his mark, a slain dove. When he is defeated the threat is over. You must gird yourselves."

The angel loomed before us, at least nine feet of terrifying beauty, as my mind spun frantically around the words, "gird yourselves." Suddenly, my awe and amazement went to scared, then careened clean across my line of terror into "the land of nothing-to-lose."

"Uh, I'm sorry but you can't...be asking...*me* to do this. I can't do this. I'm not ready to do this...fight a *Demon Destroyer*?" I felt the hysteria building. Once again, the light surrounding the angel grew brighter, yet there was no threat in it, and immediately, I began to calm down.

"There is one you must seek out. She will be your guide. She lives among you, but *she is different*." As he finished speaking, his hand came up, and I automatically coward. Then in a quieter voice he said, "Come forward." Jack was the first to move slowly toward the light. I rose through no will of my own but hung back and watched from behind.

The light intensified, but the angel's voice remained quiet, almost soothing. "You must do battle, Jack, now more than ever. You are a soldier of the Almighty. In you He is well pleased." Jack dropped to his knee, but as the angel continued speaking, there was no audible sound to anyone but Jack. And I was fine with that. In fact, for the first time, I began taking a lung full of oxygen. Then, Jack rose, and the angel spoke for several seconds longer. That's when I got the unmistakable sensation *I* was being discussed. This is not a perception I get wrong very often. I narrowed my eyes at the bright 'light show' and sure enough, he looked back at me with blinding bright eyes that terrified me, but also verified my suspicion. I couldn't see Jack's eyes, or I would have been doubly certain, but his session was over. Without turning, Jack was stepping back. It was my turn.

As in a trance, I moved forward, realizing that this miraculous yet very scary dream was just not going away. I was doubtless risking the wrath of God, but the way things looked, I'd been doing that for quite some time. "You see..." I said, fighting the temptation to simply fall on my face and instead shaking my head and commanding my lips to move. "I *can't* do this!" Unexpectedly, the angel reached out and touched my shoulder with just the very tip of his luminescent index finger. It felt as though a cool river of fire ran through my entire being. I relaxed, and fear began draining out of me like so much sludge.

Still, I fought. "I'm sorry, but...how dangerous? Can...um, is it possible for us to get...hurt?" I just couldn't go along without something to control the terror his words had poured into me. To my amazement, this incredible being of light didn't get all huffy-bright and stoic. He actually seemed a little surprised, but he answered me—even if it wasn't the answer I was hoping for.

"The greatest danger lies in doing nothing," he paused, "yet great danger remains in going ill-prepared. If you train well, there will still be danger, but you will be 'the head and not the tail.'"

There was no logical reason for my next request except that I could feel myself slipping. I was giving in to...the light, and this really made me mad. "What do I call you? I want to know your name," I said gruffly.

At that moment, the most amazing thing happened. The radiant light began to pulsate, and automatically I moved to cover my face with my arm. But before I'd raised it over my eyes, I realized this magnificent angel-being wasn't angry. Instead, he was emitting something close to laughter. I looked at him in amazement, and he simply shook his head.

"Cassie. I begin to understand, even if you do not," he said, shamelessly creating yet another question for my already over-heated brain. Then he said, "Believe me when I say, you would be unable to pronounce my actual name...but you may call me *Hamaliel*."

"Really? Wow, that's not so hard...Ham...a lie lee lay. Crap... I'm sorry! I mean crud. Could you tell me one more time?"

"Hamaliel."

"Right, Hama...LEE...el. Right?"

"That's right." Hamaliel was watching me intently, and when he spoke next, it was to change my life forever.

"Awaken to the call. Sleep no more." His voice sounded far away and yet it echoed in my bones. "God has sent me to deliver to you, his beloved daughter, Cassandra Elena Connor, this message: *'You may not know Me, but I know everything about you. I desire to establish you with all my being, for you are my treasured possession. I know the pain you have suffered, and although you haven't known it, when you are brokenhearted, I am close to you. I gave up everything that I might gain your love. Come home. I have always been Father and will always be Father. I am waiting for you.'"*

Something thick and dark, that had been wedged between my rib cage and heart snapped and began to melt. It was strange. I'd never realized that anguish had the taste of salt and felt like a broken throat.

Hamaliel stared deeply into my eyes, and his face grew tender. "I bestow upon you the gift of *eleeo*, the gift of compassion. You will not thank me for it until you learn to use it but using it will make you wise and strong."

I'm sure he noticed the state I was in and was hardly waiting for anything from me—let alone a "thank you". Then he simply began to fade from our sight. As the last vestige of light disappeared, I heard him say, "He hears your cry in the night. Come back to Him, Cassie. Your future and...n...you love...depen...on...t" The last part of the sentence was all but lost, and then so was I.

"Tessa! Jack!" I called, frantically. I was on my back. I

opened my eyes as wide as I could but there was only darkness. Someone was holding my head.

"It's OK. Your eyes will adjust in a minute. You fainted." Jack's voice said above me. Slowly I began to see outlines and sat up.

"What happened?" I put a hand to my face, I guess to check if my head was still attached.

Tessa walked over with her flashlight, and kneeling beside me took my hand. "Jack, help me get Cassie back to the house. We have to talk." Without a word, Jack lifted me off the ground and into his arms.

"Let me down; I can walk," I protested, hating how strong he was, and how utterly weak I felt.

"You sure?" Jack asked, as he set me on my feet.

I wanted to say—all right, carry me—but self-respect won out. Instead, I stammered, "Y...yes, I...I'm sure, b...but what just happened?"

"You met an angel..." Tessa replied, and then I heard her add under her breath, with what I could have sworn was a touch of a smile, "...and he knocked you down and struck you blind."

Chapter Four

Jack and I followed Tessa back through the woods toward our house, her small flashlight throwing a weak glow against the ground. As I watched its bobbing beam, I couldn't help wondering if mankind shouldn't have come up with more than one word for "light." This little beam was so different than the blaze of white radiance emanating from Hamaliel, that it hardly seemed to classify as light at all, and if it did, it should have been classified as "pretend light."

I found it reassuring to massage this thought, in much the same distracted way I found myself massaging my chest just above my heart. Both my brain and heart had been badly stressed, and I could feel the effects of shock beginning to either set in or wear off; but I couldn't be sure. All I knew was the impossible seemed real, and I couldn't let the thought that kept circling round and round my mind like a vulture over a carcass, settle. If this really happened, my life, as I knew it, was over.

Upon reaching our porch, Tessa and I dropped down onto the steps. Jack leaned against the railing and closed his eyes.

The night had turned cool, drying the sweat that earlier stood on his forehead and stained his shirt. I realized that, if Jack had broken a sweat, then I wasn't the only one to see a colossal angelic being speaking the warning to "gird" ourselves against the evil attack of demon warriors. Strangely, I'd have preferred doubting my sanity to having this particular vision confirmed.

Luckily, no one spoke for several minutes, and my rising panic tapered off to a mere two-alarm alert. Finally, Tessa said, "Pretty amazing, huh?"

I must have looked at her as if she were deranged. "Gee, I guess you could put it that way," I said, feeling irritated by her understatement. At the moment, I'd forgotten this was old-hat to Tessa.

We sat in silence for a few more moments. Then Jack said, "I wonder when all of this is supposed to start...how much time we have?...And I wonder who the *Link* is? Did he tell you, Cassie?"

"Me? You were there! I was wondering if he gave you any special information when he turned the volume off? What was happening then?" I asked, my eyes narrowing, wondering again why I'd have been talked about behind my back, right in front of my face, so to speak.

"Ah...so that happened with me," Jack said, nodding. "Yours went silent, too..."

"*Tell me* what he said to you," I demanded.

Jack looked at me for a few long moments. "Yea, I will, but not yet. Right now, we need to talk about other things. The angel—that is, Hamaliel, said the *Link* was a leader who will someday bring change to the world."

"*Important* change." Tessa interjected.

I sat there, stupidly looking at them both without a clue, when it suddenly hit me. "Oh, my Gaw...I mean, Oh my gosh!" I quickly corrected. Surprisingly, I was sure I knew who Hamaliel was talking about. *It had to be Nathan!* "Jack, there's a guy who goes to my school. He's a senior. I think he's the *Link* Hamaliel's talking about. Someone in a position to make important... Listen, I'll tell you more in the car, but I need a favor..."

~

As Jack drove following my directions, I tried telling him about Nathan several times. It was harder than I thought. Finally, I blurted, "Well, um, there's a guy, and he's nice. And, well, he's very smart, involved in school, wants to go to law school, and get into politics."

"So, what?" Jack asked, looking sincerely puzzled and a wee ticked off.

Of course, this made it worse, and I got flustered and huffy. "I thought we're trying to figure out the *Link*, and I am giving you my opinion based on, based on...well, if you'll let me finish you can decide."

"Fine. You like this guy, don't you?" Jack asked evenly.

"Um...Yes." And I was proud I said it with so little hesitation.

"Does he believe in God?"

"How should I know? Does it matter?" I asked indignantly. "He's a good person." Tessa snorted in the back seat. "What? He is!" I said defensively.

"Cassie, whether Nathan Gregory is a good person or not, isn't the issue..." She never got to finish her thought because the car veered to the side of the road, coming to a screeching stop.

Jack turned on me, his face dark but composed, his words clipped. "Nathan Gregory?" he repeated, unable to disguise his disdain.

"You know him?" I asked, rising up and staring him down.

"Oh, Cassie. Everybody knows Nathan," Tessa said from the back seat, sounding good-hearted and probably trying to make up for seeming the traitor.

"Sure, *everybody knows Nathan...*" Jack stated mockingly, piercing me with his eyes. "That ought to be enough by itself to send out the forces of heaven—to protect Nathan's popularity! What does it matter whether he believes in God or not; he's a nice guy! Everybody will vote for him! Why, he must be the *Link!*"

"Stop it!" Something close to tears welled up in my eyes. Jack turned back to the steering wheel, still fuming but headed the car back onto the road. I turned straight ahead too. "I don't know what your problem is, and right now I don't care. I didn't ask for any of this," I said, hiccuping. I hadn't meant to get upset, but obviously, the evening's stress had caught up with me—and then some.

Tessa reached into the front seat and patted my shoulder. "Cass, it's all right. I'm sorry if I haven't been nice about..." She obviously didn't want to say Nathan's name again around Jack. "It's just hard to picture him as the *Link...*but who knows?"

I quietly looked straight ahead.

By the time we reached the cabin drive that wound past the lake, things had mellowed in the car. I could tell Jack felt bad he'd made my eyes tear up, and I knew now was the time to ask him for the real favor. "Jack," I said, keeping my eyes lowered. "I need you to be with me when I go up to the cabin. Jack's mother doesn't like me...she hates me. I don't have the right pedigree." I ended, with what I hoped had the right amount of suffering, minus the self-pity. Truly an art form to manage that.

Jack turned and looked at me with his unreadable face

firmly in place. "So, I'm your cover," He stated flatly. His eyes were dark and gleamy, communicating his irritation well.

"Look, I'm sorry. I'm in kind of a tough spot here. I have to tell him I can't meet him later tonight."

"I thought you were going to spend the night with...Brit...tany..." Tessa's words faded off as the obvious answer became clear.

I was too tired to glare at her. I just sighed.

Jack continued looking at me. It was a strange penetrating gaze, and it made me feel odd. I shrugged my shoulders, as if to ask, *what?*

"I heard Hamaliel say something to you as he was leaving—right before you passed out. I think he said, '*Your future, and the one you love, depends on it.*' If Nathan is your future, and he's the one you love, I guess he's the guy we're going to have to protect. But Cassie, in your heart, do you *really* believe Nathan's the *Link?*"

"He *is* special. Why is that so hard to believe?" I asked, feeling strangely defensive. Jack stared at me for several more seconds.

Then, as if deciding something, he said, "OK, wait here." Opening the door, he strode toward the cabin.

I rolled down the window. "Jack, wait. What are you going to say?" I called after him, but he just kept walking. All Tessa and I could do was sit and watch as he climbed the steps and casually rang the bell. To my horror, Mrs. Graham answered, and in total keeping with the rest of the evening's shock-inducing events, she embraced Jack as she ushered him inside.

Jack and Nathan did not appear for an infinite, perpetual, eternity. Honestly, it was that long. Tessa tried talking to me, but all I could do was stare out the window toward the cabin like a faithful dog. When the front door finally opened, Nathan and Jack walked out, followed by Mrs. Gregory. She hugged Jack again and waved goodbye. It was surreal, which made it rather in keeping. The guys walked casually to the car, only exchanging a couple words. Jack opened the door and slid behind the wheel. Nathan came up to my window. "Hey, Cass, this is a surprise. I didn't know you two knew each other," he said, leaning in.

"And I didn't know you two were such buds, either." I replied, not as successful at hiding my frustration.

"Yea, since we were kids," Nathan said, looking over at Jack, and smiling, but only with his lips.

"Yea." Jack agreed shortly.

Nathan peered in the back seat and gave Tessa a wave. "You guys don't mind if Cassie and I talk in private for a minute, do you?" Opening the door before they could answer.

"Not at all." Jack said, smiling like his lips were glued on.

Walking beyond the other side of the drive, we stood behind a stand of pines for privacy. I couldn't help noticing that, even though it was dark out, Nathan casually checked to make sure his mother couldn't see us through any windows, but he was so annoyed he wouldn't look at me for a few seconds and stood clenching and unclenching his jaw in irritation. I should have hurried to explain about Jack, but for some strange reason, all I could do was stand and observe how great his jaw muscles looked when he was ticked off.

"Why are you here with Jack?" He finally asked. "We weren't supposed to meet...for another hour," he added, glancing at his watch.

Shocked it was so late, I said, "It's nine already? I need to go, but..."

"Not so fast! You just got here," Nathan replied, his irritation abruptly changing and his voice suddenly low. He moved toward me slowly, backing me up against the tree. "I haven't been able to get you out of my head, Cassie. Tell me we're going to be able to see each other tonight..." I started to answer, but he leaned in and kissed me. Normally, this was when I lost control of most of my faculties: speech, hearing, walking, and definitely rational thought. But tonight, I pushed away and untangled myself.

Instantly, his face registered surprise.

"I'm sorry, Nathan, I can't tonight." I was overwhelmed with everything I needed to tell him. I wasn't sure where to start, and I knew now wasn't the time. "I need to talk to you," I continued, "so much has happened that we need to talk about..."

Nathan's face darkened. "You better think about what you're doing." He turned and began striding away, then halted and turned. "I can't believe it! What did he tell you, anyway? Ya know what, it doesn't matter." He exclaimed angrily.

I stood listening to Nathan rant, trying to read between his words. I was completely at a loss until he said, "If you're breaking up with *me* for a loser like *Jack*, you're a fool."

This was one of those times when the ability to hide emotions by mastering facial expressions came in handy. As exhausted as I was, I did an inner eye roll, as well as a glare, and something close to a hyena face. However, outwardly, I was the queen of serene. I looked at him with complete composure and said, "What is wrong with you? Are you out of your mind? Jack gave me a ride as a favor so I wouldn't have to face your mother alone—for your sake. He's my neighbor. And if I want him for my boyfriend, I'll let you know. But Nathan, this has nothing to do with him." I turned and started back to the car.

"Cassie, wait." He grabbed my arm and hauled me around. Searching my eyes, he whispered gruffly, "I'm sorry, I thought..."

"Yes, you made it pretty clear." Drawing me close, he put

his arms around me, and without wanting to, I felt myself slacken under his touch. In a softer voice, I said, "We can talk later...Monday at school." I smiled up at him, "Of course, there's always tomorrow. Your mother could invite me up to the cabin for a little brunch," I added teasingly.

"My uncle is coming in the morning," Nathan said quickly, worry instantly reflected in his eyes. I couldn't help being amused.

"I can see my sarcasm is completely wasted on you." I replied smiling. "You probably need to get back, too..." I didn't finish. Nathan bent forward and kissed me again, his lips soft and his mouth tasting like wintergreen. He'd tightened his embrace, kissing me more deeply when I heard a branch snap. Pulling away, I looked over to see Jack standing in the shadows, a broken twig in his hands.

"Time to go," he said, then turned and walked back to the car.

"Man of few words, our Jack." Nathan said, with a half-smile. "I wish I could call you—you'd think by now we'd have reception up here—I'm starting to hate this place. If I get home before it's too late, I'll call tomorrow."

"Don't worry. I'll see you on Monday. We'll talk then." Suddenly, I remembered all the dark, evil forces Hamaliel had warned us about. Could they be lurking even now, waiting to destroy the *Link—Nathan*? I wondered. And I realized I needed to warn him.

"What's the matter? You look like you've seen a ghost," Nathan ventured.

"Close enough...but never mind. Just please be careful up here...believe it or not, you could be in danger, and I don't have time to explain it all now," I said speed-talking, "but if anything happens that makes you think you're in danger, get out of here. Get home and call me!"

He smiled down at me with laughter in his eyes. "The

only thing I've ever been in danger of is you. My mom warned me about girls like you, and she was right. But if you're not going to be here, then I'm pretty sure I'll be safe. So, get outta here so I won't have to call the cops...Oh, that's right, I can't. In that case, come with me..." Nathan started pulling me in the direction of the trees.

Laughing, I pulled away. "I'm not kidding, Nathan." I said, composing myself. It was clear he was never going to believe me, but then, I hardly believed myself. "Oh, never mind. Just be safe. *Promise me.*" I added, sounding exactly like the extra mother he didn't need.

"Sure, I promise. Does this mean if I stub my toe, you want me to call you from the store?" He teased.

"Very funny. I had that coming." Reaching up to give him a quick kiss on the cheek, inspired no doubt by the recent "mommy role" I'd just taken on, Nathan turned and caught my lips, kissing me hard. It took every ounce of effort I could muster, aided by the vision of Jack and Tessa walking up and dragging us apart, to push away. Nathan's eyes were on fire as he looked at me. And then he said my name, "Cassie. Cassie, I ..."

I stood, mouth parted, heart beating wildly. For at least the umpteenth time that night, my heart was in my throat. And then he said, "...I want you."

I could have sworn a cold breeze blew his words at me. "I...I...know." It was all I could get out. Turning, I quickly walked out of the trees and back to the car. "Let's get going." I commanded, even before the door closed behind me. Jack had the car idling, and he pulled out of the drive without a backward glance.

"Well, did you tell him?" Tessa asked, leaning forward into the front seat.

Jack looked around at her and answered with rare

sarcasm, "*Oh yea,* she told him all right." I glared at him but didn't respond.

"Well, what did he say?" Tessa asked, not understanding.

"He said he'd be careful." I answered, surprised how quietly it came out.

Jack looked at me suspiciously. "What else did Nathan say to you?" I was silent. "Did he tell you he loved you?" Jack asked, surprising me with his prying.

"No—those words weren't mentioned," I answered, feeling suddenly overcome. I covered my face with my hands, unable to control all the emotions surfacing as I commanded the tears rising inside me back into the well where I'd stored them for so, so long.

Chapter Five

The next morning was Sunday, and, as usual, Tessa rode her bike to church. I watched out my bedroom window as she pedaled away in her best Sunday outfit, the only group of clothes she wore together on a regular basis. And it was probably the only group of clothing known to mankind, outside of a theme park, that could transform a normal human body into the caricature of a dressed mouse. Disney had nothing on my sister.

I knew Jack would probably meet her there, but I couldn't force myself out of bed. I told my mom I was sick, and truer words have never fallen from these lips. I wasn't just sick I was undone... I'd been severely flaked.

I was aware my mother checked on me several times, because I heard the door open and close. Tessa probably looked in too, but I didn't move the cement block that was now my head to make certain.

Other than the two of them rustling about downstairs, the house was probably quiet, but it was hard to tell. My mind was filled with noise. Not the clamor of answers presenting themselves, oh no. Instead, it was filled with the echo of self-ridicule and the static of a thousand questions slamming into each other like people on a subway after someone yells, "Fire!"

It seemed as if something big inside my mind was trying to get out, but the opening was too small. Some unnamed fear I couldn't identify at the time was boxing it in. Looking back, I'm pretty sure I was afraid of who I'd become.

I felt stupid and blind because for so long I'd refused to believe in anything. And although I obviously didn't consider myself a brilliant thinker, or even all that good at Jeopardy, I was at least proud of the fact I had a grip on reality. Then, to leave no doubt as to who actually had a grip, and who was in a pretend world, Tessa's angel appears. And he was a big one. It might have left some room for doubt if it had just been Tessa and me. But then Jack was there. If he hadn't been, I could have chalked it up to the fact that we Connor women were officially out of our collective minds. But he'd seen it too, and even with what I'd considered Jack's weird fanaticism over God, and pig-headed determination to be his own person, he was not nuts. In fact, Jack was the sanest person I knew.

Then there was Nathan. I had no idea what was happening with Nathan. His amazing good looks, in fact, just his presence made me weak. I felt addicted to him, but not so much last night...and I realized that, for a moment, he'd even repelled me. It was a quick emotion, only a fraction of a second, but I couldn't lie to myself.

It was that blasted angel! I stormed, as the noise raged. When I couldn't stand it any longer, I held my pounding head, broke down and prayed for relief. I honestly couldn't remember my last prayer, and it felt very uncomfortable, but I was desperate. "All right, I give up. Help me, God. Please,... help me." Slowly the pounding subsided, and the noise began to quiet. Unbelievably, a scripture from childhood bubbled up. *"The Lord is my Shepherd; I shall not want. He leadeth me beside the still waters, he maketh me lie down in green pastures, He restoreth my soul..."* As the words echoed within me, I fell into a deep sleep and didn't wake until the next morning.

~

Tessa usually took the bus to school, but unexpectedly, I got up earlier than usual. So, I decided to drive her across town to the junior high. I saw her eyeing me closely and figured she was trying to decide just how much brain damage I'd suffered since Saturday night. Of course, I wasn't sure either.

Since Monday was a special rally day, I wore my cheerleading outfit, which gratefully relieved me of any wardrobe decisions that day. I could tell I hadn't fully recovered from Sunday's migraine marathon, and hair and makeup pushed me to my limit. When I looked in the mirror, I was happy to see that, except for slightly bloodshot eyes, there was nothing to give away the weekend's mind, spirit, and soul-bash.

As Tessa got out of the car in front of her school, she turned with a worried expression and asked, "So, do you want to comment on my Hawaiian shirt?"

"Your what? Oh, your shirt. Sure, it's really...ah bright," I said, squinting my eyes against the neon glare as I actually focused on it.

"OK, Cass. Now you're scaring me. Tell me I look like a sale at a Hawaiian thrift store,...or tell me you're suddenly allergic to bananas...anything! Just don't sit there, it's scary!"

"Sorry, sis, you look positively..." I gave my sister "the once over" and smiled. She had chosen a pair of hideous purple pants, cinched at the waist, and rolled at the cuff. I knew nothing in Tessa's closet fit because she refused to buy her clothes in the little kid's section. So, everything was always too big. Under her multi-colored parrot and banana shirt, which hung open, she wore a green and yellow t-shirt with the words "Go Ducks" emblazoned across the front. Her socks were pink, and her tennis shoes silver, with a red Nike emblem. To top the entire outfit, she'd pulled her hair into a puffy bun, which amazingly, appeared a lot like a sleeping brown poodle, and she'd placed small multi-colored clips around the napping pooch in hopes of holding any stray curls down. The really weird thing was, that for the first time I could remember, I thought she looked wonderful.

"I don't mean to scare ya, Tess, but honestly, you look just right. I'll see ya after school."

I watched Tessa blink quickly. "Wow. Thanks." She stood, stunned.

"What's your first class?" I asked, in an attempt to snap her out of her confusion. It did the trick.

"Ah...science. You know what they say, 'A day without fusion is like a day without sunshine!'"

Her face lit up, and she was grinning from ear to ear. And to think, I had just thought she was so darn cute. "That's a real knee slapper, Tess. I'll see ya after school," I said, smiling a very fake, yet practiced, and believable smile as I pulled away from the curb.

"Thanks, Cass. See ya after school!" I watched in my rearview mirror as she actually skipped and ran to her first class. Somehow, making her feel good didn't make me feel so bad today. That was interesting.

∾

As warm and fuzzy as all that might have been, being at school was suddenly very difficult. I couldn't get my bearings. I went from class to class feeling as though I was walking and talking under water. Everything was distant and muted. When Nathan said "hello" to me in the morning, I sensed he felt it, too. Of course, proof to this was, he began ignoring me. At least it seemed that way—it was hard to tell from beneath the ocean.

At the morning rally, the exercise pumped some much-needed blood into the old brain, and I was able to focus a little. Nathan watched me intently from the bleachers as we cheerleaders did our routines. But when I waved to him, he pretended not to see me, looking away and talking with the guys next to him. Strangely, Nathan was acting like...he was acting like...he was acting like he knew how weird I was acting. I decided I'd have to do a better job at covering how strange I felt, but it seemed I was losing the power I'd so carefully built up over my facial expressions and emotions.

At lunch we met up outside my class. "Hey," I said, "You want to go somewhere so we can talk?" Of course, I still felt strangely underwater, and I might have sounded a little bleary, because he looked at me for a second before answering.

"Let's wait 'till after school. Jake's holding our lunch spot."

I smiled up at him, a slow smile that should have been hidden, would have been hidden, had I been myself, which said, *"Wow, what would we do if we didn't have our spot held?"*

"What?" He asked, obviously annoyed.

"Nothing, I'm *starved!*" I lied unconvincingly and felt myself swimming up the corridor air toward the lunch yard.

We sat together with our friends, all the kids in the "A" clique. They were also called the "snob" clique, a title we all secretly loved. Nathan sat across from me and made no attempt to speak to me directly. Usually, I'd have taken the next step, but today I just couldn't make myself. It's not that everything felt phony and conceited; it did. But I'd loved feeling that way. Truthfully, I just didn't have the energy.

"Cassie, are you alright? You're acting a bit 'draggy.' In fact, we should give you the exalted title of 'Draggy Queen,'" Jenna said, laughing and watching Nathan out of the side of her eye.

"Oh no, she can't have that!" remarked Jason, another friend. "She'd take the crown away from poor, 'Lil' ole' Mark'! That would mess with his world!" He said, conspicuously pointing out a rather thin, well-dressed boy in brown and white wing-tips leaning against the wall.

"*You're terrible,*" Sabrina laughed, "but it's *true.* He's a *real* 'drag queen!' I heard he wears his mother's *night gowns* to bed!" She said loud enough for the boy to hear.

This was met with peals of laughter. I was the only one who didn't find it humorous at all, and honestly, I didn't know why. I looked over and found Nathan staring at me. "OK, what's the matter?" He asked, silencing everyone.

"What do ya mean? Nothing. I mean, I'm...I'm... nothing's the matter!" I stammered, knowing this wasn't true, but not knowing what the matter *was.*

"I don't believe you; you've been acting strange."

"Well, you're the one ignoring *me.* I'm not the one ignoring *you,*" I said, grasping at *that* thin straw.

"Uh-oh, love spat. Can't eat with all the tension. You two need to take it outside. Never mind, we *are* outside! Well, when there's trouble in paradise, guess it's time to get a room and...work it out!" Our friend Michael quipped, pumping his arms to everyone's amusement but mine.

A tall, slightly heavy freshman girl sat on the edge of a bench watching us. She wasn't someone I, or my friends, would have given a second of our precious time to—or even noticed. She'd have been invisible to us. Except that now she dangerously continued staring in our direction—until Brittany couldn't take it any longer.

"What is going on today? How am I supposed to even drink my soda with that elephant over there watching me? Well, that's it. It must be a sign—I'm not eating another thing all day!" She said, tossing her soda and unopened lunch into the garbage can. Everyone started laughing again, twisting around this time to stare back at the unknown freshman. The girls' face flamed, and she turned away, but not before catching my eye.

Nathan was staring at me too, waiting I suppose for me to join in the laughter, but something strange was happening. I felt myself slipping, spinning into a tunnel. When I came back to myself, I was slumped forward onto the table. Nathan was beside me, and Brittany and Jenna were calling my name.

"Cassie!"

"Cassie! What happened? Are you alright?"

"Yes, I'm fine; I...think I'm fine," I assured them, but inside I was trembling. Truthfully, I wasn't fine. I looked across at the girl sitting at the other table. She was staring wide-eyed and our eyes locked.

"Come on, I'm taking you to the nurse." Nathan stated, gripping my arm, and helping me stand.

The freshman girl continued observing me even when Brittany told her to, "Go find a car accident, you freak..." And I knew she continued watching me until I was out of sight.

The nurse's office was empty except for a guy lying on his side on the small couch. "Sit here," Nathan commanded. "I'm going to go see where Nurse Stiles went. She's probably in the teacher's lounge." Then he spied the kid on the couch.

"Hey buddy, where's the nurse?" He asked. The boy turned his head and looked at Nathan steadily, then without speaking, turned away.

I didn't know who this particular boy was, but I knew *what* he was. He was known as a *Cholo,* a term given to the Mexican kids who belonged to gangs. The fact of the matter was, he and his kind had always been beneath me: acting and dressing like tough guys, speaking their annoying broken English, trying to scare me...scaring me.

"Hey, I asked you a question," Nathan said again. This time, the guy didn't move. I could see the anger building in Nathan, and I took his arm just as he began to curse.

"It's OK. Maybe he doesn't speak English. All I need to do is sit here and rest a minute. She'll be back soon enough." I told Nathan, trying to sound calm.

"Yea, well, I'm not leaving you alone in here with *that.*" He said, motioning to the silent boy on the couch just as Nurse Stiles walked through the door carrying a folder.

"Well, Nathan, Cassie, what's the problem here? Is somebody sick?"

"I'm OK. It's Cassie. She had a fainting spell, or something, at lunch..." Nathan began.

"You better get to class then; the bell rang two minutes ago. I'll take care of Miss Connor."

Nathan nodded. Searching me again with his eyes, he mouthed the words, *"I'll call you."* Then he looked back one more time to shoot a challenging glance toward the Mexican kid. But it was wasted; the boy had covered his eyes with his arm as though warding off an invisible blow.

"Are you OK for right now, Cassie? I need to talk to Mr. Dos Santos for a minute." Nurse Stiles said.

"Sure." I answered.

The boy sat up, lowering his arm. I was surprised to see fear in his eyes. He'd held himself rigid while Nathan was in the room, but his hands now began to tremble. "I couldn't get a hold of your parents...is it Raphael?" Nurse Stiles asked.

"Yes, but all my friends, they call me Santos." he said in a quiet, accented voice.

"All right. Well, Santos, I understand that both your parents are working. Do you know another number where I might reach one of them?"

Santos bent his head and answered quietly. "My father is at a lot of different places during the day. My mother works at a motel. But she doesn't have a car. I can get home by myself."

Nurse Stiles turned to look at me and I pretended to read a flyer. She turned back and answered Santos in hushed tones. "I can't let you walk home. I'm sorry, but I need an adult to come and get you."

She sat down and moved closer for more privacy, but I could still make out her words. "I want to help. Really, I do. Could you explain a little more clearly what happened? Your teacher...I don't know why he'd say this, but he said you acted like you saw a ghost...or *something* frightening. But I want to know; did someone threaten you?"

Her words were muffled but I heard them. I looked up just as Raphael Dos Santos looked over at me, and I knew. There was no reason for me to know, but I was as certain of this as I was that an angel appeared in a grove of trees that grew in a circle—that is, I was firmly and confidently almost sure.

"No. I can't explain it." Santos said quickly, lowering his eyes from my shocked stare.

"Has this ever happened before?" Nurse Stiles asked.

"No," Santos said, but I could tell he was lying. "Mrs. Stiles, I just need some time until this...passes." He said, gritting his teeth.

Nurse Stiles patted his clenched fist. "Lie down and rest. You're probably suffering from a panic attack. They're more common than people realize. You said earlier you had a headache. I'll give you a couple Ibuprofen and a towel for your eyes. You can return to class when you feel better."

Standing up, she turned to me. "Now, Cassie, what seems to be the problem? Nathan said you fainted at lunch. Do you need to lie down?" She asked, suddenly concerned.

"No, I think I'll be fine in a few minutes, too. I don't really know what happened. I..." Suddenly, the event began swirling around me again...thoughts and emotions that weren't my own; memories of a life I'd never known, an existence as foreign to me as my own was becoming. But this life had been hard and sad in ways I'd never experienced, *and there were dreams...*

"Cassie, are you alright?" Nurse Stiles was leaning over me and had taken my wrist. "Your pulse is quite high. I think I'd better call your parents. Is anybody home?" She asked, worry creasing her brow.

"Ah, yes, my mom." I answered, feeling dazed.

"OK, I'll be right back. Meanwhile, you'd better lie down in the other room."

"Thanks. I do think I should go home, but I'm OK sitting." I replied.

"Fine, sit tight." She said, going out the door. Santos was watching me, but turned away when I looked over at him. I noticed his hands still trembled.

"Excuse me," I said, leaning forward in my seat. "Your name is, Santos?" Of course, he didn't have any warmer feelings for me than he did for Nathan and decided to cold-shoulder me. "I heard what the nurse said to you, but I think you're seeing things," I ventured, wracking my brain for the words Hamaliel used to describe one of the Guardians. Then I remembered and spoke aloud, "One will have *'sight that extends beyond the veil,'* which means, they'd also see forms of evil," I translated.

At those words, Santos jumped to his feet. "What did you say?" he almost shouted.

"I know what's happening to you. You're one of us." I said, reaching out to grasp his hand.

Santos' face went from frightened, to embarrassed, and finally to angry in a flash. "I don't know how you know this, but one thing is sure," he said, wrenching his hand free, "I'm *not* one of *you!*"

I quickly wrote my name and phone number down on the flyer I still held. "Here, take this. Call me if you decide you want to know what's happening to you. Believe me. I'm just as blown away by all this as you are. And...I'm sorry about my boyfriend. He shouldn't have treated you that way...I shouldn't have..." I couldn't finish.

As I spoke, Santos looked only at my mouth, but when he finally moved his gaze to my eyes, he stared with such intensity it took my breath away. After a long second, he nodded, then, standing up, walked out without a word.

Nurse Stiles came in and looked around. "Cassie, your mother is here. Did Rafael Dos Santos return to class?" She asked.

"Ah, yes, I believe he did." I said, not really sure where Santos had taken off to. Walking out, I bumped into Jack. He stood talking to my mother and I almost didn't recognize him. His hair was combed, and his perfectly faded jeans didn't even have a smudge of motor grease anywhere. He was wearing an old, pale-yellow sweater over a t-shirt, and I could feel a flush rising to my face. Of course, being as everything else in the day had been geared toward making me appear an idiot, I found it impossible to change course now, and blurted out, "Oh! You didn't need to come with my mom..."

Thankfully, Jack ignored my comment and asked, "How are you feeling? Your mom said you fainted?"

"Yea, I think I just need to go home and lie down...I'm OK though," I answered, taking my mother's arm.

"Come on, honey. I'll take you home," she said to me. Then turning, she added, "I hope you like going to school here, Jack. You and Cassie can share rides now." I couldn't help it. First, I stared at her stupidly and then at Jack.

Jack smiled. "That might work out great. Thanks, Mrs. Connor. Hope you're feeling better, Cassie. I'll see you later. I don't want to be late for the next class." With that, he held the door open for us. Then, he walked down the hall, his class schedule in one hand, and a backpack in the other.

Chapter Six

"Alright," I said to Jack and Tessa, "I need to know if either one of you have had anything happen out of the ordinary today." It was after dinner, and Tessa had called the three of us to a meeting outside on the porch.

"Nope, pretty normal day for me," Jack said, smiling his mysterious smile. I knew he was lying. It was the first day he'd attended public school in his entire seventeen years, but *"Nope, pretty normal day for me"* was all he was giving up. I decided that was *fine*. I sure wasn't going to *ask* him about it if he wasn't man enough to bring it up first.

"So, Jack, are you going to talk about your first day at school? I mean do you even want to?" I asked, clearly bent out of shape that he'd forced me to break my firm commitment, a micro moment after making it. There was no end to his insensitivity.

"No, actually I don't; so why don't you tell us what's eating you?" Jack said, narrowing his gaze. Tessa squirmed in her rattan chair.

I raised my eyebrows. "OK. How about, does either one of you know what we're supposed to be doing here? So far, I have not seen one incident, which would make me think Nathan is in danger at all. The only one in danger has been me," I said, still stinging from a day of weirdness with me in the leading role.

"How's that?" Jack asked, amused.

"It's very hard to...well, I had a strange 'woo-woo' attack at lunch today," I admitted.

"Are we supposed to know what a 'woo-woo' attack is?" Tessa asked, pushing her glasses up on her nose.

"You know, something like, 'woooo...'" I hauntingly clarified.

"Sounds pretty scary," Jack said, unable to keep from smiling.

"It was—*very*. And the really strange part? It's like I went *into* someone else." I said tentatively.

"Wow. Sounds kinda like possession!" Tessa said, her eyes growing large behind her glasses.

"No, your goofiness, it was scary, but not *that* scary. I just felt like I was looking into someone else's life and feeling their feelings. And there were memories...Oh, my gosh," I said, things suddenly coming clear. "It was the freshman girl across from us, looking at our table! Brittany made some crack about her, and strangely, I didn't really think it was funny. But I knew my friends were watching me, and that I ought to be laughing—and then, whoosh! My mind...it was like a whirlpool...and I passed out. Later, in the nurse's office, I remembered the things I saw and felt."

"That must have been the effects of the gift Hamaliel gave you; he called it eleeo; its Greek, I looked it up..." Tessa was saying in her thoughtful yet enthusiastic voice.

"Tessa, thanks; but honestly, I'm not too fond of what our 'angel friend' likes to call a 'gift,' even if it does come from Greece. This little present he gave me leaves me swooning in front of my friends while I experience someone else's pitiful life. Like mine hasn't become pathetic enough," I complained, just like the warrior-princess-of-God, I'd become.

"So...the part about 'not appreciating the gift until you earn it' is probably true," Jack said, pretending he wasn't giving me a hard time...and *loving* it.

"Well, for your information, I'm not the only one who isn't too fond of their gifting," I said. "His name is Raphael Dos Santos, Santos for short, and he's seeing things that are scaring him pale—and that's saying something. He wasn't real keen on sharing, but I gave him my phone number in case he wants to talk." I gave them both my most knowing look. "And guess what else? I think the girl—the freshman at lunch—she may be the other Guardian. One of the impressions I got was that she was watching me because of a dream. We can't be sure, but if it's true, that would only leave one more...the one with nothing to offer. And in my experience, we have nothing to worry about. The kind of people that don't seem to offer anything always have a way of finding you," I said cynically.

"Remember the other part," Tessa said earnestly, "the offering it all part."

"Right, sorry. I guess I'm just tired. I need to go in, finish my homework, and get to bed; it's been a long day," I said, just wanting to be alone with my depressed thoughts.

"Shouldn't we talk about finding the special person Hamaliel told us would guide us?" Tessa put in, "I think we need to find her."

"And how do you purpose we do that?" I asked feeling perturbed. Again...still.

"We pray...God will lead us. He has so far," Jack said, looking at me. I had the distinct feeling he'd been tempted to add "Duh," to the end of his sentence. But then, maybe it was just my mood. At any rate, it didn't make me feel any better. I knew I had to buck up, put on my face-shield, and keep my unstrung emotions unreadable.

"You're right; let's pray," I said easily, and bowed my head and folded my hands. Jack gave a surprised smiled. Tessa cocked her head and narrowed her eyes before giving herself over to the order of business. Her prayer was straightforward and easy as she thanked God before He'd even done anything for her...us. I supposed that was one way of getting something from your Father; I mused. It would be pretty hard to turn down someone as sweet as Tessa when she was already so darn grateful. And, I reasoned, it was a good technique to remember...almost simultaneously realizing that my motives probably disqualified me immediately. It was becoming increasingly clear how unqualified I was for Christian-hood-ship, and I was pretty sure that wasn't even a word. Everybody sat silently with their eyes closed for a moment afterward, and I assumed they were still praying. So, I just let my mind cruise.

Jack was staring at me when I opened my eyes, and he changed the topic, saying, "You know, I wish something threatening *would* happen, so we could know whether Nathan's really who we're supposed to be defending."

"Ah, I'm sure that's coming from a purely scientific standpoint, Jack. Is that why you enrolled at the high school, so you wouldn't miss out on any of the good stuff...the bloodshed?" I said, my face serene. A small smile curved my lips and my voice was even. I was in the process of recovering some of my dignity.

"Oh! Do you think there will be blood?" Jack said, pretending to be excited.

"OK you two, the fight is supposed to be against the forces of darkness, not against each other!" Tessa said in exasperation.

"Tessa, we're not fighting. I just need to ask Jack one

thing while we're on the subject of Nathan. What do you have against him, I mean, besides the fact that *I like him?*" I said, looking steadily at Jack.

His face darkened instantly, but he returned my look without blinking. "What did he tell you?" He asked calmly.

"Nothing. We haven't had time to talk about it. Besides, I want your version, Jack," I persisted.

"Well, that's what you'd get. My version. I think I'll let you figure out what's true on your own," he said standing. I stood too, not wanting to be left sitting while Jack walked out all superior.

"Fine. I think I'm up to that. I'll say goodnight, too," I said. I was on the step above him, and as our eyes met, they locked for a brief second. His were glowing in a way that could only be attributed to the reflection of the moon, but they burned into me nearly destroying the shield I'd raised. I turned quickly, *trying* not to hurry into the house and up the stairs.

After finishing my homework and my bedtime beauty regime, I walked over to my sister's door and peeked in. Tessa's little body leaned over a large textbook on her desk. Her hair looked excited, and her be-speckled face was absorbed. There were papers in piles with scratching's that could not have been more foreign to me had they been hieroglyphics. She was so tiny, and the book, way too big. She was deeply focused, so I tiptoed back, leaving her door ajar.

I'd had a hard day, and the love which had filled me since my encounter in the pines was fast slipping away. The girl who'd recently decided to go along with—no—had actually *wanted* to be a part of God's plan, seemed to be someone who called herself by my name but only inhabited this body at random intervals. I crawled into bed and pulled my Bible from the shelf, and, for the first time in years, I allowed myself to open its cover page and read the inscription:

To my **daughter:** I **love** you **more than** the **univer**ses w**ith**in the u**niverse.** Ca**ss**ie, your answers **lay within th**ese **pages. Always look** deep, deep, **d**eep. **You'll find** God **even** in the molecules. Love, Da**d Colossians** 1:14-17

I stroked his writing, feeling the old pain well up inside me. I recognized the struggle it had taken him to write this. There was a time he could have helped me understand, told me what to do; without him, nothing felt right, and none of it made sense.

Since I'd needed the appearance of an angel to make me believe in God once again, shame still held me hostage when it came time to pray. I wasn't sure how long it would take...I wasn't sure if I would ever *feel* like my faith was real...

I flipped open to the verse in Colossians and read:

"...in whom we have redemption through His blood, the forgiveness of sins. He is the image of the invisible God, the firstborn over all creation. For by Him, all things were created that are in heaven and that are on earth, visible and invisible, whether thrones or dominions or principalities or powers. All things were created through Him and for Him. And He is before all things, and in Him all things consist."

I finished, and then read it again. Something was wrong. *I* was wrong. I knew it wasn't supposed to be like this. This book was supposed to hold my answers. These words weren't supposed to affect me like the hieroglyphics on Tessa's homework.

Chapter Seven

As I grappled with my newly commissioned role as "Christian warrior," the rest of my life continued on a downward spiral. It felt like I was swimming against a rip tide as one minor disaster followed another.

My friends couldn't seem to talk about anything besides the hot "new guy" at school named Jack, while I searched in vain for Santos. But he wasn't at school, and he didn't call. I even tried slyly asking around but got nowhere.

Of course, the delightful gift bestowed on me by Hamaliel made my life at school and dealings with my friends a real treat. Just when I'd begin to relax—to let the worries and concerns of dark warfare slip from my mind, and maybe enjoy a joke for a moment or two—I'd get nailed. The fact that it happened when we were having fun at someone else's expense wasn't lost on me; it just ticked me off. I'd never been someone to *verbally* insult anyone, with the exception of my sister, (and everyone knows sister abuse is a right and privilege). I chose to abuse people in the privacy of my mind. I couldn't help myself on that count. Thoughts happened before I could stop them. And it was how I amused myself.

Besides, in the past few days I'd even reformed my verbal cruelty towards my sister. But since that first day back at school after the Pine Circle, when strangely nothing was amusing, I'd found myself falling back into the pattern of enjoying a joke or two my friends shared at someone else's expense. And some of them *were* funny.

Now, the best part of the gift with which Hamaliel so graciously saddled me was that, just when my friends were having the biggest laugh, they would see me standing and staring off into space like the killjoy I'd become.

I must admit, these jokes weren't as entertaining when I'd suddenly find myself experiencing what our "targets" felt. And usually, a victim's memories were being created by the hurt that "yours truly" and all my darling friends were inflicting. It didn't take very long for my fun to be ruined. It became impossible to look at anyone as though they didn't matter. And if I dared, I was in danger of becoming them, if only for a power-packed emotion-filled minute. It was a nightmare.

If this weren't enough, Nathan and I were struggling where we'd never struggled before. He was jealous of everyone, namely Jack. Then, in some bizarre turn, which highly resembled "keep your friends close and your enemies closer," Nathan decided to renew his friendship with Jack and make him his best, best, bud. As a result, in the last few days, we hadn't spent any time together, and now, *I* was jealous of *Jack*. So, I decided one more unthinkable thing must be in order.

~

Approaching the girl during a break, I slid in next to her on a bench. "Hi. I don't think we've ever met..." I began.

The girl's eyes opened wide. "You're Cassie Conner." She blurted out, and then looked embarrassed.

"Yes, I am, but I don't think I've ever met you...at least not formally..." I admitted.

"I'm Hailey." The girl replied. She began to say something else but closed her mouth quickly as if to keep the words from flying out.

"What?" I asked.

"Ah, nothing. I, um...do you already know?" She ventured, peering at me as though waiting for a sign.

"About the dreams?" I asked, taking less of a chance than she could have known.

"Yes! Yes!" Hailey reached over and grabbed my hand. "I dreamt about you, and the new boy that hangs out with your boyfriend, and the funny little girl in glasses, and a Mexican kid that goes here!" she exclaimed, relief flooding her face. "It was so real! Then the other day...for a second...it was as if... when you looked at me, you knew...and you knew me...and..."

"You have no idea," I broke in smiling, just as Brittany, Jenna, Nathan, and Jack walked up. It couldn't have happened any other way for it to be made official. I was now a leper. Brittany came to a dead stop, halting everyone behind her. She stared at me as if I'd lost my mind. Without a word, she kept going and Jenna followed, the same look of surprised indignation on her face.

Nathan at least controlled his disdain and said, "Hey, I've been looking for you. So...you coming?" He finished, keeping his distance in case of contagion.

"Yea sure. But in a minute," I answered, unable to keep from coloring. Nathan nodded and kept walking. Only Jack stood where he was, smiling. It was a smile that would have melted my heart if I hadn't been in love with Nathan, and yet, it melted a little anyway. He walked over and sat down beside me.

"I'm Jack," he said, smiling at Hailey.

"Hi," she managed, shyly looking down at her book bag.

"Um, Jack, Hailey says she's dreamed about us, and Tessa, and the kid, Santos, too. I think we all need to get together and talk."

"Definitely," Jack answered.

"What about?" Hailey asked, seeming astonished at the circumstances she'd found herself in.

"It's a bit of a story, really. I think we need to talk... somewhere else," I said looking to my left and right, and then launching. "The only thing I can tell you is that the group you dreamed about Jack, Tessa, me, you, Santos are a part of it except I don't know about Santos, the Mexican kid, I can't seem to find him and there's one other too we don't know who but it's all about protecting someone although nothing's too clear yet." Stopping before I passed out.

Jack smiled. "Can you meet us Friday after school?" He asked Hailey. "Maybe you already have plans?"

Hailey had a hard time looking Jack in the face without coloring and turned to me. "Oh no, I don't have anything planned! I mean, I can meet for sure, after asking my mom, that is."

"Good. Give me your phone number, and I'll call you. I can pick you up if you need a ride," I offered.

"Um, OK," Hailey answered, scribbling her number on a napkin.

"Oh wait, what am I thinking? There's a football game Friday. I'll have to be here. Maybe we could get together after. Do you go to football games?" I asked her.

"Well sure...I could." she answered, still looking dazed.

"Good. I'll pick you up if you need a ride," Jack offered.

"See you Friday then," he added, taking my elbow, and standing.

"Yea, see you then," Hailey replied, in a tone of utter disbelief.

To say my warm and adoring friends treated me with "cool reserve" following my chummy acceptance of Hailey gives "cool" and "reserve" expanded meanings. An Eskimo would have taken chill. A cloistered nun had more conversations. Still, I blundered through the day, optimistically ignoring their pointed rejection of me. I don't know why; I knew there was no way they could forgive or forget the fact that I was hopelessly entrenched in weirdness. I'd been breaking the unwritten laws of my peer group like they were rules our parents had set. And by Thursday, I knew it was over, one way or another.

I had spoken with Nathan every night that week on the phone, and he'd asked me again and again to explain what was happening to me. I wanted to tell him in person, alone, but that didn't happen. There was never enough time with all our school activities and his hectic schedule. Finally, I explained it all, the angel, the Guardians, everything, over the phone—and, surprise, surprise—it didn't go well.

He immediately decided we should meet, even if it meant he'd miss part of practice, and I'd be late for cheer squad. I couldn't help cringing as I remembered my attitude toward "crazy Tessa" when she'd told me about the angel. Karma is an ugly word when it's you it's getting ready to slap. I knew Nathan was serious, and I was nervous.

I dressed carefully that morning, taking extra time and wearing an outfit I'd been saving. I knew I looked good, and if I'd ever needed to put my "assets" to noble use, today was probably the day. I was tired of everything going wrong. Obviously, it was up to me to make things right. I hadn't cracked my Bible for days and was actually starting to feel I could balance these two worlds if I just didn't go too overboard either way.

Jack was waiting at the car when I came out, and we drove to school together. I was always so surprised to see him looking...for lack of any other way I wanted to describe him... school worthy. He wore a pale blue, t-shirt that turned his grey eyes a darker blue, and pale, nicely worn Levi's. I wondered how he knew what looked so...decent together. Did he even look at magazines? As we drove, I decided to throw him a bone. "You look nice today, Jack," I said, keeping my voice light.

"Really?" He was looking at his homework and didn't even look up. That really bugged me, and I wasn't about to say, "yes, really." That would amount to a steak, not a bone. After a couple seconds, he looked up and said, "So, where're you going?"

I turned and raised my eyebrows. "School."

"You look like you're going somewhere else, too— something special today?"

I wasn't wearing anything all that different, so I honestly didn't know how he knew exactly what to say. "No, just school, but thanks."

We turned into the parking lot and found a space. Nathan saw us from the lawn and headed over. I grabbed my backpack and turned quickly to Jack. "And yes, you *really do* look nice," I said, ducking out and slamming my door. As I headed toward the lawn, I could see different emotions play over Nathan's handsome face. Miracle; he was eager to see me—he *was* worried—but he *liked* what he saw. At that moment, I was glad of two things. I was grateful for my assets, and I was glad I'd thrown Jack, well, a little steak.

My last class was supposed to be forty-five minutes long, but it seemed to take twice that for the teacher to take roll. By the time it was over, I'd aged ten years. After seeing Nathan at the beginning of school, he'd avoided me the remainder of the day. By the time the bell rang, and I'd walked to where he'd said he'd meet me at the end of the office building, I was a wreck. I took a deep breath and closed my eyes. When I opened them, I saw Jack walking toward me. I wanted to scream.

"Nathan wants to meet you down the hall—in the music room. He wanted me to tell you."

"Oh swell." I said, my tone decidedly ungrateful. I hadn't bothered to notice that Jack didn't look any happier than I felt. As he turned to leave, I quickly added, "I'm sorry, Jack, thanks." He turned back and looked at me.

"Don't do it."

"What?" I asked, honestly perplexed.

"You can't be two people, Cassie."

"I'm not trying to be!" Surprisingly, I felt tears welling up inside me, and this made me furious. "Shut up, Jack. You don't know what you're talking about."

He turned and walked away, his shoulders and neck stiff.

I made my way to the music room trying not to think about what Jack had said, and my mean and awful response to him. I couldn't help wondering if the woman Sybil I'd read about in psychology class felt this way before finding out she was nine other people inhabiting one body.

When I got to the music room door, I could hear a piano being played. I knew it had to be Nathan. He sat alone at it in the corner, head bent, his fingers moving effortlessly. I went up and slid beside him. He kept playing but turned to smile at me as he continued. As usual, I was confused, but completely captivated. He was everything wrapped up in one package. As he finished the piece, his fingers ran down the keys in front of me, and in one fluid movement, he threw his arms around me—the music abruptly ending. But my heart's pounding took over. If he'd wanted to keep me guessing, he was doing a good job. He continued holding me, breathing the fragrance of my neck but not kissing me.

"So, you're *not*...upset with me?" I finally asked, hating to break the moment. His arms slackened. I leaned back to see his face, which revealed nothing. "What then? Is it over?" I asked. "Because if it is, you don't need to end it with a concerto. A simple, *it's over*, will work," I managed to say with a small smile. I couldn't stand waiting any longer. He dropped his arms.

"I guess that's really up to you. I talked with Jack. He backs up your crazy story, but c'mon Cassie. Even if it were true, I'm not sure I'd *want* to believe it."

"What do you mean?" I asked, knowing exactly what he meant.

"It's a decision isn't it? To believe in that stuff? If I do, my whole life changes and I don't want my life to change. I like my life. And I want you in my life. So, if you want to be in it, if you don't want this to be over, you've got to give it up." His blue eyes had never been so blue; they'd never been so serious.

"I think I can do both...have both," I said, my stomach beginning to feel sour.

"You can't."

"I think I can."

"Sleep with me. This weekend, after the game." His eyes had turned steely.

"Gee, that was romantic. Nothing like a command to get me all tingly," I said, with a smirk. He didn't smile, as his eyes remained fastened on mine. "Fine! Will that prove something to you? Will that prove I love you as much as God?"

"No, but it might prove something to you," Nathan said, softening. Suddenly, I was sick. Sick at heart. I stood up.

"You know, I'm not a prude. I've just been waiting for the right person—you. And the right time." I said defensively.

"Yea, well I've been waiting, too." Nathan countered.

"Then do something about that watchdog-mother of yours," I shot back, walking toward the door, angry and not sure why.

Nathan's silence said more than any heated reply would have. Just as I got to the door, he said, "Wait." I turned and realized he'd gotten up to follow me, stopping a few feet away. "Cassie—Cassie...I..." There it was again. And immediately my heart began to pound. It was more than the way he said my name. It was something in his eyes... "You are *so* beautiful..."

Once again, less than I needed. "So, what?" I shot back, realizing instantly my own false vanity.

He smiled, "Come on, you know I..." I stood waiting. Finally, I broke the silence.

"Yes, I know, '*You want me.*' I'll see you tomorrow...after the game." I walked out the door and to my car without looking back, even though I knew he'd followed me part of the way and watched until my car rounded the corner.

Chapter Eight

I was driving *me* nuts. It used to be that almost everyone else in the world was, in one way or another, either by extremes or increments, oddly irritating. And in general, I treated irritating people with a modicum of kindness, only lacerating them mentally while finding ways to avoid contact. The exception, of course, was Tessa. Here, sister-rules applied, and once in a great while extreme irritators, where I was left with no choice but to dispatch whatever justice was necessary; however, now I had become my own worst offender. And, I could find no mercy. Not to mention, face and voice modulation did not work. Thus, began the torture.

I couldn't understand why everything had been so easy only a week earlier. Now, *everything* was so hard. I couldn't make decisions, keep a friend, or hold onto a boyfriend without selling my soul. Granted, it was my body. And all right, I was only letting him use it so I could keep him. Still, it felt extreme. And my whining was so annoying.

The next moment, I'd begin on things I didn't like unless, of course, I could act like a crybaby, goody-two-shoes psycho.

Case in point, I *loved* being pretty; yet, right now, I *hated* that this was exactly what Nathan liked and wanted. *Wha-waa.* Obviously, I had grave mental concerns.

Then there were my God issues. Now that I knew there *was* a God, I told myself, *I wanted to do His will.* But my other very irritating voice would pipe up saying, *if I were honest, I'd admit I always knew God existed, and that I'd just been mad. And the truth was I didn't want God now any more than I did before because God wouldn't take care of me, and I couldn't trust Him. Also, MY will was more FUN, and God was BORING.* At which point I'd put my hands over my ears and start yelling, "Lalalalalalalalala..." as loud and long as I needed to shut myself up. Pinedale's crazy crown was mine.

This fun lasted most of the afternoon. It was now after 9:30 in the evening. I'd muddled through dinner and homework and, completely exhausted, somehow found my way into bed. Tessa had silently watched me throughout dinner. I was amazed she'd stayed quiet, and yet, miraculously, she had. She hadn't even slipped into my room after her prayers. Here was final confirmation on the existence of God—so, I thought I'd take a shot and give Him a chance to give me a break before I was completely broken, done, ...kaput.

Nathan's request had actually been an ultimatum, and I knew it. He wanted me to choose between him and...Him. But could I sleep with Nathan and *not* make a choice? Maybe I could, even if my gut felt funny about it; but I didn't want to let my belly be my only guide. Goodness knows I never would have learned to swim if I'd listened to my stomach. And I'd never been in the school play, I argued, if the heaves beforehand had kept me from my stage debut. So, I decided just to ask Him, saying, "*God, give me a sign. If you don't think I should sleep with Nathan...the 'Link,'*" which I added in case it had some sway. "*Please give me a sign.*"

Then I realized, that since my life had become so extraordinarily strange, I might not recognize a sign if God actually decided to give me one, so, I had better choose something myself. I wracked my brain for an event similar to an asteroid shower, or the earth standing still for a day, yet still in keeping with my own needs. My math teacher would be grading our last exams. I pondered asking for an 'A,' realizing that would rival Earth at a standstill any day...but I doubted he'd have them back by tomorrow...*Bummer*. I wracked my brain. Suddenly, it dawned on me.

"If Santos is at the game tomorrow night, and You let me speak to him, I'll know You don't want me to sleep with Nathan." It wasn't a tsunami in Pinedale, but it would do. The guys in this group usually hated football players, they had no school spirit, and I'd never seen even one show up for a football game since I'd been at Pinedale High. Of course, I'll admit, I'd never, ever, looked.

I was late for school the next morning; meaning; I had missed my ride with Jack, and Tessa took the bus. Both worked out well for me. The rest of the day was a study in tardy. I showed up late both in mind and body, missing questions by either mere fractions of a second, or sections of my brain. I was late to classes by several minutes, and missed Nathan almost altogether for so many various reasons it became comical.

By the time the game had begun that evening, and I was in the middle of a cheerleading routine, I remembered I hadn't told Jack that I wouldn't be meeting with them that night. I tried not to think about it and just have fun—there were too many other things I was trying to stay on top of, and I couldn't worry about those three now.

For one thing, I could have sworn my highly annoyed friends had begun to thaw a tiny bit. Whenever I approached their airspace, the crackling sound, which surrounded them when they were displeased, seemed to be lessening.

But as they say, the game wasn't over. Don't get me wrong; it was looking good for our team. Nathan had passed for three touchdowns, and we were winning. And the girls threw me higher than we'd ever accomplished in practice; so high, that as I flew through the air, visions instantaneously flashed through my mind of them winking at each other as they acted out terrified gasping screams and let me fall to the hard earth. The fact that I landed safely and heard each of them inhale deeply in relief as their grips held, restored my faith—if not in their humanity—at least in their clear understanding of the importance of being the best darn cheerleading squad in the district.

No, as far as the football team, Nathan, and my social status—things were looking up. But then, I looked up. Santos stood at the top right-hand corner of the bleachers with about ten of his Hispanic campaneros, his eyes glued to my face. Since we were right in the middle of a yell, nobody noticed when I let out a slightly different tone of surprise; but they all noticed when I set my pom-poms on the bench and took off around the bleachers. It's true, I thought I saw him nod at me, but suddenly I couldn't fathom why I'd set off chasing him. When I looked back up to where he'd been standing, he was gone. He'd probably run for his life. I remembered saying to him, *"You're one of us,"* and by now, I must have begun to seem like the lead character in an alien invasion.

As I desperately searched for him, my mind would not relent. I could envision the headlines in the morning paper: "Mexican American student missing after being chased by insane white cheerleader." And what could I tell the rest of the squad about my abrupt exit that they would ever believe? Obviously, it would need to be something critical. Nothing else would be acceptable. I was deciding between "tear in my undergarment" and "severely torn fingernail" when I saw him. He'd come down alone and was standing under the far bleacher in the shadows. I slowly made my way over to him like an animal rights advocate trapping a feral cat.

"Hey, it's Santos, right?" I asked lamely. He looked drawn and thin. Beneath his eyes dark hollows had formed.

"That's right. You're Cassie," He answered.

"You wanna talk?" I countered, getting right to it.

"Just tell me what you think you know," he said, moving deeper into the shadows.

I looked around. I'm proud to say, there was only the slightest hesitation on my part, not really enough to mention, considering I knew nothing, and I mean absolutely nothing, would repair my reputation if I were seen entering the underbelly of the bleachers with a gang member.

"OK, this is what I was told...It's going to seem very weird to you, but obviously something weird is already happening. Otherwise, you wouldn't be here looking like you do. At least I hope that's why you're here...well, not that I *hope* something weird is happening to you..." I mentally slapped myself. Santos *was* looking desperate. "Sorry, OK, here it is. There are six of us. Three of us have been given special gifts: One girl, Hailey, dreams of things that are going to happen in the future. I was given something that lets me see how other people feel, and your gift, at least the gift the other Guardian is supposed to have, is the ability 'to see beyond the veil.' In other words, you can see into the realms of the spirit world. And right now, what you're seeing are the dark forces getting ready for a battle. A big one."

"How do you know this?" He asked, gripping my wrist.

"OK, I was hoping not to have to tell you until maybe you trusted me a little more. But here goes... An angel told us. His name is Hamaliel." At the look on Santos' face, I continued more quickly. "I know, I know; I didn't believe it either. I gave my sister so much...never mind. But believe me, it's true. I saw him. He called us the Guardians, and he said we were chosen to save someone, and something, the forces of darkness want to destroy. Someone he called the *Link*. We think it's a kid our age that's supposed to grow up, and become important, and make great changes in the world. I don't know why you've been given this awful gift; I hate mine too, and I don't know why any of us were chosen..." As I said this, I heard someone calling my name in a loud whisper. It was Jack and following him were Hailey and Tessa.

"We saw you take off, so we came to find you. Come on, let's go somewhere else to talk," Jack said, looking directly at Santos. To my surprise, Santos followed him without a word.

We sat facing each other in the middle of the Pine Circle. I had insisted on a lantern, so it was easier to see each other's faces. And what a collection we were. It was hard to believe that this was the best God could do in forming a group called the Guardians. In fact, you could say that an angry, scared, gang member; a twelve-year-old brainiac; an overweight, embarrassed freshman-outcast; a born-again Christian; and most questionable of all, a peer-conscious high school cheerleader, made us an, assorted, contrasting, dissimilar, not to mention, motley group. So, it made it stranger still that, as we sat together in that circle, I felt a current of warmth hugging us. Weirdly, I liked them all, and I liked being with them.

After becoming more comfortable, Santos began telling of his experiences with what he called the "creatures." The first time he'd seen one he was helping his father.

"I'd just taken the grass carrier over to the back of the trailer and dumped it in. I was thinking what a beautiful day it was," he said, his eyes clouding in memory, and his voice low. "The air was cool, but the sun was warm. I almost enjoyed being out there working, but I had better things planned with my homeys.

"I got word that Sal, this friend of mine, had scored some good stuff. I was tired of only hearing about it. So, I decided it was time. I had never done drugs before. In fact, I still haven't," he said, quietly. "I promised my mom I wouldn't. She'd been real worried about me hanging out with my homeys. She used to pray over me before I went to bed every night when I was little. But lately, I even found her praying for me in the middle of the night." He looked up. "She works hard and doesn't get to sleep much. I knew it was hard on her, my being in the gang—but my parents—they will never understand. They don't know what it's like to go to school in this place." He looked away.

"People treat us like we're nothing at school," he said defiantly. "My parents expect me to grow up and take care of white people's lawns or houses...just like they do." It was obvious he had other ideas.

"Anyway, I was standing there, dumping the grass when, from the corner of my eye, I see a movement, like someone sneaking around the house. I dropped the carrier and went to see. My father was coming around the corner with a bag of leaves in his arms and I almost bumped into him. So, I ask him, 'Did you see someone running real fast-like around the corner?' And he smiles and says, 'No, only just me.' So, I looked around, and didn't see nothing. But then I turn to follow my father and there it is." Santos stared blindly ahead, a bead of sweat on his upper lip. "It wasn't very big, but along the wall, crouching like a tiger, was this thing. It was pale and looked almost human, but it had fangs and stood on two legs with its small front claws against a big ole' bulging chest. It was snarling and saliva dripped from its mouth and teeth. Its eyes slowly came up my body to my face, and just for a minute, it seemed like it was smiling at me. A real evil smile."

As we sat listening, I knew I wasn't the only one whose neck and arm hair stood at attention. Leaning forward, shallow breathing, everyone's body was on red alert for the instant we might need to rise shrieking and run helter-skelter into the night.

Santos shook his head, and we watched his body relax. "I admit, I opened my mouth to scream, just nothing came out. Then, right before my eyes, that creature, it vanish. I could not believe it. I wonder if maybe I was crazy or something, but I knew I never did no drugs," he said, staring into the lantern's light. "But since then, I've seen more. First a few, then more, and now I see them everywhere. It's getting worse, and I can't stand it. They're on people now—they're even on some of my friends!" He said, his voice urgent, his eyes large.

Tessa's eyes were as round as his, which meant that magnified by her thick lenses they were approximately the size of two regulation eight balls. "Exactly what do you mean, when you say, 'they're *on* people'?" She asked, barely breathing.

"Nobody sees them but me! Even the big ones can be right next to someone, and they don't see it!" He said exasperated. "But they hook onto people. It's really awful. Today, I saw a man with a small one on his back, and it was sucking on his neck. It was really..."

"Gross!" Hailey finished for him.

"Yea, and terrible. But the man didn't know, and I couldn't do nothing."

"Wow, I don't think there's any doubt that you're our man," Jack said. "Can you handle being part of the Guardians if we promise to help?"

"I really thought maybe I was going crazy. Then I met you, cheerleader Cassie... Cassita Bonita, that's what we call you," he said, looking over at me, with a small smile. "So, then, I'm thinking, maybe there's a reason for all this."

Now, I had an idea that "Bonita" was a type of tuna fish. I also figured it was better than a few of the names I'd heard the gang members labeling a few of us, shall we say, with fairer complexions. So, I was pleased; although, I thought some kind of bird might have been nicer. But, then I reasoned, at least it wasn't a carp. It was amazing what my mind could reflect upon in the middle of being scared stupid.

Santos continued, "So now, even if you guys aren't crazy, how you gonna help me?" He asked. And I wondered the same thing.

"I don't know yet. But I know that you wouldn't have been given this—weapon—if you weren't strong enough to use it against the 'creatures.' I promise, I'll stick with you until we figure something out together," Jack said.

Santos sat up taller, and for the first time since I'd initially seen him, there was an emotion besides fear or anger in his eyes. He looked at Jack, and I could tell something passed between them. *Leave it to guys to bond over the word "weapon,"* I thought to myself. Still, I couldn't help feeling encouraged, too.

"Then you're willing to help us?" Jack asked, still looking intently at Santos.

"Just what are we supposed to be doing?"

"All we know is what the angel Hamaliel said. There will be six of us, and so far, there are five. He described you and Hailey as having exactly the, well, he called them 'gifts,' that you both have. He also explained that we've been chosen to protect someone that will grow up to be a leader: someone who will be given the 'mantle of power.' The forces of darkness are planning an all-out attack to keep that from happening."

"Who is this *Link*? This chosen one?" Santos asked.

"We think it's Nathan Gregory," Jack said, sounding unconvinced.

"Who is Nathan Gregory?" Santos asked, revealing the vast chasm existing between our worlds.

"You remember. He's the guy that was with me in the nurse's office that day..." I admitted, realizing he'd find out sooner or later.

Santos stood up. "I'm outta here, man. There is no way that *chingasa...*"

Innately I knew I would rather be a fish than whatever he'd just called Nathan...

"Hold on, Santos," Jack said. Then turning to the rest of us, "I'm with him. How do we know for certain it's Nathan? He'd be about the last person I'd choose," he finished, deliberately looking away from me.

"Gosh, and you two are *so* close now. I would have thought you were devoted to the cause," I said, letting sarcasm stand in for my anger.

"There are a lot of people I'm friendly with that I wouldn't vote for as bathroom monitor, let alone believe they'd grow up to be key players in world peace." He said bitingly, staring at me as though he thought me reckless enough to continue engaging him in this particular battle.

"Well, guys, we don't know for sure," Tessa put in, "I mean, his uncle is in Washington, and Nathan plans to go, too...and we don't really know anyone else..." she said, trying to diffuse the situation.

"Anybody can become powerful with the help of God," Hailey offered, making it sound as much like a personal pep talk as a statement of faith.

"Look, Jack, ...Santos. If you don't think it's Nathan, fine. I mean, why would either of you want it to be him? He was simply the most obvious choice," I said, needing something that wasn't an overt defense of myself, but vindicating my position. I thought I'd done splendidly.

"Yea. Then there was the part about you protecting 'your future and the one you love,'" Jack said, still looking at me as though I were responsible for this whole evil-on-the-rampage-business.

"Yes, there *was* that. But may I remind you, I asked—*no, I begged*—not to be a part of this!"

"What Hamaliel said to Cassie was, 'Your future and the one you love depend on it,'" Tessa explained to Santos and Hailey.

"So, you *love* that guy?" Santos asked, a look of utter disbelief on his face. When I didn't answer, he shook his head. "Maybe he's the *Link*, but I don't think so. If we can, we need to put it to some kind of test."

"I think so too, and if we can figure out a way, we will," Jack agreed. "Meanwhile, are you in, Santos?"

"Yes. I'm in. But for the record, I don't like that Nathan guy."

"Yea, we kind of got that," I said under my breath. We sat in silence for several minutes, each caught up in our own thoughts until I found myself looking at Hailey. Her black hair was pulled back, and I couldn't help noticing her surprisingly beautiful green eyes. They were slightly tilted up at the corners, gleaming in the light. She had a strong straight nose, and if she ever decided to cut some bangs and lost a few pounds... Sensing she was being watched, she looked up and blushed. Jack must have been studying her, too.

"So, Hailey, what about your dreams? If you'd like to share, ...well, right now we need all the help we can get," he said.

"I've had some amazing dreams, that's for sure." She answered, without her usual embarrassment.

"Go on, tell us," Tessa encouraged, anxious to hear what Hailey had seen.

"Well, the first one was about a week and a half ago. I saw a shepherd. He was in a big field, and there were all kinds of animals...mainly sheep, but not just sheep. And the different animals were forming rings—like around each other..."

"Concentric rings." Tessa added. I'm sure believing that word might be helpful to the rest of us who managed to stare at her blankly.

All except Jack, who nodded and said, "Right—keep going Hailey."

Well, in the middle of all the...herds, was a pen made of something shiny..." She looked off for a moment. "Something like a silver chain; it was in a perfect circle. I knew some animal was inside this pen, and there were dogs, lying nearby guarding it. To tell you the truth, I kept trying to look into the pen, but I couldn't get close enough to see the animal. But I knew it was special, the shepherd said it had to be protected. That's what the dogs were for. They had collars on, and what looked like a small compass hung from each of their collars like a tag. I knew it meant that even when they didn't know which direction or path to take, they would be guided—or maybe they would be guiding the others. I'm not sure. There was only one dog lying a little further off, with its head lowered that didn't seem to have a collar. That part isn't too clear. Boy, this sounds silly when I say it out loud." She said, stopping.

"No, keep going," Tessa encouraged, leaning forward intently. We all murmured in agreement.

"Well, except for inside the pen, I could see everything; the valley, the hills, and the surrounding towering mountains weren't familiar at all, but I knew I was looking at Pinedale. It was lush, beautiful, and peaceful, until I looked toward the mountains and saw something coming over the ridge. They were wolves; or at least something like wolves. I thought they were coming for the animals, but then I realized that what they really wanted was the animal in the pen. I knew because the dogs got to their feet, and now they were huge and fierce with shining eyes—and they weren't afraid at all. But I was scared because the wolves were large. And there were lots of them. I'm telling you, I got so frightened, I woke up."

We looked at each other. "OK. I think that's pretty freakishly self-explanatory, ...except for the part where the dogs are all fierce and aren't afraid, and of course, the whole concentric circle business," I added.

"Tell us another one." Tessa said, enthralled.

"About a week after that, was a dream about you, Cassie," she said, looking at me. "And the rest of you were in it, too," she said, sweeping her gaze around the circle. "My dream was exactly what happened at school when Cassie and her friends were sitting across from me. Everyone had begun making fun of me," she said, looking down in embarrassment. "But in my dream, Cassie came over and told me not to feel bad. You were standing next to her, Jack. Santos and Tessa, you were there, too. Then Cassie said to me, '*Hailey, God has heard you, and you have been chosen.*' It was so real."

"*I* was the one that said that?" I asked, amazed that I'd been leader of the "Onward Christian Soldiers." Of course, I knew it was just a dream and it hadn't actually happened that way. Still, how *very* unexpected, and somehow, *cool*...

"Uh-huh, and then you told me to, '*Remember this dream.*'" And I woke up. "The next day when everything happened, I couldn't believe it. When you looked at me, I thought, my gosh, she knows!" Hailey ended, shaking her head, and smiling.

"Have you had any more?" Tessa asked, irrepressibly.

"Well, I've had the 'wolves coming over the mountain' dream several times, but it's always the same—except last night it was different." She looked at each of us. "This time in the dream, the wolves were one mountain closer. Also, the five of us were sent looking for someone. The shepherd told me we should find someone who he named, the 'Master of the Call.' And somehow, I knew it was the person who'd train the dogs to guard the animal in the pen. Anyway, we went into the forest on the west edge of town and began calling out the name *Darius*." She looked at our rapt faces, and when we remained silent, she added, "That was it."

"That was it?" I asked, hoping for a little more closure on our next move. I knew *I* wasn't going traipsing around the forest calling out a name like *Darius* without a little more to go on. I could see it now: Sheriff Riggs, happening upon us, *"Excuse me, kids, who are you looking for?"* *"Why, the 'Master of the Call,' Sir. Have you seen her around these parts?"* No. Uh-uh, I needed a bit more.

"How about going tomorrow? If everyone can meet at the high school parking lot at 11:00, we could all go together," Jack reasoned, primarily looking at Santos.

Santos agreed, and both Tessa and Hailey nodded vigorously. So much for my not traipsing.

"Hailey; Santos. I don't know too much about your spiritual backgrounds or your faith, but it's clear God has great faith in you. He is in us as we work together. So, before we go, I think maybe we should all pray together," Jack finished, a little tentatively.

"Cool," Tessa agreed, walking over to Santos and Hailey, and taking each of their hands. This was happening a little fast for me, but I knew I wasn't any more uncomfortable than Santos who stood looking ready to run. I went over and took my place next to him figuring if he decided to bolt, I'd be right behind him.

Once more we made a circle, and Jack took Hailey's and

my hand, so Santos and I took hands, too. "Cassie, would you say something for us?" Jack asked.

"Sure, I will." Turning slightly to my left, I said, "Uh ... Tessa, would you please lead us in prayer," and as Jack's eyes were closed, I completely wasted a malevolent look on him. However, when I painfully squeezed his fingers, I caught his smile.

Tessa nodded sweetly and closed her eyes. "God, thanks for all Your help. We'll wait on You. We know that You'll somehow make everything clear to us. Be with us tomorrow as we try to find someone we don't know named Darius. Don't let us forget to thank You all day long. Oh, and God, thanks so much for bringing Hailey and Santos to us. Amen."

During her short prayer, something strange happened. I looked up and saw each face fill with the same look of wonder. A current of tingling power had coursed through us, running from one hand to the next.

"Did you feel that?" Santos asked, his eyes wide.

"Uh-huh," I uttered, shocked into semi-speechlessness.

"Wow," Jack said, looking closely at his hands. Hailey smiled brightly and Tessa beamed. "OK, tomorrow at 11:00," Jack restated.

We all agreed and turned toward home. Tessa stood for a moment longer deep in thought. Then she called to Hailey, "How many dogs were there in the first dream?"

She tapped her chin remembering. "There were five closest to the pen...but...let's see... another one was a little further out in the field... six." Hailey answered. Tessa nodded thoughtfully and started walking.

I lay in bed that night and knew I'd made a major decision without thoughtful consideration. Actually, that's usually how I did my best work. God had done his part. Asteroids, in the form of gang members, had showered down on Pinedale High's first home game of the season. And now wrath, in the form of Nathan, was going to shower down upon me because I'd chosen God and not him.

There were seven missed calls and two messages on my phone when I got home. There was no doubt Nathan was going to dump me, and it made me feel a multitude of things, including sad. Not simply because he'd changed my life at Pinedale High for the better, and not just because he was about to change it again for the worse. And it wasn't even because he was an amazing kisser. Being denied our make-out sessions would alone have been enough to create withdrawals and severe heartache. No, there was something else. Yes, I would miss being associated with all his admirable qualities and all his great accomplishments just by being his girlfriend, but that wasn't it either. It wasn't even the fact that all the other girls wanted him and now he'd be available; although, I realized this last reason made him devastatingly desirable, and harder to give up. In truth, it had nothing to do with him hurting me. Strangely enough, my sadness had more to do with the knowledge that I'd be hurting him. And I didn't want to wound his heart.

Nathan had a good heart; heck, it was good enough to be the *Link*. But I knew myself—and I knew myself with him. If I stayed with Nathan, neither of us would be as good together as we'd be apart. We were too much of the same stuff. Granted, I'd never be the accomplished "woman-for-all-reasons-in-all-seasons" that Nathan was as a guy, but I could hold my own as beautiful, hurt, lonely and pretending. And I knew how cozy we were keeping each other warm with those same comfortable disorders. We'd never ask each other to change even for the better...especially for the better. And I'd come to know something different...

Ever since the moment with Hamaliel, when I felt my pain melting and something else filling up that space, I'd found it very hard to pretend anymore...about anything. And boy, not only did this mess with my inborn skills at camouflage, but it totally messed with what I was beginning to expect out of myself. Which, of course, helped turn my relationship with Nathan on its head. So somehow, I'd have to get over him. And somehow, I'd try to keep him from hating me too much. Otherwise, it would break his heart. Down deep, I was sure of this...

Chapter Nine

The next morning dawned clear and cold. The sun had only begun warming the crisp air when we arrived at the high school. It was 11:05 and Hailey's mother was just dropping her off, but Santos was nowhere to be seen. Realizing no one had gotten a cell number from him, we waited for another ten minutes. Then, we decided to start out without him. As we were pulling away, we saw him loping toward the parking lot.

"Hey man, glad you could make it," Jack said, smiling broadly as he drew the car up beside him, "get in."

"Sorry I'm late. I didn't realize my dad's job was so far away. We were up on Redwood Street, across the river," Santos said; breathing hard, sweat standing out on his face despite the cold.

"You had to walk all the way over here?" Tessa asked.

"No, I ran. If I walked, it would have taken me forever."

"You should have called me. I would have come and gotten you," Jack exclaimed.

"No big deal. I'm here, let's get going," Santos stated, getting into the back seat with Haley and Tessa. Before he'd even caught his breath, he said, "I seen a lot a creatures today. There's either more, or I'm seeing more. Either way, it's pretty nasty. Before, they were jus prowling, maybe hunting, but now, they're on people," he said, shuddering involuntarily.

We drove in silence, too freaked out to say much. When we got to a mountain road, a few miles into the forest, Hailey said, "Turn right up here and stop. This sorta looks like the place I dreamed about."

We got out and stood around, looking hesitantly into the forest which surrounded us. Then Tessa said, "Ya know; I think I remember some of the high school kids in my Algebra II class talking about an old lady that lives in a run-down cabin up here in the woods. They were talking about egging her place on Halloween, but they didn't know if they could find it. The rumor is she's a witch." Tessa added.

"The old brueha?" Santos asked.

"I'm not sure, but I don't *think* that was the name from last night," I replied, smiling indulgently.

"No, brueha means 'witch' in Spanish," Santos said, smiling back at me. "There is an old woman that buys tamales from my mother sometimes. She used to ask about me. My friends said she was a witch and lived in the mountains. She dresses like one. Her clothes are all old and her hair is long and messy. But my mother, she likes her." Santos finished.

"Was her name Darius by any chance?" Hailey asked.

"I don't know. I never called her *nothing*. I hid from her." Santos said, laughing.

"Well, let's go on the road. We'll head down any path that looks like there might be a house or cabin at the end," Jack suggested.

I liked the idea of sticking together and systematically checking roads, partly because I was creeped-out by the mention of the old lady being a witch and also because I'd already imagined some of the awkward situations we could find ourselves in if we were to mindlessly begin yelling the name "Darius" into the empty woods.

We automatically assigned Hailey the lead, and she accepted the position a little tentatively. I imagined that dreaming something, and then finding yourself awake and in it, had to be slightly strange. However, to be here *at all* spun the dial on the peculiar meter six ways to bizarre.

Eventually, I found we'd spread out, with Jack walking just ahead and to my right. Occasionally, I'd hear someone yell a tentative, "*Darius,*" into the air, and we'd all stop and listen for an answer. Personally, I hoped she wouldn't step out from behind a tree cackling, or the rest of the group would have to drag my dead body back to the car.

Now, I've never been a great outdoorswoman, except, of course, when it was time to model the latest winter fashions. Then it became necessary due to the extreme heat generated when you wore the apparel indoors. But I have to say, the woods were at least as beautiful as the situation was weird. And it was hard not to notice how great guys looked in the woods. The autumn had turned the leaves into all the warm vibrant colors on my fashion wheel. Jack's shoulders looked wide in the cable pullover he wore, and his dark hair was framed by the surrounding gold. I was mentally waxing lyrical, probably with a gooey look plastered on my face when Jack turned around and looked at me. I thought I caught myself in time. I hoped, I hoped, hoped, hoped. I couldn't exactly tell, although his eyes were twinkling, and he had his unreadable half-smile starting to form, so I quickly looked away. That's when I saw her.

She was standing a-ways off, high on a path to our right. Her hair was gray and pulled back, with tendrils escaping in great mass, like an uprising. She had a walking stick in her hand and was silently watching—smiling. I couldn't help feeling she'd been watching us for a while, even though the thickness of the woods made it unlikely. Jack saw me stop and point. He came over, and seeing her, called out, "Darius?" She waved, her smile broadening. Then, she turned and headed up the path away from us.

The others hurried over. "Shouldn't we follow her?" Tessa asked Hailey, hoping, like the rest of us, her dream actually contained more clues.

"I don't know...but yes. I think we should. What do you think, Jack?" She asked, her eyes wide.

"Do you see anything, Santos, that would make you think she's a witch? Or that there's evil around her?" Jack asked.

I knew I shouldn't, but I couldn't help adding, "That is, besides her very frightening hair-do." Santos thought I was funny, but Jack gave me a quieting look.

"No, there is nothing here," he said stifling his laugh, "I don't see any creatures. I haven't seen nothing, and she was clean," he added sincerely.

Jack's eyes shot over at me. "What?" I asked, "You don't think I'd make a joke about *that*, do you?" I asked feigning deep hurt. Tipping his head to the side, he gave me another one of his looks, which I refused to dignify by ignoring.

"Let's go." Jack led the way along a winding path, catching glimpses of her ahead, until we came to a clearing on a small hill. Smoke was rising from a chimney not too much further ahead. We could see the old woman's figure leading in the direction of the rising smoke, her pace quicker than I would have thought possible for someone of her years. When we finally reached her cabin, I understood why, outside of the obvious bad hair and icky clothes, the witch story had begun circulating. It was a stone and log cabin; something you might see in a storybook. There was a well out front, where it looked like she drew her water, or as the case might be, held small children captive. No lines for telephones or electricity were in sight. It was very obvious to me why no one chose to live like this anymore—not if they knew about government subsidized housing—for pity's sake. I could tell she wouldn't have a dishwasher, TV, or even a microwave inside. For her sake, I thought drolly, it might be better if she could conjure up a little magic to entertain herself. I shook myself, and sort of asked forgiveness. Then, I swore I wouldn't joke around anymore, even in the lonely confines of my brain.

As I consciously sobered myself, I realized the place wasn't actually dirty. The ground had been raked and the one stretched clothesline had a few pieces of clean neatly hung laundry on it. A large bush was covered with a clean pink printed sheet, which looked almost dry. There was a row of tomato plants, each revealing a few red fruit left hanging onto their yellowing stems. Three rows of new dirt looked as though they'd been tilled under for the winter. But most comforting and fairy-tale-like were the animals. Two cats peeked from under her potting table and several birds sat in a row along her clothesline. A large dog, with a beautifully thin face, lay in the sun and lifted his head and thumped his tail at our arrival, but never got up. There was also a duck and a chicken pecking around, and what looked like a racoon sunning himself on a flat rock beside the house, belly exposed to the rays and the world. They all seemed content and unafraid.

Each of us stood taking all this in, while looking apprehensively toward the open door to the cabin. Then, quite suddenly, the old woman emerged carrying a tray with six metal glasses and a ceramic pitcher filled with *who-knew-what*.

"I've been expecting you!" She said cheerily. "Come, come. Sit down. I would invite you inside, but the day is just too glorious! I don't think we should waste it, do you?"

Without giving us a chance to mumble, or stumble around, she continued, "Come then, Raphael. Introduce me to your friends. But first, is your mother well?" She added.

Santos stood staring at her for a fraction of a second before approaching the picnic table where she'd set her tray, answering, "My mother is fine. I...uh...these are my friends," he said, turning to us. "This is Jack, and this is Hailey. Um, that is Tessa and Cassie, they are sisters." He ended.

"Isn't this nice." She patted her hair, as she gazed sweetly at us, and the gesture made me smile; though truly not in a rude way. It was just so cute.

Tessa was the first to approach her. "Hi," she said, putting out her hand. "It's awfully nice to meet you." The old lady tipped her head and studied Tessa, her eyes and face glowing with pleasure.

"So," she said, patting my sister's hand. Tessa returned the smile, looking back at her through magnified lenses, her hair a match for the old lady's any day. Tessa had worn the incongruous pairing of red leggings and combat boots, possibly shorts. Although, a tie-dyed sweatshirt falling to her knees made this impossible to tell. A portion of her hair had been restrained with clips, but what portion was also hard to determine. Around her waist she had knotted last century's ginormous white windbreaker, now the color of dirty snow.

"It's so good to have you all here," she said, approaching the table and dragging Tessa with her. "Let's sit down so we can chat." We all climbed over the benches three to a side, with the old lady sitting at the end next to Tessa and across from Jack. I strategically sat at the other end across from Santos and next to Hailey. The old woman began pouring liquid into the glasses and passing them down until we'd each gotten one. I peered suspiciously into my lemonade and smiled.

"We need a toast, which is another way of praying if you

direct it that way!" She said, winking. It sounded a bit sacrilegious to me, but then I wasn't really a theologian yet. I decided I should give myself at least another week of not swearing before I started being offended by other people's doctrine.

"So, here's to our Father in Heaven, and to those who serve Him," she said, lifting her glass, "'*Arise, shine; For your light has come! And the glory of the Lord is risen upon you. For behold, the darkness shall cover the earth, and deep darkness the people; But the Lord will arise over you, And His glory will be seen upon you.*'"

"Isaiah 60: 1 and 2," Jack said, lifting his glass and clinking it loudly against hers. Then everybody clinked and gulped. I was just glad there wasn't more lemon-to-sugar-d water ratio, since it managed to go down every wrong pipe and into my nose cavity. Leave it to me to cough and spew after a toast to God.

"I'm...I'm *so* sorry," I finally managed to get out, after everyone had taken their turn pounding on my back and venting any buried hostilities. The old woman just smiled sympathetically.

"It's all right, Cassie," she said, coming over and patting my hand. As she touched me, I knew she was talking about more than my coughing jag.

After everyone had taken their seats again, Hailey timidly asked, "By any chance, is your name Darius?"

"Why, yes, it is," she said, smiling at Hailey. "And you must be our dreamer."

"So, it's pretty obvious you know about us," I said, brilliantly.

"Yes, my dear. I have known for many years. Before I came to this town, I had been praying over it for a long time, anticipating the day when the battle would arise. I was told about each of you; although the only one I could recognize was Raphael, because of his mother, Mrs. Dos Santos."

"OK, I'm sorry, for bringing this up, right in the middle of your story about Santos' mom, but would you mind telling us something about yourself," I strategically blurted. Everyone's very wide eyes were on me, and Jack's infuriating half-smile was starting up again. "I mean, you seem very good..." I hurried, "but um...well, I'm really new to all this. I just don't know too much about Christian stuff, ...and I didn't know God used witches." The words were still leaving my mouth when I wanted them back—I could not believe I had said the word "witches" out loud—that I hadn't sugar-coated my suspicions into something more palatable, like enchantress...or *anything*...

Darius looked at each of us and said, "I know how the world views me, and I have allowed it to be so. For although I am on this earth in human form, much as you are, I am here with a special task. There are many realms which exist beyond this earth, but rest assured, I am governed by the One God, the Father. To human eyes and limited understanding, a witch is what may be seen. But in many ways, this has made my life much simpler. Those who would fear the exterior and not trust the experience of 'who I am,' over 'what I appear to be,' are almost always an inconvenience, and they tend to stay away." Her beaming smile fell on us like sunlight after rain, but all I could feel was shame. *I had trusted the exterior and not bothered to rely on what surely felt like love...like God. I was such a...* Darius' voice cut through the mounting noise in my head. "But, Cassie, I'm so glad you asked me. Only someone with the heart of a warrior steps forward with courage into their fears. *Seeking* the truth is often inconvenient, but *finding* truth keeps one's life from becoming so." I looked into her sparkling eyes, and even though I wasn't entirely sure I knew what she'd just said, I at least recognized the grace in it. I nodded, and she nodded back.

"So, you were telling us about Mrs. Dos Santos?" I said in a husky voice, hoping everyone thought was a result of lemon-aid burn.

"Yes. How come you know my mother? I mean was it because of the tamales, or was it something else?" Santos asked.

"Oh my, the lovely tamales!" Darius said, her tummy jiggling as she laughed. "Yes, those should have been enough! They taste as though from heaven! But no, it was quite by accident really. I saw your mother at the farmer's market. I recognized in her the mark of a prayer warrior. It's not something you can see on the outside of a person, only someone who knows the signs—and I know them well," she explained, looking at each of us.

"I began buying her lovely tamales, and it was then I saw you," she said, looking at Santos sweetly. "What a boy, so full of life. However, I knew your heart was sensitive, too sensitive for darkness. But your mother covered and protected you with the blood of Christ. Even so, I wondered if you could make it to the hour of our need. So many things in the world call out to man's fallen nature, and one wrong choice could have made you unfit to bear the weight of your gift. But you remained whole and strong, and we are grateful! For your gift is one we will need if we are to overcome the forces set against the Kingdom of God."

Santos looked down; his face flushed. Only I was at an angle to see the tears glint as they gathered in the corners of his eyes, and I looked away so he wouldn't be more embarrassed.

"Now, my children, what would you like to ask me?" Darius exclaimed, clapping her hands. "Our time is short and there is much to do!"

Chapter Ten

Jack looked up and took the lead. "One of the first questions I have, since you seem to know a lot about us is, I was wondering if you know that we were called by an angel to protect someone? Actually, the angel called the person the *Link*..."

"Ah, yes, the *Link*. And what evil seeks to destroy—*who* evil seeks to destroy—is the chosen *Link*, deemed worthy to inherit power; a gift given that has increased during the lives of those who have received it before." Darius stopped for a moment, as if caught up in something far away. Then she blinked and flashed her smile again. "Excuse me for interrupting this thought, but do you mind my asking which angel was sent?" she asked, her eyes twinkling with eagerness.

"Of course, I mean no...it was Hamaliel," Tessa answered, as though he was her personal friend, which in a way, I suppose he was.

"Oh my! Isn't *he* just grand!" she said, patting Tessa's hand in congratulations.

"You know him?" I asked. The strange sensation of

watching this on the sci-fi channel while not actually participating in it grew stronger.

"Oh, not personally," she explained, as though this were enough. Darius sat quietly for a moment, looking at Jack and me. "Did he, Hamaliel, talk about the mantle?" she asked.

"He said it would be a powerful 'mantle of peace' that would be given to the *Link*," Jack replied.

"Do any of you know what a mantle is? And I'm not talking about the shelf on your fireplace," she said with a chuckle.

Tessa, listening intently, answered, "I do. Technically, it's a loose outer garment; it's something that covers or conceals what's underneath it. But I think you're talking about it in the abstract, such as a blessing or a gift, passed along to someone considered a worthy predecessor. An example would be a 'mantle of power' or a 'mantle of healing,'" she ended, looking down at the table quickly; an old habit born of my past need to ridicule her when she displayed embarrassing bouts of brilliance. When she shyly looked up, I smiled and was duly ashamed to see her turn pink with pleasure.

"Yes dear, that is *exactly* what I'm talking about! This particular mantle, however, has not been in the world now for almost a generation. It has been held by a being of light...in this case...my, oh my! It's been Hamaliel! He shall hold it until the time arrives to release its power back to the Earth. We are very close to this occurrence, for there is one of destiny. We cannot know who the *Link* is. Not until this is revealed, and the time to deliver the mantle has arrived. It would be dangerous for anyone to know for certain...or for any of us to have this information prematurely. The enemy is very proficient at discovering secrets, and as you might guess, this information is extremely important to them.

"The forces of darkness have only one season—for us, one moment! When it's feasible to take possession of this mantle, after it's delivered, and before assimilation. In the earth's realm, the mantle changes properties before its power is fully integrated. This is very hard to describe unless you were to understand the structure of the molecular force of light. You must comprehend how faith, and faith alone, transposes things of the spirit world into energy which this world actualizes... realizes...ah, can use." She amended. Only Tessa was nodding her head enthusiastically. The rest of us looked as though we were hanging on by one of those molecules.

"Oh my, I *am* sorry. I do go on! But I am trying to explain that, in this instance, the forces of darkness have a rare opportunity. Thus, they must act quickly. If evil can obtain the mantle before it's assimilated, it will. If not, then just after the mantle is newly integrated upon the *Link,* evil will try and act. It is then that they can both be destroyed. In either case, this would be a very grave sorrow, affecting many lives—even the future of the world." She looked up. "There is another important matter," Darius continued. "Did Hamaliel give you any idea who the enemy will be in the final action? There will be one chosen to walk in the first spirit dimension. This is a dangerous dispensation for a demon to take, indeed it's not often given to a Dark..." Darius' voice trailed off as she considered something to herself.

"Do you mean 'the Destroyer'?" Jack asked solemnly.

"Oh dear, Hamaliel used that term, did he? Well, I suppose its best you are prepared. Still, I would have thought... Oh, never mind. Is that all, or did he give you a name?" Darius asked her wrinkled face puckered with concern.

"He said we'd know him by a mark, a slain dove, ...I think that's how he put it," Tessa answered.

"Oh my," she said, turning what I was sure was one shade paler—if this were possible. "That one goes by several names but usually, Rasvampin," Darius said, exhaling as she said his name. "Of course, he chose it for effect, ...nevertheless, he is quite powerful." She sat very still for several seconds, appearing to be gazing inward. When she finally looked up at us, her merry eyes were like cold sparks. "There are several things you need to know about this foe. He is one of the Dark Lords. He was only sent to this realm because the battle is of extreme importance."

I shot Jack a look under the cover of my brows that I was sure he could read. I mean how hard is it to decipher two words? *"Run! Run now!"* Of course, the look he returned me was unreadable; it was his "sorta-smile," which I detest, and he obviously decided to ignore my warning entirely. However, when Darius continued, it was as though she was the one who'd caught my look. "But children, I entreat you, don't grow fearful or despair! Although he is deadly dangerous, he too can be destroyed! And God must believe you are the ones to do it..."

Again, she seemed to be looking within herself, while speaking outwardly to us. "Rasvampin... as he likes to call himself, leans toward the dramatic, as evidenced in his choice of names. But he holds a secret that can render him powerless. I am not allowed to reveal more, for if I did, it would not assist you. You must find it yourself in order to defeat him. But I can tell you this. Often, he will carry something that is the embodiment of his power, like the mantle. And like the mantle, it can take on a physical form until he has re-assimilated it."

"Huh?" Instantly I wished I'd phrased my question with just a bit more thought behind it.

Darius lowered her voice as though the great demon was near—and I couldn't help cautiously looking over my shoulder. "He will sometimes carry a weapon—and he will use his power to terrify. Disarm him and you will not only defeat him, you could then destroy him. But beware; in four thousand years of battle, this has never been achieved...

"This power, in a different dimension, can take on a physical form when it enters either the earth's plane or a spirit realm above the earth. The form is but a mere representation, but it helps humans understand, and also aids in assimilation. Now, until this object, which is power, is fully assimilated, it can be anything. A ring, a cloak, a sword, you name it. It will be made of a pure substance, and it will contain power until molecular change enables it to be taken into the person for which it belongs or is bestowed upon.

"In the case of a mantle—not a Dark Lord's weapon, mind you—once its power is assimilated, it can be used for its amazing healing properties; however, this healing ability remains available to the *Link* for but a single hour." Darius sighed, and then smiled, "Now, there have been a few instances—but only a few, thanks be to God—where a mantle was destroyed. However, the one Hamaliel brings has been around for eons." Darius stopped and stroked her chin lost in thought. "A few have even been lost within Earth's sphere until another bright soul comes along worthy and able to claim it."

"Like in the story, *The Sword in the Stone*?" Hailey asked.

"My goodness! That's a wonderful example!" Darius beamed, "but, the mantle cannot not remain as a physical substance for long in this world. Its purpose is to be assimilated and deliver the virtue it contains. However, just as you so properly illustrated, the mantle is used as a metaphor in myth," Darius said, smiling at Hailey, who smiled back shyly.

Darius' voice changed subtly and became lower. "However, while the object is above Earth's plane, it can remain unassimilated for much longer periods. Time is so different there. Now, the weapon Rasvampin carries from the underworld is different from the mantle in one major way. The energy released from this object is entirely negative. Which makes it highly volatile, and very dangerous. This unassimilated power is quite difficult to control. Rasvampin loves to play with this power, which makes him perilous. But remember...it also makes him vulnerable."

Somehow, I'd missed exactly *how* this made the "Dark Lord," Rasvampin so vulnerable. He didn't sound very helpless to me, with adjectives like "highly volatile and perilous" being tossed around. I was still wondering just how real all this could be when Darius turned toward me and asked:

"There are two others. One...a *young man*—your friend—has he come around yet?"

"Well, no. I wouldn't say Nathan has 'seen the light,' so to speak," I answered, looking down at the table.

"I believe he has a great destiny to fulfill. You must be diligent in your prayers for him. All of you," she said, gazing at each of us, her eyes lingering on Santos and Jack. "You are responsible for more than you realize. Each thought has power. Much rests on his decisions."

"Why would someone who once believed in God, but doesn't anymore, be chosen as the *Link?*" Jack asked, trying, but failing, to hide his disdain.

Darius smiled. "We, none of us, can afford to look upon our own understanding—our own righteousness—so to speak," Darius said kindly, looking steadily into Jack's eyes. "Your faith has been called upon, and this is the truest battle."

"Yes, I'm sorry. I know that, and I'll remember," Jack replied, his voice quiet but firm.

"I know you will," she answered, and it was as though Darius bestowed a blessing on Jack as she reached up and touched his forehead with her pale, parchment-like hand.

After several seconds, Hailey tentatively raised her hand as though we were in the classroom.

"Excuse me, but what is there to do?" she asked, and then quickly added, "I mean, you said there wasn't much time, and we had a lot to do..." she trailed off.

"Oh, what an excellent girl you are! No wonder you were chosen!" Darius exclaimed, clapping her hands together. Hailey went the precise color pink of my favorite cashmere sweater. It looked quite good on her, too. I decided to find that exact color in something for her at Christmas—amazed again by how ready my mind was to embrace anything besides the challenge facing us.

"The first thing is the memorization of scripture," Darius explained. "And this is not to be taken lightly."

Quite frankly, I would have taken the employment of field artillery with less grimness than memorizing verses from the Bible. A long time ago, I'd found this was decidedly *not* my strong suit, and felt it was just another sign pointing me toward the inevitable choice of heathenism. Now, I wondered if I would ever be assigned any state higher on Heaven's dance chart than "Christian-pagan."

"Because you must always remember that your *struggle will not be against flesh and blood, but rather the spiritual forces of evil in the heavenly realms.* It's imperative you are ready! You must arm yourself with the word. *Put on the full armor of God, so that when the day of evil comes, you* will *be* ready *to stand your ground. After you have done everything you can possibly do,* you will continue to stand.'" She looked at each of us, and I felt the power of her words sinking in. Then, she continued. "Now, I have a list of scriptures you can start with. If you already know them, learn others," she said, looking at Jack. "The realm of the demonic world can hold mortals frozen with fear unless they are equipped. These are quite literally the swords you will carry."

Immediately, I envisioned myself decked out as Cassie, warrior princess, pointy breastplates, and all. I didn't mean to chuckle out loud, but I must have, because when I looked up, I was surprised to see every eye on me. "Oh, sorry, I just had a vision of myself actually doing battle...you know, shiny sword...great leather outfit...never mind, sorry," I finished lamely.

Darius smiled her wonderful forgive-anything-smile. "I'm so glad you brought that up," she said with enthusiasm, "because that is almost exactly how you'll be doing battle!" Every mouth seemed to fall open on cue. Even Jack, mister-manly-man, and Santos, the used-to-wanna-be-knife-wielding gang member, looked stunned.

"Come over here, and let me show you," Darius said, rising from the table. We followed her to a clearing a short distance from the cabin. "Take hands and form a circle," she commanded. And we did, much the same way we had the night before with the exception that Darius was now part of our circle. "Do you each know a Bible verse you can recite?" she asked.

Everyone did, even me, because I'd had a couple verses beat into my brain early on. But the one who surprised me was Santos. Obviously, my doctrine of snobbery was well-ingrained; for some reason, I never imagined a gang member memorizing scripture. I caught myself before I beamed him my entirely patronizing smile, saving it for my own splendid accomplishments.

"Oh good!" Darius said happily, "Now, we all need to recite our verses together out loud, at the same time. This will help accustom you to all the outside noise and distraction, teaching you to focus. As you get better, you can do this silently. But for now, speak the words aloud. All right then, let's begin!"

I started saying my verse, growing confused by the

jumble of words I was hearing from everyone else and ending with, "...now I lay me down to sleep," which, I was almost positive, wasn't a scripture. Darius had begun laughing, a deep resounding sound that had me joining in, holding my sides.

"All right, all right. I can see we need a little work! But let me try to explain what is *supposed* to happen," she said after a minute, still chuckling and drying her eyes. "Your focus must be on the content of your scripture, and your focus must be total. Your mind cannot wander. If you can achieve this, you will split off. You will still physically have a body, but your spirit will enter another plane. It will seem, very realistically, as if you are inhabiting your physical body there. However, it will be a spiritual body. The more power you give the scriptures, the more substantial you will feel, and the more power your sword will have. The demon fights in much the same way. He will tear down the scriptures and your faith —as well as your confidence. The more focused he is, and the better he is at finding your weakness, the stronger his weapon."

"You must stay in a circle, calling upon God and using his Word. This will be your shield and your sword. And Cassie, you can even wear your lovely leather garments if you can imagine them," she said, chuckling again as she looked at me. I glanced around, but I couldn't find a hole *quite* big enough.

"Now, let's try it again. Concentrate," she added.

I tried again, only this time, a different verse bubbled up out of *who knows where*. I remembered it as one I'd discarded as part of "the great lie." It was Psalms 145:18-19, and I think my dad had me memorize it for Sunday school. As I recalled, it had taken *forever*, but now I said each word, concentrating as I spoke them, wondering at their actual meaning. "*The Lord is near to all who call on him, to all who call on him in truth. He fulfills the desires of those who fear him; he hears their cry and saves them." Who knows...maybe Dad had been saved in a different way, different than I'd hoped for,* I thought. I said the verses again, and then again, concentrating so hard I lost track of where I was and what was being said next to me. Suddenly, I was standing in the center of a shiny circle, a blade, long and sharp, with light glancing off its silver edge clasped between my hands. I could hear soft murmuring around me and saw the outline of someone else with a sword next to me. Then, I was instantly back, holding hands in the circle, reciting the same verse and ending with, "...*who fear him; he hears their cry and saves them,*" just as though nothing had happened.

Darius had her eyes open, and she beamed a radiant smile at each of us. "Now, that was more like it!" she pronounced, "Did any of you enter the circle?" she asked, hopefully.

"I did," Jack stated proudly.

After waiting a moment for someone else to ante up, I finally said, "I did, too." I was not happy when so many of my team members looked shocked. When I say *so many*, I mean, *all.* "What? You don't believe me?" I asked indignantly.

"Of course, they believe you!" Darius said, clapping her hands together. "Oh, Cassie, it's just that when someone such as yourself has pretended for so many years *not* to be a warrior—and it is so obvious to me that you have never been anything else—it surprises them. But, as I said, it does *not* surprise me. You were chosen because you will be such a *mighty* warrior!" she ended.

If the rest of the group had offended me with their looks of disbelief moments before, it was nothing compared to the look my face now held. I stood in shocked silence, trying to let her words sink in.

"Will we be able to see who...what we are fighting?" Tessa asked.

"Yes, very clearly. In fact, that brings me to another point. Raphael, come here. Tell me about the demons you have witnessed so far," she directed, taking a seat on the ground as though she were young and not the ancient, bent, woman she appeared to be.

Santos walked over and sat down next to her. He began describing the same ones he'd told us about the night before. Then he added, "I thought I saw a different one today, though: Less animal-like, more human. But I couldn't be sure. It was larger, but it still wasn't solid. I could see that he was really tall and had big muscles. He walked bent over like, and his face was ugly, a little like a lizard. Pointy, sort of. And carried a sword in his hands; they were like claws," he added.

"Ah yes, the Malthorphs. These are Rasvampin's personal army of demon underlings. He sends them ahead, and these you will fight—in another realm—with your swords. They haven't fully arrived, but the time is quickly approaching. I would say you have approximately two weeks to prepare, more or less." She looked at Santos. "Right now, you're the only one who's able to see these demons, am I correct?"

"That's right," Santos agreed.

"Not exactly," Darius said, smiling as though she had a surprise for him behind her back. "If any of the Guardians, or the *Link,* is with you, all they need to do is touch you, and they will be able to see the demons, too. If you form a line touching each other, you can all see them together. But I warn you; you mustn't let on that you can see them for two reasons. These minor demons, not the Malthorphs, but the Siphon demons that attach to people, are basically stupid creatures living off instinctual need and simple orders. You can fight them without these creatures ever knowing you see them—that way you can destroy them."

"But how do we fight them if we have to pretend not to see them?" Santos asked for all of us.

"Kindness toward their host. They attach to those who feed them with their negativity...their sorrow, un-forgiveness, pain...their anger. It's a cycle that, once begun, becomes much more difficult for the host to break—especially once these demons attach. Kindness, a word, even laughter if it's joyful, can make a demon uncomfortable. As a result, he will release his grip. But here comes the tricky part. One of you must decide to be the 'keener.' Oh, my that's just a terrible word, really," she said, pressing her finger to her nose. "Let me see, what's a better... I know! Someone must decide to be the *healer*! Yes, that's really much better," she said beaming. "Once the demon detaches, words must be spoken in the hearing of the demon. The healer will know which words. This will seal both portals, healing the victim, and at the same time destroying the demon."

"Do you know who the 'healer' should be?" Hailey asked, timidly.

"Oh, my goodness child, no. That is something the heart decides. Anyone is capable, but it is a desire, and it must be! This is difficult work to begin with, and the words are essential.

"In the next two weeks you must work diligently at releasing those around you of their Siphons. When the main force of Maltorphs arrive, the Siphons—who literally suck and store negative energy for these larger warriors—will hopefully have been significantly reduced, and the Maltorphs' source of energy greatly diminished."

"You said there were two reasons not to let them know we can see them? The first one, so they'd release their victims; but what was the other?" Hailey asked.

"Why don't you tell them, Cassie," Darius said, turning her smile on me.

"Well, Hailey, I imagine that's to keep you from being voted 'Queen' or 'King' of the Leper Ball," I said, fake smiling all around.

"Oh Cassie, I knew you would have the perfect way of explaining it!" Darius said, a laugh gurgling in her throat. "People just don't realize there's another world existing in a different dimension. You will have a difficult time persuading people you're not crazy, as I'm sure Raphael can attest."

"You can say that again," Santos said nodding, "*I even thought I was crazy!*" We all joined him in laughter.

"However, no matter what precautions you take, this war will not make you popular—as I'm sure our dear Cassie can already attest—for you are fighting for God. All you have to do is read about what happened to his Son, or to the apostles, to find out how quickly defending the Lord of the universe can turn others against you..." she said before turning kind eyes on me. "But be of good cheer. *You will not be left or forsaken.*" Then, smiling at everyone cheerfully, she finished with, "and there's always a chance, you won't get run out of town on a rail, either!" And laughed heartily. The others laughed with her, and I assumed they were caught up in her merriment and not chuckling out of sheer idiocy, since these same jolly people were the ones I'd be depending on in this battle against evil; and when it came to evil, I didn't know if I was talking about Satan, or my old girlfriends.

There was another reason I wasn't feeling quite as cheery or optimistic as my compatriots appeared. Rasvampin lurked in the recesses of my mind, and while everybody else seemed secure that we had better than a snowball's chance in a blistering abode to beat this demon, I wasn't convinced. Not even a little. So, of course, I asked.

"Ah, Darius, I'm sorry, maybe I missed something, ... probably I missed something, but I really don't understand," I said, looking at her glowing face of wrinkled cheer. "Just how exactly are we, ...mere humans, and high school kids, at that, ...how can we, how are we...supposed to destroy a Demon-Lord-Destroyer?" I asked, feeling glacially cold fingers scale my ribcage and squeeze my heart as I called out his title.

"How?" she repeated, looking at me with eyes as bright and dark as obsidian. "Well, first you must practice. As it says in Ephesians, you must '...*Stand firm then, with the belt of truth buckled around your waist, with the breastplate of righteousness in place, and with your feet fitted with the readiness that comes from the gospel of peace...*' You will, as it goes on to say, be able to '*extinguish all the flaming arrows of the evil one.*'"

"But most importantly you must realize that you do not fight alone. You fight *with God* because, '*He is in you, and He is greater than he that is in the world,*' ...or even he that is coming to face you in the spirit dimension," she added, her eyes twinkling.

"So, remember: pray, study, learn. Spend time together and spend time apart in prayer. Find your faith...not the faith of anyone else. You must have your *own* faith, your own *relationship*. It must be personal and intimate.

"Rasvampin doesn't just believe God exists. He *knows* God exists. But he's chosen to follow Satan. If you are going into battle in the name of God, you must know Him at least as well as your enemy does. Rasvampin doesn't have the power of love. He doesn't have the power of Christ's blood, but he has faith. He has faith in evil's ability to draw man away from the Creator; he has faith in chaos over peace; he has faith in all those who believe one god is as good as another —because he knows they won't know who to call on when he meets them in everyday battle—and he knows he will win. Your faith *must* be greater than his.

"But remember, you would not have been chosen for this great battle if our Lord did not have great faith in you. And, at some point, you also must have given your life to Christ," she said, looking, I was sure, straight at Santos and me at the same time. "Do not look so worried. Remember what it says in Second Thessalonians, the third chapter, third verse, *'The Lord is faithful, and He will strengthen and protect you from the evil one.'* You will find your power in God; without Him, there will be no defeating a foe such as this. But then," she said, suddenly smiling, "without Him, things much less fierce in the world than Rasvampin will be your undoing. So, as they say..."

"...Gird yourselves," I finished.

"Exactly!" she replied, beaming.

Chapter Eleven

The next day was Sunday, and I was surprised to see Santos show up at church with Jack and his family. On the way home from our visit with Darius, Hailey had asked if she could come with Tessa and me in the morning.

Seeing us, Jack and Santos came over. Both squeezed into our pew, so there we sat, the five of us. I think the sermon was good; although, I must admit I didn't hear as much of it as I'd meant to. My mind kept wandering back over Darius' words about Nathan, and I was filled with confusion. *"Has he come around yet? He has a great destiny to fulfill... Be diligent in your prayers for him... You are responsible for more than you realize... Each thought has power..."*

I wanted to help Nathan fulfill his great destiny. I wanted to be the person who brought him back to God. Maybe I'd been rash, and I was supposed to be his angel. Today I kind of liked that idea. Not in the sense of Hamaliel of course, way too scary, but in the sense of radiantly, luminously, resplendently... A thought suddenly interrupted my holy ruminations. The truth was, the thing both of us enjoyed most in our relationship had been the perfectly *un*spiritual nature of it. Besides, Nathan would never fall for me in wings. And though I wouldn't allow myself, it made me want to cry.

The sound of singing began penetrating my melancholy. Hailey's voice was deep and resonant; Tessa's rang clear and bright. Slowly, I began singing the words displayed by the overhead projector high on the wall in front of us, and I felt my spirit lifting. There was a welling up of love and pain within me—a place I didn't go often, and never in the light of day. But instead of allowing it to control me, I sang. I let the emotions flow through my voice, and when all the songs where finished, I felt better. I was nowhere closer to knowing what I really felt, and even less of an idea about what to do. But for the moment I'd let go. Amazingly, the turmoil of thoughts about Nathan had changed into six simple words from the final song ringing over and over in my head, "Bless the Lord, oh my soul. Bless the Lord, oh my soul."

When the service ended, the five of us meandered out and copped the free donuts from the tables outside. Then we sat down together under a tree to talk.

"So, how'd everybody sleep last night?" Jack asked, sounding every bit the boy scout camp counselor I'd imagined he'd grow up to be.

"I was too excited to sleep very well," Hailey said, excitedly.

"I was nervous, but I slept, OK" Santos said, looking better than he had a few days ago.

I decided, what the heck? I'd play along. "Well, I was nervous, and am nervous. And I will-be-forever-more nervous, if I don't get a handle on some of the scriptures Darius gave us. And here I thought she was such a darling old thing," I said, exposing my sincere worry.

"Oh, Cassie I'd be glad to help you, but I don't know

when I can these next few days. But I will after Thursday," Tessa offered.

"Me too," Jack said, "Could I help you, let's see, next Wednesday?"

"Thanks, guys, but I've got to get help before then. I'm swamped too, and I can't get the picture of wolves pouring over the mountains out of my mind. Not to mention fighting Rasputin-Rastnasty-vampire guy, whoever his evilness is, with only a couple scriptures, and a nursery rhyme or two."

"Wait, I've got an idea," Jack said, jumping up and heading toward a group of young people. I noticed Tessa's eyes getting wide.

"I hope it's not what I think it is," she said, in her less than reassuring voice.

"What, Tessa?" I asked, but she kept staring after Jack. "What's he up to?" I looked at both Hailey and Santos, and found they were deep in discussion and paying no attention to my particular plight whatsoever. I turned back to see Jack with his arm resting on the shoulder of one of his brothers. Instantly I understood the reason for Tessa's concern. "He wouldn't be thinking of recruiting one of the 'cretins', would he?" I asked her. She looked at me with dread in her eyes, and with Tessa and her glasses, that also meant dread *magnified*. It was unsettling. "Oh my gosh, does he have a broken leg?" I asked, as Jack's brother, decked out with cast and crutches, made his way back with Jack to where we were sitting.

I smiled and jumped up to greet him, trying to be charming. I knew, momentarily, that I'd be in the process of denying my need of his services—and wracked my brain for his name. "Hey, Chip, is it?"

"Yea, hey Cathy," he said, his bright blue eyes twinkling.

"I'm Cassie," I said, trying not to act offended, since we'd been neighbors for a year and a half now.

"Yea, and I'm Chris," he said, smiling back.

"Sorry, Chris. I should've known that…" I was sunk.

He looked over and spied Tessa. "Hey Tessa, lookin' good today," he said. For the life of me, I couldn't tell if he was making fun of her or giving her a compliment. Tessa seemed to think it was at her expense because her eyes narrowed, and she didn't reply, which was very unlike my sweet sister. I decided Chris needed watching since he was showing signs of an attitude which I knew all too well. "How come you haven't come over lately?" he asked, pointing his chin at her.

"Really? Gosh, I wonder, Chris. The *first* and *last* time I was invited over—for a game of chess? —Do you remember that?" Tessa's usually composed voice had taken on an interesting tone.

"Ah, yea," Chris was smiling broadly. "It was great…" He began before being interrupted by my sister.

"Yes, we ended up playing field hockey in the yard, and I was the puck. Does any of this ring a bell?" I had never seen tiny little Tessa look so mad. In fact, I didn't know she could get so mad.

"Oh, come on. You were beating me at every game of chess; and you weren't the puck! We were kidding around. Besides, it's a ball—and you're so tiny. The guys were just having a little fun, and face it, you didn't take directions that well."

Tessa was looking at him in complete dismay before putting her hand up and pretending to smile, "Look, can we just let it go?"

"Sure. And come on over anytime," Chris said. Tessa dropped her hand, the pretend smile slipping into a look of dismay.

Jack shook his head. "OK, Chris, you already know Tessa. These are some new friends of ours, Hailey and Santos." The two had gotten up and were saying hello. Santos asked Chris about his leg, discovering he'd broken it rough housing. Wow was I surprised; and I could only imagine how astonished Tessa was.

When the conversation lulled, I said, "You're what, Chris? The second oldest?" I'll admit I'd guessed, since he was tall, and nearly the same height as Jack.

"Nope, I'm the third," he said with a tight grin. "Jack talk about us a lot?" he asked sarcastically. Jack slugged him lightly on the shoulder.

"Whenever your checks clear, I do," Jack said, fists up and feigning a boxing match. "And don't let him give you a hard time. He's the second oldest." Chris tried to respond to the boxing but stumbled over a crutch. Jack and Santos caught him before he went down.

"Darn this leg. I can't do anything!" he moaned.

"Not true—and that's why I asked you over. It's true you can't have fun by messing around for a while. You can't do chores around the house and yard, either. So, you and I know Mom will be setting up some major homework for you to take up your extra time. Something epic. ... On the other hand, you could help us with a project that Mom would love and totally approve of."

Chris stood, looking suspiciously at Jack. "What is it?"

"Cassie needs help memorizing scriptures, lots of them. And we both know you could help her."

He distorted his face, giving the impression the job was beneath him. So, I gladly took this as the perfect opportunity to give us both an easy out. "Honestly, Chris, if this isn't something you want to do..."

"I'll do it," he said too quickly, "but..."

"But what?" Jack asked, his eyes narrowing slightly.

"OK. Here's the deal. I've been meaning to talk to you, but I wasn't sure when, or how," he said, looking up sheepishly at his brother. "I want in; I followed you to the Pine Circle the other night." When he saw the look on our faces, he began talking faster. "I couldn't go to the game, and I didn't have anything to do. So, when I saw you guys come home early,"

"You followed us and spied on us." Jack said, heatedly. The two brothers faced off; their wills locked in a grim battle.

I could see that, at the very least, Jack wanted and was waiting for an apology; but Chris was just too stupi... Suddenly, I again found myself ...spinning, falling soundlessly into a young heart or was it this man's mind? Entering through his pain, his feelings of ...never quite enough ... wanting to be a part of something besides his brothers, something besides the will of his mother, wanting to do something great, wanting to be chosen ...prayers in the night, God please, God, let me be chosen. Choose me ...working hard, smart, ...why not enough? ...Why is there never enough, ... please God, ...I'm so alone... whirling...

I was always surprised by the extent of pain everyone seemed to experience; most of the time you could never tell by someone's looks. But thanks to the big guy, Hamaliel, I was lucky enough to slide down a stranger's rabbit hole and experience *so much* of it all at once. *Boy, what a gift.* I came back to myself in what had to have been only moments, with no one the wiser, except of course, hopefully, me. Santos was stepping in between Jack and Chris, and I sincerely hoped I hadn't missed anything too juicy.

"Chris, what is your full name? Is it Christopher?"

"Huh? No, it's Christian." Santos looked over at Hailey and nodded. She was nodding her head and smiling back at him. Chris looked at them both and asked, the question the rest of us were wondering, "What?"

"Well, you see, Hailey and me, we been talking, even before you come over. She told me she had another dream—and it's about the other Guardian..." He turned to Hailey. "You tell them Hailey, it's important." Santos sat back down, and we all did the same while Chris leaned against the tree.

"OK, I was going to tell everyone. It's just Santos asked first," she said. "Anyway, it wasn't much of a dream, at least I didn't think so when I woke up. I saw a sign and that's all. It was a sign hanging on a tree right before we come to the Pine Circle; it said *Christian*. All I saw was a sign on a tree. That's it. I didn't know what it meant, except maybe the obvious. We should all be Christians, or all of us are Christians; I didn't know. And I didn't even think of Chris having the name Christian—that was Santos. But now, I think he's right."

Still angry, Jack looked to Tessa, and then me for confirmation. Tessa shook her head as if to say she wasn't sure, but her face said, "highly unlikely." I gave her foot a nudge and smiled at Jack.

"I think he *is* the other Guardian. Didn't I tell you he'd find us?" I said, giving the kindest look to Jack I could muster, in consideration of the older-sibling-indignation-impulse, which let's face it, is pret-ty hard to control. Then turning to Chris and locking eyes with him, I said, "You didn't choose us, you were chosen because somebody up there thinks you'll make a darn good warrior. So, I'll pass on to you, what someone who knew what he was talking about said to me, 'God has heard your cry.'"

I'd felt good after coming home from church. I was becoming so *wise,* so Yoda-ish. I was so very worthy of my "Guardian" status, that when Jack said he needed to talk to me about something right after I'd gotten home, changed clothes, and before I'd bothered with lunch, I slipped; I wasn't nearly suspicious enough. I did try putting him off, but he said it wouldn't wait—that should have been clue enough. When he came over we sat down in the living room with a couple cans of soda—and he dropped the bomb.

"I talked to Nathan, and he seems pretty upset. He wants to work something out." Jack was looking at me very intently so I couldn't let him see my heart scudding in my chest. I doubted there was much I could do about eye dilation.

"Really?" I said, as slowly as I could, hoping it didn't sound contrived.

"Yes, r-e-a-l-l-y," he mocked.

Seeing modulation hadn't worked very well, I took a deep breath and tried again. "OK, and how does he propose to do that? He made it clear I was supposed to choose between him or God, and I obviously chose God. He left me several very angry messages with little doubt that I was the one who'd have to change. You realize he broke up with me? Now, suddenly, he wants to work something out. And why didn't he call me? Why on earth are *you* the go-between?"

"I'm getting to that part. He says he wants to meet you— at least halfway." I raised my eyebrows in response. "He wants to have you up to the cabin this afternoon to meet his mom and uncle."

Luckily, I'd swallowed my sip of drink. Otherwise, I'd have spewed it out all over Jack's face, which wouldn't have bothered me as much as the overspray on the couch. "His mother will have a live kitten if he introduces me as his girlfriend," I said, trying to keep that image from actually playing out in my imagination.

"That's why he wants her to get to know you first. And, I don't know, I think maybe if you do this, we just might be able to reel him in. Or at least get him into dialog with us. It's really hard to carry on anything meaningful at school, so the weekends are actually the best. We're getting down to the wire here."

"Wait a minute, you said '*we*' can reel him in and get him to dialog with '*us.*' What do you mean by that?" I asked.

"Nate's invited you to an early dinner, and he's elected me to be your boyfriend for the date. You know, to break his mom and uncle in slowly."

I wasn't sure if my outer body was contorting, but my inner self was grimacing, twitching, and sneering in any number of distorted configurations. However, while experiencing this, I had a few lucid thoughts. One was that I wanted to strangle Jack. This action was averted by the simultaneous realization that, before the impending battle against evil, it probably wasn't a wise move to choke out your partner. And yet, sitting and even looking at Jack was making this downright difficult to suppress. Not only did he have the nerve to call Nathan, *Nate*—which, I'm sorry, not even *I* was allowed to do—he was also just *groovy* with the idea of being my "boyfriend for the day." But this was only once he'd been given *"Nate's permission."* It made me want to... I think I already mentioned what I wanted to do but let me add...with my bare hands.

"So, are you up for it? Can you do this for the cause?" Jack was asking, probably wondering why my pupils were twirling.

"For the what? I'm supposed to go to Nathan's cabin and lie about you being my boyfriend, all in the name of God? Are you kidding me? I know I don't have the longest track record for being a Christian, but I *am* trying here," I said, "What's really going on, Jack? Are you trying to catch me in some sleazy-sin-trap?" I asked, looking at him sideways.

Jack started laughing. "Wow, a sleazy-sin-trap, huh? No, I promise you it's nothing like that. I'm honestly just trying to get behind the wall Nathan's put up. I think you've been the one person he's let in. Plus, I know you still have feelings for him. He called *me*. It was his idea, and I was willing to go along for both of you. But if you don't want to, no problem. We're a team. If I've offended you, I'm really sorry. Forget I brought it up." Jack got up and started for the door.

"No, wait. Let's do this," I said, once again revealing the calm, rock-like certitude of my nature. "But I'm doing this for Nathan, not the team. Understood?" Jack looked at me for a long second before responding.

"Cassie? Are you sure? We'd have to be ready to go in an hour. That alone might make it impossible for you."

"How dare you. Are you saying I don't look just fine the way I am? Now get out of here. If I don't hurry, we *will* be late," I said, pushing him out the door.

Chapter Twelve

s I dressed for the dinner, I spent the hour making everything on the outside look flawless. Though, for the life of me, I couldn't find a cubby anywhere in my mind to tuck away a single thought. They just flew around in disarray, bumping into each other and making a mess of my brain.

I couldn't believe Jack had actually gone along with Nathan's plan, and had me going along with it, too. However, I did appreciate the fact that I could blame it all on him. But to complicate matters, I knew if I were going to do my part in pulling off this whole charade, I would have to practice being extra nice to Jack, and "nice" is an icky thing when it's all gummed up with insincerity. And believe me, these concoctions were something I knew about first-hand. I was furious with Jack for no reason that made a lick of sense, but there it was.

Strangely, I wasn't sure how to be in a relationship with Nathan anymore; yet once again, it was being dangled in front of me. And I hadn't refused... but then, I couldn't refuse, I reasoned with myself, not if I could help him, and not if he was the *Link*, and not if, like myself, he just needed to find his way back to God. These were convincing arguments, but no matter how many times I replayed them, I couldn't get that vision of myself in feathers and light back.

Jack stared at me when I came down the stairs. I watched him swallow when he said I looked nice, which may be the only thing that kept me from punching him in the nose as my greeting. Tessa was waiting for us by the door.

"You going to be alright? I mean, I know you're OK, it's just that, well..." Tessa said, looking at me like she wanted me to read her mind and spare myself the humiliation of having it spelled out.

"If you're worried about my meeting Nathan's mom and uncle, don't worry. I'll be strong!" I said in a jesting way.

"No. Not exactly..." she continued, still being evasive. I could tell she was dying to give me advice, but afraid to clarify my obvious wrongdoing. She'd found out about the lying; I just knew it. I shot Jack a dirty look, and suddenly I was sick and tired of it all. Don't ask me why, I just was. Trying to be good, and failing, simply has its limits when you're new at it.

"Oh, leave it alone, will you?" I said, grabbing my jacket, and heading out the door.

"See ya, Squirt," Jack said, grabbing her up and spinning her around. "Don't worry. Cassie will figure it out," I heard him say as he set her back down. Maybe those words should have soothed me a little, but instead, I really wanted to extract one of his good teeth.

The whole way up the mountain, Jack kept looking at me as though he had something to say. I sat next to him, pretending to be in deep thought, but in truth, all my crazy thoughts an hour earlier seemed to have flown out my ear. A fly would have had brain matter to spare after pondering my thoughts. The car was warm, and I was sniffing Naugahyde. Finally, Jack ventured a word.

"So, what exactly do you want to do once we get there?"

"Huh?" Once again, I'd used my deeply intelligent question.

"I said, what do you want to do once we get there?" Jack repeated.

"You mean besides the, '*Hi, howya doin?*'" part? Well, there's the acting like we can't get enough of each other, making out in the driveway, and gazing deeply into each other's eyes—that's definitely *OUT*. So, I guess we just act like our normal selves. I think that will probably do it. I mean, come on, Jack, Mrs. Gregory isn't exactly expecting us to make a spectacle of ourselves!" I ranted. Jack was quiet, and I could tell he was mad. "Oh, all right. I'm sorry. It's just I feel like a criminal doing this, and I hate it. I thought you were supposed to be this great Christian. Why on earth did you go along with it?" I asked, making him responsible, and demanding the full pound of flesh.

"I'm not sure why I'm doing this," Jack answered truthfully. "But what makes you think I'm any better Christian than you are?" he asked.

"Practice," I stated.

"Well, this isn't about practice; this is about knowing who you are. Who are you, Cassie?" Jack asked.

"Well, that depends. What kind of Christian says, 'Screw you?'" I answered, hunkering lower into my seat. It ticked me off more that Jack didn't seem to take offense. Then I felt bad, and he just kept driving, leaving me to my miserable, unknowable self.

When we finally turned up the Lakeside Drive, Nathan was waiting for us at the top. Jack stopped and got out, letting Nathan in which, I had to admit was pretty darn chivalrous on Jack's part. Too darn, in fact.

"I didn't know if you'd come," Nathan said. Wow, he was so gorgeous. I'd almost forgotten... If we were going to break up for good, I was going to have to blind myself, wear dark shades, something...

"I didn't know if I would either. I can't believe you have me pretending to be *Jack's girlfriend...*" I said, trying my hardest to muster up some of my earlier annoyance. I could already feel my mind going numb around him, willing to do his will... I mentally shook myself. Where had my willpower gone in all of two minutes? I wondered.

"I knew you wouldn't like that part, but Cassie, Mother really admires Jack. If she can just meet you, I know she'll really like you. Then you can break up with Jack and be my girlfriend."

"Great plan. I see you've really thought this through," I said. The rest of my blistering observations secure in voice-lock-down for the time. The evening was going to be hard enough without commentary at this stage.

"Listen, I know I said it was over, but I've done a lot of thinking these past few...well hours. If I give up a few things, maybe you can, too. I can't ask you to be the only one to change. That wouldn't be fair."

"No," I said, looking at his perfect nose, amazing eyes ... beautiful mouth.

"And I'm sorry about the ultimatum. I knew it wasn't right. I don't want it to be that way between us."

"Me neither," I wasn't sure what he'd said, but I felt the same way.

"Come here." He reached over, pulling me close, just as Jack opened the door.

"Oh, sorry guys, but it's about the time your mom is expecting us. You want to ride in with us?" Jack asked. Until now, I'd so underestimated his concern for etiquette.

"No, that's OK." Nathan leaned his head back against the

seat in frustration. "I'll go on ahead. Wait here a few minutes. Give me ten. Oh hell; give me five and then drive on up. I'll meet you out front." He slid out and walked away without looking back.

"Sorry, didn't mean to break anything up," Jack said, without even trying for sincerity. I just gave him a look, and let it go. At least I was here, and so was Nathan. I wasn't going to let Jack get me riled up now. But the five minutes flew by, and I convinced Jack we should wait a bit longer. I knew by this I was not looking forward to what lay around the bend, because if I had been, I told myself, God would have seen to it the minutes turned into hours. I'd already begun blaming God, and I'd spent less than five minutes with Nathan. This was not a good sign.

We came up the drive and rolled to a stop next to where Nathan waited. Jack got out of the car and was coming around to open mine, but Nathan didn't wait for him. He opened it and pulled me into a hug. "Come on, I want to introduce you to my uncle," he said, nuzzling my ear. "You remember my Uncle Thaddeus," he said, turning to Jack.

Jack had the strangest look on his face, cool and pent up at the same time. "Sure," he said, moving between us, and pulling me to his side. "How could I forget?"

Nathan was staring at Jack the way one dog stares at another that's edging toward his side of the street. "Oh, sorry," Jack said, with his peculiar brand of insincerity. "Your mom is watching us from the entryway. I thought maybe I should save you from yourself." I looked up to see Mrs. Gregory wave from the door, so we all smiled and waved back.

"Thanks, Jack," Nathan said, slapping him on the back, all jovial good will. I looked up and watched as Jack smiled in return, knowing both their smiles had cost them a great deal. *Oh boy*, I thought, this was going to be a *really fun* afternoon.

Inside, the cabin was a thing of beauty. Mrs. Gregory had the fine good taste only money can buy. Everything seemed to glow or exude in that understated way of a luxurious lodge. I tried my best not to seem unsettled by it; after all, this was but their weekend abode. Their house would probably have me babbling. I was praying I wouldn't break down and do that here.

Jack introduced me to his mother, and she greeted me... coolly. I guessed she'd already seen me at school, and I suspected she was aware of her son's *past* interest in me. Jack's and my performance was going to have to be very convincing if her 'hello' was any indication of her susceptibility to my many charms. She embraced Jack, telling him she was "so happy" to have him come for the day—just a mite more warmly I should add than she had been towards me. Jack reached into his pocket and pulled out a very tiny, slim cardboard box with a simple red string, and handed it to her.

"Jack, what on earth is this?" she asked, a look of sweet pleasure filling her face. I could see the power of great beauty had once been hers...a beauty that had begun hardening over the years.

"It's not much," Jack said, watching her take out a very small cellophane envelope. "It's a forty-cent Tomas Paine... blue and white. I remember how you were always looking for some of the earlier stamps to add to your late husband's collection. I hope you like it..."

"Oh, Jackson. You are the most thoughtful boy I've ever met," she said, taking his arm and leading him through the door. It appeared to me that Jack had mastered the art of brown-nosing even from the confines of home schooling. Then again, maybe he really was that thoughtful. Either way, it was irritating.

Nathan's uncle had come down from upstairs, and after

slapping Jack on the back with a hearty, "Hello there, Jackson! Great to see you again!" turned to me with a small bow and a careful smile. Nathan came up from behind to introduce me, but Jack must have remembered his role and backtracked.

"Senator Gregory, this is my friend, Cassie Connor," he said, interrupting Nathan mid-sentence.

The senator stood at least six-feet-three and leaned back to peer down over the however many inches his horrendous nose added, allowing his bloodshot eyes to graze, as opposed to gaze, upon my personhood from head to toe. It was a lovely experience and left quite an impression. I felt like excusing myself to find some wet wipes.

"Has anyone ever told you how much you resemble, oh what's her name...?" he rolled his bloodshot eyes upward.

"Katie Holmes?" Nathan piped in.

"No, no. I don't even know who that is; ...she was a classic...Claudia Cardinale! Has anyone made that comparison?"

"No, I don't think so, ...and no one has ever compared me to Katie Holmes *either*, ...but thank you both very much. My father used to say I reminded him of Boo-Boo though, on Yogi the Bear cartoons," I said, widening my eyes and smiling big, to help with the whole cartoon image. "Of course, I was little, and my eyes and stomach were a bit bigger then," I added, only half kidding. Luckily, Jack and Nathan thought I was funny. Senator Gregory on the other hand, wasn't sure what to make of me. But I could tell by the sound of his laugh he didn't use it very often, anyway.

We sat in the sumptuous living room in front of a blaze that, had it been outside, would have qualified as a forest fire. The plush couches were filled with down, and once again, lethargy set in as I listened to Jack, Nathan, and the senator debate politics. Meanwhile, Mrs. Gregory diligently ignored me by going back and forth to the kitchen overseeing the help with the meal. It was interesting listening to the differing opinions of the guys, though, and I was surprised how knowledgeable Jack was. It was fascinating how he held his own against Nathan and the senator.

Still, Jack must have noticed that the fine glaze spreading from my brain, to my eyes, to my entire being was beginning to solidify. Very soon I'd be rendered immobile, so he said abruptly, "Nathan, would you mind showing Cassie the rest of the house? I've already seen it, and I know she'd enjoy it a lot more than listening to us. That is, unless the senator can come up with a better answer than the war of 1812, I'm about to win this argument."

"I've already abdicated...I have to, even though blood is thicker than..." Nathan stopped abruptly, and there was an uncomfortable moment of silence.

Slowly I rallied, jumping into the abyss, while not understanding but recognizing 'awkward' like the face of a bad relation. So, I figured I'd do what I could. "Oh Jack, thank you!" I cried, "I would get right up and kiss you, except I'm stuck in the clutches of the fluff. Someone is going to have to give me a hand, or I swear, it's going to swallow me whole!"

Of course, I'd been playing my role, and I was startled when Jack jumped up and pulled me out. He stood holding me with a teasing look on his face just as Mrs. Gregory walked into the room. Embarrassed, I went to give him a peck on the cheek, but he turned and kissed me on the mouth— quick, but on the lips. I could feel my face becoming red from my neck up.

"Show her the game room," Jack added, as if to make up. "She'll love that." Nathan smiled, but I knew he was mad; his back ramrod straight.

We toured the downstairs first, with Nathan using his loud directing voice. Then we got to the upstairs where he showed me his room, loudly, and went onto the walk-in-closet, not so loudly. We kissed like two people lost to each other in war rather than teenagers hiding from mom. Of course, the latter would rate pretty high up there on a scale of "Dangerous Things to Do."

"What's with Jack, anyway?" Nathan asked, finally stopping long enough to vent. We'd gone out and were leaning on the upstairs banister after I'd freshened my makeup and hair in the bathroom. "I think he's taking this acting business a little far. I'm not so sure this was a good idea," he finished, his face clouded with frustration.

"I'm glad you're realizing that. It was an awful idea. It's wrong, Nathan. I want to be with you, but not like this. Let's tell your mother the truth," I pleaded. Nathan's face went from angry to pale in a second.

"She'll never let me date you. If we tell her the truth, it means I will have to directly disobey her. Is that what you want?" He moved away from the banister and backed me against the wall. I searched his eyes trying to find the truth, but I couldn't look at him without feeling confused.

"Why aren't I good enough for her?" I asked, honestly, naively wondering.

"It's not that," he lied. "I'm all she has since my dad died, and she really wants me to make the right choices... for my career," he said, in an effort to console me. It wasn't at all consoling.

"I 'get' making right choices. I want you to make those, too. But they include more than your career. Have you thought anymore about the Guardians?" I could see his facial muscles tighten and the shutters behind his eyes begin to close. I was losing him, so I hurried. "Nathan, I believe you're the *Link*. A mantle will be given to you to carry; and not just for our nation. It's a mantle of peace. I love you, but you must accept responsibility for this power, or it will be lost..." I heard a creak on the stair and looked over to see the top of Mrs. Gregory's head descending the stairs. I pushed Nathan away and saw her pivot and come back up, calling as she came, "Nathan, Cassie, lunch is ready…"

Nathan stepped away from me and said, "Coming, Mother. We'll be right there."

"Don't keep Jack waiting, now," she replied coolly. Honestly, if you were small enough, you could ice skate on that woman's tongue.

"How much do you think she heard?" Nathan asked, worry creasing his brow.

"Probably more than you did," I said, looking sadly into his eyes. I started down, but he pulled me back, and kissed me one more time. I was suddenly afraid he really hadn't heard anything I'd said.

Chapter Thirteen

We sat down to lunch at Mrs. Gregory's beautiful walnut log dining table, which was something a five-star restaurant would serve...if stars on restaurants go that high. I'd been listening to so much talk about armies and generals that I may have confused it with how many MacArthur had. Anyway, it was beyond delectable. I could eat only so much of it though. Nerves had my stomach in a knot. My mouth was saying yes, yes, yes; my stomach was saying no, no, no. Mrs. Gregory didn't seem to notice. She was having such a fun time baiting me it took all her attention.

"So, Cassandra, that is your name, isn't it?" she asked.

"Yes, but please, call me Cassie. Everyone does," I answered.

"But I like Cassandra. It lends class," she said pointedly. "You're a cheerleader, aren't you?"

"Yes, I am."

"Does it leave you any time for extracurricular activities? Key Club, Math Club, Debate Club, that sort of thing?" she wondered in her sweetly menacing way.

"Oh yes, several of the girls are involved in different clubs. I'm not, but I could if I wanted to..." I hadn't actually finished when she turned her attention to Nathan.

"By the way, Nathan, Mrs. Randolph wants you to come and spend the weekends with her and Susan next summer—while you intern with your uncle in Washington," she announced. Turning back to me, she explained, "Nathan has put in a lot of work to achieve his goals. I'm so proud of him. The Randolphs are dear friends of ours. Nathan and Susan Randolph have been friends since before either of them could walk." She smiled at me. "It's always nice to have friends with such similar interests in life."

"Did you know Cassie's father was a big-shot microphysicist, and she's got a little sister who's a genius?" Nathan said, attempting to come to my rescue.

"How fascinating. Do you enjoy the sciences, then?" Mrs. Gregory asked. The old battleship knew right where to aim the cannon.

"Um, no. I think I'm the idiot-savant of the family, minus the savant part." I said, shooting for humor. Only Jack laughed, and then sweetly came to my defense.

"She's no idiot. She's smart, beautiful, funny, and she doesn't take herself too seriously. That's why I like her so much," he said easily. I ducked my head; afraid someone would see the forbidden tears popping up in the corners of my eyes. I quickly commanded them away.

"You're sweet, Jack," Mrs. Gregory said, not buying a word of it.

"How long have you and Jack been seeing one another?" she continued, the torture coming more easily now.

"Oh, it's been a while. Well, not that long, I guess," I answered, brilliantly shoring up the "idiot" part of the self-diagnosis.

"Well, outside of my Nathan, I don't think there's a more

charming boy alive. What's your favorite thing about him?" she asked like the nosey, nosey thing she was.

Jack was talking to Nathan and the senator, but I watched his ears perk up, and he did a quick sideways glance. There were so many things I could say to set him on his heels... but I told the truth. "His character. Jack has integrity," I said, and took a bite of food as if I'd just said he skipped rocks well. But then he turned in his chair smiling at me, and I couldn't stand it. "Of course, the other thing I really like—he's so *sensitive*. Honestly, if Jack weren't a guy, he'd be *my best girlfriend*," I finished, false sincerity glowing from my eyes. Jack kicked me under the table.

"Isn't that sweet," she responded dryly.

"Um, very," I answered, sipping my water.

"Are you two exclusive? Are you, what do they call it, 'going out' together?" she asked.

I hesitated and glanced across at Nathan. He looked like he was holding his breath. "Oh, we're pretty committed...to the same thing," I added evasively.

"Which is?" Mrs. Gregory asked, smiling tightly.

"Well, let's see. We're both sure God is leading us. ... And we try and contain the passion, if you know what I mean," I added, hoping to score points, in the *lamest* way possible.

"Oh, ho! But Jackson is a passionate young man," Senator Gregory said, eyeing me in his very personal way. I veiled an involuntary shudder, by folding my arms.

"Oh, yes, he is. In fact, his passion for stamps, wow! That's the first thing that caught my interest," I replied, unable to control myself. "He's so darn knowledgeable!"

"Hmm. I didn't know that about him, ...so you must be interested in stamps too, Cassandra," Mrs. Gregory remarked, an old trout too smart to take the bait, but nibbling it to tease me.

"Me? Oh no. I just like to go up to his room and watch him lick them," I said, sealing my doom.

Jack reached over and put his arm around me as I watched Nathan stiffen. "Very funny, Cassie," Jack said, shooting me a look filled with tenderness that screamed, *Oh my goodness you're stupid.*

"I'm interested in this commitment to God you spoke of... Tell me about that, will you?" Mrs. Gregory's said, continuing her inquisition.

"OK, Mother. Enough of the third degree..."

That was all I heard of Nathan's protests. As I sat thinking how very, very, much I disliked the woman that gave birth to my boyfriend, I felt myself *slipping... whirling.* Suddenly, I was entering the theater of her life. *I felt her pain and was aware of hurt and fear being the overriding emotions of much of her life. It was like being in a vineyard with these feelings twisted into a trunk and then love, pride and loss, twisting into branches creating within her the fruit of memories both sweet, and intermingled with bitter regret. I could feel tears falling over the loss of her husband as though on my own face.* And I knew she distrusted me; I felt that too. I knew she was afraid...especially of lies. Instantaneously, she became *a little girl, ...then my age, ...then older. I knew she'd married for love; I knew he'd married for her money and her position in society. He'd given her a son, her most cherished possession to compensate, because, although she'd loved him, he'd loved another. She'd left him—and her hopes and dreams in Washington D.C.—but never stopped loving him, or hoping he'd return—until the day he died.* Suddenly, I wanted to love her, *and then just as suddenly, I did.*

As I came back to myself, I heard Mrs. Gregory saying, "I certainly was not giving anyone the third degree. I am showing an interest in our guests, in Jack and his ...girlfriend."

"I'll admit I'm interested in that subject, too. I'd like to know if you have the same religious beliefs as Jack," the senator said, looking down that big, long nose of his.

I still felt stunned, disassociated from myself, and I looked over at Mrs. Gregory as though we remained connected. "I, well, who? ...No. ...Sorry. I think my beliefs are similar, yes, but they're mine. They have to be," I said, clearly confused, but beginning to focus.

"What are those beliefs, if I may?" Mrs. Gregory asked, homing in for the kill. She'd heard enough on the stairwell to at least make her curious.

"My beliefs?"

"You don't have to tell anybody anything, Cassie. You'll have to excuse my mother and uncle."

Something suddenly shifted. I was not only present, but I was clear. I hardly recognized my own voice when I said, "No Nathan, it's all right." I shifted and sat up straighter.

"When I was young, I believed in God, but when my father died, while he was dying really, I gave up on God..."

"I'd say that's understandable," Senator Gregory cut in.

"Let the girl finish, Thaddeus," Mrs. Gregory said, keeping her cool gaze on me.

"Honestly, I didn't think even a miracle could change my mind about God," I admitted, "because I didn't want to believe in Him; and the truth is, even if something *crazy* happened, like an angel appearing," I said, tapping Jack's toe under the table, "Well, even that couldn't have kept me believing for long. And I truly don't want to sound, you know, all Christian-cheesy, but the actual reason I know God is real, is because His *love* is changing me. But I'm not sure I'm changed enough yet to have a whole set of solid beliefs ... except for that." The table was silent and there was no way I was going to look up as long as I had such a nonjudgmental piece of cauliflower gazing back at me.

"Well Cassandra, I find that authentic and ...charming."

Mrs. Gregory said to my surprise. And for the first time she sounded sincere. I looked up at her only to find her busily attending to her own meal.

"You see why we get along so well," Jack was saying to the senator, a smile playing on his lips, his eyes teasing.

"Oh yes, as pretty as she is, I'd let her believe anything she wanted," Senator Gregory said, his condescending voice perfectly matching his patronizing words.

"I'm sorry," Nathan said, pushing away from the table. "I need to be excused," his face a mask, but his voice peculiar.

"Nathan?" Mrs. Gregory said in surprise, but he gave her no answer and left the room. I started to rise but Jack touched my arm. After a second, he rose and followed Nathan out.

"Sister, exquisite as usual. Cassie, a pleasure. You'll excuse me, too, won't you?" the senator asked, looking down at his watch. "I need to make a few pressing calls to Washington," and without waiting for a response, rose and left, going up the stairs to the back rooms.

"I hate it when he calls me that," Mrs. Gregory said under her breath, her eyes narrowed, and her lips thin.

"Well, I can't blame you for that!" I blurted, then quickly covered my mouth with my napkin as if I could capture the escaped words and stuff them back in.

She swiftly looked at me, and then burst out with an abrupt guffaw, also covering her mouth with her linen. We sat looking at each other, smiling behind our napkins.

Lowering them, I said, "I need to tell you something." Mrs. Gregory's smile quickly changed to cool reserve. "I'm not Jack's girlfriend. But don't worry, I'm probably not Nathan's either—at least not anymore."

Mrs. Gregory's eyebrows rose, and she said in a cool tone, "I already knew about you. Someone pointed you out to me at school. So, what are you doing here, Miss Connor?" I swallowed hard. Now I was Miss Connor, the liar, infiltrator, wanna-be-Christian, and Nathan-hunter. I couldn't remember why I was there... I sat looking at her for the longest moment...

"Oh, sorry. I'm here because Nathan wanted you to meet me. He thought that, if I came with Jack, you'd like me more; that is, you wouldn't like me at all if you thought I liked Nathan, which I do, which I did..."

"Which is it?"

"Do...but I won't change for him; because I'm changing for me, and gosh, I don't know, it's confusing. It used to be that he was everything to me. Now he's not. But when I'm with him, I get confused," I stupidly admitted to *his mother*, wondering if she'd put something in the water.

"Why are you telling me this?" she asked, looking squarely in my eyes.

My face turned red, and all I could do was mumble, "I think I explained the level of genius I attained in my family."

"No, dear. I mean, why didn't you just go home, and play this out? Why did you tell me now? You could have left believing I was none the wiser," she said, gazing at me intently.

I pondered that for a moment and said, "It's always been important for people to like me. I used to be popular...you know, Nathan and all. But now, it's more important for *me* to like me. When I go home, and crawl into bed, I say goodnight to my Father, and I know he's seen everything I've done. ... God, not my dad that died." I added, thinking I'd given her plenty of reasons to think I was a bit eccentric.

"Yes, dear," she said, letting me know she hadn't needed clarification. "And thank you for being honest with me, Cassand...Cassie," she amended. "Now, let me be honest with you. Nathan's destiny is not in this town. He will end up marrying someone who can further his career. I know that must sound very cold to you. The young are so passionate.

But believe me, you have a lot to learn about the way life works. In the end, I will not be the one to determine whom Nathan chooses. At most, his uncle may have some slight say, but you can bet it will be for his career that he marries. I can only hope love follows.

"What I do is as much for your sake as it is for his. I can't stop him from having a girlfriend at school; I've always realized this. But I do believe not allowing him to openly date is doing what is best for him, as well as what is best for the girls of this town. If I'm wrong, so be it. But I don't believe so."

I understood everything she said—from her point of view —but from my point of view, no matter how I screwed my head around to look at it, it seemed twisted. I mean, didn't she get how poorly all that marrying-to-further-the-career business had worked out for her? I watched her sitting straight backed, her head high, and silently gazing out the window as though deciding something.

"Jack is a very special boy," she said finally, adding quietly, as though only to herself. "We owe him more than I'll ever know how to repay..."

"Do you mind my asking about that?" I said, knowing very well I was being intrusive, but taking the shot anyway, because of the nosey, nosey thing I was.

She looked at me for a long moment. So long I wondered if she had psychic powers and was looking at my aura. If that were the case, after my last hot and heavy kissing bout with Nathan, my colors weren't going to help me out much.

Finally, she said, "Maybe this will pay him back in some small way. I know he will never say a word. You are right about his integrity." She looked off toward the lake as if remembering.

"When the boys were young, they played together a lot. I encouraged it. Jack was such a good influence. Nathan's father wasn't home...much—I'd decided to move from D.C. It was a better atmosphere here. And when Nathan's father died, Jack was the person Nathan wanted to be with. One day, they'd taken the little boat out fishing on the lake. Both boys were excellent swimmers, but there were water skiers, a wake, and when the boat capsized it hit Nathan on the head. Jack saved Nathan. It was miraculous, really, how that small boy pulled Nathan to the surface and all the way back to shore, but he did. I'd been keeping an eye on them periodically from the deck, and when I looked out and saw the overturned boat, I rushed to where I found Jack dragging Nathan to land. Several other people were there too, asking questions, and wanting to help. Anyway, I got them in the car and before I even got back to the cabin, Nathan had regained consciousness and was fine. I decided to take him to the doctor in town, but Thaddeus wouldn't hear of it. He called his specialist friend here at the lake to come over, while I took Jack home. But while I was gone, reporters showed up. The next day it was in our local newspaper and had hit the AP. There was a local hero—he'd saved a drowning boy; but it wasn't Jack, it was Nathan who was named the hero— Senator Gregory's nephew. Thaddeus claimed it was a simple typo; the press had erred. He'd told nothing but the facts. Nathan would never talk to me about it, which was answer enough. I tried to make it right, but Jack and his family said it didn't matter. What mattered was afterward. Nathan left off being friends with Jack. I realize now that Nathan has never again been the same loving boy he was ... since the accident, since Jack had been his friend."

She looked at me. "Maybe I'm wrong, but I sense something real between you and Jack, despite your ploy." She must have seen my face begin to color because she quickly looked away. "It's been nice meeting you, Cassie Connor," she said standing.

"Nice to meet you too..." As I stood and reached for her hand, again I *felt* her, a remnant from my earlier encounter. So instead, I reached up and kissed her cheek, something that a few hours ago would have been as unthinkable as an A in Calculus; in other words, impossible. She said nothing, but as I turned to go, I saw her touch her face lightly.

I walked out of the cabin feeling strangely detached, and almost bumped into Senator Gregory. "Oh, excuse me," I said, side stepping quickly.

He moved to intercept me, and this time condescended to grab my arm. His breath was laced with more than phone calls to Washington when he said, "Cassie, just a word of advice. You can take a word of advice, a smart girl like you?" The look in his eyes was anything but friendly, and I stood very still, as though facing a rattler.

"You should leave Nathan alone. I know all about girls like you. Leave the boy alone. Are we clear?"

I pulled my arm from his hand and looked him up and down, "Senator, you need to wake up. Time is running out for you. It's your choice: see the light, ...*or go to Hell.*" Jack came up behind me and took my arm.

"Goodnight, Senator. See you again sometime. Come on, Cassie. I'd better get you home before your curfew," he said, turning me and leading me away.

"Wait, I need to say goodbye to Nathan," I said to Jack, not caring whether or not the old goat heard me.

"Come on, we'll talk in the car. He'll see you tomorrow. It's better, really," he said, opening my door and helping me in...by shoving me.

"OK, OK, I'm going." I smoothed my clothes and hair and sat silently as Jack drove away. He was the first to break the silence.

"So... I think we've established evangelism is not your

strong suit," he said, looking sideways at me, a smirk on his face.

I couldn't help smiling a little myself. "I'll need to talk to God tonight about that. I think maybe that was less about leading him to the light, and more about telling him to go to hell... By the way, I'm sorry for using the term 'screw you' when I could have said 'go soak yourself.' I still need work. Things like that shouldn't feel so good."

"Yea, I know what you mean," he said, smiling straight ahead. But hey, here's something you should feel good about. Nathan's in. We talked, and he wants to embrace Christianity again. He knew Jesus as a kid. After his father died, he started coming to church with me, and he really seemed to feel God's love."

Jack was quiet for a minute, so I prompted, "What changed?"

"Ah... something happened ...and he quit. He changed." Jack was quiet again, remembering, "Tonight, after you said what you did at the table, he either felt something real, and decided to give God a try in his life again—or he decided it was his last chance with you. Honestly, I couldn't tell."

I listened to him stunned. Then, happiness, joy, and relief flooded over me. "Jack," I said, "Thank you." Then, like a goose, I began to hiccup—which kept the tears at bay.

Chapter Fourteen

The alarm went off the next morning, and I was surprised to find it was already time to rise and shine when I felt like my whole body was still set on snooze. It was dark outside; I rolled out, looked longingly at my bed, and carried on. I couldn't help wondering if Xena ever slept in.

I didn't want to admit that one of the reasons I'd been forcing myself out of bed fifteen minutes early was to take Tessa to school. I had to admit that, whereas before I'd winced at her appearance, now her outfits had a cheering effect on me.

She'd decided on polka dots and plaids today, layering the many different pieces for warmth. It looked like she'd tried to straighten her hair with one of my flattening irons and had given up on the job part way through; pieces of each ironed ponytail longer and straighter than the surrounding frizz—I mean, it could have been the look she was going for—if she'd been going for shock-rocker. It was hard to tell. Her book bag leaned against the chair and was nearly half her size. It was decorated with fabric paint in rainbows and flowers. A key chain teddy bear hung from the zipper. I leaned on the kitchen doorframe and tried to imagine her swinging a sword, and found she was actually easier to imagine as a hockey puck—which reminded me of Chris.

"You mentioned Chris came over yesterday after Jack and I had already left. Did he leave a message?" I asked, finishing my orange juice, which combined with toothpaste residue, ended up tasting like oranges mixed with sour lemon chaser.

"Well, if you can call it a message, I guess so." Tessa's face automatically screwed itself up into a look of painful distaste when Chris' name came up in conversation—either that, or she'd just brushed too.

I smiled at her through my pucker. "I know you have a hard time with him, but you must admit. He's awfully good looking—for a malamute," I said, hoping for a little sisterly "cute-boy" exchange. What I got was a look of horror.

"What is wrong with you? Do you think I'm interested in boys? I'm twelve years old! Chris is fifteen! That's three years! I won't be interested in things like that for...for... well, I don't really know, but not at twelve!" she said emphatically, as though it was a mathematical equation beyond her ability.

"OK, sorry! I feel so mortified—as though I've tried to entice you into a world of evil desire. But honestly, from a purely artistic point of view, considering only his eyes, the structure of his nose and those perfect teeth... that's all I meant," I said, a little ashamed of myself, a little suspicious of my sister. At her age, I knew a cute guy when I saw one— even if I didn't like him, or even if I didn't want anyone to know I sorta liked him. But then, that was me.

"He said he wanted to come to the high school today—to see you, I suppose. I told him he wasn't allowed—that he had to be enrolled. He got very insistent. No, pushy. Actually, bossy is a better word. He said, 'he didn't care, he'd go anyway.' He's very…irritating. Nothing like Jack, that's for sure."

"Is that all?" I asked as we headed out the door.

"Basically," she said, lowering her gaze.

"Come on, what else?" I asked, knowing he'd said something more to bug her, because after all, that's what he did. She kept walking, so I pulled her to a stop and looked at her until she met my eyes.

"He said—Oh it's so stupid!"

"What?"

"He said, '*One day, I was going to marry him*'!" she cried, her eyes huge with distress. I had to admit, even without magnified lenses, mine probably matched hers in size.

"What did you say?" I asked, trying to keep horrified laughter from rising unsolicited.

"I told him just what I told you!" she said desperately.

"And…"

"And …he said he'd *wait* for me. I told him he'd have to wait *a hundred years*, but he doesn't listen. He said he 'knew the first time he saw me…'"

"Really? And knowing that, he used you as a hockey puck?" All I could think was, *those weird homeschool kids…* when, as if on cue, God's special warrior showed up. It's strange, but my stomach did a little flip.

"Hey guys, thought I'd hitch a ride if it's OK," Jack called, walking up the drive. "I can't drive mine until I fix the carburetor. I should be done in a day or two, and then I'll be glad to taxi."

"No problem," I said easily, trying to recover both from Tessa's news, controlled laughter, and the stomach gymnastics he'd brought on. I knew Jack could spot signs of weirdness from a mile away, and if I needed to recover, I knew poor Tessa really needed time. "Tessa, would you please grab my blue binder for me? I forgot it on the counter,"

I said quickly. She turned and fled into the house, returning a few seconds later empty handed, but composed.

"Are you sure, Cassie? I didn't see it."

"Oh, I'm sorry, Tess. Here it is," I said, as she looked at me with the eyes of a pup saved from euthanasia. Granted, she already looked a bit like a pup whose eccentric owner had gone overboard putting clips in the poor thing's extraordinary pelt. But there was no getting around how easy it was to make my sister appreciative.

"We need to meet with Hailey and Santos today," Jack said, as we piled into the car. "When do you get out of school, Squirt?" he asked Tessa.

"My last class is at the high school. I have to be there longer today for testing," she added quietly.

"I think they just need to get over it, and send you to MIT," I said cheerfully, but Tessa looked at me, and again she was anything but cheery.

"Like I told you, I'm only twelve years old! I *don't* like boys, and I *don't* want to go to Harvard *or* MIT. I don't want to do anything but stay right here and grow up—*slowly*." She said completely exasperated and turned sideways in her seat to look out the window.

Jack looked at me questioningly, and I nodded knowingly. "OK, Tess. Then you won't go anywhere. You'll stay right here and be exactly who, and what, God intended you to be," I said resolutely. She turned back, her eyes hopeful, reminding me again of her great vulnerability despite her intelligence. "I mean it. You'll stay here as long as you want, and just be ...*slow*," I added, finally getting her to smile.

After a few minutes, Jack, obviously dying to bring up the topic again, said, "So, the three of us will meet with Santos and Hailey today," clearly firming up our intricate plan.

"Aren't you forgetting something?" I asked. When Jack

stared at me blankly, I re-worded. "Aren't you forgetting some*one*?"

Jack closed his eyes and sighed. "Right, I forgot Chris. OK, the six of us will meet."

"Oh right, I forgot about Chris, too." I looked at Tessa in the rearview mirror and wondered if it would be fair to blackball a Guardian due to fraternization rules...but no. Considering my own conduct, that wouldn't work. "Actually, I meant Nathan... Don't you think we need to include him? He needs to get to know everybody as soon as possible. We've got to get going on this."

"Oh, right. I guess the *Link* should be included in our meetings; however, Hamaliel never mentioned the *Link* fighting. But I guess especially now we should invite him," Jack said, trying to sound enthusiastic. "Have you and Chris worked out a schedule for studying your verses yet?" he asked, changing the subject.

"Not yet, but we will today," I said, hoping this was true.

"How're you doing, Tessa?" he asked.

"Well, I'd like to have more time, but I've memorized the ones Darius gave us," she answered.

"You what? That's over forty-five verses you know already!" I exclaimed, appalled at myself, but completely mortified at her overachieving.

"Cassie, I didn't even get into the circle the first time with you and Jack. I don't know what you're griping about."

I have to admit this made me feel better, but in an unrefined, unintellectual, Amazonian sort-of-way. Still... "OK Einstein, I'll see you at school later. If you're there in time for lunch, come and find me," I said to her, as we pulled up at her school. The look of shocked surprise was replaced with joy. I wondered, had she always been so easy to please?

As we drove off, I realized why Jack had made my tummy twirl, and I wondered if he'd done it on purpose. Once more he'd managed hot. This time his Levi's were darker but still had just the right amount of fade. Under a black zippered sweatshirt, his gray t-shirt was the color of his eyes. He'd done "just right," perfectly, *again.* I knew Jack well, and he wasn't the type of guy to spend time worrying about his clothes. So, it only made sense he was trying to impress me. He was even tapping unused resources, which were looking more and more diverse, making him, well, impressive. And I was touched. But I couldn't help teasing him just a little, so I said, "Who's the babe you're trying to impress with the duds?"

Jack smiled his unreadable smile, the one I had an aversion to, and said, "Do you know Lisa Taylor?"

Somehow, but just barely, I kept from slamming my foot down on the brakes. Did I know Lisa Taylor? *Please...*

"Sure—of course I know her. She's on my cheer squad," I managed, applying the phony face with much more difficulty than usual. It was amazing how quickly I was losing my abilities. Jack didn't say anything else, so I asked, "Are you telling me you have the 'hots' for *Lisa?*" My voice raising several decibels even as I inwardly reined back my vocal cords like a Wild West stagecoach driver.

"Well, there's no doubt the girl *is* 'hot.' And she asked if I would go to the backwards dance with her in three weeks," he stated, calm and civilized. I pulled into the high school parking lot and made a big deal of smiling and waving to some of the other kids. When I didn't say anything, he asked, "So, what do you think?"

"About what?" I asked, smiling with my lips sealed so the scream that shockingly wanted release, stayed put.

"Do you think I ought to go with her?" He asked, turning to look me straight in the eyes. But there was no way I could let him see what I was feeling before I had a chance to examine it myself.

I gathered up my purse and backpack from the back seat,

straightened up, and said without looking at him, "If you like her, you should go—I would—well, you know. I wouldn't go with her—but *you* should," I said, slamming my door a tiny bit too hard, ...making sure it closed properly.

We walked to our classes without another word, parting without saying anything in the hall.

~

I didn't see Nathan for the first three periods of school and was strangely relieved. The rest of my so-called "friends" avoided me like the plague, and the static started up again whenever I came anywhere near their vicinity. It was an aggressively hurtful form of revenge, and I knew full well that anyone choosing to take a path other than the "Snob' path," or go by rules other than their sacred orders could expect exactly what I was getting. I also knew Nathan was at the core of their displeasure with me. Something told me Nathan hadn't divulged the same information to the "A" clique that he had to Jack the night before. I had a sneaking, staticky feeling that whatever it was, had less to do with God and more to do with me. And whenever one of them looked at me, I had a strange feeling come over me, probably something like a horse that refuses to take a bit and is destined for the glue factory.

Then, I saw him on the way to our separate classes. The look in his eyes as he found me from across the crowded hallway told me my hunch had been right. If he'd chosen Christ with Jack, he'd made another decision concerning me. I wasn't sure what it was, but I knew he was in turmoil. He came over, but kept his distance, and I instinctively knew to keep mine.

"I'm..." Nathan looked off without finishing his sentence. I waited.

"Am I supposed to guess the rest?" I finally asked. He continued looking off over my head. "Glad to see you?" I ventured, "how about, 'so happy that you finally met my mom?'" He stood looking over my head, silent, his eyes unblinking. A minute passed. "Nathan, maybe just the truth. I know it's hard to say, but how about, 'I'm confused.' Is that what you're trying to tell me?"

"I'm ...breaking up with you," he said, but not before he looked down at me, his eyes now filled with anger.

"Nathan, I'm *so* sorry..." I reached out to touch his arm, and he backed further away, a snarl of a smile forming on his lips.

"What are *you* sorry for? I'm breaking up with you!" he snorted, turning, and heading down the hall at a jog.

That was the period before lunch. I came into my class a minute tardy, but I must have appeared so stunned that Mr. Peters never said a word to me. I heard every tick of the clock during that class, but I don't remember anything else. I don't believe I had a single thought. Amazing, the survival modes we develop; and I'd developed mine well. It would take a long time before I'd be able to process any of my true feelings.

When the bell rang, I walked to the tables in the courtyard and spied Hailey. She was hunched over her lunch alone. Santos stood against the wall by himself, waiting for Jack, who looked to be in the middle of a very enjoyable—and ha ha, so, so amusing —conversation with Lisa Taylor. Seeing him with her grated on me. I realized these feelings were nothing less than despicable on my part, considering Jack certainly wasn't *my* boyfriend, and had every right to have a girlfriend of his own. I certainly couldn't explain these feelings—well, maybe I could. They *were* despicable, and there was nothing I could do about them. I went over and sat down next to Hailey.

"Oh Cassie, Hi!" Hailey said, as soon as she saw me. The

shirt she wore was too tight and her pants were sloppy. Her hair was a bit mussed and unremarkably combed back in a loose ponytail. I *really* didn't want to be cheered by her, but strangely, I was.

"How ya doing, Hailey? And if the answer to that question is "happy," and has an exclamation point anywhere near it, please don't answer," I said, warning her of the gloom I intended to share.

"Oh Cassie," her hand came out and touched mine, and I felt comforted. She waited an appropriate few moments before asking, "Guess what?" and I was grateful she hadn't asked what my trouble was. In fact, she looked distracted, as though she'd hardly paid any attention to my difficulty at all.

"What?"

"I saw them," she said, her green eyes large.

"You saw...the...demon-sucking-hell-hounds?" I asked, automatically shooting a look over at Santos. He was glancing our way and nodded toward us. "Where? I mean, when? I mean, where? I asked, suddenly excited by the fearful idea of them lurking nearby.

"Right here. ...They are here! Santos is waiting for Jack, and then he will show you. *They are everywhere*...I almost fainted. Cassie, it's much worse than I thought... I'm not kidding."

Chapter Fifteen

I sat across from Hailey in the quad, my mouth agape, as though catching a fly would be right in line with the highlights of my day so far. I quickly snapped it shut. "And I had another dream," she continued, just as Jack and Santos walked over and sat down. It took everything I had in the way of self-control to contain a crack about Jack dragging himself away from 'Miss Hottie' to join us in the battle against evil. Thank goodness I was endowed with *some* restraint.

I looked over at Jack with a sweet smile. "Nice of you to *finally* join us," I said with just the tiniest bit of spite...hardly any. After all, I wasn't a *master* of restraint—that took years.

"Nathan won't be joining us. Is Tessa here for lunch?" Jack asked, choosing to ignore my little zing, and deleting anything he knew about Nathan and me.

"We haven't seen Tessa yet," Hailey offered.

"What's going on with that Nathan, dude?" Santos asked, having been told Nathan had finally decided to come aboard.

"I'm not sure, except it looks like he's having a problem with the decision he made last night. I don't know if his uncle got a hold of him, or if this is just Nathan not being able to commit. We need to do what Darius told us: pray for him. I'm going to try and get him to come with me later today and meet with just you and me, Santos," he said, turning casually in my direction and looking me in the eyes. Instantly, I knew he was aware of what happened between Nathan and me, and I quickly looked away. "We'll see if it makes a difference. They say, 'seeing is believing,'" he finished.

"Yes, but *belief cometh of hearing, and hearing by the word of Christ.*' So, if this 'Nathan dude' you're talking about needs a few lessons in scripture, my services are available," Chris said, leaning on his crutches and smiling at us from the next table.

"Hey Chris, how'd you get here?" Santos asked, clearly pleased.

"I have my ways," he said smugly, as he hobbled over to our table.

"Mom bring you?" Jack asked, dryly.

Chris lost his self-satisfied air, and admitted, "Yea. I told her I would check the school out for a few extra credit classes."

"Are you going to take classes here?" Hailey asked, sounding pleased; but her eyes remained uncharacteristically anxious.

"Not if I can help it. This place is lame." Jack shot Chris a corrective look. "Sorry, I shouldn't have said that." He amended. "It's just I get twice as much done at home, and still have time to break bones," He added smiling.

Just then, I saw Tessa's tiny polka dotted form elbow her way around the table and was suddenly very grateful to have her small but admirable little person as part of our team. "Hey, Tessa; come on and sit down. Now that we're all here, Santos you can begin," I said, with a dramatic flourish of my hands.

"I won't bother to try and explain," he said, "Instead, I'll just let you see for yourselves. OK, take my hand," Santos instructed, reaching out and taking Hailey's and mine under the table. I noticed Hailey hesitating for a fraction of a second, first closing her eyes and wiping her palm against her thigh before accepting his. This should have been my first warning.

Hailey then took Tessa's hand—and Chris lumbered over into a semi-comfortable position, mashing a few of our toes in the process. He took hold of Tessa's other one. I couldn't help stealing a look at Tessa, but she wouldn't meet my eye. Jack shook his head and took my hand. His brother tried to take Jack's other hand and form a circle, but Jack slapped it away. Chris started laughing. He so dearly loved to rough house.

"Get lost. I'm not holding your hand," Jack said, trying not to smile.

"Please, Jackie. I *want* to..." Chris taunted.

Tessa looked over at Jack, her face completely white. "If the two of you would quit horsing about, you'd see you don't need to form a circle for a conduit to be created. Look around you."

My momentary embarrassment at holding hands with these guys at the edges of the quad like some weirdo Kumbaya Club was short-lived. I looked out, and the images beginning to materialize before us made me gasp. I was frozen, staring for several seconds at impossible hallucinations. Then, with a muffled yell, I let go. And so did everybody else.

"What the heck...I can't...do this," I said quickly, breathing hard. The others were silent, their faces reflecting different emotions. Jack had a puzzled look tinged with fear, as though he couldn't believe what he'd just seen. Tessa's face was blank, white, her eyes filling the frames of her large glasses. Hailey had a look of quiet alarm, as if she couldn't quite believe the creatures she'd seen earlier were still around.

Chris leaned back on the bench his mouth open, his eyes wide, a ghoulish smile across his face. He spoke second, "No frigging way! I did *not* just see that..."

Santos laughed gruffly, "This is nothing, man. These are the little ones."

"Luckily, we don't have to see them if we choose not to," Hailey remarked, looking sympathetically toward Santos.

Jack wiped his forehead, looking out at the school and back at Santos for a long moment. "Wow. She's right. That's quite some gift you've got." Then he turned towards me. I guess we have to make up our minds... Cassie?" Jack said, with intensity, "Can you do this?"

"All right. OK," I said, my voice quivering. I looked at the others, and they nodded, without looking any more thrilled than I felt. I took Santos' hand once again. "I'm sorry Santos. It must be hard. I don't know how you hold up. It's surreal watching these horrible, malformed, revolting creatures roaming the school grounds. And I'm not referring to my old friends in the 'Snob' patrol," I said, shooting for a little levity. Santos and I began laughing. The rest of the Guardians seemed not to know a good joke if it kissed them on the lips, but they smiled as if in condolence of us. And, of course, I stopped laughing when I looked over at my old group of friends—and was horrified to see several getting sucked on by the creatures.

Jenna had a thin, gray hairless demon with ears that looked like bat wings, clinging to her back, and whispering in her ear. There was a connector from the creature's chest attached to the back of Jenna's head, pulsating. Feeding. I'd never realized before now how unhappy Jenna's laugh was. Whenever someone said something to make her burst out, the pulsating began in earnest. Whatever made her laugh, was also causing her pain. It was strange…

Brittany had a pale, rather fat Siphon. Its tiny eyes were red. It had fangs and long dirty claws. It periodically drove its incisors into her neck, and shortly after, I'd see Brittany frown. It could have been a coincidence, but it happened over and over with clockwork regularity. A part of me still loved these girls. I knew they'd have died a thousand twirling, screaming, hacking, spitting, deaths, if they could have seen what I was seeing now. I'll have to admit, the visual of this dance made me smile just a little …and then I was ashamed.

"Can we let go for a minute," I said, dropping hands whether anyone wanted to or not. It was exhausting. "How are we going to do this? I'm not sure I'm made of the right stuff for this job," I said.

"Maybe you just don't want to do this," Chris said easily —too easily.

"Well, maybe I don't, Chris. Maybe that's what I'm saying," I said, stepping over to where he stood.

"Then say that. Don't say you're not made of the right stuff. That's baloney. God made you and chose you. If you don't want to—I don't blame you. It's scary, I'm scared…" He said, looking me straight in the eyes.

He was such a punk, and he'd called me out in front of everybody, and what was he? Fifteen? A feral-homeschooled-broken-legged-cretin professing future love to my twelve-year-old sister? I wanted to let him have it. The problem was there were beings of evil all around us, and we could finally see them. Suddenly, we weren't playing games anymore. This was war; and Chris was right, even if he was a punk. Still, he needed to know.

"All right. Maybe I am scared. But I see people everywhere with things on them that are horrible. *Right now,* I should be *willing* to go. I should be willing to say, 'I'm the healer!' But you know what? I'm not willing! And you know what else? I'm not only scared of the demons—and believe me, I am—I'm also terrified of my old friends and what they're going to think of me! So, how's my warrior status looking to you now? Because excuse me, I'm having problems with it," I said, staring Chris down, ticked off at myself and taking it out on him.

He licked his lips, not looking as sure of himself anymore. "I think you're doing OK. It's not easy to be so honest," he said, shrugging.

I watched for even a tick of insincerity, but knowing demons were sucking on people all around us, made me want to make up fast. Plus, I felt heaps better getting my frustrations out like that. "Well, thanks for that, Chris," I said, smiling slightly. He cocked his head at me, as though wondering if I were teasing him.

Hailey spoke up in a quiet voice, "Listen everyone, I must admit I feel the same way. I'm freaked out, too. Cassie just said what I was thinking, and if I had been honest, then you would have been saying that to me, Chris..." she admitted. I knew her confession was the truth, but also a mark of her loyalty to me. I looked at her with what I hoped conveyed my appreciation.

"Becoming the healer, that comes from the heart..." Jack was saying, just as Tessa cut in.

"I know this isn't going to be easy," Tessa said, her face earnest. But one thing Darius said keeps going around and around in my mind. She was talking about Rasvampin and how he doesn't believe God exists. He *knows* it. And we have to have more faith than Rasvampin does. Well, if the power of love, and the power of the Blood of Christ are the two weapons we have to use against him, and those are also the only weapons we can use against these demons, then it makes sense that this school is our training ground... These creatures can't fight back—and even as ugly as they are—if we can't stand up to them, what are we going to do in a week from now when we have to face the Maltorphs, and then the Destroyer?

Everyone was quiet. "OK, Tessa. We know you're right," I said, "and, I *suppose* I can stand up to the ugly creatures, but it's the demons sucking on their necks I'm worried about." Santos was the only one to laugh outright. "Sorry, Tessa. I was almost kidding," I added, "and I want to be willing to be the heal..."

"No. Listen, I'm not done making my *whole* point. I'm the healer," she said quietly. We all went silent again.

"You know this?" Jack asked.

"Yes, the words, keep repeating themselves over and over. And, of course, they make perfect sense: *Jesus Christ* and *by His Blood.*"

"What's this about a healer?" Chris asked, and we all remembered he hadn't been present when we'd met Darius and so much had been explained.

"One person must choose to be the healer—they just know it. You see it's not that hard to make a demon release. Just talking to someone, sometimes just a word," Jack explained.

"A kindness," Hailey said.

"Even laughter—joyful laughter, that is—can make a demon uncomfortable and detach," I added, "but it's after they detach that's important."

"Once the demon detaches, the healer must speak words, words given by the Holy Spirit, in the presence of the demon, and only the healer knows which words work. These seal the portals of the victim and destroys the demon," Tessa concluded. Chris nodded; his eyes serious but sparkling as he looked at Tess. She turned away.

"Jack, I think we need a plan; I'm still not sure I know how to go about this," Hailey said, looking as uneasy as I felt.

"I think you're right. For one thing, maybe we need to work in teams," Jack said, looking out into the quad, his voice controlled. "A person to get the demon to release, with Santos as the roving eyes, and Tessa, to speak the words. This can only happen once Tessa knows a demon's off. That means you'll need to rove with Santos," he said, looking at Tessa. "Does that sound OK?" Everyone agreed. I was going to offer to hang back and take minutes, but sadly, I figured they'd assume I was trying to be humorous.

Jack turned to Santos and asked, "Is there any type of demon that's different than the one's Darius told us we'd see?"

"Not really, they're all Siphons. Although, there is a type that is a little different. I think they are worse. They don't look so gross, but they are hard to be around. They seem frightened themselves, and they make you feel afraid. We will have to take hands and I can show you some."

Santos directed us over to a group of his friends, and a different group, standing underneath the stairwells where darker creatures, with fearful expressions, lurked and attached themselves to their victims. I looked around and found other kids where these same darker demons were attaching.

"I've been watching my friends," Santos said, "and I been noticing these demons always attach to the one's that smoke weed, and do drugs. All I can tell is they must wait for some kind of opening. They have a hook on one long arm, and as soon as someone gets enough of a buzz, they reach up, like this," he said, letting go of my hand and arching his own over his head and down to the crown of his own, "and in at the top, and hook them somewhere by the forehead." He sat back down. "See that dark thing on that guy over there? It looks like a beanie, but that's the creature's suction. But these creatures are paranoid; always afraid. They're lookin' around all the time. They always know I see them. Some of you guys got to go there cuz you won't be able to see them. They know when I see them. They hiss louder too," he finished, scaring me a little too much for the good of the cause.

"Oh, that shouldn't be a problem...walkin' on up to the homeys, chattin' 'em up, making them feel all warm and cozy, then letting my little sister walk over there so she can say— what was it, Tessa? *'Jesus Christ* and *by His Blood?'* This ought to work out nicely," I said, modifying my sarcastic inflection into something a bit softer. It was bad enough my thoughts were being made flesh.

"I'll be fine. God won't let us down. We don't fight alone, you know," Tessa said to me, making me remember why I so often wanted to kill her moments before realizing she was what I wanted to be when I grew up. Would it always be hell getting where God expected me to be, I wondered?

"You're the one needs to be goin' over and talkin' to my home boys. I told them I know you, and they say, 'No way man, you mean, Cassita bonita?" Santos said, working his hands in a very Mexican dance-ish way. He could be incredibly charming.

"Hmm, so they like the fish, do they?" I said, not sure why, and not sure I was brave enough to test those waters, tuna or not. Santos smiled but in a funny, questioning way. Jack laughed outright, but when I looked at him and said *"what?"* with my eyes, he just smiled and shook his head. I figured he was being lame, and I wasn't going to beg.

"Anyways," Santos continued, "there are even worse. Black and really scary, but they usually come around when someone starts drinking, or doing harder drugs. ...There are sex ones too," he added, turning as red as his olive complexion allowed. "Over there, that one." Santos let go momentarily, and pointed to a beast of streaky pigmentation, attached to a boy sitting alone, quietly studying his laptop.

The demon's veins looked as though they could be filled with paint of odd colors, exposed through paper-thin skin. Its hair was orange and thick, running down the center of its back. A large bulbous belly hung on both sides storing nourishment. Long talons drove themselves deeply into the boy's flesh, feeding the monster. Green eyes slanted above a thin pointy nose, while its tongue shot out, licking inside of the ear and the along the neck of the boy he gripped. He was a greedy, horrible demon. Occasionally, the student would look up and gaze around, completely unaware those claws were deeply imbedded into him. If I hadn't seen the monster, I wouldn't have believed the kid was a living feast—or that the quiet student—fed the creature on pornography.

It was hideous, and looking around I saw I wasn't alone in my revulsion. We were all repelled by it, so when I heard, "This is terrible. Let's get busy and *help* these people!" I looked over in surprise. The emphatic words came from Chris. Furrows had formed on the perfectly smooth skin above his eyes as he watched the boy sitting alone with his demon. Fear and repulsion hadn't been the only emotions to grip him. Concern was written all over his face.

"All right, let's do this. We'll start with the boy and the sex-demon. Who's going in first?" Jack asked.

Chapter Sixteen

T he moment of truth was upon us, and everyone sat looking at everyone else. Now maybe it was because I was co-elder, and therefore, in a sense co-leader; but for whatever reason, everyone suddenly seemed to be looking at me. I shifted and looked around; I smiled. Nothing worked.

"Look, I'm sorry, but I'm not going near that thing," I responded with my usual bravery. Everyone remained quiet. Jack smiled at me with his despicable half-smile. "OK, what I really mean is, I'd rather not." This was also met with complete silence. "Come on, ...*oh, all right!* But honestly, and I'm being honest now, I think this is a guy's job. That kid is obviously lonely—and if he needs a friend..."

"Cassie's right," Jack said, this time with a full smile. "But Cassie, I don't think anyone expected you to go. The truth is, I'd like a crack at this one. I just wanted to give everyone a chance to think about it. And we'll use this demon as our test. Santos, if you're willing, I'd like you to come with me and we'll talk to him together," Jack finished.

"Actually, could I go first?" Chris asked. "Then, if I can

get the demon to pull out his claws, you and Santos can come over with Tessa."

Oh right, I thought to myself, *now they're all gung-ho, after I'd made my declaration as a "scaredy-pants."*

Jack looked at his brother and smiled. "Have at it, bro, and good luck—no, God bless," he amended. "We'll stay here, watch, and pray.

Chris shambled over on his crutches, looking back once. I could have sworn he looked at Tessa—who prayed silently while moving her lips as she watched. I copied but wasn't very effective, deciding then and there I'd practice at talking to God. I started reciting my two scriptures and remembered the twenty-first Psalms, delighted to have three under my belt.

While Chris headed for the wall across from where the boy sat, he didn't look at the kid once. When he got there, Chris slid down the wall, his crutches clambering beside him. The kid looked up, seeming a bit nervous, and half-way closed the lid on his computer, but the demon took no notice —until Chris said something. It happened quickly, the boy's laptop slowly clapped shut, while the demon's pointy face and green eyes snapped to attention. Then, it began to writhe. His bulbous belly worked back and forth, as Chris kept talking. The boy sat listening, and started smiling. It was exciting but awful. It was obvious that the creature couldn't stand what the boy was feeling, and its contortions made it more horrible than ever. One claw came out as the boy laughed, dripping with a greenish-blue fluid. The other claw stayed part way in. Santos, Tessa, and Jack got up, and began walking toward Chris, no one looking at the demon at the same time. They walked over to Chris—and as far as we could tell, said hello.

Of course, once Santos was gone, Hailey and I were left in the dark, so to speak; at least as far as watching the demon was concerned. About this time, the strangest thing happened. I suddenly decided I wanted to see it all. If I could've surprised myself more, I honestly don't know how, unless maybe I'd found myself swinging a big shiny sword—and that had already happened. I gave Hailey a nod, and she nodded back. Game on; we headed over.

Jack was introducing himself, "Hi, just came over to introduce myself, and say hi to my brother. I'm Jack," he said. The kid got to his feet.

"Hey. I'm Kurt. You go here?" he asked, obviously aware of most of the student body.

"New actually. Only been here a week. What grade you in, Kurt?"

"I'm a sophomore," he said.

Tessa had been standing behind Santos, all but invisible. The edges of her polka dot, plaid ensemble peeking out around his legs. So, when she decided to walk over, we knew the demon must have dis-engaged. Hailey and I came up and touched Santos as he leaned an arm to help Chris stand. Both Kurt and the demon saw us as we looked over at them.

Evidently, it takes a while to be off a porn site before everything female, breathing, breathless—probably even female and unbreathing—isn't instantaneously coal for the fire of the lust-demon. I take that back. Apparently, certain outerwear will act as a steel shield against this soul-sucking Siphon. Unknowingly, my sister had geared up. Unfortunately, neither Hailey nor I had. But I was hardly imagining either of us as fuel for this creature's desire. I wasn't even wearing my tight jeans; but it seems this demon was hungry. Kurt, who'd begun to focus on Hailey and me, became distracted by Tessa—but not so the Siphon. Its face contorted with a feral craving like a cat seeing its prey in front of him. He stretched his claws out readying them to reinsert.

Watching as the lust-demon carved us up with his

grotesque eyes, I contemplated running and jumping into the nearest bush. It was almost as gruesome as Senator Gregory. "Anytime, Tessa," I called, frantically. Funny, for some reason, my psycho-demeanor made Kurt nervous, and we watched as the demon slid one long claw into the boy's neck again. Tessa looked at Santos who shook his head from side to side and mouthed the word, 'No.'

Jack placed a calming hand on her shoulder, and Tessa smiled. "That's my sister, and obviously, she's in a hurry to go," she said, "but I'm Tessa." And reaching out her hand she touched his. The scream of the creature was hideous. We jumped, and assumed everyone in the entire school could hear it. Just Tessa's touch caused the Siphon to extract its claw again. But she remained touching Kurt's hand for a moment longer, causing its wail to change to hissing. Kurt seemed strangely oblivious, but Jack had seen our startled reaction to the scream from the side of his eye and looked to see Santo's giving the high sign. He squeezed Tessa's shoulder.

"I'm in a youth group, and I have to say five specific words to at least twenty new people to win a game called, 'Battle the demon Siphons.' Do you mind if I say it to you?" My nerdy sister asked, in absolute believability.

"No, if that's all. I mean, if it helps you win," he said, smiling at the little frizzy headed person in front of him. "I love games. Is it like Dungeon and Dragons?"

"It's way more realistic. And I think we've got it in the bag. All I have to do for this part is say, "*Jesus Christ! By His Blood!*" Kurt took two steps backwards.

It was incredible watching the creature immediately fall from him onto the ground as the words left Tessa's lips. The hissing had changed into a horrible low-pitched scream, which would have been a moan except that its mouth was open and dripping blue saliva. But it dried up and disappeared within moments, the whole ordeal taking less than five minutes.

"Weird thing to say. What's it about? What's the game about?" Kurt asked, rotating his shoulders, and cranking his neck. Chris smiled, and hobbled over to him, ready I'm sure, in a Nano-second with some goofus, almost believable story about demons and their soul sucking ways.

The rest of us met back at the table. "That was intense. And how about you, Tessa! Wow, you were amazing!" Jack said.

I had to admit; she totally saved the day with her nerd game; something so random you had to believe it. We all gave her high fives, and, of course, she turned three shades of pink.

"But we're going to have to step it up if we expect to get enough accomplished in the next week," Jack continued, "even though I think we all needed to be in on this first one," he finished.

"Why don't we each pick someone and start out?" Hailey asked.

"Great idea," Jack said. "Santos and Tessa, you stick together; go to the first person that looks like they're having success. Then Santos, if possible, make contact so we can see how we're doing. At that point, Tessa, you take over. As soon as one person is free, look for the next, OK?"

We took hands, looked out among the crowd of milling students, and again I was struck with the overwhelming horror of it all. "You think those things can jump on us?" I asked, in a purely fact-finding mode.

"If it could've, that sex-demon would've been all over you. Did you see how he was licking his greasy chops?" Chris said with his amazingly, deep sensitivity, clomping over and sitting down behind Hailey and Santos and reaching over to touch them. "Gruesome, isn't it," he said, looking out over the creepy-crawly quad.

"OK. I've got my guy. I'm going in," Jack said, heading for a group of guys with at least three hideous demons attached and sucking. The students stood kicking a hacky sack between one another.

"I found someone I think I can talk to," Hailey said, looking in the direction of a short, heavy-set boy. His nose was buried in a textbook while he ate his lunch. On his back a large droopy-eyed Siphon with long fang-like teeth gouged at his neck, sucking, gurgling, gouging. Sucking, gurgling, gouging. Every few seconds it would reposition its fit, clamping sharp tubes into the boy's side where greyish green matter flowed into the demon.

Yuck. That's all I could think...*Yuck.* "Good luck, Hailey," I managed, "I mean, God bless!" I said, remembering too late, and almost shouting it across at her. Not the best way to stay incognito, I thought—and I wasn't just thinking about hiding from the demons. Santos was keeping his eye on Jack, and now he also had Hailey to keep an eye on. Tessa watched too, while gripping his arm. Meanwhile, Chris got up and headed for a group of five girls. Each one having a different demon attached. This I had to watch.

I'd just decided this course of action, as Santos got up taking Tessa with him. I'd been holding on to Tessa, but I knew I should've been finding my own demon to slay, so I stayed where I was, too embarrassed to tag along this time. They were heading for Jack, and in seconds, Tessa was talking to one of the boys. Turning, she began speaking to them all. They were laughing, and then she must have said the "words" because three of the five took steps backward, like they'd been hit by a blast of air. And now Tessa and Santos were walking toward Hailey.

I looked over at Chris, who had the group of girls laughing with him. But after a moment's thought, I figured it was more likely they were laughing at Chris. Whichever was true, Santos and Tessa looked in his direction, and veered towards him.

I glanced over at Hailey. She was smiling and conversing with the same guy being glommed-on by his sucky Siphon. But she looked up to see if Santos and Tessa were coming. When I looked back, amazingly, they were.

Chris was hobbling over with Jack. "That's eight between us, nine including the sex-demon. Not bad..." Chris said, his cocky smile fully engaged.

"How's Hailey?" Jack asked, looking out at the table where the three were now gathered around the kid. In another second it was done. Tessa and Santos were on their way back, and Hailey was saying goodbye to a guy who didn't need to give another piggyback ride to an ugly demon sucking him dry and leaving him depressed.

"So, can't make up your mind, or are you still scared?" Chris asked, all charm as usual. Jack shot Chris a look that almost made me feel sorry for him. However, it was necessary to do something more to take the little bugger down a notch. So, I did what I do best. I got on the biggest horse, even though it didn't have a saddle and I didn't know how to ride.

"Oh, I've made my choice. I just needed Santos back to get a little help. I was going to ask him, but he needed to leave, and I didn't want to interfere. I'm going to the stairwell, and I need to know which of those boys... Ah...you know, the gang boys—Oh Santos, I'm sorry—I mean, which of those friends of yours should I approach?" He and Tessa and Hailey had just walked up. "I'd like to round up the lot of them with the Siphons attached if I can, and talk," I said, calmly; that same calm that comes before a hurricane whips in, destroys the house and kills you, your family, kittens, dog, and takes your car. That calm.

"No, Cassita. I was just funning with you. These guys are

not very nice. Especially with the dark demons... They say things... they are mean... you would not be..."

"Cassie, Santos is right," Jack cut in, his voice commanding, and making it even more imperative for me to go. Chris cleared his throat. "Ah, don't go. We can go together," he added while his brother skewered him with his eyes.

"No...I've decided. I'm going alone. And besides, I won't be alone. God will be with me," I mimicked, standing up, but not before I saw the "uh-oh" look passing between Hailey and Tessa. I took hold of Santos' hand again, straightened my shoulders and found the group standing beneath the stairs. I had to steady my knees so I wouldn't fall back in my seat.

"The one over there, on the far left. That's the one you want to talk to," Santos said, his voice low. I wasn't paying too much attention because I'd seen the group of them standing together, and as far as I could tell, they were all wearing black scary beanies. There were at least ten, not counting the one standing by himself on the left. I started walking.

"Please help me God. I know I'm stupid, Lord, and I know you don't honor stupidity, but God, oh God, please help me. One of the scriptures says you help us if we call on you...and I'm calling. I don't know the *exact* scripture, but Lord, please don't make me stand on formality now—just help me. You said you would, so help me. I'm calling on you... help me...they're going to kill me, Lord, and you wouldn't want that, so this is the last chance..."

I was standing in front of the stairwell looking at the group of Mexican guys. Strangely enough, they didn't all look the same. The tallest, leaned against the wall, but I could tell he wasn't the leader. The boy standing on the far left, alone, certainly wasn't the head of this bunch, and I knew Santos had tried to send me there to save me. The leader was the guy looking at me with a half sneer, half leer.

And remarkably, he was handsome in a dark, dangerous, Latino way.

I mentally smacked myself. The demons. Remember the demons—the reason Santos wouldn't go around his friends any longer. These Siphons were *that* awful. And then I began to sweat. This was something I distinctly disliked, and I was proud of the fact that I didn't sweat. I knew it was the doing of the *diabolical realm*, and they had messed with the wrong cheerleader. "Hi, guys, you don't know me. My name is Cassie; Cassie Connor. I'm friends with Santos," I said, directing my words to the head honcho, or at least the guy standing in the center, sneering for all his life like "leader of the pack."

"Hijo de tu puta madre. What do we have here?" His sneer became an ugly smile. Santos sent us his puta, ...Cassita bonita."

I ignored what, considering the tone, I assumed was not flattery. I had to, because no demon made *me* sweat, I told myself. Besides, I had no idea what he was talking about, except of course, the fish part.

"Yes, that's right. I decided to come over...swim as it were, the gulf that's between our two groups," I said smiling. I noticed a few of the guys had come closer. One stood almost behind me. I felt a drop of perspiration fall from the center of my back just above the waistband of my jeans. This was really starting to tick me off.

"What d'you mean by, '*swim the gulf*'?" he asked, the smile that had never made it to his dark eyes dropping from his lips as well.

"You know... what you guys call me. I don't really know why you'd call me a tuna, but I guess it's better than some things," I said, raising my shoulders and eyebrows in unison. They all looked bewildered.

"Bonita is a tuna fish, right?" I wondered aloud for the

first time. The mean-handsome-looking one observed me closely. Then, suddenly smiling, said something in rapid Spanish, and they all burst into laughter.

Obviously, the joke was on me. I stood my ground, feeling an overwhelming desire to run and hide. So, I tilted my head up and tried to smile. Just then, I felt Tessa's hand in mine.

"Another pescadita," the Mexican said, still smiling.

"Yes, I came to say one thing, '*Jesucristo, con su sangre*,'" Tessa recited, and looking up at me, smiled, turned, and walked away.

My guess was the little smarty-pants had said "the words" in Spanish, and that whatever silly thing I'd done had worked as well. And I knew that, once again, God had heard me when I called. Holy mackerel... Bonita that is...

The guys standing around were staring after Tessa like she was a phantom. One, no, two of them were crossing themselves. "Who is that little girl?" The tall leader asked.

"Who are you?" I asked, causing him to stop and look me up and down again. While he was surprised by my forwardness, I think he was more amazed that he wasn't feeling angry.

"I'm Salvatore. Sal," he said, tipping his head back.

"Nice to meet you, Sal," I said, turning as I heard the lunch bell ring. "Gosh, I've got to go, but we'll talk again sometime... maybe?"

He watched me walk away. They *all* watched me walk away. It was like having ray guns shooting at my back in pairs. "Cassie," he called. I turned.

"Bonita. It does not mean fish. It means pretty," he said, and turning, walked away with the rest of the homeys following. A few shot back lurid smiles, and a few spoke unintelligible Spanish words that sounded dirty—but because of my impeccable understanding of the Spanish tongue, were probably the rosary.

I didn't care. I didn't even know how many of the dark demons had been slain. No, Cassie the warrior princess of God was no longer Cassita-tuna-girl to the Mexican guys. I was *pretty* Cassie to the whole lot of mean, marijuana smoking, gangbangers; and that made me ...happy. Yes, I was pleased with my new title. Not that I hadn't been called "pretty" before, or even that being pretty was even as important to me as it used to be. Yet there was something eminently satisfying about being significantly upgraded to the equivalent of "lovely" by a group of people you'd assumed considered you equal to canned lunch meat. It was just gratifying. In fact, so gratifying, I managed to walk right past the rest of the Guardians standing watch at the side of the building. As I sauntered on by, Jack grabbed hold of my arm, and I almost wet my undies.

"You scared me to death!" I said, grasping my heart as though it were coming out of my shirt, and not jumping out my mouth like I felt it might. Hailey, Santos, Tessa, and Jack, and even Chris gathered around me for a crazy, unmanageable group hug in which there were too many arms and elbows, and we just ended up laughing.

"Sorry about scaring you, Cassie," Jack said, the only one to still have an arm around me, "but after watching you with those guys and the *ugly Siphons* they had on them, we didn't think anything could scare you. In fact, we started wondering if maybe you weren't using some clever act to try and make us believe you've been afraid when all this time you've been fearless," he said, smiling at me.

"Very funny," I said smiling back. "But, by the by, the last lunch bell just rang, making us all late. We've got to go! But thank you guys, especially you, Tessa, and you, Santos," I said, looking over at him. "It's got to be terrible not being able to get away from this." I did feel ashamed of my aversion to it all, as well as my relief at how much cleaner and brighter the whole place looked when I no longer saw what he experienced all the time.

"Yes, it is terrible. But I am getting stronger. I am praying and learning my scriptures. It makes a big difference. I think I could make it into the circle now," he said, looking at Jack.

"As soon as school is out, we need to practice. We'll meet in the parking lot or at the Pine Circle. Can everyone be there?" Jack asked.

Everyone could, and the time was arranged.

Chapter Seventeen

I t had been a long day, and I was grateful when the last bell rang. I headed out to the parking lot to meet Tessa and Jack. As I walked to my car, two seniors, football players, and friends of Nathan's came over towards me. I figured that somehow, they hadn't gotten word yet that I was a pariah.

One of them asked if Nathan and I had *really* broken up, and I answered, "Yes, *really*." After which, he asked me on a date. I spared him the problems associated with that particular death-by-social-suicide, and politely refused. I told him I just wasn't ready; however, I was also kind enough to spare him the part about feeling absolutely nothing, barely even flattered. But we chatted, and it was nice to know they weren't afraid to buck the "Snob" system, even if they weren't aware exactly what that might mean.

"Well, there's a party in a couple weekends—and it's gonna be great. Everyone is planning to be there," he said. "If you go, it might help take your mind off things—and remember, I invited you first. In fact, if you go with me, I'll make sure you don't just have fun—it'll be *ecstasy*, if you know what I mean," he said winking.

Wow. "Thanks," I said, smiling, and lowering my lashes so they couldn't read my true feelings of yuck. "But I know about ecstasy, E, the big X. The drug, right?"

"Yea, cool! Keep it on the down-low. It's awesome!" his friend enthused. "Thanks, but I'm doing *fine* without all that. In fact, I'm doing *awesome*," I said, remembering how I'd just called on God, and kicked the hinny ends of a dozen evil-soul- sucking-Siphons. To top it off, I was called "pretty" by the tough guys in the school—all in a hair-raising six-minute stretch. Now that was my idea of ecstasy; *that* was awesome. "Take care guys," I said, smiling as I waved and spun lightly on my toes. I quickly sat back on my heels. Nathan was sitting in his sports car a few feet away, his windows down gripping his steering wheel, staring straight ahead. I closed my eyes, sure he'd heard just *how awesome I was doing* only hours after he'd broken up with me. When he pealed out of the parking lot, I was certain. Santos and Jack arrived a few seconds later watching Nathan careen around the corner. "I hope he comes back," Jack said. "He's supposed to be our ride home. He's agreed to join us in the Pine Circle."

I stared at Jack, once again trying to catch that pesky fly with my mouth. Thankfully, having no luck, and coming to my senses, I said, "What? Nathan? *What?*" Stringing together those three questions with such skill, Santos was forced to ask,

"Is something wrong, Cassie?"

"No, I'm just surprised, that's all. I didn't know, he...I ... well, good. ...Is he?" Again, my prowess at extracting information was uncanny.

Jack looked at me for several seconds and said, "Tessa had to stay late to fill out some forms for the testing she's taking. She wanted me to tell you to go on home. Your mom is picking her up at 4:30. Nathan wanted to go with Santos, Hailey, and me to the Pine Circle for a little while." He stopped and waited for the inevitable flash of fury before finishing. One thing about Jack; he was a quick study. But I surprised him.

"So, what did you say?" I asked, waiting. "Told him I'd ask you first," he said. "You're the one who has to fight. We just have to keep his butt out of trouble."

"What changed his mind... about getting involved again?" I asked.

Santos smiled. "We held hands for a little while. ...He don't like it very much, though. He break up with me too, Cassita Bonita."

I smiled despite myself. "Fine with me. I need to study my scriptures anyway. Tell him he's got half my time. Chris can help me for a while, then I'll send him over while I study on my own. He can stay if he wants, but I need to practice some, too."

Jack looked up and motioned to Santos. Nathan cruised up in his car. They got in just as Hailey ran up.

"Come on. Get in, Hailey. I'll take you home with me. Have you called your mom?" I asked.

"Yes, it's all taken care of," she said, clearly out of breath.

Jack called out of the car as they pulled away, "Chris is meeting you at your house," he said, a dead giveaway.

"He didn't tell Nathan he'd ask me. Chris is already meeting me at my house," I said, amazed at being betrayed.

"I was there. That's not what happened. Nathan said you wouldn't go along. He said you'd be mad at being left out. Jack said you cared more for him, Nathan, than that, more than he knew. Nathan laughed, and bet Jack it wouldn't happen," she said softly.

"And Chris?"

"Well, ...I guess Chris bet on you. He said he'd wait at your house." I sat for a while, mulling everything over.

"Do you ever swear, Hailey —you know, cuss?"

"No, I just never got in the habit," she said sweetly. "Do you?"

"Me, ...no, ...well, I'm learning *not* to. But it's strange. Sometimes I want to, and I don't know why. Like right now... everything worked out, right? And I did good, but I want to say something like ...*gosh darn* it all to *heck, crud, shoot*... see, none of those work."

"Go ahead. You can say something else, something *really swearing* if it helps. It won't bother me."

"Never mind. It passed, but thanks, Hailey. You're a good friend."

"You are too, Cassie."

We drove silently for a few minutes."They say God is our friend. Do you believe that, Hailey?"

She turned sideways and her beautiful green eyes became intense.

"Yes, with all my heart," she said, turning back and looking straight ahead. That was one of the things I liked about Hailey. She never asked me things she knew I didn't want to answer. And I didn't. How could I tell her that I just wasn't sure? But then again, He came when I'd called, and come *heck* or high water, that was a *boat*load more than I could say for Brittany and Jenna. And that's what I arrived at by the time I reached my house.

I pulled into the driveway and sat in the car as I watched Hailey disappear into the dense grove of trees. Finally, I got out and walked up my front steps. Chris was waiting for me on the porch, stretched out on the wooden lounge chair. His broken leg was propped on the old ottoman, and he looked completely at home. My mom had wandered out with a tray of cookies and milk, but I caught myself before allowing my mouth to drop down into fly catcher position for a third time in one day, no matter how shocking events might become.

"Wow, Mom, looks like Chris has made a good impression on you," I said, eyeing the plate of Oreo's and milk —my mom's all-time favorites. True, these weren't homemade, but that would have been entirely suspect anyway. The last time she'd baked cookies was when Aunt Hazel made some six years ago, and Mom had taken them to the neighborhood potluck claiming them as her own. She smiled at me, and I noticed she'd applied a little cover-up to her dark circles and wore a bright blouse. She was at least trying today.

"Chris tells me he's helping you learn scriptures. I know your father would love that," she said, looking at me thoughtfully. "I need to run some errands before I pick your sister up from school. I'll see you when I get back," she said, setting the tray down and taking the car keys.

"OK, see you then," I said, flopping down in a chair and closing my eyes. The last thing I felt like at the moment was facing Chris and the horrendous chore of memorizing anything harder than e-i-e-i-o. But if I opened my eyes...Yes, there he sat, with a milk mustache, staring at me.

"So, I say we get to this," Chris said, all business. He had a pad and pencil in his hand as though ready to take notes, a worn Bible marked with a bazillion tabbies in multiple colors setting beside the chair. I eyed it menacingly.

"Yea, yea, in a bit," I groaned, closing my eyes again. I heard him lay the pad down and noisily start to get up. "Come on, at least give me a pep talk," I said. "I've had rough day."

"Look Cassie," he started, then plopped back and stopped before saying what was on his mind. I wondered if it was something personal because he stopped himself as if he was using a self-improvement technique. I decided I'd be wise to let it slide.

"Well at *least* let me have a cookie, Commandant Himmler," I said, only half smiling. Chris looked at me, his eyes narrowing.

"Do you even know who Himmler was?" he asked severely. I eyed the little smart aleck for a moment before answering.

"Ah, Heinrich Luitpold Himmler? The military commander and the *Reichsführer* of the dreaded SS?" I intoned with a fake German accent. "You mean the second most powerful man after Adolf Hitler? Who is responsible for conceiving and overseeing implementation of the 'Final Solution,' the Nazi plan to murder the Jews of Europe? Yes, Chris, obviously I do. But for pity's sake, I was just kidding around. I don't really think you're a Nazi, but I am starting to wonder if you're really the same feral-rug-rat from next door or a victim of a body snatcher. Lighten up," I said, wondering what my mom had slipped the kid in his milk, but also wondering where the heck all my WWII information had suddenly come from.

Chris continued to eye me suspiciously. "I'm not kidding, lighten up!" I said again, as he persisted in looking at me. "What?" I asked.

He shrugged and looked a tiny bit embarrassed. Then with flashing blue eyes, more in keeping with his disparate nature as the arrogant king of goofiness, asked, "Do you just pretend to be dumb so guys will like you more?"

Honestly, I'm not sure why I didn't knock his broken foot off the ottoman and attempt to break the other one. I think I'd realized by that point he was hindered by a pathetic lack of social skills, and I was somewhat relieved, that in fact, this was definitely Chris; no body snatcher from another world could have digressed to such a rude state so quickly. In some ways, it was nice to know I wasn't studying with someone from a different planet. And sadly, after the things I'd seen that day, it wasn't hard to believe something so clearly sci-fi *could* happen.

I sat silently looking at him, keeping mum on all my possible responses. This seemed to be doing the trick. Chris was growing red, obviously uncomfortable, and probably trying to formulate an apology while desperately hoping I'd answer him. Meanwhile, he was trying to pull a notebook out from under himself. I wanted to help, but couldn't offer considering the delicate point of negotiations we were in. Yanking and turning at the same time, he rolled onto the porch with a loud thud. Luckily, the lounge was only a couple feet off the ground, and he lay with his leg cast in the air, clanging against the chair. He didn't hear me asking if he was all right because he was laughing too loud. It was good to see that the only thing needed was a little banging about; it did wonders for a boy who otherwise started getting peevish.

When he finally got himself back onto the chair, he actually looked remorseful. "Sorry, Cassie. I shouldn't have said that. It's just that, well you're really smarter than..."

"Shall we just get to work?" I cut in, deciding it was better to limit the damage.

"Yea, OK. This is what I thought we'd do," he said, still smiling from his wonderfully gratifying fall off the chair. "I've organized Darius' verses into power units. These are the ones I think you should start with first," he said, handing me the list.

I looked down at the paper and back up at him. "You're kidding, right? This doesn't help me. *You* need to help me. I can organize; I just can't memorize. Big difference. When I'm out there facing Voldemort...Rasputin, Rasvampin, ...see what I mean? I won't need lists. I'll need scriptures...the Word, full-on," I said heatedly.

"Ah, ...Cassie."

"Oh, for heaven's sake, and I mean that quite literally. Get it out...Say what you..."

"I need to know. What's it like?" He said surprising me. "Do you really get to swing a sword?" His eyes said more than his words. They were begging me for mercy.

"Yes. And if you *help* me, just a little, you will get to experience it. I promise. I won't torture you anymore than necessary. Let's get started—even one. What do you think the most important one would be?" I said, handing the list back to him.

"How about this one, '*The Lord will rescue me from every evil attack and will bring me safely to his heavenly kingdom. To him be glory for ever and ever.' 2 Timothy 4:18?*" He read hopefully, realizing I was not letting him off the hook.

"Nope, don't like the going 'safely to his heavenly kingdom,' part. Try another."

Chris looked at me. "His heavenly kingdom is here too, ya know. Timothy wasn't saying he wanted to die right then either," he said with exasperation. "You need to learn it, but all right. How about this, '*Be strong and courageous; do not be frightened or dismayed, for the Lord your God is with you wherever you go.' Joshua 1:9?*"

"Perfect, but it's pretty long," I complained. At the look on his face, I relented, "OK, OK it's perfect. Sorry." We spent the next hour working on this verse and two others. I think Chris hoped that changing things up a bit would keep him from losing his mind. It didn't, and I wondered if he was seeing the holes in his "guys like dumb girls" theory yet. I could finally see that the body snatchers had returned, and it would take more than a tumble from a chair to restore him to sanity.

"Chris, Chris, I'm sorry," I held my hand up after making the *same* mistake for the umpteen-hundredth time. His little face had gone an interesting shade of reddish purple, but he hadn't gone ballistic yet. I'd dodged the bullet by about a millisecond. "Gosh, look what time it is! You need to go to the Pine Circle! I promise I'll do better tomorrow..." I said, as I watched a crippled boy jet out of his chair and down three steps faster than I could—on fire.

Tucking my legs underneath me, I curled into a tight cocoon and rested my head on my hands. Sleep. I just needed a micro moment of sleep... When I woke up, it was still light, and I heard Tessa's voice coming up the porch steps. *Darn, I wish it were tomorrow*, I thought. *I wish it were any day but more of this one.*

"Hey, Cassie, why aren't you at the Pine Circle?" Tessa asked, her little face all curiosity and concern.

I looked at my watch. "Why indeed. Come on, you want to go with me?" I asked.

"Sure, but I can't stay. I have to get back early. I hope that's OK?" She asked, the group "healer" looking to me for approval.

"I grant you leave of absence," I said in my best "English Grande Dame" voice, "but why?"

"I have to be back before Mom gets a phone call. You know how Mom can be if you're not *right* there. She forgets..." she said protectively. "I have to be sure she tells them, *absolutely no press*," she said seriously.

"What's going on, Tessa?"

"They found out I was cheating," she said, voice low, eyes lowered. I stood for a moment, stunned. "I don't believe you. Why would you ever need to cheat?" I waited.

"I cheated the other way. I purposely missed questions to lower my scores. But I miscalculated and they caught me. It's much harder than you might think to average yourself out." I studied her for a second. *My goodness, if only she'd asked...* "They graph your tests over time, and evidently a few of mine were inexplicable." She looked pensive for a moment. "It must have been the move, because I was so thorough. I don't know how I could have gotten mixed up. Anyway, that's the reason. I'm sorry—it was wrong. I just didn't want to be too different; to be pressured to leave you and Mom before I was ready..."

I went over and held her for a long time; at least a full minute, which for us was huge. "C'mon, let's go." I said, smiling.

Hailey and Santos, Chris, Jack, and Nathan sat in a circle. They were all talking over each other, and even Hailey seemed totally jazzed. As Tessa and I walked up, they got to their feet. "Hey, you guys, about time!" Hailey said, running over. It was obvious she'd felt outnumbered.

Nathan stood and started to leave. "I'll see you later," he said, never looking in my direction.

"You can stay if you want to; it's OK with me..e," I said, my voice cracking at the worst *possible* time, place, pronoun.

"Come on. Stay for one more round, Nathan!"

"Yea, stay, give it another go!"

"Let's all do it together!" They chimed in equally. So, Nathan stayed. and this time, even though we'd rarely ever fought, even with words, we faced each other—with swords.

Everyone began by holding hands again. Nathan stood between Hailey and Chris, and I tried to keep my mind centered on what we were doing, instead of what it would feel like to be holding his hand, with more electricity flowing through them than usual—which was pretty amazing on any normal day. Then other feelings began bubbling... bubbling... to the surface. And I began feeling strangely sad. I pushed them down. *I can do this,* I told myself, *this has meaning.* I began breathing slowly, emptying my mind. Once Jack began to pray, the electrical surge we'd experienced before was present again. I opened my eyes for a quick second and saw

Chris. He'd felt it for the first time today and had such a goofy look on his face, that I quickly shut my eyes so I wouldn't ruin everything by laughing.

I started reciting my old scriptures first, the ones I'd used before, and all day long. I knew them, and strangely I was beginning to believe them. They'd begun *feeling* true. *"The Lord is near to all who call on him, to all who call on him in truth. He fulfills the desires of those who fear him; he hears their cry and saves them."* I began repeating this, five, six; I lost count. Somewhere along, I switched to, *"the Lord is faithful, and he will strengthen you and protect you from the evil one."* And *"Behold, I have given you authority to tread on serpents and scorpions, and over all the power of the enemy, and nothing shall hurt you."*

Saying them louder as I became surer of myself, not caring what anyone else thought including Nathan. And it happened. I was in. I felt the words resonating throughout me as I held my sword high above my head. There wasn't a tired bone in my ...body? Whatever I was in felt just like a body, and yet I was so fluid. I swung my sword, amazed by the power in my arm. I began growing comfortable with the feel of the weapon I held, and automatically I knew how to jab and thrust. And when I swung my blade above my head, I loved listening to the whistling sound it made. Looking around, I saw the others beginning to appear. More than outlines, they were now fully materializing in the circle with me; Jack first, then Santos. Turning, I saw Chris and Hailey. To my far right, Nathan appeared. He looked surprised to see me; in fact, they all did. I stood smiling, my sword swinging at my side. I was unsure what the rules were in this dimension.

Jack came over and said, "How cool is this?"

"We can talk? Well, that might just be my silliest question to date," I answered myself. "Ya wanna fight?" I said, standing with one hand behind my back, my sword at the ready. Jack stood gripping his weapon, smiling his "no one knows what I'm thinking" smile.

But before I had a chance to teach him how much I hated that smirk, Santos jumped in front of me and began attacking Jack, swinging his sword like a pirate gone mad. Chris and Hailey had begun sparring, with Chris doing mad leaps and rolls, spins, turns and summersaults. Clearly, he was enjoying life without a leg cast—life as a free cretin. All the while, Hailey had to fight back her tears of laughter, as well as this crazy kid. And I watched in amazement as she wielded her blade with grace and power. I turned and saw Nathan observing me from a few yards away. His sword hung at his side, and he was shimmering. I started walking toward him as he began turning away, but then he looked back. His face still, his eyes filled again with the vulnerability that broke my heart.

He said, "Care to cross blades?" I bowed-curtseyed, which was silly, considering I was carrying a sword of God. But like I said, I was still rusty on the rules. Smiling, I acted like I'd make the first jab. He raised his sword above his head, opening his chest to my weapon, and said, "Be my guest."

My eyes never left his, and smiling I thrust, stopping short of course. The intent was never to take out or hurt a Guardian, and never, ever, Nathan... "You know..." I began, but wasn't able to finish, because with a smile which never reached his eyes, he raised his sword; his blade fell, glinting. But right before he cleaved me in two, he vanished.

Chapter Eighteen

Jack and the others must have witnessed Nathan's crazy attack because we all found ourselves holding hands in the circle. Only a few minutes had elapsed. Nathan was walking away, but Jack turned and started after him. His body language looking as though he still carried his weapon. We all trailed at a distance. Chris limped along, and Tessa, never having had the opportunity to make it into the warrior's circle, followed along without a clue.

"Nathan!" Jack yelled. It surprised me when he stopped mid-stride, turning slowly, his eyes closed. His head was thrown back, as close to defeat as I'd ever seen. "I wouldn't have hurt her. I was on my way out." He smiled at that.

"What's with you, man? One minute you're kicking it, like I haven't seen you in years... True to yourself, strong, coming back..." Jack moved closer, and we could barely hear him, but he said, "It can't be all about her. You can't blame this on her. This is on you, Nate..." Nathan smiled slowly, his ugly smile, and started to turn away. Jack came after him, grabbing and spinning him back around. The two fought for what was only a couple minutes, not very long, considering in the movies it takes at least nine heavy-duty punches, four broken chairs, and no less than three heavy shelves full of spare motor parts crashing on a dude to get a guy to the ground. After all this, *he's* usually the winner. Still, it was awful, and we all had to keep each other from jumping in and getting involved—especially Chris and Santos—who were holding each other back at different times. Jack ended up shoving Nathan against the trunk of a tree after they'd both taken a few licks, and panting, "Do what you have to... but don't try to hurt her again." He let go, and they stepped apart, "...I mean it," Jack said, into Nathan's angry face.

"You know me better than that!" Nathan said, furiously walking away. I automatically started after him, but Santos held me back.

"Let him go. He needs some time to think—or maybe decide. He doesn't know who he is yet."

I went over to Jack. "You alright?" I asked. His face had several red marks glowing angrily—sort of in keeping with the rest of him.

"Yea, I'm fine," he said gruffly, walking away from me as if I'd started the whole thing. "Hailey, can I talk to you a minute," he asked, walking back to the circle of trees.

Tessa grabbed my sleeve, "Cassie, fill me in. I've got to go, OK?"

"Sure, Tess," I said, keeping my eyes on Jack and Hailey in case they said something I'd miss. "See ya at home," I replied absently.

"I'll walk you home," Chris said, shambling up from the tree behind us.

"Ah, no. But thanks." She turned and walked quickly away.

Chris looked at her receding back. "What's with her? I just offered to walk her home. Truth is, I was hoping to get some more cookies. I'm hungry." I looked at him and tried unsuccessfully not to smile. He was such a bonehead.

I walked back over to Jack and Hailey and sat down, ignoring the fact Jack had obviously wanted privacy. He was in the middle of saying, "I don't understand; he did amazingly in the second session. I noticed you talking to him afterwards. Did he say anything to you?" Hailey dropped her eyes, and looked like she might cry. She didn't say a word for several seconds. Then, she finally looked up. Santos and Chris had seated themselves off to one side of us, and Hailey turned away from them as though unwilling to let them hear her guilty confession.

"I think I caused this. I started talking, and I shouldn't have. It's just, I never in my whole life thought someone like Nathan Gregory would ever even look at me. And here we were together, and he was complimenting me, telling me I had good *attack au fer*. Of course, I didn't have any idea what that was." She looked down shyly and back up, "It means to get ready for an attack you're about to make by deflecting your opponent's blade. Anyway, that's what Nathan told me." Jack looked away.

I shook my head, smiling. "What a showoff. Of course, Nathan would know technical fencing terms," I remarked. Now perhaps Jack thought I said his name with a bit too much proprietorship, or maybe he thought I seemed a little too proud of Nathan's ability to use proper French.

Either way, Jack adopted a clearly chilly tone when he said to me, "I wonder what the technical fencing term for, 'slice someone in two,' is? Keep going, Hailey."

"Well, like you were saying, Jack, he'd been having the hardest time at first, taking so long to get into the circle. You know how he had to hear from all of us, telling him how cool it was; and like you said, it didn't work until he remembered what he believed as a kid. Anyway, you know ...I guess I was a little worried for him. But then, he knew so many scriptures! Who would ever have guessed? And when he finally made it in, oh my gosh. I was in awe of him. Seriously, I couldn't take my eyes off him." Hailey looked up at me embarrassed. She was completely star-struck. *Nathan had done it again,* I thought. The guys were looking at Hailey as if she was goofy. They were completely oblivious to Nathan's charisma and charm—not to mention his physical appeal. And Jack was losing patience.

"OK, we understand you *really* like him, Hailey. But what happened?" Jack asked, as curt as I'd ever heard him with anyone. Hailey blushed, and this time, I shot Jack a critical look, although, I couldn't tell if he even noticed.

"Well, that's when we started talking. He was so nice to me. And anyway, I told him he was doing awesome. I mentioned that, with his abilities, combined with the power he'd have once he was given the mantle, well, he'd be a force for God—not just in Washington but for the world." She then looked over at me sadly. Looking back down, she said, "I shouldn't have interfered. I know. And I'm so sorry." I patted her hand, and she continued. "I told him I knew that you cared for him, Cassie, and that one day the two of you could make a powerful team for God." She sighed, "That's when he looked at me and said, 'You don't get it,' ...and started laughing. He totally changed after that. I guess *I really didn't* get it. I was surprised when he decided to stay and join us back in the circle again. Actually, I was more surprised when he was *able* to get back in. ...Still, I was hoping..." Hailey put her hands over her face. "I'm so sorry. I think if I just hadn't said anything, we'd have had a few more days with him, and he'd have come around."

"Hailey... Hailey?" I said, "Look at me... this isn't your fault."

"She's right, Hailey. This is up to Nathan. He's got to

decide. We all do. Besides, he's not such a great warrior. He wouldn't last a day in my neighborhood," Santos declared, still irritated by Hailey's obvious infatuation. Hailey smiled weakly over at him.

Jack sat quietly reflecting, when Chris asked, "You thinking what I'm thinking?" his head resting on his arms, and his bright blue eyes shining questioningly at Jack.

"I don't know. What are you thinking?" Jack answered, without an ounce of vitality in his voice.

"I'm thinking I'm hungry. I'm tired of Nathan, and I want to eat. Then, I want to fight some more. Or we could fight, and then eat. Either one. I just don't want to *talk* or *hear* about *Nathan* anymore. He's lame. I really don't know why you guys go to that school if he's the best you can come up with... So, was that what you were thinking, Jack?"

"That's exactly what I was thinking," Jack said, smiling, helping his brother part way up and then letting him fall, much to Chris' complete delight.

We ordered pizza, and I attempted eating, each bite getting harder to swallow as I my throat kept trying to close down. I wouldn't be able to maintain much longer. I desperately needed alone time, breakdown time to come unglued and sling some snot time. It was not going to be pretty. Still, it had to be done...

"I'm finished," I said, "I think I'll let you warriors hack it out... five minutes in the circle, and I already feel like I've taken part in Armageddon," I smiled, hoping they'd think I was exaggerating. Chris looked at me like I'd lost my mind, and when Hailey said she had to get home too because her mom was picking her up in ten minutes, he quickly looked at Jack and Santos, fearing confirmation of his worst nightmare.

"Don't worry, man. I can stay a while, but I'll kick your butt," Santos said smiling.

"Me, too; I can stay a little longer. But Mom needs me

home soon. Ten minutes seems like hours in there, anyway. Let's hit it," Jack said, and I knew exhaustion had set in for him, too.

"Before you go, and before my mom gets here, I think I need to tell you guys about the dream I had last night," Hailey said. Suddenly, I remembered Hailey telling me at lunch she'd had another dream.

Tessa, who'd joined us for pizza on the porch, exclaimed, "Oh, tell us!" Much more excited by dreams than swordplay.

"Well, this one was about the really bad demon, the Destroyer," Hailey said, her face instantly growing tense. "I could tell, because of the tattoo—the dove—which had a bloody dagger sticking out of its breast. It was on his arm. I couldn't see it, but in my dream, I knew it was there. He was tall and wore clothes that made him look homeless— dirty and ragged—and his hair was long and greasy. I saw him standing down under the railroad trestle. He'd made a campsite, like he lived there. "Watching him, I knew he was completely evil. I would have been afraid of him even if I didn't know who he was. But I saw some kids about our age meeting with him, and he treated them nicely. He gave them beer and told them he had drugs for sale. The kids got real excited and paid him. So, he gave them baggies with pills in them, and some with powder—I don't know what kind.

"All of a sudden, it didn't feel like I was just watching the dream. I felt a part of it, and he looked right at me with an angry, kind of surprised, look. I began gasping. He then started to laugh, real evil-like. It was as if I moved far away and was now looking down at him, but believe me, it was still scary. When the kids left, he threw their money in the fire and laughed again." We sat silently for a minute, digesting, along with the meat dreamer's pizza, this new "window into the future." Neither one was sitting too well on my stomach. Just two minutes earlier, I'd felt an overwhelming need to vent. I'd felt a need to release the pent-up emotions from an emotionally packed day.

Suddenly, all I wanted to do was throw up. Of course, Tessa didn't beat around the bush using loose interpretations and dream metaphors, which might have helped my digestive condition. No, she got right to the guts of it. "Rasvampin is here," she said, showing none of the terror I felt at just hearing that name spoken aloud—especially as the evening was coming. "And he's dealing drugs. He'll use that to try and gain power to destroy us," she stated flatly, like any normal twelve-year-old fighting evil.

"Hailey, you didn't mention this, but the guys buying drugs, were ...they...Mexican?" Santos asked, "I need to know."

"What does that matter?" Jack asked. Santos didn't respond; his eyes still glued to Hailey's. Hailey sat quietly looking at him.

Then, staring down at her hands, she said, "In my dream, I knew there would be others who weren't, but I'm sorry, Santos. The ones I saw were Mexican," she said, apologetically. Santos looked away for a moment and then back.

"I know about the drugs. Salvatore and Manny are all jacked up over the good buy they just made. Some high-quality stuff for cheap. They've already sold a lot and made some good money and they're going back for more. It's ecstasy and cocaine that they bought."

"Sal?" I said without thinking.

"Yea, he was the one you talked to today. Did he tell you his name? Santos asked, clearly surprised. I nodded, not knowing what else to add.

"I don't believe it," Santos said, smiling and shaking his head. I was concerned for Sal—Salvatore, and not sure why since we were hardly bosom buddies. I couldn't be certain he wouldn't slit my throat, or worse... the next time I met up with him in a dark stairwell, but there it was. I didn't like hearing he was meeting with the Destroyer. Again, my reaction tended more toward the ticked off, instead of "Oh no!" which completely baffled me. The second thing was, I'd heard about ecstasy earlier that day, and knew it would be at the "big party" I'd been encouraged to attend, because *"everybody was going..."*

"You know, I was invited to a big party the weekend after this one. According to the guys I talked to, ecstasy will definitely be there. They assured me 'everyone' is going." I said.

"I heard about it too, and if you ask me, it sounds like the perfect place for demons to wreak havoc, especially if Nathan's there," Jack said. "And Darius didn't seem to think we had very long—two or three weeks at the most. It sure seems like a good strategy on their part to entice someone into having a big party at the time the mantle is supposed to be passed—if they can lure the *Link* there," he put in.

"But I thought they didn't know who the *Link* was," Hailey said.

"That's the point. In all the chaos, with all the people partying and doing stuff that opens their realm, the mantle and the *Link* will probably stand out like a beacon. Plus, Rasvampin knows it will be hard for us to stay away when we know the damage they plan to do to all the kids there," Jack pointed out.

"Still, if we can somehow keep Nathan from going, our problem is solved. The mantle is passed outside of all the chaos." Hailey remarked.

"Can we still get him to join us?" Tessa asked. "It seems like that offense could be our best line of defense: the mantle gets passed safely, while we guard the *Link's* safety at the same time," Tessa added.

"I don't think that's going to happen on either count," I said. "I know Nathan, and he's pretty mad. But even if we could make him come around, or even kidnap him, according to Hamaliel, if Rasvampin's still around, he'll continue to attack the *Link* even though we keep him from destroying the mantle before it's passed. And by then, he'll know who it is. Unfortunately, we need to get to Rasvampin right when the mantle is passed. When he's most vulnerable. I think it's the only way we'll be able to destroy him. Ultimately, it's the only way to protect Nathan, I mean the *Link*," I quickly corrected.

"Are we sure it's going to happen so soon?" Chris put in, unable to adequately hide his excitement at the prospect.

"It felt soon in my dream, as though things were building up fast," Hailey said.

"And I've been seeing a lot of bigger demons. They come and feed off the little ones. They suck the juice out of them. Then they look around for someone to attack. They have big rusty swords, and when they use them, the person doesn't seem to feel it. But, it sure makes them mean. Also, I've been seeing a different kind then the Siphons, and different than the skullcaps. They are the Black Ones. These make my blood go cold. My friends almost forced me, one night not too long ago, to smoke with them, but I wouldn't. They had no idea I was seeing these demons floatin' in the shadow and waitin' for me to smoke some meth. What happens is they hover, dark, and more than empty, more frightening than the Siphons. I don't know, they, remind me of Hell, and I never been there. When someone does these drugs, at least with something like meth, it opens them up, and these things, they slip in—into their brains or minds. And the Black Ones say things in whispers in a strange, horrible language, like static electricity. Something gets done to the person...like it snuffs out a light. And I'm watching this, and the whole time the guys are going, *"Oh, this is good stuff, man. You gotta try this, it feels great...*" and I'm thinking, "Get me outta here, man. That thing is freaking scary, and it's eating your brain!" We sat silently, too horrified to speak, until the fear was too much for me.

"Wow. I finally understand what's been happening to me in math class," I said, amazing myself at the lengths I would go to relieve terror. Only Santos laughed, and I realized there were at least two reasons I liked Santos as much as I did: we shared the same twisted humor, and he was as scared as I was.

Chapter Nineteen

We'd eaten all the pizza. Hailey's mom had come and taken her home, and Tessa had gone back indoors. Meanwhile, I stood on the porch watching Santos, Chris and Jack walk back toward the woods into the waning light after their re-fueling. For at least twenty minutes I'd tried getting up so I could go inside, take a bath, and be alone. But feelings—feelings I didn't like the texture of —were brewing. They felt like something I used to know how to avoid, and I found myself torn between retreating to the house and joining the guys in the circle to face Jack in a fight. Not because I was mad at him, but because I was, I was... And that's where it fell apart. I didn't know what I was. I didn't know what I was thinking. Heck, I didn't know where I was going, and pretty much, I no longer knew who I was. I turned around and went into the house.

Tessa was sitting on the couch in the living room alone. Mom was nowhere to be seen, which meant she'd already retired to her own room—early, even for her. As frightened and desolate as I felt, I couldn't help wondering, and surprisingly, worrying, whether things had gone all right for

Tess. Her little face, surrounded by hair-gone-wild, was pinched, and her glasses helped magnify the uncertainty in her usually assured gaze.

The television was off, and there were no books or magazines anywhere in sight. I walked over and sat down next to her in my dad's old chair, inhaling the musty leather and hoping to sense his lingering presence in his space, where his image just might be awakened by a whiff.

Before I'd had a second to say a word, Tessa remarked, "Boy, you look terrible. Are you alright?" But there was no energy behind her words.

"Nice try."

For a second, she looked surprised. Then, she sighed. "Yea, OK I guess I'm a little...I don't know, how do I look? Can you tell?" she asked.

"You looked worried. So, what happened?" I asked, "Mom blow it?"

"Uh, well, not exactly. At least I'm not worried I'll have to go anywhere else for school right away. But I'm nervous about the newspaper that called. I'm afraid they might not keep their promise and they'll print something. But, oh well. Mom tried. And at the end, she read something from the note I wrote for her, even though she didn't want to. Mom means well, but she doesn't always understand. Anyway, I hope it'll be enough." She said, resignedly, then added, "I just don't want to be a freak around here," and lowered her eyes.

I'll admit. Several responses popped into my mind; great hair and clothing zingers could have, and oh my goodness, would have been used with relish just a short time ago. But I simply couldn't. In fact, I even felt bad for still finding them amusing. "Tessa, being *who you are*, being *special*, is always going to cost you something. I think you know that," I said, seriously shocking myself for both recognizing this ...and for saying it kindly. Even Tessa looked momentarily stunned.

"I guess, hmm. ...I guess you're right," she said, as though realizing this for the first time. "I've always been aware I'd suffer for my faith. I mean, anymore, Christians are considered in almost the same terrible light they were during the first century. And I've been willing to pay the price for my faith. But I hadn't thought about having to pay a price for being what God designed me to be...and yet that's so simple. Thank you, Cassie. I needed to hear that," she said, smiling over at me, her eyes grateful and bright. After a moment she asked, "So, why do you look so..."

"I believe the word you used was *terrible*. And for the record, I don't *ever* look terrible. Do we have that straight?" I said, smiling as though I was joking.

Tessa smiled back. "Yes, clear. I didn't mean it, honest. I just couldn't think of the right word. You look sad, but not quite...and you're not mad, but kind of. I don't know!" she said, smiling in her exasperation. Then, lowering her voice and looking at me more intensely, she said softly, "I could always tell before. You're not easy anymore, Cassie. You've changed so much."

I didn't say anything, but as if to prove her point, I could no longer stop up the tears. One after another they began to drop, heavy single tears sliding down both sides of my face. It was all I could do to keep from going into an ugly cry. And then, there was no longer any good reason to keep the craziness locked up anymore after a day when screaming, swearing, crying, or puking, on any number of occasions seemed in perfect order. As self-indulgent as sobbing had seemed for so long, I knew an unstoppable storm had been brewing. The rain would have to fall sometime, somewhere. I rushed the sofa, grabbed a throw pillow, and let the tempest inside me blow. Torrentially. Gushingly.

At least the misery I felt was being jettisoned into the throw pillow. It was all hot emotion and no thought. Once a large portion of my misery's weight was dissipated, I began to imagine tackling another day—another day as the incarnation of a high school Carrie-Buffy combo. Of course, this thought brought on another crying jag as I mourned into the cushion the mess I'd become as a combination pariah/slayer. Then, as crazy-unleashed-minds will go, came thoughts of how this might possibly even affect my college transcripts. ...Not to mention losing all my friends! All gone! And the worst, I told myself ...*the absolute worst* ...was losing *Nathan*, my ticket out of No-Where's-Ville. As I put my self-indulgent thoughts toward my pain, the tears increased again. And then slowed, and then there were none left.

Tessa, with scads of homework awaiting her nimble mind, chose to sit through the entire episode without speaking or moving a muscle. When I looked up at her from my soggy pillow, her forehead was wrinkled in concern, her eyes troubled; but all I could think was that I ought to take back the statement I'd made a half an hour earlier about never looking terrible. Without glancing into a mirror, I knew beyond a shadow of a doubt, I looked the definition of horrifying. I was a hot mess—the result of the ugly crying she'd quietly observed for almost half an hour. Only a sister, a really good sister, would do that. I certainly didn't know whether I'd be capable of it without at least tiptoeing out for a snack.

"Sorry, Tess," I snuffled, my nose completely congested, and my eyes swollen. "I feel better. I just wish I could explain all this. I mean, cripes, I didn't cry this much when Dad died," knowing I hadn't cried at all, and had decided never to cry again. She didn't say anything for a minute. Instead, she got up and fetched a box of tissue off the bathroom counter.

"All the marks haven't been made," she stated, returning, and handing me the box, as though I had her brilliance and

I'd understand her meaning as easily as I understood the need to use tissues over throw pillows.

"You gotta help me here, Tess."

"Well, when I sit and watch my math teacher put a problem on the board, I begin to deduce as he writes it. You know, following along, ...I'm working it out as he goes. Then something really significant or difficult is thrown in, something that seems to negate... um, take away..." she unnecessarily clarified for me, "the earlier conclusion. It makes me look at it in an entirely different way. And then, right when I think I'm close, my teacher will go back and put some final marks, parenthesis, or powers, or signs. All that figuring ahead, it's senseless if you don't wait for the entire equation. ...I trust math. It has rhythm and reason. But it's nothing compared to God. God loves you. Wait for his last mark, Cassie."

I didn't say anything to her; I didn't need to. We hugged and she went up to her room. I followed, after unzipping and dropping the cover to the throw pillow into the laundry basket and placing the soggy insert directly into the machine. I'd deal with them in the morning.

As I lay in bed, I heard my mother's nightly exploration begin downstairs. She opened, rifled, rustled, and closed the same cabinets and drawers she'd rummaged through for almost two years. And strangely, I was comforted by the sound. I began reciting several scriptures, determined to memorize them, no matter how long it took. One in particular, Micah 7:8, spoke to me, and I repeated the words over and over...

"Do not rejoice in me my enemy; when I fall, I will arise; when I sit in darkness, the Lord will be a light to me."

...And as I lay in the darkness, my spirit rose, and the Lord was a light to me. And I slept.

At lunch the next day, we all sat together again, secretly holding hands under the table, and looking around at the people we'd affected the day before. It was pretty amazing when we saw the same people, and they were still without their ugly, energy-sucking escorts. Still, there were so many that needed help, and a lot that still needed to be done.

Once again, we began working systematically. If I wasn't actively engaged in Siphon removal, I found myself dodging the darts and arrows—not of the demons, but of the group I used to call my friends. I was becoming stronger though, and managed to ignore the insults tossed my direction when they knew I could hear, and the critical looks fixed on me whenever they could catch my eye. However, it slowly became clear this only happened when Nathan wasn't around. If he was, they ignored me completely. I wish I could say this was a relief, and in some ways, it was, but it also brought a bit of misery. I decided to focus on the job at hand, and tried to ignore the impoverished state of my popularity.

I had just finished talking with a group of lonely freshmen, cheering them up by telling them I thought their idea of forming a sewing/knitting/crochet combination club was a great idea. Meanwhile, I silently prayed for forgiveness. I openly told the girls I'd love to come, and had to pray again, realizing I'd have to go at least once to make up for my white lie. And then of course, they'd kick me out anyway, once they were unable to teach me how to grasp the yarn and the needle, needles, needlei at the same time. There were Siphons on three of the five girls, and they were all different and all disgusting—and surprisingly ugly —considering the girls themselves were so innocuous. Truly, one would never have guessed. Tessa came up, asked if they would help her with her school, "God project," and even though only one acquiesced, said her peace. I bade them goodbye, and they were a happier, different group...in ways they would never know.

I watched Tessa walk up to Santos and touch his arm. Then, rather than heading toward Jack, Hailey, or Chris, she approached a girl no one had talked to yet. I recognized her as being in one of Tessa's advanced classes. She was in my grade, a tall, gawky-looking girl of Middle Eastern decent. Her arms had some kind of pale rash on them. She sat a short distance from two other socially challenged girls and pretended to eat. Of course, I didn't know her—for two reasons. First, she was decidedly unpopular, and second, she was in the advanced classes. As for the first, I had never stooped to lower *my* standards, and as for the second, anyone in the advanced classes refused to lower *their* standards for me. It had seemed so fair. Now I wasn't sure things were meant to be that way because I was finding *I* wasn't supposed to be that way. I walked over and touched Santos' hand.

There instantly appeared a Siphon-beastie about the size of a large hand puppet with bristle-like hair and a bulbous, veined tummy, attached to her. It had a set of three pincers on each hand for fingers, and it was picking at the girl's skin. Whenever she reached over and rubbed or scratched the area of irritation, the Siphon would howl with glee, and a grey-pink liquid would pump into its stomach.

I couldn't hear what was said to the girl, but I saw her smile as Tessa slid in beside her. Oh, how the fuzzy-itch-Muppet began to whine. The two shared a laugh about something, but then Tessa must have decided she couldn't waste any time. She laid her small hand on the other girl's thin shoulder as she stood to go, and I watched her lips moving. The girl's face was still and intent. A howl went up, and the Siphon simply disappeared. Popped right in front of our eyes like the nit of a louse—and just that gross.

Santos squeezed my hand and directed my attention to Hailey. She had been walking toward us, totally focused on Santos, and not the group crossing her path, when they accidentally walked into her. I cringed, and started to go to her defense, but Santos held my arm.

"She's amazing. Watch her," he said, his voice an octave I'd not heard before. I looked at him quickly but didn't have time to make an opinion. Hailey was in more trouble than he knew. She'd just walked into Chuck, or Chucky, or even Upchuck, as he was known on the football field, and he was a piece of work.

Large and rather intellectually challenged, I'd had him in a class last year. The only thing I was grateful for was he'd made me look highly intelligent. Even then, I'd been amazed at his unlimited capacity for cruel fun. And although I was known to enjoy a spot or two of that myself in days gone by—OK, a few weeks ago–this guy was in a league all his own. He made fun of just about anybody and everybody, with the same five adjectives sprinkled into his vocabulary: loser, fat-ass, dipstick, butthead, and gonad. At least those were the five he could use without fear of immediate suspension. He had several others that he used outside the earshot of teachers that consisted mainly of four letters and always of disgusting body part combinations, dick-face being the kindest and least offensive.

It was no surprise that Chucky was being sucked on by demon. And this one was a large, pale Syphon with a snake-shaped head. Its bulbous eyes rotated in its bony looking skull as its body wrapped and draped itself, clinging onto the large boy with suctions. When it saw Hailey, it lifted its suckered mouth off Chucky's neck long enough to hiss. I was so grateful she couldn't see anything any more frightening than the Neanderthal boy standing in front of her. I knew he'd be scary enough without the bug-eyed-snake-demon hissing at her from his back.

Chucky had bumped into Hailey, and three of his challenged friends were laughing as though they knew why this was so funny.

"Hey 'fat-ass.' Get out of my way, 'loser,'" Chucky sneered, standing in her way. Hailey unsuccessfully tried to step around him. Even from where we sat, I could tell she was turning red. But then she stopped and turned to him.

"By the way, you did a really good job out on the field ...at the game last Friday," Hailey ventured, taking the offensive. The boys standing with Chucky started to hoot and laugh. Now it was Chucky who turned red.

"Like I care what a fat-ass, dipstick like you would think. Get lost!" He answered angrily. I watched the creature on him sigh, its translucent eyelids half closing over its bulging eyes as it gulped—the juice of humiliation and anger obviously sweet nectar to the beast.

I assumed Hailey would walk away in embarrassment. She was standing stock still, her eyes closed. I could hear the soft patois of Santos' prayer, and I began to pray, too. But then, she opened her eyes, and smiled shyly back at the big dummy of a kid. And it shouldn't have made any difference at all. But it did. The instantaneous forgiveness she directed at Chucky was like a laser light at the demon. It had the same effect as Tessa's healing words. The horrid Siphon squealed, shriveling before our eyes. It slipped off Chucky like a deflated inner tube and then disappeared. As Hailey walked past a momentarily stupefied and silent Chucky, she was surprised to see Santos and I doing a jig and high-fiving each other. She had no idea what had just transpired.

Chapter Twenty

s one week turned into the next, we fought on and off the school campus. In the Pine Circle we all became better with our swords; we were becoming stronger and faster. I was even learning scripture, due in large part, I must admit to my handsome, if socially challenged, gimp of a neighbor Chris. And fight it as I might, I couldn't help finding things to like about him.

At school, the most grotesque, frightening, and horrifying encounters were becoming almost commonplace. We were walking up to Siphons and kicking their slimy tails. I was *amazed* at us. We were actually adapting to these abnormal circumstances and to surroundings that, let's face it, were a bit more than creepy. In fact, at one point, it became clear to me there was real danger of my becoming *too* desensitized. But then, of course, I still had remnants of my gift...

I'd seen a group of emo-goth girls with several Siphons, all different, all ugly, draped and sucking on them. I knew these girls had a particular dislike for cheerleaders, for my type, for my old crowd, for me. Still, someone had to do *something*, and everyone else was doing *something* in other places. Santos and Tessa were with me when I drew a bead on the girls. Seeing what I was up against, they said they'd keep watch and come over when they could. But I wasn't concerned. I was stoked and walked confidently toward their circle. I could've sworn, however, that even without Santos, I heard hissing, and hoped it was the demons and not the girls. As I got closer, I could feel the air change temperatures and their eyes boring into me.

"What do *you* want?" The girl with the black hair, black sweater, black pants, and black tie-up boots, all coordinating with her lip liner, asked as I approached.

I don't know what I'd been expecting, but open hostility wasn't it. Unfortunately, I figured it probably hadn't been demons I'd heard hissing. "Hi, I um, I wanted to... just say hi," I answered, like a total cheeseburger. Obviously, I'd needed to prepare a little better for this encounter. The "spooky girls," as I'd called them—only to myself, and before realizing God expected more of me—stood staring like I'd just slipped my straight jacket.

"What? Are you running for Homecoming Queen? You want my vote? What's your problem, cuz you are sooo out of luck..." One of the girls taunted. She wore black from tip-to-toenails too, and it coordinated well with her disposition. The rest of the girls snickered.

I couldn't keep the flush of blood from flooding my face, but I tried with all my might to stay focused, and tried remembering that the beastie-beings, the horrific, gunky Siphons, were still sucking on these girls. But all I could manage was to stand, stutter, and stammer. It was crazy that I couldn't get a grip in front of these girls. Girls that only days ago I wouldn't have given a hoot or a holler about—considering how far beneath me they were on their color charts alone.

OK, I told myself, *close your eyes and pray*. But I couldn't.

All I could do was stand like a cardboard cutout, my feet nailed to the turf, and my mind as empty as a ping-pong ball.

"Did it look like we were inviting you over here?" The girl with a ring through her nose and black eyeliner the width of sidewalls asked. The sneering laughter of the other girls broke me out of my momentary coma.

Oh, screw it, I thought, looking at the mean girl right in the eyes. *You deserve to be sucked on.* Getting angry gave me nerve, but I also began to feel the queer and uncontrollable sensation of slipping away from myself and ... *Stop it...no, no, stop it right now*, I thought. *I like her...really...I...* flowing into her. *She was so alone. Fear, lots of fear, and then the sensation of being left by people she loved, wrenched at her, at my heart. ...There were so many different families and different homes ... Then, we were looking in a mirror and wondering what it would feel like to be pretty, wondering if it would make a difference... Surface images and feelings filled me, but deeper things touched me too, ...and all in mere moments. I wanted to somehow leave something of myself inside to assure her she was beautiful. I wanted to help her not be afraid...* Suddenly, I was back, standing stupidly in front of them as they waited for my reply.

Inwardly, I shook myself from top to tail like a dripping dog on the shore of a lake. "No need to be testy girls. Like I said, I just wanted to say, 'hello,'" I said, coming back to myself with fresh dignity. "And no, I didn't think your super sweet smiles meant I was invited." A couple girls laughed. "I just came over because I've been banned from the 'snob' clique for not obeying them, but don't worry...I'm not wanting to join up and contaminate you with my urban ugly. Besides, black's not my color; although, it's the bomb on you..." I said, pointing to the only girl in the group who had the right coloring and used it appropriately. "And I'm not running for prom," I said, sauntering around the group and sizing them up. "But now that you've brought it up, let me add that, although *I'm* not running, if one of *you* had the courage to run, who knows? Maybe you'd spare the school this year from another pom-pom, pabulum queen. Just a thought," I said, looking directly at the girl with the nose ring.

"Why would any of us want to demean ourselves by condescending to *that* ritual?" she asked, "and by the way, it means to degrade, humiliate, or disgrace ourselves," she finished with a smirk.

"Yea, I know the definition of 'demean.' I also know '*balk, balk, balk,*' when I hear it," I said, sticking my neck out, figuratively, and literally, "and I've got a pretty good grasp on what a social statement is, which, if you weren't so *chicken*, you'd see that by, considering the challenge, you'd be asserting a different value system for posterity. Uh, the succeeding generations, heirs, successors, you know... All those coming up after you that aren't in the popular crowd but have worth and importance and a right to be recognized."

I stood, completely out of breath, looking at the goth girls' shocked faces. I could tell they were impressed, but as I looked over at Tessa, I saw her standing and watching with Santos. She was ready to come as soon as the Siphons released, which meant; I'd failed. I turned and started walking away.

"Like anyone would vote for *us*," the girl with the nose ring called out to me.

I turned back and spoke the truth directly to her. "I would."

If *I* hadn't been shock treatment enough, Tessa passed me on her way to speak words that would undeniably blow their minds, and without a doubt, collapse the demons preying on their despair. As with so many of her other endeavors, my little sister was a genius at slaying the creepy things...and that genius was rubbing off.

The fact was, the creepy things, Siphons of every size and shape were noticeably beginning to disappear. And as we worked, other students began inadvertently working with us. As the demon population diminished, so did the angst that had recently shrouded the school. With Santos' help, we watched as people started speaking happily and kindly to each other, disengaging some of the creatures from their victims without even trying. As diligently as Tessa worked, she couldn't be everywhere at once. Out of desperation, Hailey tried and discovered she could also speak the words for healing. Then I tried, and watched as Santos gave me the enthusiastic thumbs up too. Soon, we all began using the healer's spoken words, *'Jesus Christ, by His Blood,'* and watched as the portals closed and the demons deflated and disappeared. It was *amazing*.

Chris had been allowed to take a few special classes. Astonishingly, one was the same biology class Tessa was in. And for a puncture-wound waiting to happen, he had proven to be massively effective at detaching Siphons. Even I hadn't remained immune to his pathetic charm; however, it seemed Tessa had access to a boatload of that antidote.

As I watched Hailey from day to day, it was obvious to my easily entertained mind she'd shed her flimsy mortal disguise to become She-Ra: Princess of Power, barely hiding her secret identity from the student body as she attacked the "Evil Horde." It truly wasn't difficult, at least for me, to become overly fantastical in my imaginings. We were slaying demons at lunchtime, for pity's sake. Anyway, I had *loved* watching She-Ra when I was a girl, and I loved watching Hailey assume more and more power. It also seemed to me, Santos was enjoying it too, and that he watched her just a bit more closely. Her triumphs brought him a little more thrill than anyone else's. At any rate, I loved thinking this.

As expected, Jack had been kicking butt every time he

approached either a single person or a group. And even though I hated noticing, he was especially fast at changing the atmosphere around any girls that were mean or negative. I found this humorous in a not-so-funny way since he'd had the opposite effect on me lately. The truth was, he was nice to everyone, including me. He just wasn't crazy about me anymore. I hated to admit that this had an effect on me. Surprise, surprise...

It seems when the universe quit orbiting around the gravitational pull of my charm, worse yet, when I realized it never really had, I was forced into living a different version of life. It certainly wasn't ego gratifying, and in most ways, it wasn't as fun. But in other ways, my new worldview included the novelty of looking in the mirror and liking more than the just the image. I actually kind of liked who I saw *behind* my eyes, instead of just my awesome mascara job. I'd also found the unique pleasure of going to bed with a feeling of peace encompassing me, something I was becoming used to. As weird as it was, I found I didn't want to give up who I'd become for who I'd been. And just as this school day was about to end, this truth came home to me in no uncertain terms.

Although the day seemed particularly long, strangely, I wasn't tired. Stranger still, I hadn't let thoughts of Nathan, my old friends, or any of the usual head-banging frustrations steal my increasing enjoyment in demon-destruction.

I'd been reading scripture like we were supposed to, and honestly, wondering about a lot of it, but doing my best to let stuff sink in. And during a break, one verse I was reading made sense. It pretty well summed up what had recently occurred in my life after deciding to give up my cool world, for God's frankly uncool, but let's face it, surprisingly happier one: "*This is my commandment, that you love one another, as I have loved you. If the world hates you, you know that it hated me before it hated you. If you were of the world, the world would love his own: but because you are not of the world, but I have chosen you out of the world, therefore the world hates you."*

Now that made sense because it was absolutely true. Boy, did my world hate me ever since I had been chosen out of the world. The only tough slice to swallow was the first part, where we were supposed to love one another as He loved us. *Bummer,* I thought. Because this meant that, even though I'd never treated my old friends badly, I was being commanded to *love* them. It was pretty twisted. But I knew God loved me when I'd hated Him, and that He'd loved me first. And so, I ended up deciding I would do what God was asking of me; or, at least, I would do my best. As I sat contemplating all this, I caught Nathan watching me from across the quad. I looked straight at him, and he turned away; and although my heart did a thump and pang, I realized there was nothing more I could do on that point. Nathan needed to choose, and the next move had to be up to him. However, after school, Jenna gave me a chance to flex my oh-so-rock -solid resolve—and practice the loving bit.She approached me as I stood at my locker, deciding on which books to take home. We hadn't spoken for so long that I'd almost forgotten she wouldn't be as excited to see me, as I was her. Before I could control myself, I managed looking totally pathetic by almost jumping for joy at having her stop and speak to me.

"Hey Cassie," she said, leaning on the locker next to mine.

"Jenna! How are you?" I asked, just a wee too ecstatically. Her perfect eyebrow shot up, and a condescending smile came to her lips. "*I'm* fine. The question is, what's up with *you?*"

"A lot," I answered truthfully. Suddenly, I knew I wouldn't be able to repair the tear in our relationship without changing back into who I was. I looked down, realizing for the first time the complete defeat I would encounter if I ever tried to justify my actions with the truth.

"Nathan thinks you have a thing for Jack," she said. I didn't respond because I was still admitting to myself how far away I was from being able to explain anything to her. When I just stood there, she added, "How could you? I mean, its *Nathan*, not just anybody! And what makes you even more pitiful, is the fact that, if it weren't for Nathan, Jack wouldn't even be alive."

I looked at her, and then I looked away. I badly wanted to set her straight, but I knew I'd be doing something Jack wouldn't thank me for. I was too mad to think why this would be, so instead, I used my new inner guidance system. If something inside me was dying to get out, and I deeply yearned to spit the words all over someone, then it was probably better not to. When I continued to stare at her in silence, she foolishly went on.

"You do know? Nathan saved Jack from drowning when they were young. I mean, I don't blame you for having the 'hots' for Jack, but why would you give Nathan up for him? You must be nuts...you're sure acting nuts," she said, not bothering to use her fake saccharine voice. Miraculously, I continued to hold myself in check. Time was running out. Nathan needed to reconcile with Jack, and I needed to love Jenna because God wanted me to...

"Jenna, Nathan broke up with me. Jack and I are friends. So, would you please give Nathan a message for me? Tell him he needs to come back... tell him, ...well—just tell him that... I guess," I said, ending on a weaker note than I'd intended, but smiling at Jenna with as much sincerity as I could muster.

"You're kidding, right? After you dumped him for Jack? You really are crazy!"

"Jenna, Nathan broke up with me," I answered, gritting

my teeth, in an attempt to hold back the barrage. "And like I said, I don't have anything going on with Jack except friendship." I turned back to my locker boiling, but proud I'd contained myself.

Alas... Pride, they say, cometh before the fall; and the fall came when Jenna snorted... It wasn't a loud snort, just snortie enough... I whipped back around.

"That's right, I said, *'friendship.'* Jack and I are friends. But maybe I need to explain it to you...the word friendship? I'm not sure you ever passed that word on a vocab test. You just might want to look it up," I said hotly, slamming my locker and walking away without looking back.I knew if there'd been a negativity-sucking Siphon attached to me, I'd have been lunch, literally. What made it worse was there was no getting around how great it felt delivering a zinger like that on cue, rather than ten minutes later when it would have been of no earthly good. Still, in the end, I knew I'd failed.

I tried imagining God placing my performance in the same light as "Casting out the Moneychangers from the Temple"—and could almost hear Him laughing. The truth was, I didn't really feel any love for Jenna after she'd begun going off on me. Truth is, I'd kind of hated her. But strangely, when it was all said and done, more than I enjoyed my comeback, I hated failing at the love bit. The episode left no doubt; I needed to work on my anger. We were going into a major battle, and I couldn't allow resentment to endanger me, to endanger all of us. After all, the *one I loved* was at stake...

The six of us had been meeting continually in the evenings, and we were all becoming more adept at focusing our scriptures and prayers. I'd never admit this to the others, but I was really starting to feel like Xena, well, minus the whip. And at night before bed, I'd stand in front of the mirror practicing my snarly smile. I was getting good.On the unsnarly side, my prayers were finally starting to feel real, too.

And somehow, very slowly, it began dawning on me that God wasn't asking me to be different, He just wanted me to love him more, which translated, of course, into other people. And, notwithstanding Jenna, I surprisingly did, at least for the most part. More surprising still, I was memorizing scriptures. They were coming faster, and I was able to recite them better. In fact, I hardly ever mixed them up with nursery rhymes anymore. I felt good. I felt strong. And then I met a Maltorph.

Chapter Twenty-One

Our second week of slaying had come and gone, and the big party was taking place the coming weekend. But besides Hailey's dreams, all the nasty Siphons which had been dispatched, and the other evil creatures that only Santos had seen, we hadn't any proof Rasvampin was planning an evil rampage—or that the hour of the mantle's passing was at hand.

It was Rally Friday. I was on my way to third period English when I caught sight of Santos standing behind a pillar. Even at a distance, I could tell something was wrong. I made a detour, calling his name as I approached him from behind. When he turned, it was with his body first, his head last; his eyes were large, with fear dilating his pupils. Automatically, I took his arm, and standing in front of us, not five feet away, was a creature that vaporized my self-confidence in one hot breath. He was at least nine-feet tall and muscular, but bent slightly at the torso. His skin was opaque and veined. Within his hands, which were a lot like claws, he carried a sword. And I knew, he knew, I'd seen him.

Everything in me wanted to run. Yet, nothing, not an

ounce of courage, a wit of concern for Santos, or a smidgen of desire to do battle in the name of God, made me stay where I was. Only terror rooted me. I couldn't have moved to save my life, which is exactly what I felt I was about to lose.

Santos was scared too, but evidently these were the creatures he'd seen before, because he managed to speak. "It's a Maltorph. They're here. He's been watching me, but I don' know what we're suppose' to do," he said breathlessly. I couldn't answer. All I could do was look at the horrible face on the demon, mapping and charting it for future nightmares. "Cassie!" Santos whispered, "What should we do?"

Slowly, I looked away from the creature and back into the face of my friend. "Dear God, are we supposed to do something?" I asked in horror, "Now? Here at school? I mean, look at him. Can they hurt us?" I babbled.

"I don't think so, at least not physically. He's been watching me, and so far, he hasn't tried to get me. I'm not sure why. But his sword, it is very big." As though he'd heard us, the demon walked over to one of the seniors walking down the hall, lifted his sword and slashed downward. The boy stalled for only a fraction of second, and then his own arm lifted in the same arc, slashing down on a passing student and knocking him to the floor.

"Get outta my way!" The older boy yelled, ignoring the younger student's cry of pain. The senior kept walking, but I saw him shake his head as though perplexed as well as angry. The demon smiled and hissed his laughter, while using the back of his sword to slap at the student still on the ground. With every whack, although not seen or felt physically, the kid grew more and more upset, until he finally found his legs and stormed off, vowing muttered revenge.

"Come on, let's go find the others," I said, suddenly more angry than afraid.

"Look! Over there, it's two more!" Santos said, gesturing

in the direction of the north hallway. Two Maltorphs had just come around the side of the building and were looking down the hall. "We're gonna have to wait until lunch break. Hailey and Jack are going to class, and Chris and Tessa won't be here 'til then," Santos said, unable to look away from the creatures' looming forms.

Suddenly, I didn't want to let go of Santos' arm. "Will you walk me to class? I can't stand the idea of having to walk by one of those things, and not know." I said, realizing blindness, whether figurative or literal, no longer held the same kind of charm for me.

"Yea, I know what you mean," Santos agreed. We walked to class together, looking over our shoulders and down the different locker rows in fear of seeing more. Luckily, there were only the three, and one more in a classroom we passed. I got to my room without running into anything terrifyingly malevolent. That is, almost. Just as I said goodbye to Santos, Brittany walked up.

"What on earth has gotten into you, Cassie? Are you completely deranged? When Nathan told us you had thrown him and the rest of us over for another crowd, we at least thought it was because you had a thing for Jack," she said, casting a disgusted look toward Santos' retreating back.

"Brittany, we're just friends," I stated, wondering if my, *"You just might want to look that word up in the dictionary,"* could be used again so soon.

"Yea right. You hold hands with all the friends that walk you to class?"

"I don't have time to explain right now, but if you really want to know what's going on, I'll be *glad* to tell you later," I said, not caring if the details I shared blew her out of her phony universe or not.

"Like I care. Save your explanations for a qualified psychiatrist. I'm outta here," she said, flicking her hair over her shoulder and into my face. She opened the door to our English class, where I followed her in and sat down. And I didn't even spend the next thirty minutes of class, as I would have in the past, perfecting an, "if-only-I-had-said," dialogue aimed at scalding her wedges off. Instead, I comforted myself with the fact that *she really was clueless*. I had bigger more important things to agonize over: Melville and his big white whale now, and the Maltorphs waiting in the quad later.

As soon as class was over, I went to find the others. I was standing next to Santos who was easily a couple shades too pale, when I saw Jack approaching. I knew he could tell something was up before he was ten feet from us. His eyes narrowed, the smile dropped from his face, and he set his jaw. Tessa and Hailey were coming together from the direction of the gym. Chris came up from behind, clanging his crutches against the stone bench, which nearly caused both Santos and me fatal heart attacks.

"What's got you two so jumpy?" Chris asked, smiling widely. He loved scaring people almost as much as he loved being scared himself. I glared at him as Hailey, Tessa and Jack arrived together.

"What's the matter? ...Wait. They're here, aren't they?" Chris asked, his voice just above an excited whisper.

I nodded. Santos said, "Come on, you all need to see this." We sat down at the table and took hands. I couldn't believe it. There were now at least nine of the sword-carrying Maltorphs milling about the quad, watching and sizing things up. The smaller ogre-like, parasite Siphons were present too, but their numbers had been greatly diminished. Occasionally, one of the Maltorphs would approach a Siphon attached to an oblivious human. Without tearing it completely off its victim, and while the smaller demon screamed like a wild banshee, the Maltorph would suck out whatever energy the Siphon had stored. It made eating lunch completely out of the question.

We all watched with our mouths hanging open, looking, I'm certain like a group of patients just wheeled out of a frontal lobotomy ward. Finally, I broke the spell. "Let's all go to the old chemistry lab. It's empty, and I think we could get some privacy in there."

"Great idea. I think the time has come to test our abilities," Jack said, looking less confident than he sounded.

"Yeah, let's see if we can kick some Maltorph butt..." Chris added, but now his voice was barely audible.

"I'm concerned with one thing, though. How do we keep an eye on Nathan and be in the chem. lab?" Jack asked.

"I don't know. I never thought of that," I stated.

"Does something seem a little funny to you guys?" Hailey asked.

"I don't know that I would necessarily use the word, funny..." I countered, "but seriously, what seems off, besides the fact that we're surrounded by giant gargoyles with swords?" I asked.

"I'm not sure...but doesn't it seem like they're all just standing around waiting for something?"

"She's right," Jack agreed.

"You guys have an assembly today after lunch. I wonder if they're waiting, and hoping to do some damage during that?" Tessa offered.

"Could be. My homeys like to make a ruckus during those things," Santos added. I looked over at the other side of the quad where Sal and the rest of Santos' old gang hung out. They stood in a circle doing that shady pass around thing, where even a stick of gum looked suspicious. Then I looked past them, and I saw...him. A dark, slightly opaque figure stood near the entrance to the parking lot. He leaned against the wall and watched the goings on of the schoolyard.

Hailey saw him too, and wheezed, *"That's him!* The guy in my dream!"

Chris said his name out loud, "Rasvampin?" And instantly, as though he'd heard it even from that distance away, Rasvampin turned his dark, cold eyes on us. I believe I started to whimper. He had an ugly questioning look on his face as though he was trying to figure things out. For a moment, I was afraid he was going to come toward us. And then, I seriously would have wet myself. This guy made the Maltorphs seem merely misguided. We all sat silent and motionless for at least a minute; our eyes frozen to the frightening figure of evil that had us locked in his sights. Thank goodness Jack pulled himself together and broke the spell. In a quiet but firm voice, he began quoting Ephesians 6:10-13:

"...be strong in the Lord and in the power of His might,
put on the whole armor of God
that you may be able to stand against the wiles of the devil.
For we do not wrestle against flesh and blood,
but against principalities, against powers,
against the rulers of the darkness of this age,
against spiritual hosts of wickedness in the heavenly places.
Therefore, take up the whole armor of God,
that you may be able to withstand in the evil day,
and having done all, to stand."

I felt blood begin flowing through me again, and we all looked at one another. Each of us realizing, I think, that the actual war was about to begin.

Tessa became our strategist. "Hailey's right. They're waiting for a command. We have this lunch period before the assembly. I say we go to the chem. lab and pray together. One of us needs to physically be with Nathan during the assembly. The Maltorphs will be attacking people and it could cause a riot. Who knows what could put Nathan in danger, but they obviously have a plan, and Nathan may need to know where to find you guys," she finished. Her small face was swamped by her large glasses and surrounded by giant frizzy curls. I wondered if the Maltorphs would ever guess that their toughest enemy just might be wrapped in this crazy little package. I guess I wasn't the only one amazed at the precision of her mind because we all just nodded in agreement.

"I'll go to the assembly," I offered, "I'm supposed to be there for cheer squad anyway."

"No," Tessa answered, looking at me. "We need you. You're too good with a sword. I'll go. I can maintain a focus of prayer, and the rest of you need to fight. Fighting is the one thing I'm not that good at," she admitted. Once again, we looked at each other and silently nodded.

"OK, let's go," Jack stated. "Recite your scriptures as you walk, and the Maltorphs probably won't follow. But I think we should go two at a time. Chris and I will go first. We'll meet you there." We watched as Jack and his brother made their way around the other kids and the demons they could no longer see. And Jack was right. Whenever they came anywhere near the Maltorphs while whispering a scripture, they moved away.

"Tessa, you want to come with me?" I asked, hoping it sounded like I was being protective of her and not the other way around.

"Sure, let's go," she said, not a quiver in her voice. *Man, it was tough being the big sister to this kid,* I thought. I couldn't help taking hold of Santos one last time and glancing back at the dreadful dark figure against the wall. Unfortunately, he was still watching us. I quickly let go and walked with Tessa through the students milling around us, reciting under my breath to beat the band. At that point, I really wished I'd thought to repeat my verses without moving my lips. Tessa was ahead of me, and I'm sure it looked like I was being escorted out of the school by my bizarre baby sister after having lost my foil-antenna-headgear and shopping cart. But comfort lay in the fact, that no matter how crazy I looked, it wasn't half as crazy as what was really happening.

By the time we got to the old chemistry lab on the opposite side of the school, I was actually trembling—but not with fear. As strange as it seemed, even to me, I couldn't wait to get my hands on that sword. We slipped inside unseen and found Jack and Chris waiting for us.

"Check the schedule and see if any teacher has signed up to use this classroom today," I told Tessa.

She walked over to the clipboard on the wall. "No, only one teacher is down, and that was for second period. It looks like we're in luck."

Just then, Hailey and Santos walked in. The five of us moved some of the desks while Chris made a general nuisance of himself trying to hop around and help. We made a space toward the back where we took hands and started praying.

Immediately the power began building, and I began with my scriptures. Suddenly, I was in the circle. Jack and Santos, then Chris, and finally Hailey glimmered and appeared. We were together, and each of us had our hands around a sword of lightening-bright silver. My lips were still moving to the words I was repeating in the circle, "*Keep me as the apple of your eye. Hide me under the shadow of your wings, from the wicked who oppress me, from my deadly enemies who surround me...*"

"So, Tessa's not coming?" Hailey asked, her voice muted and distant.

Jack shook his head. "No, she'll leave for the assembly in a minute. Come on, let's rock those lizards."

When I heard his words, instead of anxiety, my heart leapt with anticipation. But I wasn't sure where to move. Jack looked at me, and I could tell he was wondering the same thing. Santos took a step toward the perimeter of the gray circle, but it was Chris, with a yell like the wild- gooney-bird he was, who leapt outside and disappeared. We heard a muffled shout, and without any hesitation, Jack and Santos followed. I looked at Hailey and smiled. She smiled back, but I could tell it was without the eagerness I was feeling. "Come on, Hailey, Warrior Princess," I encouraged, my voice muted to my own ears. "We've been chosen, and '*He has made you bold with strength in your soul,*'" I paraphrased from Psalms.

"You're right!" she said with more enthusiasm. Together we walked out of the wall of gray light and into the day.

There wasn't a feeling of traveling. We simply found ourselves standing outside near the entrance to the school's auditorium. The five of us were together watching our fellow students make their way through the wide double doors. The Maltorphs were there too, and suddenly, with a cry sounding both shrill and angry, one spied us.

The other Maltorphs, standing on both sides of the advancing students, looked in our direction and joined the first in its attack. I moved away from the students, as it was disconcerting to have them walk through me anyway. I held my sword at the ready, just as if my dad had been D'Artagnan by night and a microbiologist by day. One singled me out. He was a particularly disgusting demon, with slime dripping from his front teeth as he smiled. I couldn't help but shudder at his hygiene. Other than that, my only emotion was a deep desire to put him away.

The beast bellowed as he neared me, and when I lifted my sword without flinching, he stopped. "Who are you to defy the warriors of darkness?" he asked and swung his heavy blunt sword above his head and down toward my body. *Ah, I thought, what an opening...*

I sliced upward, stopping his blow, and spinning easily away from him. Then I smiled up at him. Once again, he bellowed, unable to fathom what had just happened. "I *will* make you afraid!" He roared.

I stood unyielding, and with a quick move to the left, swung hard and knocked his sword from his claws. "*The Lord is my light and my salvation*; so, come on! You think you can make me afraid? *The Lord is the strength of my life*, and you think I should fear you?" I ad-libbed while reciting. He looked at me, his red beady eyes actually startled. Then, as he screamed in anger and fear, I put him away. There was no blood, thank goodness since I get a little squeamish when it comes to runny stuff. But when I drove my sword into him, he exploded into dust.

I looked over in time to see the others dispatching their Maltorphs as well. Hailey even did it with her eyes closed. I gathered she was a little worried about the bodily fluid thing, too.

Then I saw Nathan. He was walking toward the auditorium and following a few feet behind was Tessa. Several Maltorphs began to advance, their swords above their heads. Jack took out two, and I took out the other one. I was getting ready to take out another Maltorph when Chris came sliding in like Jack Sparrow and chopped him into powder. I suspected he was having way too much fun for the seriousness of the battle. I started to say something to him but stopped—the boy was nothing if not effective.

As Nathan passed, I noticed he was leaning toward and laughing with a new girl. I hadn't met her yet because my group of ex-friends had adopted her as their newest 'snob.' She was wearing a cute outfit, and her soft blonde hair was cut in a bob. She was delicate, and not quite my height; and she looked naturally sweet. In other words, she was my opposite. Nathan seemed interested in what she was telling him, and I felt something turning in my stomach and squeezing my heart. Suddenly, I found myself standing back in the chem. lab reciting my scriptures with everyone else deeply into their own. *All right,* I thought, *no more distractions.* I focused again, and in a few seconds, I was back.

Of course, a myriad of Maltorphs had shown up and were doing battle with the other four Guardians. Jack looked at me as if to say, "Where were you?" I shrugged and started swinging. Some of them were more difficult than others, and I supposed it depended on how much Siphon gator-aide they'd been able to fill up on before the fight. We were outnumbered at least ten-to-one; yet we were winning. A few kids had come into contact with our warfare, and a fight almost broke out between two girls for no reason that they'd be able to explain later. Luckily, a teacher stepped in to stop it, and the few others who were inadvertently hit walked away angry and confused, probably blaming their sudden rage on random thoughts.

I tried to draw the action away, but after a while, I noticed my sword wasn't quite as quick. I looked over toward Santos and Hailey and saw they were tiring too. One of the students passing us was furtively handing another kid a plastic bag. I knew instantly it was drugs. I looked up quickly and saw the figure of Rasvampin leering at me from the shadows. Without thinking, I slashed my sword down through the pocket of the boy who'd been slipped the baggie. My sword passed harmlessly through his jacket, but to my astonishment, the baggie fell to the ground. A passing teacher bent over and picked it up, regarding it suspiciously. I looked up and watched Rasvampin's face go dark with rage, anger seeming to swell him like a toad needing to croak.

I spun quickly, instinctively sensing something behind

me. Two more Maltorphs were bearing down on me, and I yelled out Psalms 138:3, "*In the day when I cried out, You answered me, and made me bold...*" I gave them my best snarly-smile and sliced them—one... two—then finished, "*... with strength in my soul.*"

Most everyone was already in the auditorium by now, and it was obvious that the demons' hopes of starting a riot were being frustrated before they'd even gotten started. Suddenly, a voice rang out into the melee. "Stop!" It sounded as though it was echoed through a large reverberating pipe, and the Maltorph in mid-swing with me stopped dead. Of course, I made it literal.

"Fall back," Rasvampin commanded his army of mutant sword swingers. I looked at Hailey and saw her lower her sword, relief spreading across her face. When the remaining Maltorphs retreated, Rasvampin walked into the center of the outdoor walkway and out of the shadows. He was larger, and uglier I might add, than I'd first thought. And he was really ticked off.

"Well, well, well, I have underestimated Heaven's plan," he said, strolling in front of the five of us and taking our measure. "I wasn't expecting this. But don't get too cocky just yet. I *will* beat you at this game," he said, eyeing us with a sinister smile. "I will find the one I'm after. I will find the *Link*. Do you really think a group such as yourselves will stop me from completing the job I was sent to do?"

"Bring it on man..." Santos said, fear cracking his voice. Rasvampin threw back his head and laughed.

"Let me tell you why I will prevail, if not today...then tomorrow," he said, facing Santos menacingly. "You are a lazy, good for nothing Mexican, *coward*," he spit, his hot black eyes boring into Santos. Santos tried to respond, but I could almost see the words freezing in his throat. The demon swirled his long overcoat and walked away, stopping in front of Hailey. "Ah, the dreamer—I remember you," he said, sneering. "I laughed at you then, and I laugh at you now. You are an undisciplined, self-indulgent *slob*." Hailey made a soft noise in the back of her throat—and by now I was seeing red.

Moving on, he came to Jack. "You may have been the only one that had the power to fight a good battle, but I always win if there is self-righteousness involved, and son, you have assured me of success," he said, smiling. Jack started to say something but then looked away in shame. Chris had taken a step back, and Rasvampin pinned him with his terrible eyes, boring into him until Chris stuck out his chin. "*Who* are you? You aren't even worth my time. You will never be anybody. You weren't even chosen, so why are you even here?" he asked with disdain. Chris looked offended, then stricken. Rasvampin then turned toward me.

"And you! You're the least. You will never love anyone, or anything more than you love yourself. A self-serving..." What he said was true, and I didn't care, because something inside me snapped. He'd already fried me to the core by unjustly battering my friends.

"I have two things to say to you," I said, cutting him off. I saw shock bloom in his sneering eyes. "*The Lord will perfect that which concerns us* —me and my friends," I added.

"And the second?" I couldn't believe he was stupid enough to ask.

"And you are tacky. Your overcoat is pretty cliché, don't you think? OK, that's really saying three things...but I would think the forces of evil..." I didn't get a chance to finish because with a roar that shook the rafters he disappeared, taking with him, thank goodness, all the leftover demon Maltorphs. Seconds later, we stood together in the chem. lab holding hands. The four of us dropped into chairs and looked at each other in disbelief. Then we all started talking at once.

It took at least five minutes before anyone listened to

anyone else. Just as we were settling down, Tessa came in from the assembly. We began telling her everything that happened, ending with Rasvampin. And I noticed Santos looking away as we told Tessa about the remarks he'd made to each of us.

"He used your fears against you," Tessa said.

"What do you mean?" Santos asked, obviously uncomfortable with the conversation but hoping to understand.

"He used what frightens you or makes you the angriest—the phrases that go through your mind that make you hate yourself—or hate how people see you," Tessa answered.

"She's right," Jack said quietly. "I hate the thought of being self-righteous. I can deal with just about every other weakness I have, but that one scares me."

"It's true. You don't know how many times I've used those exact same words to privately describe myself," Hailey admitted, looking down at her lap, her face scarlet.

"Well, what about me? Is it true about me?" Chris asked.

"What do you mean?" Jack asked, puzzled.

"He said I wasn't chosen, and that I shouldn't even be here. Was that true? Do you want me to leave? Because I know I sneaked in, but if you guys don't want me here, I can go, you know," he said, just a mite belligerently. Obviously, still upset over Rasvampin's remarks.

"Do you ever think those things yourself, Chris?" I asked, knowing for a fact he'd often felt that way in the past.

"No! I mean, well, I guess I wonder sometimes if I hadn't snuck up on you guys in the Pine Circle in the first place..."

"He knew you were afraid Chris, and it's *not* true," Tessa said in a quiet assured voice. Chris looked at her for a moment and nodded. Coming from her was all the confirmation he needed.

"Well, it's different for me. I don't think that way," Santos said. "Everybody else thinks that about Mexicans, but I don't think that. It's such bull," he added, standing up and walking away from the circle. "He called me a 'lazy, good-for-nothing Mexican,' man. That's just not right," he continued, turning toward us angrily.

"I know, and when he called you a coward, I almost choked," I responded. "In fact, that's the reason I got so mad. When he said what he did to me, well, I mean...he was right. It didn't even upset me. But I'll tell you, what he said about you, and the rest of you, were such gross lies! By the time he got to me, I was so steamed," I said, my temper flaring again.

Santos looked at the floor. "I don't want to think of myself as a coward no more," he said, not looking up. I don't know why, but I stood up, too. Jack stood. Then Hailey, and Chris and Tessa followed suit.

"Then let's agree; we'll face the truth about the lies we believe," Jack said. "That's all they are, lies. Let's all have the courage not to believe them. Remember, Rasvampin can only use those lies if we let him." And he put his hand in the center of the circle. Tessa took hold of his hand. Chris put his on top, while Santos and Hailey placed theirs over Chris'. I alone stood with my hands to my side.

"OK, but what if it's not a lie?" I asked. "I mean, 'yes' for you guys; they were obviously stupid. But to be honest, I knew what he said about me was the truth." Jack looked at me strangely for a moment, and then everyone in the circle started laughing. "What's so funny?" I asked.

"You don't get it, do you?" Jack said, looking at me with a tenderness that made my stomach feel squirrely. "What he said about you was the biggest lie of them all."

Chapter Twenty-Two

We each left the chemistry lab and went our separate ways to finish out the school day. When the last class finally ended, I went to gather my things out of my locker and head for home. The thought of my quiet bedroom gave me comfort. But I had to admit, as crazy- frightening as the day had been, it was also more-crazy-amazing than I *ever* could've imagined. I wanted to go home and contemplate it and figured it couldn't hurt to bone up on a couple more scriptures. My weapon would need to be swift and sharp for the coming onslaught.

I found myself flexing my sword arm, and wondering how it could possibly feel tired. After all, I hadn't actually used it. I'd been standing in a vacant schoolroom the entire time holding hands. And yet I could have sworn I'd just done the shot put for the last hour. As I stood in front of my locker, lost in thought, I felt someone...or something... behind me. I spun around ready for ...well ...I'm not sure. All I had in my hand was my binder. Nathan stood in front of me and any tough I was trying to conjure went to taffy in a split second.

"Oh, uh, hi," I said, utilizing all my brilliance to dazzle him with word play.

He didn't answer very quickly. Instead, he leaned on the locker beside mine until I'd finished pulling out the rest of my ...two books. Finally, he asked, "Where were you? I noticed you and Jack didn't make it to the assembly. And the others didn't either," he added. He'd lumped Jack and me together. His words were easy, but his eyes weren't.

"Hmm. I'm surprised you noticed, considering how much you were enjoying little, miss blonde-twinkie-pie," I said, feeling myself slip back into my old "mommy-dog" ways, like sliding down a spillway of slimy water. I could tell Nathan was surprised. "Look," I interjected quickly. "I'm sorry. I'm sure ...Alice? Is that her name? ...I'm sure she's nice," I said, trying to pull my reactions out of sewer land, "and it doesn't matter anyway," I said without pausing, "Because come to think of it, we're not together anymore. So, you can flirt with, date, and go out with anyone you want...as long as your mom doesn't find out..." I added cruelly, still mucking around the cesspool.

He smiled and looked off down the hall. "Is that how it's going to be?" I looked away, unable to truthfully answer. I was the *last* person to answer that question. Surely mercury ran through my veins instead of blood. Nathan turned back to me, with new interest. "So how did you see me? ...Were you guys there?" He asked, peering into my eyes, and I realized he knew what happened.

"Yes! And you could have been with us; you should have been, Nathan!" I exclaimed, moving toward him. He started to move away, then he lowered his head and sighed.

"Come on. Let's go outside so we can talk." I looked around, and sure enough, several people were openly watching us. He took my elbow and steered me out and around to a bench on the side of the building where our conversation wouldn't echo down the hallway. "Cassie, this is crazy. What was wrong with us before? Everything was good, wasn't it?" he asked, heatedly, looking at me with eyes that pulled and pushed at the same time. I couldn't tell if he loved me or hated me.

"Look, Nathan; I didn't ask for any of this. I only wanted us to be together. But things change; I've changed, and I'm still changing. Maybe you could understand if you'd been there, Nathan. Then, maybe you'd get it. Don't you even care?" I asked, amazed he could be so blind, that he'd choose to be blind...just the way I used to be.

"No, Cassie...I don't care about all that! What I care about is..." he stopped. I watched his jaw clench, and I couldn't help reflecting once again, on his great facial muscles, especially when he was angry. ...*Stop it! Stop it! Stop it!* I closed my eyes and silently scolded myself. "What I'd like to do," he said, frustrated, and turning his face away. Then he tried again, "Can't we just forget about all this? Forget about Jack and ...well everything. We could go back to the way things were. Come to the party with me tomorrow night. Maybe you can remember what it was like to have fun again," he said.

His voice was controlled, but his eyes held an almost defenseless plea; eyes I'd never been able to resist before. "Oh, Nathan. You know if I go, I won't be going to *party-down*. Don't you see, Nathan? We have a chance to do something—something amazing together."

"Nice try. You're not interested in doing something *amazing* with me. You're just doing your 'Guardian thing,'" he said shrewdly, turning his face away again.

"I'd think you'd care a little more about that yourself. It's about you! Help us, Nathan—help me keep *you* safe..."

He turned back, looking at me with those eyes again, and moved toward me so unexpectedly my books and binder fell to the ground. When he took my arm to pull me close, his individual fingertips felt like sparks from an electrical circuit. "Cassie," he said again, and this time his breath was on my ear. His nearness was exciting, and comforting. I'd missed him and I'd begun wondering if he hated me. "I was angry the other day, but I'd never hurt you. You know that, right?"

"Why did you act like you wanted to, Nathan? That hurt me, too."

"You forgive me." It was stated like a fact and not a question, but I took it as though he was asking me. I'd let him off the hook. I couldn't help myself. My arm was all tingly and he was still clenching his jaw.

"Of course."

"I've never told you," he whispered, "but I've wanted to. I love you; Cassie. I love you, and I don't care if ... I ...love you."

A wave of heat passed through me, and I closed my eyes. And I wanted him to love me. Just him. *I didn't want my new friends; I didn't want peace. I didn't want any other love, and I didn't want God. ...And I didn't care either.* I opened my eyes. Yes, I did. I wanted and needed all those things...and I cared. Nathan looked down at me; his eyes had become darkly intense. And as I looked into those wells, I admitted to myself—I no longer recognized what I saw.

"So? Aren't you going to say anything? Isn't that what you've wanted to hear all along?" He asked, smiling at me for the first time in what seemed a million years. I took my time answering, wanting to remember everything about him at that moment. I hated when the smile began to fade, first from his eyes and then his lips.

"Nathan, I've loved you, too," I said, "and I still do. But I don't need to tell you. So much has changed, and there's more..."

He dropped my arm. "Meaning Jack."

"Nathan, you know I'm not talking about Jack..."

"You don't even know it yet, but you are! Anyway, you might as well be; you act just like him," he said, and I marveled at how quickly his great smile changed to a smirk.

"You know what, Nathan? There was a time I would have slapped you silly for saying that;" I answered, my fists on my hips, "But," I ended, mumbling, "I had no idea how hard it was... Let's just be honest," I said clearly, "The real reason you don't join us is because it's so hard." Nathan looked away. What I deleted, thank goodness, was the rest of my unspoken diatribe, *"Because if you'd ever nerve-up and admit you're a Christian, you'd have to change things in your perfect life!"'* It had been a long day.

"OK I'm sorry; Maybe I got carried away," I sincerely admitted, "But the truth is, I'm not like Jack at all. He makes being a Christian look easy and believe me... it's not. That is, not if you do it right. And I'm always stumbling all over myself and getting things wrong...obviously," I said.

"So then why... why go through it when it doesn't have to be this way?" Nathan said, his voice quiet.

"Nathan. It's real...I can't give it up."

"But you can give 'us' up?" He asked incredulously. "What you have now is more real than love?" His face changed and his eyes got dark with passion. "All this sword play is more important than we are!" He asserted angrily.

"You've forgotten," I said, finally tired, and extracting my arm. "You gave up on me. Remember? Let's face it. I'm not who you want me to be anymore. I don't fit in with our clique, and that's 'way' inconvenient." I looked over at a group of girls walking toward the parking lot and spotted Brittney and Jenna among them. "I need more now, and I'm not talking about a person..." I said, unable to finish and continue putting into hokey words anything as important as what I was feeling. After all, I'd become one of those *dreaded believers*, a high school misfit, a teenage Christian *zealot*: an adolescent who loved God and risked the ridicule of her peers. I was growing integrity, sprouting it like feathers in down. It was horrible, but true, and all it cost was every bit of cool I'd worked so darn hard to beg, borrow, buy, steal, grab, glom, seize, snatch and grasp. Now, I was about as uncool as it got. Nathan was silently staring at me, and I looked him squarely in the eye. "For once, please, be honest. Your reputation is more important than '*we are*,' and more important than '*love*.' So, quit laying the blame on me," I said softly.

"I wasn't the one to change everything."

"And I'm not the one ignoring the truth."

"After this party, when nothing happens to me, or anyone else, you'll come to yourself again," he continued as though I hadn't spoken, "...And just maybe, it won't be too late for us," he said, standing abruptly and turning to leave.

"Nathan, for some reason that's making no sense to me right now. You're a part of all this. If you are the *Link*, and you go to that party without accepting your role, you'll be putting yourself and the rest of us in danger," I said, growing angry.

Then looking back over his shoulder, he said, "Call me if you change your mind. The party is at Rachel's house, and I'll be glad to pick you up."

"Nathan, listen to me. What about the things you've seen? What about the Guardians?"

"If you don't come, I won't wait for you. By the way, it's not Alice, it's Alyssa, and she'll be there. And you'll end up spending the rest of your junior and senior year with your new friends—because you won't hear from me again—I mean it. This time is the last time."

As he walked away, the old unreformed, untransformed, un-transported, whatever, part of me—wanted to chase him down the walkway and beat him with my binder. But that same old unreformed part of me would never allow herself to look that desperately stupid. No siree. I liked to save the desperately stupid looking stuff for the new, improved me.

I suppose I walked to my car with a modicum of poise, but it felt like I staggered there under an oppressive weight. And I was grateful my "old-ex-friends" had already left, and that I didn't run into anyone I knew very well—because at the moment I was feeling a bit bi-polar. I was sure the old me would have won the battle of this identity crisis and tried to rip someone a new ear hole.

By the time I got home I'd settled down, amazed that the constant recitation of scripture was now second nature and seemed to function a lot like the anti-anxiety pills my mom took. Jack had given Hailey and Tessa rides, so I wasn't surprised I'd beat my sister home. I set my backpack down on the table and wandered down the hallway in search of my mom. She was sitting on the edge of the bed in her room, looking out the wide sliding doors onto the back deck. The afternoon light fell on her face, and I saw the myriad of minute lines like dry tributaries webbing their way across her perfect features. She sat motionless; her eyes open but unseeing, and I wondered what she was thinking about, or where she was.

"Hey, I'm home!" I announced with forced cheer, hoping to snap her out of her reverie. It took several seconds before her head turned in my direction. I could tell this was not one of her better days.

"Oh, Cassie." There was a pause, and then she said quietly, "How was school?" I knew she didn't really want to know any details, but I couldn't help wondering what her reaction would be if I told her the truth. *Well, Mom, I didn't do so well in algebra, but I totally kicked the crud out of the forces of evil. Then Nathan—you know, the "real keeper"— well, he makes fighting evil seem easy.* ...No, maybe not. I came over and sat down next to her.

"I guess you could say my day was really, really good ... and really, really bad. How was yours?" I asked.

She didn't answer but looked a little more closely at me than usual. Finally, she said, "What's happened? You've changed." She spoke listlessly, but I was surprised she'd noticed.

"What makes you say that, Mom?" I asked, wondering if I could keep her engaged for a few more sentences.

"I don't know," she said, looking away. "I think I need to call the doctor again. The pills he gave me make me so tired. But at night, I still can't sleep..." She stared ahead vacantly. "But I'm tired all the time..." and then she added, "and I can't find ...a thing."

"What are you looking for, Mom? Maybe I can help you," I said for the hundredth time.

"No," she said, looking off into the yard. "I don't think you can help. I think I've lost it," she answered quietly.

My mental response was always the same, *"Yep, you've lost it for sure,"* I couldn't help it. And usually that would be that, but for some reason I asked, "Mom, what is it you're looking for?" She didn't answer.

"Would you go bring me one of the little pills in the second bottle over there? I'm starting to get one of my migraines. That's a sweet girl. ...Thank you," she said, as I went to fetch her a pill. I came back with it and a glass of water and tucked her into bed. She gazed up at me, and I noticed the dark smudges beneath her once sparkling eyes— eyes now dulled by medication and confusion.

"You rest. I'll bring you some soup in a few minutes," I said, sliding out of her room and wondering whether she had headaches or just needed to be left alone. Either way, it made me want to cry. I knew it was an improvement from my past reaction. All I'd ever wanted to do before was scream. Still, I wasn't sure I appreciated my change.

I heard a door slam outside and looked out the window. It was Tessa and Jack. I watched Jack for a long moment, and I could tell he was standing beside his car a fraction longer than necessary, looking in my direction. I knew he couldn't see me, but I felt my face begin to flush. What the heck was happening to me? I decided I was losing my mind if I was seriously having feelings for both Jack *and* Nathan. At the same time disliking them both—by the time I figured any of it out, they'd probably both be gone.

"Fine!" I said aloud.

"What's fine?" Tessa asked, dragging her huge book bag over the threshold. She wore a chartreuse shirt layered under a blue and pink floral sweater, and a red and black plaid pleated skirt with saffron tights and brown chukka boots. The remarkable combination brought me great joy, and I smiled inwardly for at least the fourth time that day. I actually had to turn away, so she didn't see the outward amusement in my eyes.

"Oh, nothing really, I was just thinking that if the boys of this world decide they can't wait for me to figure out who I am, and who I like, then that's just fine!" I stated, a little more emphatically than I'd intended.

"And 'the boys of the world' just happen to be Nathan and who?" she asked, a smile coming to her greatly magnified eyes.

"Nathan and anybody ...everybody!" I said, walking past her into the kitchen.

"The rest of us call him, 'Jack,' but you can call him *anybody*, or *everybody*, if you want to," Tessa called out as she headed up the stairs. I heard her giggling as she went. Being a smart aleck wasn't her finest quality, and I grumbled over my hot tea waiting for my mom's soup to warm.

Tessa changed her clothes, and I heard her come

downstairs and open the door to Mom's room. She closed it after a short minute. "Is she eating the soup?" I asked.

"No, but she's sitting up looking at it. I think she will. It's probably still a little hot," Tessa answered, looking at me curiously before asking, "You feel like taking me somewhere?"

"I suppose. Where do you want to go?" I asked.

"Let's go see Darius," Tessa stated, heading for the door. I don't know why, but it sounded exactly right.

It was still early enough in the day for a few more hours of light in the forest, and this time we drove further up several logging roads and got closer before having to walk. When we neared her small cabin, we saw smoke coming from the chimney. Once again, I couldn't help noticing how tidy her place was, and I also observed that she had piled more wood against her house for the coming winter. There were no animals in sight; only a few birds on her clothesline, and I wondered where they all might be. I found out when she opened her door.

Before we could knock, the door swung open, and Darius stood before us with a smile like an open invitation to a party spread across her face. Her hair was electrified by the static in the air, and a few single strands stood out from her head as though they were scared stiff. As usual, light shone from somewhere behind her and she patted at her halo as though she had just emerged from the beauty parlor, running a wrinkled hand over her clean, colorfully tattered clothes. There was just nothing about the woman that didn't make me smile.

"Come in out of the chilly weather, girls!" she said, bustling us into the warmth of her small dwelling. On every chair, and stretched around the hearth, were creatures great and small. At least five, and probably six, graced the room, and I wondered where we were going to find a place to sit. "Now, Simon and Thaddeus—I want you to meet Cassie and her sister, Tessa," she said to the dog and coon lying near the hearth. And I swear, the mangiest racoon I'd ever seen, and the old greyhound, both animals present at our first visit, lifted sleepy heads to look at us. Again, the sweet dog thumped his thin tail in quiet welcome. A small Bantam Rooster spread his wings in a show of might before flying to the top of the counter for what seemed a better view. "Oh, Frederique. I know you must have a front row seat to everything, mustn't you?" Darius chuckled. Turning, she addressed the others. "But it would be ever so polite if a couple of you children would offer your seats," she said to the two cats and duck occupying both of her extra, overstuffed chairs. Chuckling, she proceeded to roust them and fluff the cushions clean. The cats stretched, and advanced on us with tails raised like flags on sailing vessels, rubbing up against our legs. The duck merely waddled over and settled down on the hearth, where the cats followed, stretched, and encircled its feathered body with their own. "Thank you, Dorcus, Naomi, and Ruth. Truly, you are queens," she said to them sweetly.

Tessa and I shared smiles over this strange menagerie, and then took the seats they'd vacated. Darius went to the small counter dividing the kitchen from the rest of the room and turned back to us carrying a tray. On it were three cups, a pot of steaming cocoa, and a plate with three large, oatmeal raisin cookies.

I stared at it for a moment before deftly stating the obvious. "You knew we were coming..." and then smartly asked what I didn't want to know... "How?" Darius smiled sweetly without speaking, and I added, "Never mind!" At which point we all laughed.

"Such an amazing day you've had!" Darius exclaimed, looking at both Tessa and me, and clapping her hands in front of her mouth. "You should be so proud of the work you've done, and how far you have all come in such a short time!"

Tessa smiled over her cup of hot chocolate, her large glasses steaming up. I smiled too. A sense of joy and a feeling of accomplishment beginning to well up inside me. Darius definitely had a way of bringing the best out of a person. We ate our cookies and drank the rich sweet cocoa, and I felt like an entirely different being.

"How did you feel, Cassie? Were you frightened?" Darius asked, a twinkle of excitement in her eyes.

"It was strange. I was scared when I first saw the demons, but after we started fighting, I wasn't at all. I was a little grossed out, of course. Those Maltorphs are *so...disgusting*," I said, unable to think of a better description, "but after I put the first one to a dusty death, I really got into it. I was wondering though," I continued, "What would have happened to me if they'd been stronger? I mean, what would have happened if they'd had more of those little vampire, mood-sucking gargoyles to get energy from? And what if they'd been able to get a blow in? Would I have felt it? I know my body wasn't there, but everything sure felt real," I finished.

Darius had been sitting patiently listening to me and nodding. Then she smiled. It wasn't her happy smile, though. It was more like a sympathetic one, and I got a little nervous. "Actually, I'm surprised no one asked that question earlier," she answered. "Yes, I'm sorry to say, if the Maltorphs had been stronger, and you had been weaker, you could, and most likely would have, been injured. It would feel physical when it happened; quite painful, actually. But then, you'd find yourself back at the circle, and although your injury wouldn't appear physically, you'd probably be unable to continue fighting. You can heal from these blows, but it's not quick or easy, which is why it is so important to stay strong in the power of the Spirit. *All* actions and *all* thoughts are important to the well-being of a Guardian. Prayer, and the recitation of scripture is key, but more important still, is a personal relationship with God. Only this will give you the assurance and the strength to beat the forces of evil," she said with emphasis. "Hamaliel did well in choosing you six, but I must tell you, your next battle will not be as easily won. Now they know you are here—and they will be better prepared."

"Um, what do you mean by that? I asked, releasing my lower lip from the grip of my right incisor.

"Tomorrow night the heavens are readying for the *Link's* assimilation of the mantle. You must all be together. Seven is the number of completion. They will find you, and the battle will be...well, it's of extreme importance to both realms. Rasvampin will bring all his influence, weight, and power. Do not expect today's battle to be an example of tomorrow's force.

"What if one of the Guardians is ...um...unavailable?" I asked, wondering for the first time to myself if Nathan was the *Link*...

"You have all been chosen for specific purposes. Each of your decisions will determine tomorrow's outcome. The transfer takes place at a large gathering," Darius explained, looking as if she was watching something behind her own eyes.

"I think she means the party," Tessa interjected.

"Yes, oh my, but of course it is a party!" Darius said, smiling as though the obvious fact had been before her all along. "And such a fun-seeking group of young people, too!" she exclaimed. "But there will be a lot of darkness surrounding them. They will probably be using substances that allow easy access to those of the dark dimension. If they only knew, they would never be so careless," she said to herself, as though in their defense, "But they are young, and they do not realize so much of their lives are shaped at this time. So many important things... Forgive me; I'll get to the point.

"The first attack was not meant to be a final assault. It was setting up a situation that would result in demonic chaos. This chaos would have fueled their next attack, which is planned for the capture of the mantle and, their hope, the death of the *Link*. Your interference has only caused that plan to be altered slightly but not changed. This time it will be imperative to defeat them completely. Otherwise, believe me, Rasvampin will return. He will not give up easily."

"But how do we beat them completely? There were a lot of them and there could be so many more. There are only six of us!" I said, feeling entirely and completely overwhelmed.

"You must defeat Rasvampin," she repeated, looking steadily into my eyes. "Do not fear, there will be *others* fighting alongside you. You must maintain your courage, your worth, and focus during the onslaught of his evil assault; then you should be able to win," Darius concluded.

"*Should* be able to win?" I asked, a shiver of fear running down my spine. "And what happens to us if we aren't able to maintain our courage, focus, and what was it you said, ... worth?" I asked, feeling angry and afraid at the same time. "And what happens to the *Link*?" I added, "What happens to ...Nathan?"

"Dear me. Important questions, to be sure. There is always a risk. You should all survive. But without courage and focus, you *can* be harmed. Those are the risks. We all face them when we do battle with darkness. But light will heal you. As far as the *Link* is concerned, whoever that is, I do not have that answer. Though if you are not successful, death is very possible—if not probable. To the world, it will appear an accident, but it will happen with all the intent of Hell behind it. And as far as Nathan is concerned, the young man must come to terms with his calling, or none of this has much chance. But as we know," she said, looking over at Tessa with a gleam in her eye, "all the marks have not yet been made! So, there is hope; there is always hope! And you must not lose it now, for '*we know that all things work together for good to those who love God, to those who are called according to His purpose.*' *Romans* 8:22," she recited, a beatific smile spreading across her face.

I tried, but there was no pretending. I wasn't feeling hopeful, or even comforted by her heavenly ability to eavesdrop. "So, let me get this straight. You're telling me that if we can't beat Rasvampin tomorrow, we'll not only be responsible for losing the mantle, but also the chosen *Link's* life?" I said incredulously. I couldn't believe how long it had taken me to grasp the gravity of our situation.

"My dear, you are not responsible for the outcome, only for doing your best. Death has already been beaten; do not let it frighten you. There are so many things worse than dying that befall man every minute of the day, yet they walk about unaware that they are in such perilous shape. It will be a loss to mankind if Rasvampin should win this battle, but remember, the war has already been won, and he has already lost. Never forget this. Stand without fear against him. This alone will assure his defeat. He has a secret, and when you find it, you will be able to thrust your sword into the heart of his weakness."

I looked over at Tessa who sat leaning forward, listening it seemed, with every muscle in her body—her brain, however, being by far the largest. She didn't look the slightest bit afraid, but suddenly I was frightened for her. "I don't know about anyone else. I mean, they may all feel up to this, but the idea that we could lose tomorrow, and someone could die, leaves me without a whole lot of courage," I said, bowing my head. "Darius, I'm scared."

"Yes, dear one. And well you might be. But fear is the fight, not the things we see with our eyes, but the things we fear in our hearts. Remember this," she said, lifting my chin. "Now, finish your cocoa. Chocolate is so restorative! And I have made up some to share with the others," she said, holding up a large thermos. "Sit together and laugh! Drink your chocolate and share with each other the good news. Say the name of Jesus! Then go to your party and put the fear of God into those horrible creatures!" she said with a smile. "They aren't dealing with just anybody, you know!" she added.

"Yea," I said, finally smiling back at her, "They're dealing with the misfits of Pinedale High School!"

"Oh, that's the spirit! Now, give me a high hand!" she said, lifting her palm toward us. "I've wanted to do this for the longest time!" she added in a confiding tone, as Tessa and I laughingly gave her "high-fives."

As we walked away from Darius' little cabin, I glanced back and saw her wrapped in a threadbare shawl, light pouring out between the crooked doorframe and her tattered, lovely self, and waved. But as she held up her hand, she said, "Wait." Not in a loud voice, but almost as if she were listening to something herself. "Cassie, Tessa," she called, "What do you know about a leather satchel?" We looked at each other, shook our heads, and lifted our shoulders and hands as if to say, "nothing?" She simply smiled and waved us goodbye, going back inside to the fire, and the "children" resting beside it.

Chapter Twenty-Three

I didn't sleep very well that night. Most of it was spent fighting Maltorphs, "dusting" them over and over again. It was exhausting, and there was no end to them. By early dawn I must have been getting weary because one of the mutant lizards came up to me and took a swack at my leg and I watched it turn into baby powder. It even smelled like baby powder. Another one was heading for Jack, so I yelled to him. He turned, smiling his despicable I'm-sort-of-laughing-*at*-you smile just as the Maltorph swung. Jack's head exploded into a pile of sand. I woke up with a start, my stomach twisted and my heart beating out of my chest.

Early that morning, I decided to call Hailey.

"Hey, girl. How ya doing?" I asked, just needing to hear her voice.

"Cassie? Hi! I'm fine; well, I'm OK I'm working on being fine," she added, cheerful, but covering.

"You can't fool a fool. Wait, I guess you can... so I'll stick with, 'you can't kid a kidder!' Anyway, come clean," I said, once again wasting my dazzling humor on Hailey's overly cautious responses.

"You're no fool, Cassie, but I'll admit you're a kidder," she said, a smile in her voice. "I had a scary dream last night; that, and things are a little tough at home right now. Anyway, I'll get through it. Though I must say, it's great to hear your voice."

"I know what you mean on both counts. I had a scary dream, too, and I called just to hear yours," I responded.

"OK, now I know you're kidding," she said shyly.

"Actually, my humor isn't that subtle; so no, I'm not kidding. I called because there wasn't anyone else that, well, reassures me the way you do. But I'm having second thoughts about the reassured part... *You* had a scary dream?"

"Yea. ...Do you want to hear it?" she asked. I could hear something close to hesitation in her question.

"Of course. I need to, right? I mean we're getting down to it, Hailey. There's no fooling around. Of course, I want to hear it. Hold on just a minute though, I'm going to grab a chair and a pencil and paper and write this all down," I said, realizing in my attempt to stall for time that it might not be a bad idea.

I set my phone down without waiting for her reply, bent over and took in a lungful of air. *Anything* scary Hailey had dreamed last night meant it was ominous for real. *Crap! Crap! Crap!* In retrospect, these unbidden words were quite an improvement on my past vocabulary outbursts, and I apologized with a quick, "*Sorry Lord,*" followed immediately with another: *Crap! Crap! Crap!* "All right, I'm really sorry, Lord," I said aloud, feeling ashamed for the fear I'd already succumbed to before any fighting had even begun.

I grabbed a notebook off the table, and a pen from the drawer, picked up the phone again and sat down. "Go ahead, Hailey. I'm ready," I said, not feeling ready at all.

"Well, it's about tonight."

"Right."

"There were a lot of kids, and it was obviously the party." She began. "Unfortunately, that was the only obvious thing about the dream. One of the worst things about it was how different this dream was. It felt real, like I was there. Although, nothing was clear. I know that doesn't make sense," she said, sighing.

"It's OK, go on. What happened?" I said, proud of myself for encouraging her when I really didn't want to.

"We were there, all of us. Nathan was there, too. The Maltorphs were everywhere; so many of them. There were also other demons, and it was different. It was frightening. And Rasvampin was there."

I could tell this was getting hard for her. "Go on."

"Everything was dark—kind of foggy-like. I could see one minute, but not the next. You were fighting; Chris was fighting. Santos... Jack... But it was Nathan, something about him." I could hear Hailey breathing hard.

"Tell me, Hailey. Does he get hurt?" I asked.

"What? Oh, Cassie. I don't know! I couldn't see... All I know is he is either going to be hurt, or maybe he hurts someone, or... honestly, I couldn't tell," she said, and I thought she was hiding something.

"What do you *think* happened, Hailey?"

"Honestly, I couldn't tell! It was so misty, so confusing! The demons were different...hideous and more demonic. Nathan seemed to be on our side, but then I saw him with Rasvampin. It seemed strange. Then, everything went hazy again. Chris, Santos, and Tessa were beside him. Rasvampin was there. I was there and you and Jack..." she began to weep. "I'm sorry, I didn't really see anything; but it got so frightening; so terrible. Finally, I woke up. But not before I understood that someone, got...hurt."

"Jack?"

"...I don't know."

"Hurt or killed, Hailey?"

"I think, I'm pretty sure, someone dies."

"This is important, Hailey," I said, trying to keep my voice even. "Do you have any idea, even a hint of an idea, who it is... who will be in danger tonight?"

She was quiet for a second, which felt like an hour. Finally, she said, "I know what you're asking. But I don't know who it was. I really don't. I was afraid for every single one of us, Cassie. Believe me when I tell you that we were all in trouble, which means, we're all going to be in danger. And if Nathan *is* the *Link,* and he decides not to be with us, then Heaven help us."

"I guess that's what we're counting on ...Heaven helping us," I said, sounding to my own ears like an entirely different person had abducted my vocal cords.

"You're right, Cassie. Thank you. I've been so afraid since this dream—and I haven't been able to get perspective on it. I really needed to talk to you—because I know *Heaven is* helping us. It's just ...it was so different from my other dreams. I think that's partly what made it so scary," she added.

"Maybe that's a good thing. The rest of your dreams were so accurate. The fact this dream wasn't as clear could mean there's a chance it won't happen the way you saw it. You said it was foggy, so maybe one of us won't get hurt..." I said, the reality of her prediction starting to sink in.

"I hadn't thought of that," Hailey remarked, sounding less convinced than I needed her to be.

"Well, we should probably tell the rest of the group when we meet today; but I'm glad you told me first," I said.

"Do you think we ought to tell them? I mean it was so confusing. I feel like it could cause more harm than good," Hailey said, voicing my own fears.

"I was thinking the very same thing. I honestly don't

know. Let's pray about it and maybe the dream will become clearer. If it does, one of the others may have more insight."

"You're right. OK, then. Thanks for calling this morning. I really needed to talk to you. Do you want to tell me your dream?" she asked, amazing me with her unselfish concern.

"No, one scary dream talk before nine in the morning is my limit. I just wanted to say, hi," I said, realizing I didn't need to share after all.

"OK. I'll see you around three o'clock at the circle?"

"I'll be there. Are you going to be OK at your house? I mean, if you need to hang somewhere for a while you're welcome over here," I said, sensing she needed more consolation and a deeper sense of security.

"Thanks, Cassie, I'm fine. But pray for me, and I'll be praying for you," she responded. I realized then, I was the one who really needed more bolstering. "Oh, by the way, before I had the horrible dream, I had two more shorter dreams. But they didn't seem to have anything to do with each other, and they seemed to be about you or maybe Tessa," she said.

"And you're only just telling me *now*," I said, teasingly.

"Actually, I'd forgotten about them! The first one was about a silver necklace. Do you know something about a silver necklace— a chain?"

"No, not really. I have a few; nothing special. I lost a nice one in seventh grade, somewhere on the soccer field ...before I moved here. And I haven't seen Tessa wear one in years, but I'll ask her."

"No, never mind. It was hardly even a dream...just an image. The one about you, or I'm pretty sure it was about you —when you were younger—had to do with a man. I think it was your dad. He looked so nice, and he was holding your hand. I saw him walk over to your garage and open the outside garage door—the one you say you never open. Then, he pointed somewhere off to the side. All I could see was a thin leather folder-thingy."

"And then what?"

"That's it. I told you they were short. That's why I almost forgot them. Anyway, do you know what it is?" she asked.

"Not yet, but you're not the first person to mention it. Darius asked Tessa and me about a leather satchel, and I have no idea what it means. Anyway, I'll fill you in later. So, I'll see you today?" I said, cutting it short.

"Great. See you later. And thanks again, Cassie."

I had to give myself a serious talking to as I was sorely tempted not to shower, or moisturize, or brush my hair, and just throw on a pair of sweats. All I wanted was to run outside and open the garage door. I wanted to begin ransacking every box in sight until I found whatever satchel Darius and Hailey were talking about—and I had no idea why.

I couldn't think of anything my family or dad had ever owned that would mean a hill of beans to me when it came to fighting evil. Just as I was toweling my hair dry, Tessa barged into my room and pounced all forty-nine pounds of energized body parts onto my bed.

"I just figured out what Darius was asking us about last night!"

"Well, I just figured out *where* it is," I said, raising my eyebrows, in my futile, yet continuing attempt to stay competitive with my overachieving midget of a sister.

"Where!" she breathed, all excitement.

"You first. What do you think it is?" I asked, narrowing my eyes, as though suspicious of her claim.

"It's Father's leather case! The one he had under his

pillow the last few months of his life...the one he kept the will in, the one with our house mortgage stamped 'paid' across. You remember!" She said, seeing the perplexed look on my face.

"Honestly, I don't. I don't remember anything about that time," I answered, possibly experiencing unhappiness over this fact for the very first time.

"Then how do you know where it is?" she asked, her little face scrunched in puzzlement.

"Hailey had a dream," I admitted.

"Wow, I wonder what it could mean. This must be important. Let's go get it!" she said, galvanized once again.

"I'm almost ready. Just let me finish drying my hair." At her look, I added, "I'll be quick. I promise! No extras, just go down and see how Mom is doing today. I'll be right there!"

We stood back and opened the garage door, praying nothing would fall on us that would cause serious bodily injury. The garage-sale-that-never-happened waited as patiently for us now as it had when we'd planned it a year and a half ago. Each of us had added things as time went by, and our orderly assembly was now a haphazard arrangement of junk that needed to be hauled away. But, of course, Mother wouldn't hear of it. Neither would she hear of a garage sale on the weekend mornings she wasn't feeling well. In three more years, there would be no choice. Tessa and I would have to burn it down.

I scanned the top of the boxes looking for anything remotely resembling a satchel. Then Tessa and I began looking in the boxes. Tessa called Hailey to get a clear description of the location Hailey had seen in her dream but came back as stumped as she'd left. It simply wasn't where

Hailey had seen it. "She said, Father pointed to the top of a box on the right side facing the house," Tessa said, slouching in one of the lawn chairs we'd set out on the drive. It was only then I noticed it looked like she'd detonated small explosives among her ringlets throughout the night. She still wore a combination of articles known to her as pajamas. But her normal clothing choices made this assessment harder than one might imagine.

"Why don't you go in and get dressed? I'll put everything back, and I'll keep looking while I do. Does Mom want us to do any extra chores today?" I asked, figuring we'd have to get things out of the way before three o'clock.

"Just raking the lawn. Darn, I really want to find it. It's got to be here," she said, getting up, and looking around one more time.

"It's here, and we'll find it," I said, more confidently than I felt.

"OK."

Tessa went indoors, and I started putting things away, rechecking every box, looking under all the piles of collected paraphernalia, and despairing that anything of any value could be found anywhere within that garage. I couldn't think of a place we hadn't looked, and I hadn't checked twice. Finally, I gave up and went back inside to gather up my laundry. When I came back down, Tessa was already outside raking leaves.

The climate had become a touch warmer, and the meteorologist on the local TV channel, our own Sandy Gale, no kidding—and called, unfortunately, by all the locals, Windy Beach—said we could anticipate a break in our unseasonably dry weather by Sunday. It had been one of Pinedale's longest dry spells. I could almost visualize the clouds finally brewing up a mix of wind and water, because the air felt full of static and crackle. Tessa's morning hair made sense, and I couldn't help imagining the fright Darius' "do" would be in by now; it made me smile.

However, as I gazed out through the front window at my sister, I gasped, and sitting down on a kitchen chair, started laughing. She'd taken an old pair of pink tights and cut off both the legs. The panty part had gone on her head like a skullcap, with her hair sticking out the two thin, short, leg holes in a massive explosion of frizzy curls. The rest of her attire was comparatively drab. It consisted of a long white tee shirt, Dad's old green and yellow argyle sweater vest extending past her knees, orange leggings, and her favorite pair of combat boots. But the hair, yessiree, it did win the prize.

"So, what-cha doing?" I asked, after containing myself and wandering outside, making sure I'd wiped the tears from my cheeks.

"Just raking. I want to get my chores done early today. You know we need to be..." she'd started seriously but stopped to look up at me. I couldn't help it; I tried to hold it in but started busting up again. "I don't know what could be so funny," she said, narrowing her eyes at me, which only made it worse. "Aren't you at all worried about what we'll be facing tonight?" she asked, beginning to get angry.

"Well...well...I was," I gasped, barely able to get the words out, "but demon warriors are nothing compared to that hair of yours!" I laughed, falling on the ground, and holding my sides, in tears again.

"What's going on over there?" Jack called, walking up the drive. I tried to sit up, but the tension of the week had culminated in this cruel laughing jag, and I couldn't stop. As soon as I'd open an eye, I'd see Tessa, and begin again. It was as painful for me as it was for her. Well, almost.

"She thinks I look funny in my new hair invention," Tessa remarked, gamely smiling despite herself.

"Is that what this is all about?" Jack asked, smiling back.

"I'm...sorry. It's just...it's just...you look like a tiny... pink...human moose!" I wailed, breaking into howls of laughter. I couldn't bring myself under control, and even while I laughed, I knew it had to be all the stress. Suddenly, Jack was on the ground holding me down, while Tessa piled leaves on top me. I screamed and laughed while Tessa wreaked her revenge. Opening my eyes, Jack's laughing face came centimeters from mine. His arm was a steel band across my body. While the other held my arm down to the ground, one of his legs was thrown over me in a locked hold.

"OK, OK; enough! I give up!" I yelled, the laughter dying in my throat as I frantically struggled to no avail against Jack.

"Do you apologize to your sister for being so... hysterical over her hair?" he asked his lips almost touching my cheek.

"Yes! Yes! Anything! Just let me up!" I cried, my panic beginning to mount, and realizing too late, I needed to control myself.

"I don't know, Tessa. What do you think?" Jack asked, still facing me, his eyes clear and smiling.

Tessa must have realized my state because she relented. "OK, let her up. But no more comparisons to wildlife when it comes to my looks," she announced.

"Sorry, Tess. I promise," I said, still struggling not to laugh when I caught sight of her and wondering how long she meant to hold me to that preposterous promise.

"And that includes, Minnie Mouse," she added... undoubtedly referring to her Sunday best. Jack's eyes were looking into mine...

"Yes, yes! Just let me up, Jackson Graham, or I swear... I will make you pay!" Of course, *that* was a big mistake.

He tilted his face above mine and smiled wickedly down on me. "Now this should be interesting," he said, and shifted his weight as though settling in. "Just how do you plan to make me pay?" I stifled the rising panic.

"Really, Jack, you're hurting me," I lied.

"No, I'm not," he said quietly, and preceded to hold me prisoner for another very long three seconds. His eyes were fastened onto mine, before jumping up and pulling me to my feet. I didn't know whether I was relieved or not, but I couldn't walk very straight.

Tessa was hiding her giggles behind her hand, and I shot her a quelling look which she ignored completely. In fact, she lowered her hand and chortled out loud. I supposed I more than had it coming.

"Let's go in and get something to eat," I said, trying to shake the leaves out of my hair and clothes, and awkwardness off my demeanor.

"Sounds good to me," Jack stated, walking to the door, and holding it open for us. Leaning down, he nabbed the newspaper off the stoop on his way in. Opening it at the table, he began reading the headlines as I made my famous broiler cheese sandwiches. "Local Girl..." he stopped abruptly and closed the paper. Both Tessa and I stared at him. "You might want to sit down," he said to us. "Tessa, I think this is about you."

"Oh, great!" she groaned, slapping her head in exasperation, and sliding onto a chair. "I knew I was getting off too easy."

"It's probably not so bad. Go on, Jack. What's it say?" I prompted.

Jack looked at me for a second before opening the paper again, but finally he nodded. "'Local Girl Genius,' that's the heading. It goes on to say: 'Local girl, Theresa Conner, who turned twelve-years-old last March, has an IQ of at least 150. Her teachers, Mr. Julian, from the Pinedale Junior High, administered the ISIQ test, and Mrs. Gurley, of Pinedale

High School, administered the Wechsler IQ test. Both suspected Theresa had been purposely hiding her exceptional intelligence. Upon speaking with Theresa's mother, she informed us that it didn't surprise her to find this out. She knows her daughter Theresa 'wants to live a life of an average girl.' Her teachers don't know how long this will be possible, however, since she has tested above the school's curriculum. 'We've always known Tessa was brilliant, but we didn't realize until recently, how brilliant,' Mrs. Gurley told us. Both scores for these tests ranged from 149 to 152. Anything above 142 is considered genius. Theresa lives in Pinedale with her mother and older sister. She attends the junior high while taking several classes at the high school. According to testing scores, she could attend college classes in several, if not all, areas of study. Her highest marks were in math and science." Jack folded the newspaper and laid it on the table.

"So..." I said, looking at my sister's pale face, "that wasn't *so* bad." She stared at me, and if her hair hadn't still been sticking up in those silly stockings, I swear she would have broken my heart. As it was, I had a hard time keeping a straight face, so I tried making up for it. "Look, I told you. You don't have to go anywhere, or do anything, you don't want to. You're Tessa Connor. Why on Earth would you dumb-yourself-down for anybody? Dad would be so mad at you right now," I said, fuming for her benefit.

"Dad would be homeschooling me. I wouldn't have to go away," she said sadly, a tear forming in her eye and slipping down her cheek—this time breaking my heart.

I pulled her close, her bushy antlers brushing my nose, and said, "You're smart enough to teach yourself. You're as smart as Dad ever was. Just don't be afraid of it, OK?" She threw her arms around my neck and hugged me tight.

"You're right. I'm not going anywhere until *I* decide!"

"No! You're not! Now get out of here!" I said kidding, but she smiled and ran up the stairs to her room. Jack and I looked at each other and started laughing.

When I got silent, he looked over at me, took another sandwich off the plate, and asked, "What's wrong?"

"I'm pretty sure she even dumbed herself down on *those* IQ tests."

Chapter Twenty-Four

Jack didn't stay too long after eating my famous cheesy broil. I began feeling uncomfortable around him after we'd been alone for a few minutes with nothing in our mouths to chew on, and I think he could tell. It was ridiculous. I'd look at him and start feeling awkward. I'd known him all this time, and now, right before our big battle, I was getting strange. Perfect. He gave me his annoying half-smile a couple times, the one where I couldn't tell what the heck was going on in that brain of his. I was just plain relieved when he said he needed to leave and I didn't have to sit and speculate, because, honestly, if I'd had to guess, it would have been, *what a silly sap you are, Cassie Conner*. Of course, as soon as he'd gone and I was left to myself, the minutes began to drag.

I finished every single chore I could think to do with unprecedented speed. I knew I needed to spend my time preparing for the coming night, but no matter how I tried to get ready, my faith wandered in the garden of Gethsemane. Instead, I found myself unconsciously attending to the things that soothed me. In other words, I primped. I'm not proud to have discovered myself in the middle of a hair conditioning routine—a surefire recipe used by Princess Charlotte of Monaco—according to one of my old fashion magazines—but I will say my hair was wondrous when I finished. I would have stopped there, realizing the shallow nature of this pursuit, but there *were* my nails to consider. After all, I would be wielding a large sword, and my hands would be in full view. I stretched that little endeavor out as long as possible, but it still seemed as though time moved at an altered speed, and I wondered how long it would take for the sound of my scream to reach the ears of another human. It had been a while since I'd thought of interesting problems that my dad would have formulated for me...and I smiled.

One good thing, I realized, was that I was reciting my scriptures non-stop. But I couldn't figure out why I was avoiding prayer. This question hung in front of me, but it was hard to look at directly. Finally, when I'd run out of everything else I could consider, I faced it. As I looked at it squarely, I knew. It was the little matter of faith: Faith in God and his master plan. Because how could I trust Him when he'd let me down once already?

Sure, I knew there were things worse than death ...*didn't I?* I asked myself; *no, I guess I really didn't,* I answered. Because even though death might not have been the worst thing that happened to my father now that he was with God, I personally couldn't think of anything worse than losing him. After all, now he wasn't with me. Eventually, I had to ask myself the question, *what if someone else I love died?* ... My mind began to reel. The words Hamaliel said about my willingness to do battle came back to me: "Your future, and the one you love, depends on it." *The one I loved. The one I loved.* The words kept repeating themselves in my mind. Suddenly, I wasn't sure it was Nathan. Yes, I loved him, but not the way the words resonated. Who was Hamaliel referring to? ...*Tessa.*

The very thought froze my heart. *No God,* I pleaded, *not Tessa. Take me. Take my future, just not Tessa.* I got up and went to her room. She was sitting on her bed cross-legged, her hands folded in prayer. Her eyes were closed, and a small smile curved her lips. I was relieved she'd removed the inspired hair contraption, so I wasn't tempted to laugh. Then I noticed something lying on her lap. I couldn't tell what it was because the folds of her shirt covered it, but the longer I stood looking at it, the more it seemed to shimmer. I was frozen, and then Darius' words came back to me. *Whom Evil seeks to destroy, is the one chosen to be worthy of the mantle.*

"Is it you?" I asked loudly, unable to keep the anger from my voice. "What are you doing hiding this from me! Why didn't you tell me?" I yelled.

Her eyes popped open in surprise at my exclamation, and I saw her take a long indrawn breath. "Cassie... What?"

"Sure, act all innocent, but I've caught you. Give me that thing!" I yelled, trying to grab what was on her lap. She deftly moved and I fell across her bed.

"Here, you want this? You can have it," she said, looking at me, I imagine, with the same expression I'd had not long ago when I assured her that she was just outside of Crazy Camp. She handed me a small crystal rosary.

"What is this?"

"It's a rosary..."

"I know that! What are you doing with it! Is it the mantle? Did Hamaliel give it to you?"

"I got it five years ago in San Luis Obispo. You were with me. It was one of Dad's last trips—we went to the California Missions? You really don't remember?"

"No. I told you already," I said, half sheepishly, half of me still inexplicably mad.

She raised her eyebrows. "What's going on?"

"I got scared. I thought you might be the *Link*," I said, sitting down on the edge of her bed.

"And what if I am?"

"Are you just saying that? Because so help me…"

"Finish that sentence, Cassie… 'Because so help me, *God*?'" she asked, unsmiling.

"Don't mess with me right now," I said, not feeling even the slightest bit chastened.

"Alright. I'm sorry. None of us know, and as far as I know, it's not me. But Cassie, what if it is, or what if it's you?"

"Don't worry, it's not, me." I said, confident I wasn't cut out to wear a mantle of world peace unless it was ermine. Besides, I could see trouble brewing over *that* accessory even as I imagined it.

"The thing is, it could be." She said, "and it could be Jack, or Hailey, or Santos, or even Christian." We both looked at each other and smiled. "Well, OK, maybe Christian's stretching it a bit. But I still think it's Nathan. Truth is we don't know yet. And Cassie, any one of us should feel honored to be chosen…right?"

"Right. Big honor. Sounds more like getting stuck with evil's homing beacon on you right up until the last minute. Then when it's finally converted, absorbed, whatever…you can still be annihilated for a short while. Great honor," I said, purposely setting my mind against the honor of it. The fact was that it was a mantle of power given to the Earth and passed along through generations of souls working toward love and peace, like Gandhi and Mother Theresa. However, my sister knew me very well.

"Cassie, you don't fool me. I know better, and I know when you're scared. And you're not scared for yourself; you're scared for me. But Hamaliel trusts you. He knows you have the faith to fight for this cause, protect the others, and me. Most importantly, you have the faith to protect the *Link*. And you can handle the burden of being chosen when, or if, that time ever comes," she said, her eyes shining. My insides suddenly felt loose—and I knew neither Hamaliel or Tessa realized how weak I really was.

"I'm glad you've been coming to more sword practice," I said, trying to smile.

"Yes, well, I figured I'd better do my part. Even though physicality has never been my strong suit. Still, being in a spirit body is different, and I've found it so freeing."

"The fighting?"

"No, but I'm getting better."

"Are you afraid for tonight?"

"Yes." Tessa shivered slightly, "But there've been worse things..." she said.

"Oh really," I said sarcastically, "And just what would those things have been?"

"Doubt. Doubt and fear. Doubt that God wasn't real, and fear that I was alone," she said, looking at me intently. "Rasvampin and his demons are nothing in comparison to that. In fact, even though I'm afraid of them, and this sounds like a contradiction, their being here has given my soul courage. 'Blessed are those who believe without seeing,' but I have seen, and believing is pretty easy now. Evil is a very simple truth that even my mind can't refute."

I was shocked. I never knew she'd ever doubted a moment in her life, or that her brilliance had, at times, been the enemy of her faith. But her words were like arrows finding the bull's eye on my heart. I took her hands, and one of the Psalms I'd repeated to myself throughout the morning surged through me and I repeated it aloud. "*...You have delivered my soul from death. Have you not kept my feet from falling, that I may walk before God in the light of the living?*" Tessa's smile seemed filled with light.

I smiled back, and stated, "Still. You know how I overrate my importance in almost every situation, so I want you to stay close to me tonight. You're not to go anywhere, or do anything, without me along, understood?"

She smiled. "I'll stay close, I promise," she said, adding just the slightest bounce on the bed. It made me look at her once more, and it dawned on me again that twelve years old was very, very, young to be facing mean monsters, let alone this kind of evil.

After my talk with Tessa, I went back to my room and began praying. I was still afraid, and I didn't have any assurances Tessa or I would live through the night—or that either Jack or Nathan ...or any of the Guardians would. In fact, I think I felt one of us probably wasn't going to make it. Still, I knew I could trust God. Don't ask me why; it's still a mystery to me. All I know is my prayers became pleading. Then, I cried as I begged, until finally something inside me let go, and I began feeling at peace. He'd heard me. He'd heard me all along. He'd always heard me, and He loved me. And that was enough.

When my phone rang, it almost went to voicemail before I came to my senses and answered it. Hailey was on the line. "Hi, Cassie. I just wanted to let you know that Raphael, I mean Santos and I; we'll be headed over in about thirty minutes. We spent the afternoon praying together, and it's been great. He went home but he's going to come back and pick me up. By the way, I told my mom I was staying over with you tonight. Will that be OK with your mom?"

"Sure, in fact she'll love it," I said, thinking about the many times my mother had asked why my friends never stayed here... "Um, did you say thirty minutes?" I asked, a bit befuddled.

"Yes, I know it's a little late. We'll try and get there sooner if we can," she said, apologetically.

"No, no, I'm sure that's fine," I said, completely taken off guard by how much time had passed. "By the way, what are you wearing tonight?" I asked, snapping back to my superficial self with record speed.

"Well, I'm not sure. I mean, we're not actually going into the party or anything—except in the spirit realm—are we?" Hailey asked uncertainly.

"No, but if I'm not mistaken, did you, or did you not, refer to Santos as Raphael?" I asked pointedly. There was silence and then, unable to hide the smile in her voice, she answered, "What do you mean?"

"Hailey, do you really think you can hide from me?" I chided.

"Oh Cassie, please don't say anything...we're only friends. He doesn't like me that way. But it's nice to have a guy as a friend. I've never had one before."

"No, of course I won't say anything. I know how important friends are," I answered truthfully. "But how long do you have before Santos is back?"

"About twenty, maybe twenty-five minutes."

"Right. So... back to my first question, 'What are you wearing?' Because if you haven't considered it yet, I might have a suggestion or two," I added.

"Oh! I would love your help!"

"OK, your green blouse is cool; the one cut on the bias. And wear your darker washed jeans and those short black leather boots you wore once. I really liked those. Lighten up on the eyeliner just a tad. Use a dark gray if you have it, to bring the green out in your eyes. Let's see...part your hair just slightly off center, and don't wear a ponytail—your hair is so gorgeous. Oh, and your small silver hoops, and last but not least, just a dab of whatever your perfume is. I love it whenever I get a whiff—one's outfit isn't complete without a sweet scent," I ended, not wanting to *completely* overwhelm her with support.

"Oh, Cassie; thank you. You're amazing. There's just one thing, though. You know those boots...well, they're not real leather," she admitted.

My eyes wanted to roll backwards, but I don't think my voice betrayed me. I decided to imitate Darius, my new female "friend role model," conjuring what I thought would be her content, if not her tone. "Isn't it amazing? A person would never know by looking at them. What a good eye for quality imitation you have!" It wasn't a lie, but my personality was stretching into areas of benevolence it had never known, especially regarding fashion—as if Tessa hadn't stretched me enough.

"Really? Oh, thank you, Cassie. I do care how I look, I just never..."

"I know, and you're welcome, but you better hurry. I'll see you soon."

"Right, I'll see you in a little while. Bye!"

Yep, time had finally decided to move while I was not watching, and a lot like boiling water it had made up for its pokey ways by racing ahead. It was already 2:40. I looked in my own closet and found for the first time in the remembered history of my life as a fashionista—which I'll admit, memory-wise only went back as far as my father's death, but I was certain extended into childhood—I was completely, and crazily, uninspired. It was as if all my style-juice had been poured out onto Hailey; oh well, it was fashion well served. Ignoring my own advice, I grabbed a pair of faded jeans, my softest black t-shirt, an old "cozy days" Stanford sweatshirt my dad had given me in junior high, and put on my most comfortable tennis shoes—which I'd *never* worn for anything accept running or PE, *ever*. When I looked in the mirror, it was almost shocking... Shocking that I could still be so cute. Well, also shocking that I was completely without style. But, I reasoned, tonight, I was headed into battle. I needed the assurance of comfortable clothes. If anybody had a problem, they'd just have to deal with it. I was going as Cassie Connor, *new and improved*. I smiled at myself, straightening my shoulders, and turning sideways in the mirror. Then I sat down on the side of my bed and took my tennis shoes off and put on a pair of really great leather boots—which helped my faith.

At a couple minutes to 3:00, Tessa and I decided to head for the Pine Circle together. Chris and Jack were heading into the trees when we came out of the house. Jack walked in front, and Chris kept trying to trip him with one of his crutches. Tessa and I both looked at each other at the same time, but she looked way more disturbed by his antics than I felt. I just thought, as usual, he was funny in an undomesticated way.

"You and Chris doing OK? I mean, you two getting along as friends?" I asked.

"Sometimes," Tessa answered, unconvincingly.

"What do you mean?"

"OK, I'm going to tell you, but I hate putting it into words," she said, stopping, and looking at me seriously. Then she held up her hand and began counting off on her fingers. "One, he's critical of other people. Two, he's a know-it-all. Three, he thinks he's cute. Four, he's too, I don't know, too ... boyish-like."

"Boyish as in puppy-ish? I know, but Tessa, he's only fifteen..." I said, feeling like the last critique was a mite harsh coming from a twelve-year-old acting like Methuselah.

"I already know you think I'm wrong for feeling this

way," she said, looking down, "because *I* know I am. But I can't help it. I pray for him, I pray for me, and I still feel the same way."

"Maybe it has something to do with what he said to you?" I peeked around Tessa's turned face, trying to catch her eye, but she avoided mine. "I mean, I would understand if that sort of freaked you out. Maybe that's what's kept you from seeing him clearly?" She remained silent. "When someone tells you that you don't have a choice, it can be hard. I mean, if he'd just come around being his charming feral self, who knows? Maybe you would have naturally fallen for him in time, but now you've kind of set yourself against him. All his flaws are magnified," I said, thinking, that in her place, that's how I'd have reacted.

She looked up at me and nodded. "That might be possible."

It's hard to understand how the impulse to strangle someone can leap upon you in an instant, until that someone is a twelve-year-old saying something like, "*That might be possible,*" to your sage sisterly words of wisdom. I managed to restrain myself. "Come on, let's go," I said, walking down the steps and heading toward the Pine Circle.

Chapter Twenty-Five

When we got to the Pine Circle, I sat across from Chris, and the four of us began talking about Rasvampin. Everyone was on edge, and we dove in, not waiting for Santos and Hailey before discussing things we thought His Demon-ship might have as a weakness. These were basically the same ideas we'd come up with since the day Hailey first dreamed about him. Pride was the obvious choice, but then Chris presented the new idea that Rasvampin himself could have a weakness for drugs. I couldn't help it. I cracked up and said, "He most likely has a weakness for sin too," and laughed some more.

Chris didn't like my joke, while Jack and Tessa thought we were both crazy. The truth was that nothing we came up with sounded right.

It had been obvious from the moment we sat down that Jack kept staring at me, something he'd never done before. I wanted to tell him to stop—it was so annoying. At the same time, I didn't want him to know I'd noticed. Achieving these together was a difficult task. Thankfully, we saw Santos and Hailey coming through the trees. Jack stood up to greet them, but then moved over next to me when they came and sat down. It was as if he wanted to make me nervous. I knew I didn't need to be thinking of anything except what was coming down later. The last thing I needed was Jack Graham distracting me and making me lose focus. Heck, I might end up "dusting" myself.

After we said "hi" to Santos and Hailey, everybody commented on how *nice Hailey looked*. Of course, I silently congratulated myself on my masterful accomplishment. It took time, but Hailey's color returned to a natural shade of pink. Finally, Jack took over.

"OK we're all here now, so I thought I'd tell you why I wanted to meet this early before the battle tonight," Jack started. "We know how to use our weapons, and I don't think we need too much more practice in the circle, but I think we should talk about strategy. And I also thought we should get together and talk about anything that needs discussing...and of course, pray together," he said, looking around.

I peered over at Hailey as she cleared her throat. "I had a dream last night I should probably share," she said, her brow creased with concern.

"Great, let's hear it," Jack said, and all my overly optimistic compatriots voiced their agreement.

"It was different than my other dreams. It was very foggy. I spoke to Cassie about it this morning. I prayed about it and asked God to tell me what it meant. Anyway, what I believe God told me is that nothing is clear about the future... But you should all know that tonight, like in my dream, we *are* going to be in danger. Someone, any one of us, maybe all of us, could be in danger of being hurt. Someone might be in danger of... of... something more," she said, stalling. "I felt in my dream, that even though I didn't see it happen, and I didn't see who—um...I felt someone might die." She rushed ahead with the rest, "I'm sorry for sharing all this because it doesn't have to happen; nothing in our future is for sure. But I thought I should tell you anyway," she finished, finally looking up at everyone's fixed stares.

"Um, I thought you guys would want to know," I said, breaking the silence. I sensed an immediate exhalation of breath, not of relief, but as if unaware, collectively, each person had been holding their breath, waiting for someone to say something.

"I'm glad you told us, Hailey," Santos said, looking at her with his quiet eyes, and I could tell he hadn't already been told. His reaction was amazingly calm and sounded genuine. I couldn't help being impressed. If I hadn't been warned earlier about our possible doom, my own reaction wouldn't have been nearly so relaxed. In fact, with others to support Hailey, I'm sure I would have resorted to hyperventilating.

"Yea, we needed to know," Jack said, looking strained, but sounding pretty composed. I looked at Tessa, and although her demeanor was calm, her face was pale.

Chris, his eyes wide, said what the rest were probably feeling, but not saying. "Holy cow. That makes this whole thing a lot more real for me, that's for sure."

"Maybe we all needed to come back to that. I mean, we started there. We were scared stiff the first time we saw the Siphons, but after a while, it became sort of a contest. I don't know about the rest of you, but at times I've had the feeling of being in an intense competition, especially after doing away with so many of those energy-suckers. After I started killing the Maltorphs, I really, kind of, started to enjoy myself," Jack said. "But we can't let ourselves forget this isn't a game. Evil is for real."

"I think the Maltorphs were easier than they might have been. We took a lot of their power away when we killed so many Siphons," Santos said. "They were not very strong against us. I wonder if they will have more power this time?" he speculated aloud.

"Maybe," Tessa said, "They've had time to regroup, but then again, if Nathan doesn't change his mind, we'll be at a party with a lot of the same people. And hopefully there hasn't been enough time since yesterday for Siphons to re-attach, because the Maltorphs seem to need a constant supply of energy to fight us," Tessa said.

"That's true. But all they'll have to do is bring more. I was fighting four and five at a time, and I was lucky not to get sliced," Chris said.

"First of all, let's not forget. We don't fight alone. God is with us. Second, we were all pretty busy, and they'll try to take us out one-by-one. Only then can they can get to the *Link*..." Jack said.

"So that Rasvampin can get to the *Link*..." Hailey said, gazing off as though reliving it.

"All right then; we don't let that happen. We protect Nathan from every side..."

"Ah, Jack..." I said, hesitantly.

"Yea?"

"Are we *sure* Nathan is the *Link*?" I asked, knowing when I spoke the words, if the can I'd opened had been chock full of worms, I'd have been overjoyed—but I'd just opened a tin full of maggots. Hailey, Santos, Chris, and Jack, *especially* Jack, looked at me as if I were trying to mortally mess with them. Only Tessa, who knew the workings of my outrageous brain, sat silently examining her hands.

Finally, Jack said, "You're not kidding." It was a statement rather than a question, as he'd ultimately decided even *my* humor wasn't that low.

"I know I convinced you—all of you—that he was the *Link*. But at the time, *I* was convinced! Especially after he became one of us... I mean what are the odds? Well, I guess we don't really know that... but a lot has happened since then. A lot has happened to me... and I don't know. I have a little different idea about what, or who, or what, ...I don't know!" I said, exasperated.

Jack turned and looked at me full in the face, his eyes serious and his voice gruff. "Just answer one question. Hamaliel said, in fact he told me, that a lot depended on you. So, tell me, *tell us*. Is he *the one you love?*"

"What do you *mean* Hamaliel told...?" I started.

"Just answer it, Cassie."

I dropped my head. "I care about him... and I love him *...in a way*. But when I really thought we had something, I didn't really love anyone but myself. That's the truth. So, I don't know what you want me to say..." I said, knowing exactly what he wanted me to say. But I could feel Jack's overwhelming nearness even in the presence of the group. I felt like a traitor to Nathan... and I could only take so much humiliation.

"Is he the one you love, Cassie?" Jack repeated, only this time, although his voice hadn't audibly changed, I felt emotion in his words as surely as if he'd reached over and touched my hand with the tips of his fingers.

I looked up and gave in to the inevitable truth. "No. Now that I know what love is, I know he's not *the one I love*," I stated, without revealing even a glimmer of the thrill I felt course through me when I saw the look that dawned in Jack's eyes.

Jack turned back around as though nothing had happened between us, thank goodness, and said, "Well, this changes things for sure. We've been going on what Hamaliel said to Cassie."

"OK, maybe I should already know this, but what did the angel actually say to you?" Chris asked.

"When I was leaving, he told me to *come back to God*. He

said *my future and, ...*then, it sounded like, *the one you love depends on it.* But truthfully, I was pretty out of it. Is that what it sounded like to you?" I said, looking at Jack and then, "Tessa?"

"You know, I've been thinking. Hamaliel was leaving, and it really wasn't clear, but I thought he said, 'the *ones* you love,'" she said a little sheepishly.

"Well, Jack?" Chris asked.

"Yea, I guess it *could have* been that, now that I think about it," he said, smiling grimly.

"Well, how will we know? I mean, who the *Link* is?" Chris asked, a bit anxiously.

"Darius told me and Cassie that, we all, the seven of us, had to be together when the mantle is passed. So, does it matter?" Tessa asked.

"Yea, it matters, considering Rasvampin is after that person!" Chris said, showing actual fear for the first time since I could remember. Never in a million years did I think I'd feel this, but I was beginning to relate to the pye-dog.

"There will be a mantle. It will be given to the *Link*, and there will be a war. That is what Darius told us when we went to her cabin. And all that will probably happen tonight. But don't be afraid, Chris. If you are the *Link*, I'll protect you," Santos said, chiding Chris with his grin. Chris couldn't help smiling back.

"Look, I'm not worried about me..." For just an instant, his eyes shot over to Tessa and back—and I wondered if anyone besides me caught it.

I knew he felt the same way I did, not wanting the title, but willing to take it rather than letting someone we cared about get stuck with—the honor. ...So, who was the *Link?* The question lingered on everyone's mind, but I managed to force it out of mine. I decided I didn't want to know. I was afraid.

"So, is Nathan completely out of consideration?" Chris asked again, his voice cracking under the strain, unable to pry his mind away from the question.

"No," Tessa said clearly. We all looked at her. "Any of us, including Nathan, could be the *Link*. That's what Hamaliel told us."

"So, Nathan. Is he with us, or no?" Santos asked. "He said 'hello' to me in the hall yesterday, and I was surprised. He said it in front of his friends. They all look so funny cuz they don't dare say nothing to him about me. He seemed like he wanted to stop and talk, but then he just kept going. I wanted to tell him, 'Man, you missed a crazy battle, and we missed having you!' But he wasn't ready, or he would have stopped," Santos finished.

"Well, he hasn't talked to me, either. Not since our...you know, our fight the other day." Jack said. "How about you?" He asked, looking at me. I really didn't want to answer that question, and it annoyed me to no end he'd asked me specifically. If he'd asked the group as a whole I could have ignored him.

"Ah, yes. ...As a matter of fact, I spoke with him yesterday after school."

Jack sat waiting, and I met his silence with my own. If we'd been alone, that would have been that. He was as stubborn as a mule, and I was, well, simply firm in my conviction that I had a right to privacy. Unfortunately, his younger brother was in the same family, but more closely resembled a jackass. So, of course, Chris nosed his way into the whole thing.

"What's the matter...? What did he say, Cassie? I think we all need to know—don't you?" I glared at Chris, but of course, I knew he had a point. And that made it worse, coming from the juvenile-buttinsky...

"OK! He asked me to go to the party with him. He didn't

want anything to do with being a Guardian. He wants me to forget all this, and he told me this was my last chance. I was to call him, and he'd pick me up, or it's over for good. If I don't go with him, he's planning to blackball my existence...never mind. But, believe me, he'll be at the party tonight either way. He just won't be with us fighting evil." I lowered my voice, "because he'll be with someone else." I'd controlled my emotions, not letting anger or hurt surface. Yet, I found this last sentence sticking in my throat. I kept my eyes forward, refusing to look at anyone.

Chris broke the extended silence again with his incomparable wisdom. "So, I take it ...you're not going with him?" he asked, more a question than a statement. Hailey groaned, Santos shoved his shoulder, and Jack threw a stone at him. "Hey, I'm sorry. I was just saying..."

"Yea, well, everyone else realizes, and it ought to be obvious to you by now, Chris," I said very seriously, as he looked over at me, belligerent in his humiliation, "If I were going to a party with Nathan—or anyone—I'd have dressed a lot better than this, wouldn't I?" Finally smiling at the juvenile oaf. Everyone else laughed, but since he was never quite certain of me, it took Chris a second to pick up on the fact that I was kidding *and* letting him off the hook. Finally, when he smiled, something almost caring passed between us. ...The *crazy-Graham-cracker*.

"Cassie, I hate to ask this, but would it be too awful to call and have Nathan pick you up?" I looked at Hailey and my jaw unhinged. "No, it's not what you think," she continued quickly. "I was just wondering. If you lured him over here, maybe we could talk to him one last time...convince him. I mean, even if he's not the *Link*, he's one of us..." Hailey said, sweetly and almost pleading. I couldn't help remembering how smitten she'd been with Nathan the one time he'd spoken with her. And Santos, who'd hated Nathan in the beginning, had come around after only one or two sword fights. Even Jack had forgiven him after being betrayed. As usual, Nathan seemed to have ingratiated himself into the group without putting out much effort.

"Look, I just don't think I can do it. I'm sorry," I said.

"Cassie, this may be his last chance; you don't know," Santos said.

"And I'm responsible for his last chance?" I asked, taken aback.

"No." Jack said, turning toward me again; then he sighed. "And yes. We all are. If we can give him another chance to change his mind, we should try. I think that's what Hailey and Santos mean," Jack said without enthusiasm.

"Trust me. It will just tick him off. He has no intention of helping us. He made that more than clear," I said, looking at their uncomprehending faces. "Well, maybe you had to be there!" I said, getting frustrated, "It's just, I really don't enjoy the idea of going through all that again..." I could feel myself beginning to well up inside, and decided I wasn't going to cry, even if it took stuffing pine needles into my eyes and nose.

"You shouldn't have to, Cassie," Tessa said severely, the sympathy amplified in her lens-magnified-eyes. "I'll call Nathan and tell him to come and pick you up. When he gets here, I'll wave him over to the Circle. You don't have to be involved at all," she said, defending me the same way I'd stood up for her that morning.

"No, that's not happening; and it wouldn't work, anyway. But let's get off this. Give me some time to think about it. I'll decide before I leave here today. But don't count on it," I said, warning them.

They all nodded, but Santos said, "I'm sorry, Cassita. Can we pray before we leave you with this burden? I'm praying for lots of stuff now, and it always helps," he added.

"Sure," I said, not feeling "sure," but saying so, anyway. I mean, what was I supposed to say, "Heck no! I don't want God weighing in on this?" I was very aware how unattractive honesty could be, and I needed to be as attractive to God as possible, even if He knew how I really felt. I figured it this way; when an earthly father knew how his kid felt, he probably wouldn't be fond of tantrums either. He'd much prefer control even when he *knew* his child wanted to throw one.

Now, I'd thought it would help having Tessa begin, because it seemed she was on my side. But of course, she came up with the perfect scripture to put it all into context, making me realize why I loved her so much, and why I wanted to kill her at the same time.

She bent her fuzzy little head and began. "I know you plan our steps, Oh Lord, and as your word says, '...*I now send you, to open their eyes, in order to turn them from darkness to light, and from the power of Satan to God, that they may receive forgiveness of sins and an inheritance among those who are sanctified by faith in Me.*' And this is what we pray over Nathan. Whether he comes tonight, or tomorrow, or any day after that, we pray you open his eyes. So please, don't let Cassie feel bullied, but give her the wisdom to know if she should call Nathan tonight. Amen."

Darn her.

Chapter Twenty-Six

After Tessa's prayer, no one seemed to think they needed to add anything, and we were able to go on to the next topic. I wish I could say I was relieved, but I knew eventually I'd be calling Nathan. All I could achieve for the next hour and a half was the impossible task of trying not to think about it.

Of course, Jack and Chris made this undertaking nearly impossible as they shared their thoughts on "strategy" for the upcoming demon "war party." Jack began our training by stressing the importance of "communicating, coordinating, and executing," and told us we needed to make sure we fought "on the ground we chose." He said it was important "not to give the enemy the choice," etcetera, etcetera, etcetera —or in my vernacular, blah, blah, blah. I began wondering if he'd been reading some horrible field manual on combat. This lecture went on for at least ten minutes but felt much longer—more like nine-thousand-eighty-seven minutes multiplied by some strange math like calculus.

Then Chris added what he considered his twenty-two cents about, "staying aware of the entire battlefield," and the importance of "staying alert." Now I was certain they'd come across the same dreadful volume of information. Interestingly, just as he was making the awesome point about "paying attention while the enemy was trying to kill you," as though none of us would ever have thought of it ourselves, I was in the middle of rubbing my face so I wouldn't yawn.

Although, I was sure it was *invaluable* intelligence—each and every *fascinating* detail, I realized, if I listened to much more, I'd face no worse or gruesome a death even by the demons that night. The only thing left to do was interrupt politely. I planned to, but I guess I'd waited too long. I must have run clean out of polite without realizing how low my tank had gotten. Chris was just expounding on how, "... important it was to keep moving..." when the bolts on the gates of my mouth simply burst.

"Gosh that's great. Thanks, guys. Let's remember to keep moving!" Everyone sat staring at me, and my guess is, they were probably waiting for me to say something intelligent. But honestly, I was just fed up—so I smiled.

Chris looked at me. "Can I go on?"

"Seriously, I wish you wouldn't." I groaned.

"What do *you* think we ought to be doing to prepare?" I couldn't believe it. Tessa was standing up for the "Lil' Gimpy GI"? I looked at her with volumes of unspoken bitterness in my eyes, and she had the good sense to turn pink.

"Well, gee, I don't know... *Anything* but this comes to mind," I said. But I honestly didn't want to be unkind. "Listen, guys. I appreciate all your work; but seriously, I can't take it." They all stared back blankly, except Jack, who was looking at me with his annoyingly cryptic smile. I said, "Come on, how would you like it, if I made you listen to a dissertation on shopping? Would *you* listen? Even if your lives depended on it? I think not." The three guys looked at each other.

"She has a point," Chris said, surprising the heck out of me.

"I'm not listening to no shopping stuff. Do we have to?" Santos asked, not quite understanding I was simply making an argument.

"No, thank goodness; so, I think we agree. Besides, we'd almost finished anyway," Jack said smiling. He wasn't fooling me. A couple more hours and they would have been winding down. "There's only one more thing I should probably tell you guys. But before I do, I thought I'd ask about your visit with Darius. Did she say anything you might need to share with us?" Jack asked, looking at Tessa and me.

"Oh my gosh! Hold on," Tessa said, jumping up and running out of the circle, and through the trees.

"What's going on?" Chris asked.

"She'll be right back. Darius sent a little something for everybody, and we forgot it. So...let me see. One thing I remember asking her was whether we could get hurt...and as Hailey already told you, the unfortunate answer to that is, 'yes.' If a Maltorph hits us, it's not fatal, just painful. But we probably wouldn't be able to fight anymore."

"We should make a plan if that happens," Jack said.

"There's not much we can do, but get back to the base circle, stay inside it and pray, is there?" Hailey asked.

"That's what it sounded like, but I'm coming back if I can," I stated.

"How long before you're better? You do get better, don't you?" She asked.

"Yes, you heal, but it's not quick or easy. Another thing was that all our actions and thoughts before and during the battle—our prayers and scripture, of course—are important. Oh, and like Hailey said, we all must be together. Which means that, if Nathan is inside at the party, we go inside. And she made it sound like it would inevitably happen at a party anyway. Rasvampin will bring a party to us, one way or another," I said. "He's not going to let the mantle pass easily or quietly."

They sat silently digesting this information, and I wracked my brain for the other important things Darius had told us.

Just then, Tessa arrived with the thermos and four mugs. "Cassie and I have already had a cup, but Darius wanted everyone to have some. It's hot chocolate, and it's the best I've ever had!" Tessa said, smiling, and passing the mugs around. She sat down, opened the thermos, and passed it to Hailey. When it reached Jack, and he'd filled his mug, he looked up at me with a funny smile.

"This thing is still almost full. Come on, share some with us," he said to Tessa and me. He started handing his cup over, but "Gimp-a-long" made sure Tessa had his mug before she'd even had a chance to think about accepting Jack's offer. I took a sip and passed Jack's back to him.

"Thanks. Isn't it amazing?" I said, making sure not to look directly at his face.

"Amazing," he said, in a way that made me flush.

"I don't know if Cassie told you this part or not, but I think it was the most important thing Darius said to us," Tessa began again. "I mean she told us a lot of things, —like, we needed to maintain our courage, our worth, and our focus during attacks. She also said that Nathan had to come to terms with his calling. Oh yea, and that if someone died, it would look like an accident to the world. And she even said that there would be others fighting alongside us—like angels, maybe. ...All that was good, but what stood out to me is what she said at the end."

I stared at her, unable to remember what that was, because I was still going over all the things Tessa had just infuriatingly pulled out of her little brain. The twerp went on. "Darius said not to give up hope no matter what. And she quoted Romans 8:22, '*we know that all things work together for good to those who love God, to those who are called according to His purpose.*'" Tessa let that soak in before she continued. "She said all of us needed to remember that the war had already been won, and that Rasvampin has already lost. We must stand without fear against him, because fear is the fight, not the things we see, but the things we fear in our hearts."

Everyone sat silently for several seconds. "Thank you, Tessa. We all needed to hear that," Santos said finally.

"Amen," I said, moved by it too, despite the fact I'd heard it all a mere ten hours earlier.

"Thanks, Tessa, and thanks, Darius," Jack said, lifting the mug of cocoa in the air in mock salute. Everybody laughed and followed suit. Then Jack said, "Anybody want to fight? I'm tired of talking!" The yelling seemed to make it unanimous. It was, of course, the cries of only three guys, but they made up for us girls, and then some.

I wanted to fight, but the truth is, I wanted to kill something. I knew I was going to call Nathan, and my hands had gotten clammy ...along with my heart. "I think I'll go in, and get it over with," I said to Jack, as we got up and everyone started joining hands.

"So? OK then. Are you coming back when you're done?"

"Yes, but we should probably leave by eight-thirty, nine at the latest. None of us has eaten, so I'll get something together."

"My mom made lasagna. I can bring it over to your house. But I need to tell you something in private." He must have seen the look of panic on my face because he added quickly, "About what Hamaliel told me that first night. I was going to tell the group... then I thought maybe you would want to know...alone." I tried to read Jack's eyes, but they didn't look like he was going to tell me I was about to die. So, I decided to wait and freak-out later.

"OK, after I call...my *date*," I said, smiling tightly. He smiled, too.

"Hurry and get back," he said, turning around and taking hands with Tessa and Santos.

I was glad I'd left my cell phone at the house, so I'd be alone when I called. And so, Jack wouldn't be close enough to see me, and I wouldn't be close enough to feel his eyes watching me. This was hard enough alone.

~

"Hey. I'd... almost ...given up on you." I didn't think I imagined the joy I heard Nathan quickly conceal in his voice, and it only made it harder.

"What time do you want to be here?" I asked, keeping my voice neutral, but finding the act of camouflage more difficult than I used to. He was silent for a moment.

"I'm glad you called, Cassie. I ...I hoped you wouldn't let 'us' be over," he said, as if I was the only one in charge of that happening. I didn't respond. I couldn't. I decided to end the charade.

"Oh, Nathan..." I exhaled, in exasperation. But before I could get another word out, he took over.

"I know... I know how you feel. I'll pick you up around eight forty-five."

"Nathan, wait..." I heard silence. "Nathan?" I looked at my phone. He'd hung up. I thought for a moment and then called him back. It went to his voicemail. What the heck was going on, I wondered? Then I sat down and said a prayer. *"Thy will be done, here...right now, right here, Lord, as it is in Heaven. Amen."*

~

"So, what did he say?" Jack asked—his sword poised high. I had my sword at ease by my side. I wanted to test my speed, and I knew Jack would give me a real fight.

"Hmm...well, I'll tell you, but you'll have to earn it," I said smiling, but staying still.

"Really? No problem." With lightning speed his sword swung sideways, and I barely came up for it in time with my own. We spun and struck and parried, matching each other blow for blow. We fought for what seemed like ages, and I didn't want to admit how difficult it was to stay up with him, let alone get ahead once in a while. Out of the corner of my eye, I noticed Santos and Hailey had stopped and were watching. When I spun, ducked, and came up with a blow, I saw Chris, standing to my left beside Tessa, grinning from ear to ear. Jack blocked my strike and laughing, spun away. I leaped after him, amazingly light and swift in my spirit body. But his sword was too much; for every lightning strike, his own would sing in response. I could feel laughter starting to build in me, but if I began, I was afraid I'd lose focus, and he would surely get to me. He parried three of my strikes, smiling at me the whole time. Finally, I let go and laughed. If I could never admit it before now, Jack was a lot of fun. He brought his sword up and began making circles around mine, faster and faster until he'd locked them up. Then turning around somehow, he slipped behind me. I turned ready to strike, and he was on a knee his arms outspread.

"I give up. Tell me what Nathan said, but only if you want to," he said, smiling up at me. Tessa, Hailey, and Santos clapped while Chris cheered; and my heart melted. I knew I hadn't won.

"OK, meet me back in the circle," I said, and could hear Chris shouting his disapproval. He wanted a chance to fight one of us. Tessa, Hailey, and Santos were all attacking him when we found ourselves holding hands and reciting our scriptures. The others were so intense in their prayers they didn't even notice when we slowly moved Santos closer into the center, and keeping the circle intact, put Tessa's hand in his without disturbing their recitations.

Jack and I silently walked further into the woods so we wouldn't disturb them with our talking. I grabbed his sleeve as we walked. It had gotten dark among the trees and I could barely see, realizing again how tired my arm had become! When we entered a clearing, he led us both to a felled tree so we could sit down. Grazing Jack's knee, I automatically distanced myself from him, and then moved back, berating myself for acting like an embarrassed, love-struck schoolgirl. But who was I kidding? I moved away again, and finally looked up at him. I could just make out the quizzical look on his face. "Bump on the log," I said, by way of explanation, figuring it wasn't entirely a lie. "So, you want to know what Nathan said," I began, "in truth, not much. He'll be here at 8:45. He obviously assumes I'm giving everything up for him, so he's going to be really mad and hurt."

"Really? Well, what did you say to him?" Jack asked, wondering I'm sure, what romantic whisperings had paved the way toward that delusion.

"That's the sad part. All I did was tell him to pick me up. He did the rest. I'd decided to tell him the truth, but before I could get a word out, I realized he'd already hung up. I even tried calling him back, and it went right to his voicemail." Jack was silent. It was almost 6:00. The few minutes we spent together alone would seem a lot longer in the circle fighting. The rest of the crew was bound to be coming out soon.

Jack shifted his weight closer to me on the log. I looked up at him, and he held my gaze, unblinking. "Cassie,

Hamaliel told me some things that you couldn't hear. I wondered about them at the time because I knew they were things that would...upset you."

"Really? What things?" I asked, working at keeping my voice light.

"One... really isn't important, but another is very important, and it's time for you to know." He looked deeply into my eyes. "You're the one to take out Rasvampin." His eyes remained glued to mine, and I held his, unable to move or think. The fact that it was getting pretty dim at the edge of the woods didn't help. I felt creepy things starting up my spine again. Finally, I moved my lips.

"Why did he say that?" I asked, not exactly sure what, or why, I was asking, but wanting an answer anyway. Some answer, any answer—a lie would do.

"God chose you for a reason. He knows who you are, and He trusts you," Jack said steadily.

"But Jack, only faith will defeat Rasvampin. You have more faith; Tessa has greater faith, Santos, Hailey, and Chris! Why aren't we all responsible for bringing him down? That's what I was counting on, being a part of it, but not being responsible for defeating him! This isn't fair!" I said, jumping up and storming around. "No wonder Ole' Light-Show didn't tell me! I'd have run for the hills—and he knows it! That was pretty lame, don't you think?"

"I think..."

"What else did he tell you? I want to know. What else would have made me mad?" I asked, cutting Jack off mid-sentence, and walking over to where he was now standing.

"It's not impor..." Jack started.

"I'll decide that! What did he say?"

"He asked me to watch out for you. Well, what he said was to 'watch over' you," Jack said, standing in front of me and staring me square in the eye without a blink. I couldn't help being impressed, considering I was certain he could see the blood boiling in my eyes.

"So, all this time... Nice to know." I started turning away, but Jack towed me back around and pulled me to him. And then I sobbed like a big scaredy-cat crybaby. I didn't even care, mainly because I couldn't do a darn thing about it. After all, I was meeting Nathan shortly to give him a convincing display of my lunatic-liar status. I'd just been given the angelic news *I'd* been specially chosen to overthrow a major *ugly, ugly,* Demon Destroyer who'd never yet been defeated in the thousand eons he'd existed to torment the souls of earth, and to top it off... the guy I thought was watching me with "passionate" care, had actually been "ordered" to by the same angelic-host-with-the-most who'd come delivering news of my own sure doom. Yea, it was sobbing time again, and it hadn't even been a week.

I shamelessly used Jack's shoulder to mop my face, hoping to leave mascara smudges he'd never be able to clean off. Doubt about everything swarmed me, and I wasn't sure if I was more embarrassed or terrified. I knew I certainly felt incapable of going on. I wanted to throw in the towel—and I would have—if I'd been able to determine in from out. Jack lifted my chin and looked into my eyes. I made myself look at him squarely, even though everything inside me was cringing in both fear and shame.

"There wasn't a day you were with Nathan I didn't wish... Cassie, I believe in you. You can do this. You don't have to trust me, because God is much more trustworthy than I will ever be, and He believes in you," he said, his lips so close to mine I could feel the words on my cheek.

His head came back up, leaving me light-headed and grasping his shirt for support. Something began to clear and click inside my head. Suddenly, I knew I needed to be alone.

"Jack, I have to go back to the house. I must... get ready for the party," I said, my mind still clicking away.

"You what?"

"I don't know what just happened... but something... and I'm going to go with Nathan, or at least, I want to talk to him. It's the only way he'll listen; even then, it's a long shot. Meanwhile, he needs to believe I'm still interested in...us, and that I want to go with him." Jack dropped his arms from around me. His eyes now had that impenetrable look I was used to.

"Jack? Thanks for being here. No matter why you're here, you've always been..." I dried my face. I didn't know how to finish, and I looked away. "I'm only now learning what real friendship...what real *love*, consists of," I admitted, looking at him with genuine feeling. "I suppose I have a lot of crazy stuff inside that needs sorting out before God's done teaching me ...about all this."

His eyes became warm, but he wore that unreadable smile of his, "We all do."

I turned and started for home. "Explain to the guys... tell them anything you want. I'm taking a shortcut. Do you mind feeding them at your place?"

"Not at all," he answered, "I just have one question," he said, and I turned back, wondering. "You realize you called an Angel of the Living God, *Ole' Light Show?*"

"I did? Out loud? Hmm, that's some of the crazy stuff I was talking about..." I said smiling but turning and quickly walking away. I'd seen Jack's eyes twinkle, but with his smirky-smile it was hard to know if he was disgusted with me or not. And I couldn't believe I'd actually used that nickname out loud.

Of course, I realized what ought to be concerning me wasn't Jack's response, but my propensity toward sacrilege. "OK God, I *promise* to work on *that*, but please. One battle at a time. For some reason, you've given me the job of taking out Rasvampin—*Thank you very much*—so why don't we tackle that one first?"

~

I was amazed at how well "sassy"'worked at getting me off my spin on the "wheel of terror." I only hoped my "sassy side" didn't offend God too much. There was no doubt I was going to need Him liking me tonight more than I'd ever needed Him in my life, and that was saying a lot.

As I made my way back to the house, I looked up and saw the first stars overhead. Clouds had started blowing in just as predicted, but the sky had a look of wonder about it. I usually never noticed these things, nature things. They were just distractions and caused unnecessary dirt. But strangely, as I gazed, I found my heart beating fast, filled suddenly with a crazy longing. I started to lift my hand to the sky when I caught myself. Enough! *Holy Land of Oz*, I was losing it!

When I reached the garage, I stopped and stared at the garage door. Instead of opening it, I went around to the side door and turned the overhead lights on. I tried to keep from being distracted by the colossal mess. Boxes piled on boxes clear to the rafters. The rafters. I looked over to where Hailey had directed us in her dream. The boxes we'd searched had been piled almost to the rafters earlier. But now, they were now in a different... shall we say, arrangement. I made my way to the back through the maze, and moved some clutter so I could place a rickety old ladder, not really tall enough, under the far rafter: a flat piece of wood running the whole width of the garage. I took a deep breath, and climbed up until my fingers reached the place on it where the top box had been stacked; the place Hailey said my dad had been pointing. I felt around and there was nothing, just dusty wood. I carefully moved my fingers to the right, fearing all the while an imminent broken neck was only fractions of inches away and weighed this against my probable destruction at the hand-talons of Rasvampin. I moved my body further, hovering almost in thin air between the ladder and the discarded debris of our lives—then I felt something. I scratched at it, pulled it toward me, and finally got my fingers around its edges. Moving it ever so slowly, I was back on the ladder with it crushed to my chest. I didn't look at it; I knew what it was.

Chapter Twenty-Seven

Setting the small leather satchel on my bed, I took a soft, damp rag and carefully wiped the dust from its cover; then held it to my face and inhaled. I coughed. Unfortunately, all smells of Dad were overpowered by years of imbedded garage dust. I slowly opened it.

Tucked inside was a folded piece of paper which, when opened, was a deed to our house. Along with it was an off-white envelope with a letter folded into thirds inside the open flap, and two other unopened envelopes with small stickers on the tips of their sealed edges. One sticker was a flower...a lily, the other, a yellow smiley face. I felt something inside me "ping" softly.

I knew I should show my mother before going any further, but I didn't. I unfolded it. Dad had used a computer, which surprised me because I didn't remember him losing his ability to write or talk. But then, apart from a vague recollection of reading to him, I didn't remember much of anything. Suddenly, an image of his face smiling at me from a wheelchair appeared. Wow, I hadn't seen that in, ...forever. Now I read the heading; in a simple font he'd typed: *"My dearest Maggie,"* I closed the letter. Then slowly opened it and peeked at it again. *"I loved you the first moment I saw you. I love you now, and I always will..."* I folded it and closed my eyes. "I'm so sorry, Mother," I said aloud, amazed that I was feeling, even a fraction her pain, possibly for the first time. I carefully put her letter back in the envelope.

Taking the other two envelopes in my hand, and probably even though I knew better, I slowly pealed up the lily sticker and opened the folded sheets. It started: "My dear little Tessa..." And I shamelessly read the entire thing. He told my little sister how proud he was of her heart—so like my dad, who had to know by then she was a "mega brain," but recognized her greater quality. He asked her to take care of, and honor, Mom. Dad told her to keep studying her Bible, and then he wrote what I'd said to her a bit less eloquently that very morning, *"Never be ashamed of who you are, and never settle for being less than God's delight. Do not be afraid of the talents you've been offered; trust His purpose for your life."* He continued with more about loving her, about God, and about trusting others. And then he told her something amazing.

"I had a dream not long ago, too wonderful to tell in full. You were with me, holding my hand. We came to a road that split in two, and I cannot describe the wonders I saw on each path—they were too numerous, too beautiful. I didn't want to let go of your hand, but I understood it was necessary. I cried out, "No! My daughter is too young! She still needs me!" And a light as bright as the sun shone into my eyes. I put my arms up to cover, and when I dropped them a moment later, you were walking away, hand-in-hand with another—a bright being—and I wasn't afraid. You were laughing, and even turned back and waved. I awoke feeling such joy. I didn't tell you this dream because you are so young, and would be unable to feel all I felt, but someday, you will know the truth of this

vision. *And of this you can be certain. As we take our separate paths, my heart is constantly with you."*

Dad ended by saying, *"If I have a sorrow, it is that we will have to wait to continue our great friendship and, what would have been exciting collaborations. But I'll wait for you in Heaven's laboratories with unbounded anticipation. Until then, I have left you my preliminary work on what may one day be a device in which those left here with debilitating disorders, such as ALS, can project words directly from the brain into a computer with no mechanical interface. It's a long way from reality, but someday it could be a wonderful contribution. I only wish I could better aid you on your journey(s). Remember, never limit yourself, and never limit God. I love you with all my heart, Dad."*

I looked at the connected sheets of paper and they were covered with numbers, writing, drawings and formulas that might as well have been in Latin. In fact, I think some of them were. I couldn't believe it. Tessa had barely been ten years old when he'd died. Putting it all back, I pressed the seal into place as well as I could, and sat staring at the other envelope sealed with a smiley face sticker. It seemed ridiculous and strange, and somehow familiar at the same time. Slowly, I unpeeled the silly thing, careful not to crease or tear it, and unfolded the sheets of paper.

"Cassie, my Sweet & Tart," I smiled. I'd forgotten he used to call me that. *"You, ...my brilliant daughter, must never count yourself less than God's magnificent design."* I stopped, and read the line over, deciding he was trying to build my confidence. *"Don't forget, I know you better than anyone else. You must remember, I've been your best friend for a long time now.*

"Of course, you already know that one of my favorite things about you is your natural loveliness. You are so much like your mother. So, how great has been my happiness to find

some of myself in you? However, your greatest quality you haven't yet discovered. It lies beneath your pain. Yes, my daughter, I see your pain, and I know you feel betrayed. How I wish I could take this burden for you, but I rest knowing someone greater than myself already has. You must believe that God is faithful to the end. He will never leave you or forsake you. And although I must leave you, my love will always surround you. Take care of your sister; love and honor your mother. I fear my passing will be hardest on her. But you are my warrior, and I expect great things from you. Great things.

"Now, for fun, I want to leave you with one of our little games. It is a solution, and this time you must write the formula! As I said, I have great faith in you. If you do your research, it will be the best of all the (strange, yet wonderful) formulas we've concocted together. Now, this one is a marvelous metaphor, and it's something Dr. Mark Banning, a colleague of mine, sent to me a few years ago when it was first discovered. This is a piece of science that can illustrate an amazing truth about our faith. Have fun with it. The scripture in the front of your Bible will help with this. We've shared such priceless literature these past years. Now, I ask that you read the Bible and study it for yourself. There is no greater book. Remember, I count you among my greatest friends, and will wait patiently to be with you again. Dad.

"P.S., I know the years of sacrifice, birthday parties, school dances, movies, the friends, you gave up to be with me and to read to me. But I believe God opened up this gift in your mind because you so unselfishly gave of your life—and no sacrifice is ever lost. And it gives me great joy knowing you could store the entire Bible in that mind of yours, or as you like to call it, in your 'recall nook,' after only one reading. But again, I urge you to study it. I promise you, this will be a weapon you cannot live without."

There was a peculiar ringing in my ears. My stomach felt a little funny. I made my way over to the bathroom door, and I stood holding onto the jamb. I wasn't sure, but I thought I might have to make a dive for the toilet bowl. I took a deep breath. Then, I slowly turned and made my way back to the bed. I honestly didn't remember a thing about a…a… "recall nook?" I picked up the letter and scanned it quickly. *I'd called it a "recall nook?"* Clearly, it was *closed* for business.

It dawned on me with a mixture of sadness and relief, that my father had obviously written this letter when he was further into his disease, after his brain had been affected… But even as this thought occurred, I realized it was my own mind that had shut down and closed off. Still, the idea that I had this ability remained… I searched for the right word… ludicrous. Absurd, nonsensical, ridiculous, preposterous, illogical. And I realized I could continue all night impressing myself with the many words I could think of for how stupid this was. I mean, I couldn't think of anything funnier than my dad saying it wouldn't take long for me "to have the entire Bible stored" when I'd almost driven Chris around the bend with a single scripture. But then, I remembered, the times when information would download into my brain, and I wouldn't know where it came from. Like when I hit Chris with the information about Himmler and the SS, and honestly couldn't remember *how* I knew it. And other times in school when whole segments of information would suddenly pop into my mind. …But I'd never bothered to analyze it. I took as it came, figuring it was just a lucky coincidence.

I wondered what the heck I'd thrown away along with everything that brought me pain? Well, for starters, "God." That answer popped up rather quickly, and I supposed it didn't get any more profoundly ridiculous than that. Well, I had no idea how to open the door to my little cranny, nook, bookshelf, whatever. Things just slipped out on their own. Finding out how to open it would have to wait. It was getting late and I couldn't dwell. There still had to be something here that would help me tonight with Rasvampin. Dad had included a solution, but I was running out of time, and solutions sounded good to me. I looked at the paper he'd included with the letter. It was a molecular diagram of a cross.

Above the picture were the words: **Electron microscope pictures of Laminin molecules.** I scratched my head.

Sequence diagram of the chemical structure of Laminin molecule

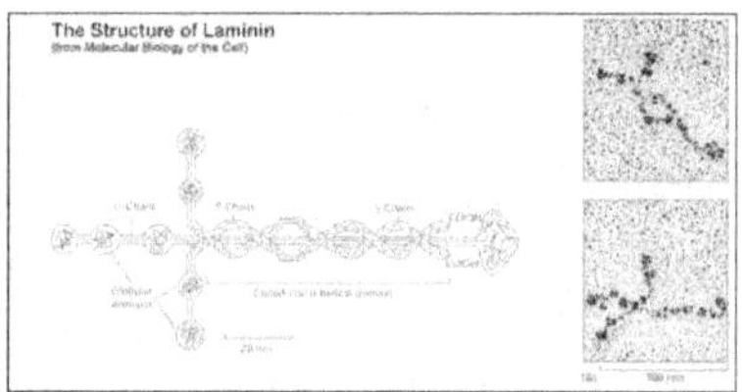

(**nm** = *Nanometer* which is one billionth of a meter)

The laminin **protein molecule** is the major component that makes up the extracellular matrix also called the basement membrane. These are the sheets of protein that form the substrate of all internal organs. Laminin assist in cell adhesion binding other extracellular matrix components together.

The laminin molecule is shaped like a cross, and has four arms that are designed to bind to four other molecules. The three shorter arms are particularly good at **binding to**

other laminin molecules, which is what makes it so great at forming sheets. The long arm is capable of **binding to cells**, which helps anchor the actual organs to the membrane.

Laminin is made up of three separate parts, called the Alpha (A), Bata (B1), and Gamma (B2) chains. That gives it a total of six ends, which accounts for a lot of its flexibility in connecting up various kinds of molecules.

The various laminins are a family of glycoproteins that is an integral part of the structural scaffolding in humans and almost every animal's tissue. Laminin is vital to making sure overall body structures hold together.

I looked at the gibberish written underneath the picture, and quickly figured I'd better start looking somewhere else. At least my dad hadn't said anything about my innate abilities in science, or I'd have known for sure his letter was a bunch of ALS brain-altered-hooey. Grabbing my Bible off the shelf, I opened it to the first page. The sight of my father's handwriting warmed my heart. He'd written the entry before he'd needed his computer; this meant he'd been planning to have me work this equation out at least a year before he'd written me the letter. I said the verse out loud as I was opening up to Colossians. I'd already memorized it, but I went ahead and read the verse, hoping the written words would help in finding a clue. " *...in whom we have redemption through His blood, the forgiveness of sins. He is the image of the invisible God, the firstborn over all creation. For by Him all things were created that are in heaven and that are on Earth, visible and invisible, whether thrones or dominions or principalities or powers. All things were created through Him and for Him. And He is before all things, and in Him all things consist.*"

I'd said this verse a hundred times; each time trying to understand it. Still, I knew I hadn't grasped it entirely. But a thought kept percolating. *Could the solution my dad wanted me to work out somehow be the key to defeating Rasvampin?* Granted, if there was a straw anywhere, I knew I'd be grasping at it, and this seemed a whole lot flimsier than a lifeline, but I didn't have anything else.

I looked at the time. Of course, now that I needed it to slow down, the hands of the clock were moving at warp speed. I didn't really have long enough to discover why the contents of the satchel were so important that Hailey would dream of it, and Darius would ask us about it. There was no doubt time was my enemy. This could take hours and then there was a little problem concerning what I was wearing. Nathan would never fall for the outfit I had on; he'd know something was fishy the minute he laid eyes on me. I decided to work on the formula first and throw something on last minute. I recognized that, as soon as I'd decided this, choosing to enter a convent wouldn't be any more revealing or convincing to God ...or myself that I'd achieved real internal changes. Unfortunately, there wasn't time to pat myself on the back.

"Where would my dad expect me to start?" I asked out loud. I looked at the diagram and read its description again. The last sentence in the last paragraph struck me...plus I understood it. "Laminin is vital to making sure overall body structures hold together." The last sentence in the last verse of Colossians read, "*And He is before all things, and in Him all things consist.*" These two sentences at least seemed similar. I went into my closet and found the dictionary Dad used whenever he studied his Bible. I was sure he'd want me to use it. I looked at the words in front of me. The one meaning in this context I wanted to make sure of was the term, "consist."

I looked it up, and read: "CONSIST, to stand. To stand together; to be in a fixed or permanent state," And then the section that jumped out at me, read: **"as a body composed of parts in union or connection**. Hence, to be; to exist; to subsist; to be supported and maintained." I sat for a minute and contemplated what that meant. It was shaped like a cross. And the cross...Jesus, his sacrifice, held it all together, and yet, He was *...before all things, and in Him all things consist.* All things. I wondered if I already knew that awesome truth, somehow, somewhere. And then I realized—of course I did—in my very being, my very cells. There was only one problem. Even though I remembered giving my dad strange problems to formulate for me, not only couldn't I recall even one, I couldn't remember how on earth he'd written them out. And even though we both knew they weren't supposed to be scientifically accurate, I knew there wouldn't be time to formulate any conclusions very well. Still, I felt as if answers were dancing inside me. They were waiting for my mind to catch up to my spirit. I looked at my watch. It was 7:50. I still had a few minutes.

I got paper and pencil and wrote the name, "Rasvampin," at the top. Beneath it, I began writing every description I could think of. Sad to say, I began with "Ugly." But then, his looks and fashion statement *were* hideous. Next came, prideful, arrogant, evil...and on and on until no matter what else I came up with, everything fell under those categories.

Next, I sat and contemplated the picture of Laminin. I knew I had been young, and my questions would have been convoluted and unscientific—but that they'd hold a deeper meaning. Dad's formulas for me would have been similar. I began to write. As I did, another scripture, Hebrews 11:1, popped into my mind and the formula evolved.

TITLE:
That Which Holds Man Together as Opposed to What
Holds Demons Together? and The Matter of It All

Matter: The Substance of things.

Now, Faith = the Substance of things hoped for and = the Evidence of things not seen.

So, Faith = Substance. Substance = Matter. Faith = Matter.
Faith is the evidence. Faith = Evidence minus all the things
unseen.
Therefore, my body consists of matter, which is faith. I am
composed of faith. The evidence of things not seen is the
Cross found in that Substance—that Matter
Holding me together.
So, What Holds the Ugly, Prideful, Arrogant, Evil etc.
Rasvampin Together?
Faith.
Faith in something...
Faith in himself.

~

It was imperfect to say the least; in fact, it was laughable. But I had a feeling my dad would have loved it, and better yet, something about it resonated within me as more than metaphor. It was 8:43. All I had time to do was exchange my Stanford sweatshirt for my brown cashmere, brush my hair—which, I had to admit, was still in fabulous condition thanks to my earlier attentions—do a last-minute touch up on my make-up, and grab my lambskin leather jacket. I still looked a bit hoedown, but it was fall. I hoped Nathan would assume I'd gone for that look on purpose. I didn't even have time to check and see if it worked.

It took all my composure not to fly down the stairs. I had the strangest sensation Nathan had already arrived and was waiting for me. He wasn't in the house, and Tessa hadn't come home yet. My mom was in her room, so I knocked on her door. She was sitting up in bed watching T.V., a vacant look about her.

"Hey, Mom. I found something in the garage." She turned and looked blankly in my direction. "I think it's something Dad left for us." Instantly, her back straightened, and the fog in her eyes seemed to clear. "There's a letter for each of us. Here's yours," I said, handing the satchel and letter to her, and kissing her forehead. "I'm going out with Nathan. I won't be back too late, I promise." My mom was staring at the letter, tears gathering in her eyes, one starting down her face. "You found it. You found it. Cassie, thank you. You found your letters—yours and Tessa's?" she asked tearfully.

"Yes, Mom. Mine is on my bed. You're welcome to read it. I put Tessa's on her desk. I started to read yours, but I didn't, I promise." I told her, walking out, and quietly closing the door. She was already pouring over her letter, and I'm not sure she even heard what I said.

I went to the window and looked out. Nathan's sports car was in the drive, but he wasn't in it. When I went out, no one was in sight, but I could hear voices. Slowly, I walked toward the Pine Circle. I was certain someone was coming through the trees, but I turned around when I heard voices coming from behind me. It sounded like Hailey and Santos were headed toward my house from Jack's. Then I heard another sound. Nathan was approaching me from the direction of the Circle, but it was so dark it was hard to see. By the time he got close enough, the streetlights were casting shadows over him. Still, I could tell something was wrong. "Nathan?" I called, but he didn't answer. He was almost on top of me as if he didn't see me, and couldn't hear me call his name. "Nathan?" I repeated, this time a little louder.

"Yea, it's me, Cassie," he said. Then before I could answer, he walked past me without stopping.

"Nathan, what's going on?" I asked. I didn't want to run after him. He'd just blown by me like I didn't exist. But, at the same time, I couldn't help wondering if some "big shiny being" had anything to do with his condition. "Tell me what happened," I demanded, catching up to him and grabbing his sleeve. He stopped a few feet from his car. His face was pale, and it was then I knew he'd seen something. "Nathan, are you alright?" I asked.

He looked down at me and shook his head "no." Then he turned, walked to his car and got in. He sat for a long moment without moving, and I stood by the door staring at him. He was incredibly handsome, and he looked back at me with deep soul-searching eyes, although, a bit haunted at the moment, and I thought to myself, he'd probably just been told by the great Hamaliel, that he, Nathan, was chosen to be the *Link*. After all, with looks like that, it was inevitable.

"I saw..." He shook his head. Just then, Hailey and Tessa wandered over as Santos came up beside me. "Hey, Nathan, my man. Are you leaving? You can't go without at least saying, 'hello, ...or goodbye' as the case may be!" Santos said smiling and putting his hand out to Nathan. Nathan hesitantly reached out, and then they did some sort of squeeze-knock-fist-thing. "I miss you, man. I wish you..."

"Yea, well, ...I can't..." Nathan said, curtly.

"Um, Nathan," Hailey started, coming up beside Santos. "I've been wanting to tell you how sorry I am if I said anything that might have upset you the other day..." she trailed off. Nathan stared at her, and I saw her face go still. She seemed startled by her own nerve. It was the first time I'd ever had a visual for the term "deer in the headlights" but I couldn't blame her. Nathan didn't seem like the friendly guy she remembered from the other day.

He sat staring at her and then, as though suddenly remembering who she was and what she was referring to, replied, "Oh, No. It's OK, really." He immediately turned his eyes away from her towards me as though erasing the memory and dismissing Hailey. For the first time since I'd known him, I was ashamed ...for him.

Santos and Hailey slowly walked away. Nathan was just about to say something to me when Tessa walked up to the car door. "Will you be at the party?" Her voice didn't carry the animation the rest of ours projected. It was all business. He looked at her for a full second, strange emotions moving over his face. I couldn't tell if he was angry, annoyed ...afraid? And then he answered.

"Get lost. I'm talking to your sister." I stared at him, shocked. Tessa didn't move. She simply continued looking at him, but he never dropped his eyes from mine. Finally, he said, "Yes! I'll be there." Tessa stepped away and turned from the car toward Jack and Chris who'd arrived and were standing a few feet away. When Nathan saw them, he set his jaw. Looking up at me he said, "Cassie, I'm sorry. I need a little time... I saw..." he turned away, before finishing, "It doesn't matter."

"Nathan, it does matter. You know it d..."

"Make up your mind. I'll be at the party...in a little while. I hope you come." He looked beyond me toward Jack, then back at me. His eyes held mine again, imploring, and I couldn't help falling into them, into their plea. "Answer me this...when you come to the party tonight, will you leave the Guardians and be with me?"

My mind was spinning. He knew I was going as a Guardian. Why didn't he insist on taking me now? What or who had he seen? "Nathan, please tell me what happened..."

"That's what I thought..." Turning away with a sneer, he started the car, put it in reverse, and without another word was gone.

Jack and Chris watched Nathan drive off. Looking at me

with a half mocking smile, Chris asked, "So, what'd you say to make him leave you in the dust like that?"

Normally, his little barbs were like gnats on a warm day: irritating and so easily squashed. Tonight, it was Chris I wanted to squash. I walked—no, I stalked—OK, I stormed back to the house without a word. I heard the sound of several tongue-lashings Chris received, Jack's voice being the clearest, but it did little to ease my spirit.

I sat down on the steps just as Jack said, "No, you stay here. I'll talk to her first." Then he shoved his brother a bit roughly, causing him to re-balance on his crutches. Something like that usually thrilled Chris, and normally made me smile, but not tonight.

Jack came over and sat beside me, but before he could say anything, I said, "Look, I don't really know why I'm so upset. It's not what I said that made Nathan leave; and it's not Chris... But I'd like to kill him, anyway. Maybe we can offer him as a sacrifice to Rasvampin."

Jack smiled. "Maybe you're upset because in about thirty minutes we're all going to war. We're about to load up in my dad's van and head over to a party where all hell's about to break loose, literally." I looked up at him and was unprepared for the effect his eyes had on me. How could I allow myself to be so induced by eyes!

"Ye...ye...yes." I stammered. Furious with myself, I stood up. Jack followed suit and moved closer to me, which didn't help. "Look, let my brother apologize. Not because he deserves to, he's an idiot. But like I said, we've got a war on. Things have to be right between all of us."

"You're right. Just give me a minute," I said, forcing a smile.

"What happened with Nathan? Why *did* he leave?" Jack asked, and I could tell Chris hadn't been alone in assuming we'd had an argument—but then, why not?

"He must have met ...Hamaliel. It's the only thing that makes sense. I met him walking away from the Pine Circle, and at one point he said, 'I saw...' but didn't finish. Then, he told me to forget it. But other than that, he wouldn't tell me anything. Strangely, he knew I was going tonight as a Guardian, and he didn't demand that I go with him. Instead, he asked me to *leave the Guardians once I was at the party* and go with him then."

Jack continued staring at me, not asking for my response. He knew me well enough to know "not asking" was the only way I'd give it to him. "All I did was answer with a question. I asked him to, 'please tell me what happened to him.' That's when he drove away." I felt something rising inside me again. I didn't know if it was sadness, or anger, or both. Jack was silent for a moment, but I could have sworn I saw a smile in his eyes.

"Well, I hate to say it, but we don't have time to worry about Nathan. We've got to get going, too. I don't know what happened, but let's pray it was Hamaliel he met. One way or the other, Nathan's a part of this. I guess we're about to find out what part he plays." He squeezed my hand. "Ready?"

I nodded, and as he took my arm, Chris headed toward us. I knew this was going to be hard for the boisterous, brawling coon because all he'd really done was blurt thoughts out his blowhole. Admittedly, it was something I'd done a time or two. I could relate to his predicament even better in the 'uncontrolled thought' department, where I silently wagered he didn't have near as much editing to do.

And as much as he would hate apologizing, I was going to hate it more. Grovel, grovel, no, no, grovel, yes, OK, Yuk! However, it looked like there was no way around it. I sure wished the little whistle-pig would quit mouthing off, at least to me.

"Hey Jack, can I talk to Cassie alone for a sec," Chris said, standing in front of us with his head down.

"Sure, I'm going to get the van. I'll pick you guys up in two." Jack gave my arm a small squeeze and headed over to tell the others. Chris looked up at me. The kid could be so darn appealing. I dreaded this part. I just wanted to say, "let's forget it."

After about three seconds, he said, "You know I'm..." He stopped and shook his head. "Cassie, I just want you to know, I've got your back tonight." I smiled. He smiled back. The little ferret played it just right.

"And I've got yours," I countered.

He looked away. "Yea, well, Jack told me about Rasvampin...about you. And I just want you to know," he repeated, "I've got your back."

"Thanks, I've always known that, Chris."

"Ah, Christian... tonight."

"Thanks, Christian." I said, and he grabbed me in a big silly hug, with his crutch falling to the ground, with me trying to keep him upright, and him laughing. Even so, I had to work to keep from getting a silly tear in my eye and embarrassing us further. OK, I had to work to keep from embarrassing myself beyond redemption. How was I going to whip anybody's tail tonight? I knew Xena wouldn't be caught sniveling. This thought reminded me of something I'd been meaning to tell Hailey, and as Christian and I made our way toward the others, she and Tessa came up and took my arms. Then I remembered something else...much more important.

I stopped and turned to Tessa. "*I'm so sorry*. I would have told you sooner, but I found the leather satchel," Tessa's eyes grew large. "There were letters to each of us from Dad. I put yours on your desk. He left me a solution, and I had to work out a formula. I did, and we'll see what comes of it..."

"He left me a letter..." Tessa's eyes were bright with

excitement. Just then, Jack pulled up into the driveway. We all looked over. "Can I go get it? Should I wait?" she asked, looking longingly back at the house and up at the window to her room.

"Tess, I think it can wait. I wouldn't tell you that if I thought you'd need it for tonight." I stopped. "Do you need it for tonight?" I asked, wondering if I was thinking too literally. She looked up at me all eyes and crazy hair. "Get in. I'll be right back," I said, and bolted into the house and up the stairs. I grabbed the letter off the desk without touching one other thing in the room, barely even the floor, and made it back down before Santos had buckled himself into the front passenger seat. I jumped in and realized that somehow Mr. Graham had changed the back seats to face each other; either that, or Handy-Jack had figured out a way to put them in so we could sit that way tonight. We shut doors, buckled up, and headed over to Rachel's house.

Chapter Twenty-Eight

We'd barely left our drive before Christian traded seats with me, and I let him. Tessa wasn't pleased, but he had a flashlight, and it was too dark in the van to read without it. Sitting next to Hailey, I took her arm. "I've been meaning to tell you something," I said quietly.

"I bet I know," she said, smiling her embarrassed smile. "A lot of people, well, they've mentioned I look like I've lost weight," she said shyly.

"Hailey!" I whispered loudly. "Of course, I've noticed, but you won't ever catch me mentioning *weight*. It's against my principles," I informed her. What I didn't tell her was just how *new* these principles were. They'd been formed in the last few weeks, after finding myself riding shotgun inside the hearts, minds, and memories of at least half a dozen overweight girls. No-siree, I did not go there anymore. "What I wanted to tell you," I continued, "was that ever since I started using a sword and seeing myself as a warrior, I've envisioned myself as Xena, Warrior Princess!" I said, sitting up straight and arching an eyebrow. Hailey laughed.

"If you could see yourself fight, you wouldn't think that was far-fetched at all," she returned, and I loved her for saying it.

"That's just it. I've watched *you*, in and out of the warrior's Circle, and Hailey, you're the real Xena. I'd love to get a picture of Lucy Lawless as a freshman in high school. I bet she looked exactly like you," I told her—and I meant it.

"Really? You're not just saying that?"

"I'm not just saying that."

"I've already decided to cut some bangs after I lose ten more pounds."

"I'd love you with bangs." I looked over and saw Tessa with her head buried in Christian's shoulder. Her letter was folded neatly back in its envelope and Christian wore the most alarmed look on his face.

"Um, could I trade with you? I think she'd like to sit with you," He said, clearly out of his tadpole depth.

"Oh Tessa," I said, changing seats quickly, and putting her head in my lap. She didn't cry, at least not in the sense of weeping, but I could tell something was going on inside her; something deeply moving was taking place and she needed comfort as it transpired.

"Is she OK?" Hailey asked, with Christian looking on in uneasy concern.

"She'll be fine. She just needs a moment to process."

"Look over there," Santos said, pointing out his side window at what appeared to be an empty garage-type building on a vacant lot. "It's where I used to go with my homey's ...well, my gang," he admitted. "They're usually there by now. But when there's a fight, or if something's planned for later, then they come after." He was silent for a moment. "I wonder if they are planning to go to the party tonight. If they are, it won't be good, guaranteed," he ended.

"Well, it's not surprising the party is at Rachel's house," I said aloud.

"Why's that?" Jack asked. And I realized he hadn't been at the high school long enough to know Rachel, where she fell in the social groupings and why this made a difference. It was nearly a science; the only discipline of such I excelled at.

"Rachel's parents have money, but it's considered 'new' money. Truth is, most of the kids are just jealous. But then, there is the problem of her taste in clothes and her lack of common sense when it comes to guys. She doesn't have a lot of restrictions on her, and if she were just economically average, she'd be on the second lowest tier of the social strata. Instead, she's second to the top. Money does wonders, but it can't help you when it comes to the kind of parents one has and where you live. Those in the snob clique take both very seriously. ...And of course, her fashion is pretty awful," I added, seeming unable to stop myself.

Santos had turned in his seat; a questioning frown on his face. Meanwhile, Chris stared across at me with a look of complete, bewildered disdain. "What? I just answered Jack's question." I responded, wondering what more they wanted.

"Cassita, how does her having money and bad parents and no good fashion, how does that make the party at her house not surprising to you?" Santos asked, clearly confused. Christian was still looking at me like I was nuts, but at least he was quiet for once. I loved how Santos called me Cassita. I'd answer him anything.

"Easy. Bad part of town..." I began.

"Cassita, I live here, too."

"Oh, I'm so sorry, Santos. *I* don't think it's bad. Really, I don't. It's just considered that by the police," I said, realizing I hadn't helped myself a bit. Chris smiled, and I imagined him enjoying my turn as the imbecile with the unruly mouth.

"OK, I'll start over. Rachel lives on a nice piece of property away from neighbors. The railroad tracks aren't far from her house. Good noise barrier. No problem with parental authority, even though she won't have any this weekend. She'll make sure there's booze aplenty, since money's not an issue. And everybody will be invited, because as I've pointed out, Rachel is not discriminating." Everybody made sounds acknowledging the sense it finally made. *Brother*, some people just needed to bone up on the basics. In fact, these social forensics should fall under the heading of social science. I knew if they did I'd certainly ace *that* class.

"OK, turn here," Santos instructed. We started down a road leading out of town, and it wasn't long before we'd come to the long driveway leading to Rachel's house. We parked on a slight incline across the road, just in front of a tall streetlight that lit up the back of the van. There were cars parked all up and down the drive and on both sides of the road, but our position gave us a great view of the expansive lawn. It was a high school "dream set" right out of *Animal House*. The grass was arrayed with lawn chairs from various plastic vintage lines, two strands of overhead Christmas lights illuminated the partially dying grass, which was already strewn with plastic beer cups and cans and, of course, all our class mates standing in groups talking, laughing, and drinking. The music was blaring inside the house and was loud enough to enjoy outdoors. We could even feel a slight vibration from its bass inside the van. It was surprising how many people I didn't recognize as we gazed out the windows at the crowd milling about. More surprising was how fun the party looked to me...

Jack and Santos climbed into the back from the front seats. Santos squeezed beside Hailey, mashing Christian to the window. Jack sat next to Tessa and me, a much easier fit considering Tessa was the size of a squirrel. "We need to take a little time together. Focus. Pray. This is it..." Jack started.

"Excuse me," Tessa spoke up. "I don't mean to interrupt, but I need to tell all of you something...well, maybe ask."

Everyone sat silently waiting. "When I saw Nathan tonight, ...I don't know for sure, but maybe he *is* supposed to be the *Link* and..."

Everyone began talking at once. Santos and Hailey both thought he'd acted strangely, but Chris felt something when he approached the car. I remembered thinking *it was inevitable* that he was the *Link*; however, I didn't mention it was because he looked so amazing.

"*And* Tessa?" Jack asked. We all stopped and turned toward her.

"Um, and um, well, I was given the mantle ...tonight. I was told I'd know when it was to be assimilated, you know, absorbed." We stared at her; our mouths open.

"What?" I asked, dumbfounded, and ticked off, too.

"It's only a symbol really; it's a silver chain," she answered, completely oblivious to my reaction.

Hailey's intake of breath was audible. "I dreamed of a silver chain. Did Cassie tell you?"

I jumped in. "Well, in a manner of speaking; I attacked her while she was praying," I confessed. "I thought the crystal rosary on her lap was the chain, and I was attempting to save her from becoming the object of Rasvampin's wrath. Obviously, it didn't do me any good! Anyway, I might have forgotten to fill her in on the details..." I admitted.

Christian was looking at me; his mouth paused in the open position just moments before spilling out whatever stupidity had entered his brain cavity. I shook my head. "Don't even," I said, smiling very insincerely. He brilliantly closed his mouth.

"I know you're worried, Cassie. But you don't need to be. We'll have help tonight, and I'll be fine," Tessa said, looking at me in all her ridiculously innocent faith; the stuff I was supposed to have in order to protect her. I sighed.

Jack squeezed my arm softly. "Tell us more about the

chain, Tessa."

"Well, it doesn't *really* exist as a silver chain, except that's how we're able to see it. Still, I can show you, but I can't let anyone touch it yet," she said, reaching deep within layers of colored garments to an inside pocket...somewhere. When she pulled out the chain, everyone gasped. It was beautiful, luminescent, and shimmering in the darkness of the van. "It helps to have physical properties define things of the spirit. We relate better to them," she explained.

"It looks real to me," Chris said with awe.

"Right, I know. But the truth is, it's only energy. I'm only keeping the form of the power for the moment, just until it's given to the *Link*. Hamaliel said it's to fool Rasvampin, but I didn't ask him what he meant. I think Rasvampin expects Hamaliel to give the mantle to the *Link*, and instead, I'm going to. I'm not sure when that will be, but Hamaliel said I would know. Of course, it's sometime tonight." She said, sliding it back inside her pocket where it disappeared. I figured if nothing else, it was strategically intelligent for her to dress the way she did, and silently prayed the layers of hideously wonderful clothing would help keep her safe.

"And so why again do you think it's Nathan? That he's the *link*?" Santos asked, not bothering to hide his uncertainty.

"*All* I'm saying is it could be. Because after I'd been given the mantle, I got up to leave, and I saw Hamaliel point. He looked down at me, and then he was gone. I looked and saw the back of someone leaving but I couldn't tell who. I left the woods at the far end toward Jack's house. That's when I saw Nathan walking down the road away from the woods. I'm sure Hamaliel was pointing at him."

"And you didn't hear anything?" Hailey asked.

"No."

"It could mean anything then," Chris said.

"Yes, it's just a suspicion." Tessa replied.

"Look you guys, it's getting crowded." Santos said. He and Hailey were staring out the window. Jack and Tessa reached across, and we all took hands. What I saw didn't make me feel any better about Tessa's delivering the mantle. The lawn was suddenly crowded. Among the kids who were talking and drinking beers lumbered Maltorphs, at least fifty of them. And strolling on the outskirts of the crowd was Rasvampin, a whip in his hand. And not just any whip. Even from this distance, it was easy to see that it undulated with its own power.

It was obvious nobody could see Rasvampin, because to any of the carefree partygoers, he'd be even more terrifying than the giant Maltorphs. His darkness was so deep that, to catch a glimpse of him, made you want to run screaming in terror until you woke from your nightmare. The Maltorphs looked restless, swinging their swords, and looking toward him as though waiting for an order. And Rasvampin looked impatient too, scanning the night—his cold dark eyes scrutinizing each group. Once, I thought he looked toward the van, but he turned away. I knew he looked for the *Link*, and the glowing chain that was the mantle.

When I dropped Tessa and Jack's hands, Rasvampin and the Maltorphs disappeared. The front lawn which had previously seemed a messy partygoers dream, suddenly looked clean, and much less crowded, as though someone had done a massive garbage cleanup. And pretty much, that was the plan tonight; that was our job. ...But not mine. I was going to protect Tessa. After all, what if Nathan decided he just didn't want to go along with all this? I mean, it was his 'God given right' to refuse. At that point, Rasvampin would go after the mantle and Tessa, which wasn't fair. No way was I going along with any of that. I'd take the chain and give it to Nathan myself even if I had to stuff it down his shirt. Then, I'd hide her. Let everyone else figure out what had to be done.

I wasn't doing anything but taking care of Tessa...no matter what. Screw Hamaliel. I felt rebellion swelling inside me, and my will began pushing itself up in the manner I'd been comfortable entertaining for so long. It felt right, ...because I was ...crazy-scared.

In recognition of my disrespectful and sacrilegious condition, lightening lit the sky. A few seconds later, thunder cracked. Well, maybe it was a coincidence, but I took it as a reminder that there were bigger things going on than my dread. "OK, I need prayer," I confessed. "I'm feeling pretty messed up right now. I'm scared, angry, and the 'hell party' looks kinda fun. At least when I'm not holding hands with Santos," I amended, "so I doubt I'll be at my best out there tonight."

"We all need prayer. Especially after seeing that," Hailey said, her voice quavering.

"Yea, but I know I need more courage than I've got. I need to let Tessa do what God believes she can do. And I need to believe I can do what Hamaliel...well, I guess what God's asked me to do..."

"Did the satchel give you any clues?" Hailey asked.

"I don't know, maybe..."

"Well, I know this..." Christian said, looking at me with his serious eyes. "You come across like you don't know anything... and don't get mad at me, this is supposed to help you. You think you're stupid, and act like you're a brainless beauty queen, but I've never known anybody who memorized scripture faster than you once you quit ...you know, acting stupid." Jack reached over and punched his shoulder. Hard.

"Thanks, Christian. Some of that actually helped," I said smiling.

"Nothing has changed, guys. We knew it would come down to this. And really, is this a surprise?" Jack asked. We looked out the window, and none of us answered. Evidently it wasn't to him. "If Nathan isn't already here, he will be. When we see him, we'll surround him and Tessa so she can make the transfer.

"I wonder why Hamaliel didn't give the chain to Nathan directly, and gave it to you instead?" Hailey asked, suddenly curious.

"It must have to do with timing. Maybe he needs to see more before he'll believe, and accept the mantle," Tessa answered.

Christian spoke up. "Why would someone as unreliable as Nathan be chosen as the *Link?* I don't get it. It's nuts!"

"God's ways are not man's ways." Jack reminded him.

"Remember Chris, Rasvampin and the Maltorphs. They all know who we are, man. Nathan is the only one they're not expecting. Remember? He never fought them. And he's never hung with us at school. That might be one reason," Santos offered. "Tessa, unless we can get Nathan back here to enter the Warrior's Circle, you'll have to go up to him like you are. You'll have to go without a sword in your hand, and in your real body if you're gonna hand it over to him. And we'll have to make sure Rasvampin and the Maltorphs don't get to him first. 'Cuz you know, they come to lie, steal—and kill," Santos reminded us. Christian nodded, somewhat appeased, but still aggravated.

Suddenly, I wanted to fight. I wanted to get my sword dusty, and hear it sing as I swung it at those ugly demons.

"Santos is right. Remember," Jack was saying, "we're all sons and daughters of the living God. We are all going into battle tonight as sons and daughters of the King," His words made me shiver; I could feel my faith expanding. "Tessa, would you lead us in prayer, and then Cassie, could you start us out with a scripture?" I nodded, realizing I didn't deserve the honor. But then, I wasn't deserving of any of this. I was beginning to understand that being 'undeserving' was the whole point.

Tessa's small but steady voice began. "We're here, Father. It's time..." She next asked God to trade our fears for His promises. "...and to *make us more than conquerors.*" She asked Him to be with Nathan, "...*and surround him with protection,*" and to help him hear, "*God's voice, and not the voice of the enemy.*" She named each of us individually and asked for protection. As she prayed, I felt God's Spirit hovering over us. She finished with, "...*your will to be done here on earth as it is where you abide. So please ...abide in us.* Amen."

I looked up. I'd been so caught up in her prayer I'd forgotten to think of a scripture, but then I knew... "*The Lord is my light and my salvation*" I began, and let my voice build, "*—why should I be afraid? The Lord protects me from danger —so why should I tremble? When evil comes to destroy me, when my enemies and foes attack me, they will stumble and fall. Though a mighty army surrounds me, my heart will know no fear. Even if they attack me, I remain confident!*" I ended, feeling every word of the Psalm resonate throughout my being.

"All right, all you swashbuckling, blade swinging, Soldiers of the Cross. Let's all begin together, and we'll meet in the Warriors Circle!" Jack yelled.

A cheer went up, and as we held hands, the scriptures began in earnest, pouring out of hearts, minds, and mouths prepared for this very moment. Lightening split the sky, but the sound of thunder was muted. I found myself standing in the foggy white light of the circle, my sword gleaming brightly in my hand. Jack, Hailey, Santos, Christian, all appeared. Only Tessa remained within the van praying and reciting, waiting for the right moment to leave the van and approach Nathan.

"OK," Jack said, after a quick head count, "if we go storming out, the Maltorphs may start wailing on people. We need to find Nathan, and make sure he isn't inside. Did anyone see his car when we pulled up?" We all shook our heads 'no.' "Well, if he's in the house, we need to get him outside. Otherwise, we need to get Tessa inside before he gets hit. One blow and he'll never cooperate. He'll be infected with anger and doubt."

"Don't you mean more?" Christian asked. I gave him a quelling look, which I knew he totally ignored—because he grinned back at me.

I shook my head. "Let's step out of the circle and see what we see. Just don't head onto the lawn yet. If the Maltorphs happen to get wind of us, at least they'll be drawn away from the party," I suggested. However, there was no way to know where this foggy circle was physically located. As far as I knew, we could have stepped out and found ourselves inside Rachel's kitchen.

"Good idea," Jack said starting out. But as usual, Christian, wildly happy to be free of his cast, leapt first. Following, we found ourselves only two feet from the end of the driveway. Luckily, no Maltorphs were in the immediate vicinity, but I knew they'd smell us in a matter of moments. I could only hope the odor of boozy humans on the earthly plain would mask whatever scent we un-intoxicated humans gave off in the spiritual realm.

There were crowds of kids, and the looming Maltorphs blocked our full view of most of them. Suddenly a small opening in a crowd at the front of Rachel's house appeared and I spotted his shirt. "Look..." I said, pointing.

"Is that him?" Jack asked, following with his gaze where I pointed.

I was pointing toward the edge of the upper lawn, and it looked like Nathan might be leaning against the wall near the door. I couldn't quite see... I began moving forward, but Jack stood in front of me. "Wait," he whispered. "If we go up there now, the Maltorphs will start wailing, and people won't have a chance. One blow to Nathan and he'll be lost to us. They're waiting for us. Let's call them out here first, and then clear a path after we get rid of a few of them. That way we can send Tessa out more safely."

"You're right, Jack." Santos agreed. "Too many people will get hurt. If the ones inside the house are doing drugs, and they come out, it will be a slaughter, man."

"Yea, OK ...Let me go back and tell Tessa. She needs to know our plan. If she knows the strategy, she won't come out too soon." I said, and Jack nodded.

"Tessa," I called softly, and she opened her eyes. Suddenly Jack quit reciting and opened his eyes, too. "Hey," I said. "You decided to come with me."

"Yea, and I did, too," Hailey chimed in. Then Christian was there and so was Santos.

"Don't think you're leaving us out there alone," Christian said, smiling widely. "I don't mind taking on twenty at a time but forty is a bit much."

"What? You mean forty? I'd only make my little guy take his fifteen. I'd take me my thirty-five, but then you made such sad sounds..." Santos teased. They began slugging each other over poor Hailey's head.

"Save it for the demons," I said, "the uglier ones," I amended.

"Oh, man. And here I come to tell Tessa I think she should wait for me, because I'm thinking maybe I should go with her. She can't see us, or any of the demons when she leaves this van without me. And maybe Nathan, he might need a little encouragement too. I don't know, I'm just saying."

"Wow, I see your point." I said, grateful Santos had thought of this.

"Yea, good. But Santos, wait until we can secure the area for you. Then you'll have to try and get back as soon as you can and suit up. Hopefully, you can get Nathan to come, too. We're outnumbered pretty badly out there," Jack added, concerned by the multitude of Maltorphs facing us.

"Yea, and don't let them see where you're going. Sneak back and get in through the far side of the van. I don't want Rasvampin knowing where our, ...you know, ...where our bodies are. ...Geez that sounds weird." I said, and gave Tessa's hand one last squeeze.

"I love you, Cassie."

"Don't *even* say that right now!" I said, "Of course you do. And stay in the van unless *I* tell you. Don't get out even when Santos does, all right?" I demanded.

"You'll just have to trust me, Cassie. I won't get out unless I feel like I'm supposed to." She said firmly.

"No, not good enough. God will speak through me, your elder, OK?" I said, growing fearful.

"Let's do this, Cassie. We can't waste any more time. I think you can trust your sister," Jack pointed out. Chris sat across from me, nodding his head.

Hailey reached over and patted my arm. "She'll be all right. She's the strongest one here," she said. And deep down I knew Hailey was right.

"OK," I said, finally yielding. Still holding Jack and Tessa's hands, I closed my eyes, and we all began saying our scriptures again. In less than three seconds we were once again standing within what had become a blazing circle, the words echoing through me... *Though a mighty army surrounds me, my heart will know no fear...* This time Jack led the way out, and we followed.

Chapter Twenty-Nine

The night seemed brighter than when we'd first left the Warrior's Circle, as though lanterns had been hung in the sky. We tried moving along the perimeter of the lawn, but it was no use. We hadn't taken more than a dozen steps when a howl went up. I hardly had time to put one Maltorph away when two more were on top of me. From dust to dust, I thought, as my blade sang through them both. Another Maltorph, huge, hairy and smelling like a decaying potato came behind them, swinging. I felt the verses of scripture singing through my blood, and I slashed him into dirt as I merely raised my sword for combat.

Our swords seemed super-charged, yet there didn't seem any way we were going to get close enough to where Santos and Tessa needed to be. And I knew that, if the Maltorphs got a good look, they'd remember Santos. He'd be able to see them, but he wouldn't have any weapons to protect himself or Tessa. Even though these thoughts raced through my mind, I didn't have long to worry. I didn't have time to do anything but survive. Rolling to the side and stabbing the beast bearing down on my left, I barely escaped being hewed in two by a particularly uncouth Maltorph and his horrendously unclean weapon. I knew if the spirit world had gangrene, and I'd even been nicked, there might never have been recovery.

Three more putrid Maltorphs took his place. Five more awaited their turns, snarling and circling, slobbering grey-green slime until it fell in long lines to the ground. I heard Rasvampin laughing in the background, but I couldn't take my eyes off the circling lizard-faced demons. I swung and sliced one into powder, but he'd been slower than the others, and even stupider, if that was possible. The Maltorphs were big, and dumb—this helped. I was quick and could dive and roll, but with so many, there was no place to go. I was hemmed in. I looked around for help. Jack was fighting four Maltorphs at once. Hailey, Santos and Christian, were back-to-back and fighting for their lives. "Lord, help us!" I yelled.

Suddenly, we weren't alone. Beings, the height, if not the girth, of the Maltorphs, bright, and carrying brilliant swords, appeared beside us, and the fight was on. At first some of the Maltorphs began retreating. But then, Rasvampin cracked his whip, and in an ugly, guttural voice, yelled a strange word which sent a cold shiver through me. Although smaller, or lesser somehow than Hamaliel—the angels—because, of course, that's what they were—stopped for just a fraction of a moment. I saw one closest to me lift his head and move the corners of his mouth ever so slightly downwards in thinly disguised disdain, as if what he'd heard was distasteful. Then he slaughtered two Maltorphs at once.

In the melee, some kids had been hit, and although they weren't aware of it, small brawls broke out in several areas; but not many were wounded. No major "spirit injuries" resulting in "partygoer violence" had been caused...at least not yet.

Rasvampin stood away from the fray, looming, watching us, and watching everyone who walked in or out of the house, as well as everyone on the lawn. He watched it all at the same time, his eyes mere slits. But I knew he had raptor eyes, and he didn't miss a thing. The angels who fought were more than equals to the Maltorphs, but there weren't as many of them as there were demons, and they didn't often go near Rasvampin. He also kept his distance, but showed little fear of them, glaring whenever any came near.

The night sky had become a light show. More and more kids were coming outside to drink and party, some of them wearing the black, skullcap-like-demon Siphons we had seen earlier. Lightening lit the atmosphere and thunder boomed. The wind blew warm but there was still no rain. I knew that if any of these same kids, reveling in the spectacle of the night, could have seen what we were witnessing, they would have run for their cars, revved their engines and sped away—never to return except in their worst imaginings. Every time lightening lit up the sky, the nightmare just got brighter.

Hailey and Santos continued to fight, often back-to-back and side-by-side. Dust flew everywhere. And more than once, I turned to find Christian leaping behind me to fend off an attack. But it was impossible to take much time to see what the others were accomplishing. However, every so often I'd see Jack leaping backwards, slicing upwards, spinning, and thrusting sideways, and the roar of a dying Maltorph would follow. Because of proximity, I ended up watching Jack's back, when, after being overwhelmed, he'd come to my aid. At least that's what I told myself. Christian was simply everywhere at once. And slowly but surely, with our angelic helpers, we were evening out the odds.

Suddenly, I heard Jack call, "This way!" and I could see a path being cleared by three angelic beings closer to the house. We managed to fight until I caught a glimpse of Nathan. I swung around after dusting a Maltorph, looking to see who

Nathan was with, but there were too many demons in the way.

I needed to get closer to his group so we could protect him from the rampaging Maltorphs. Swinging wildly, I took a chance and charged forward into a pack of them, hoping to hit as many as I could before they saw me coming. It worked, and I gained a little ground.

Suddenly, I heard a sound behind me and without thinking, threw myself sideways into a crowd of kids. It felt strange falling through them because I could feel myself quickly touching their souls as my spirit body passed through their flesh. But it didn't feel nearly as creepy as the whip that missed my head by mere centimeters. It wasn't its crack next to my ear that left the awful impression of impending agony, as much as the sound of hissing. Rasvampin's whip was alive.

Before I knew he was next to me, Jack was helping me to my feet. He then took out a Maltorph bent on my destruction. Hailey and Santos were at my back, and Christian was already working his way toward the door. Rasvampin was watching, and I yelled to Christian just as the Demon Destroyer twitched his wrist. Out of nowhere, a gruesome black snake whipped toward Christian. He dove behind the Maltorph in front of him, and the fangs of the whip bit into the demon instead, which began shrieking and immediately turned to dust. Crouching and coughing, Christian recovered from being smothered in demon debris and half smiled back at me, looking startled by the grotesque whip. But he didn't waste any time, and turning, continued fighting. We followed, and much to Rasvampin's fury, dodged or used Maltorphs as shields when his whip sailed too near. Finally, we were all together, back-to-back, near Nathan's group.

We managed to clear a neat area around them when I heard Jack call Santos' name. Jack didn't need to say anything else. Santos knew. He looked over, motioning to me, not wanting to leave Hailey alone. It would have made me misty-eyed and sentimental any other time; it was so darn sweet. But the Maltorphs wouldn't let up even for a tender moment. They just kept on, rudely swinging their ugly rusty swords at us. And they seemed doubly offended that we'd taken ground this close to the door, charging with renewed vigor.

I'd assumed it would take ages for Santos to show up, or at least it would feel that way considering the spirit realm's time warp. But it seemed only seconds had passed when I watched him, back in his physical form, walk over to Nathan—time warp, indeed. The Maltorphs saw Santos too, and recognizing him better in his earthly form, converged with added frenzy. Jack, me, Hailey, and Christian all stood back-to-back, fighting off the heavy sword blows as they pushed us closer to Santos and Nathan. The angels fought too, but they couldn't be everywhere, and it seemed to me Rasvampin had brought in fresh recruits. Several of the kids got hit and began acting out, pushing each other—the lust for a good fight welling up within them. Try as I might, I was too busy keeping people from being hit to hear what was being said, but I could tell Nathan was angry. It looked like Santos tried to take his arm, but Nathan shoved him away and started walking around the side of the house in the direction of Rasvampin. I held my breath, unable to move, watching the unholy whip sail, hissing through the air, stretching out fully. Miraculously, Nathan turned back sharply, just as dark glistening fangs snapped, not quite grazing the skin of his neck.

Jack skewered a Maltorph bent on taking off my head—which apparently, I'd seemed willing to offer the beast. "Cassie, go back. Santos needs your help. Nathan won't listen to him. Christian, Hailey, and I can hold them."

I looked at the other two. They glanced in my direction

and nodded. "Call for more help! Send up prayers!" I shouted and began myself. I could have sworn that, before everything vanished, more bright recruits arrived for our side.

When I opened my eyes, I saw that Tessa was no longer in the van and had already gone to join Santos at the party. I linked Jack's hands with Christian and Hailey's and stepped out into the night. Lightning struck overhead and illuminated the scene before me. More kids than I realized had begun getting rowdy, and I knew it was due to everything unseen happening around them. I skirted the areas I remembered seeing the most Maltorphs, then, hugging the house ran towards the area I'd last seen Nathan.

Santos saw me. He began ducking and swerving from things I could no longer see, making his way to my side and taking my hand. "Dear God," I said, as soon as the spirit world appeared again, and then added, "I should finish that sentence and not leave it hanging like an exclamation... But Dear Heavenly Father..." I said again and faltered. The place looked like a fright-night movie that needed to end. "Please help us put a stop to this. Help us make this end!" Santos looked at me, his face grim, and nodded.

Then he pointed to Nathan. He stood leaning one straight arm against a wall. Alyssa stood beneath it, smiling up at him. Several people milled around them. It was then I saw Tessa. She stood under the eaves of the house, near the door, waiting. We carefully walked toward Nathan, acting nonchalant and remarkably, remaining undetected. Then I caught sight of Jack battling nearby, and I dropped Santos' hand. I didn't think I could watch him, and at the same time do a good job convincing Nathan to come with us. Santos stepped into the shadows.

"Nathan!" I called, waving, and doing my very best to pull out *even one* of the remarkably life-like synthetic smiles I'd honed over the years when my real one wasn't available.

But I'd grown rusty. He, and about six others turned towards me. Brittany and Jenna gave me scathing looks, but Nathan faltered before his face became cool. I saw his hesitation, and he knew I'd seen it. Whispering in Alyssa's ear he walked over, his face set and his eyes wary.

"So, have you made up your mind? I'd just about given up on you." He said, moving closer. "I'm not going through any more of this, Cassie. I mean it."

"Oh Nathan," I said, taking his hands, my eyes filling with emotion, knowing he'd believe I was concerned with his desires, when in fact, there were more important things concerning him that tore at my heart. "You have to believe me," I began. It was then he saw Santos.

"What are you doing? Believe *you*?" He said, as though betrayed.

"Please, Nathan. You've got to trust me!" I said, letting go with one hand and grabbing hold of Santos. Nathan's face went white. His eyes were the size of saucers as he watched a large Maltorph bearing down on us. Thank heaven Jack was there, and leaping over, sliced the demon through the back, dust spewing toward us.

"What the..." Nathan didn't finish. Rasvampin roared, and the Maltorphs went still. Nathan's head jerked toward the sound, and when he saw the towering figure of Rasvampin, his face contorted in fear and shock. The kids watching us, stood talking among themselves wondering what had made Nathan Gregory go white in a split second.

"Begin the slaughter! The *Link* must be found!" The snake whip cracked and hissed in the air, and Nathan turned back to me.

"What's going on?" He asked, stark terror in his eyes.

"You know what's going on," I said, hoping to bring him back to himself. "You're a part of all this. Help us, Nathan!" He stood immobile, locked in terror as the Maltorphs hacked away at the crowd. Their filthy swords went through limbs and plunged into hearts. For everyone that had taken any kind of drug or intoxicant, the blow was like bitter contaminant shot directly into their veins.

Kids began squaring off, yelling obscenities. Brittany, Jenna, and even Alyssa advanced on me calling me names I'd never heard exit even their defiled mouths. I looked around and saw Jack still swinging, defending any and all he could. But the Maltorphs kept coming. Hailey and Christian were holding their own, but I feared they'd be tiring. Santos looked around. "Hurry. Let's get him to the van. Things are getting too crazy."

Nathan yanked his hand away, spinning around—his face incredulous. He turned back, and I knew—it was like he'd turned the lights on, and the nightmare was over—while actually, it still raged all around him.

Tessa was suddenly at my sleeve. "Nathan," she said, but he refused to look at her. "Nathan, I know you saw something today, and you can't deny it. You even went with Jack and Santos to the Pine Circle—and entered the Warrior's Circle. None of that would be possible if there wasn't a plan for you... something beyond your greatest dreams for yourself." Nathan turned and looked over toward Alyssa.

I couldn't believe it. Tessa was standing right under his nose, and true, she was tiny; however, Nathan wasn't deaf. Plus, there's just no missing a person in layers of multi-colored garments, with big bespectacled eyes and electro-magnetized hair—not even in this intoxicated crowd. Tessa looked up at me and shook her head. There was no getting around it; he was totally lost...almost as lost ...as I'd been.

I moved toward him. "Get away from me, Cassie," he said, his eyes frantic. "I told you I didn't want any part of this..."

"Nathan, we need you. *I need you.* Wake up! *He hears*

your cry in the night. Come back to him," I said, repeating the words I remembered Hamaliel saying to me. Nathan blinked. Then the craziest thing happened. All the rest that was spoken to me that night, that I'd have sworn was forgotten, *I suddenly knew.* "Nathan Graham, *you may not know Him, but He knows everything about you. He desires to establish you with all his heart, and all his soul, for you are his treasured possession. He knows the pain you have suffered, and although you haven't known it, He is close to you when you are brokenhearted. He gave up everything so that He might gain your love. Come home. He has always been Father, and will always be Father. He is waiting for you."*

Nathan's face was changing. Just as it happened to me, something within him was melting, and he began moving beyond his fear. He took a step toward me. Just then, I heard Santos yell, "Watch out!" And he jumped, knocking Nathan and me to the side. At the same moment, Jack sent his sword out and managed to hit the tip of Rasvampin's whip, popping out one of the snake's eyes. I heard roaring in the distance and knew he'd done damage.

Nathan instantly repelled Santos, and when I looked at him, I saw him holding his neck, and looking stunned. Although he didn't know what happened to him, anger and fear again moved over his face. Before I could reach out, Nathan turned and walked with quick strides toward Alyssa. Grabbing her by the arm, he headed into the house.

"I'm going after him!" I exclaimed to Santos.

"No man; the demons. They're gonna be thick in there! You know they are doing drugs in there...and they will be the really bad ones," he said, his eyes round.

"Worse than this?" I asked, looking around. Surprisingly, I realized we, and the "beings of light," had made progress where the Maltorphs were concerned. Now, there were actually a lot more really ticked-off kids avenging each other in brawls to contend with.

"I don't know about worse, but way more scary," he said.

Jack was suddenly beside me. "We stick together from here on out." Hailey and Christian showed up beside him.

"What's up, guys?" Christian asked, as though we were at summer camp.

Still holding onto Santos, I looked around. The Maltorphs were dwindling, and two angels battled near Tessa. She'd taken her place by the door again, as discreetly out of view as was physically possible, considering...Tessa.

"Nathan's inside. I'm going after him." I said to their stunned looks. "He was almost with us...and then..." Out of the corner of my eye I saw it coming; it was uncurling at us. It was unfurling its wicked end directly toward... me. I dove, but I knew it wasn't in time. For some reason, I felt no pain, but I heard a horrible screaming.

Rasvampin had moved in from his position on the outskirts, which had given the whip not only room to bite, but then wrap itself around Christian. How he'd moved from where he'd been standing to take the whip's blow, I'll never know, but he had. The one-eyed snake bit him unmercifully, over, and over. But before Jack and two angels raised their blades to slice its body into bits, it was gone in a breath, hissing back into Rasvampin's hand.

Christian fell in a heap. His sword quivered, and was gone. Santos and I ran over as his spirit body still shimmered. "Christian!" I cried.

"I told you... I've got ...your ...back..." and then he was gone, too.

"He's in the van. I'm going to check on him. He's probably out for the night." Jack said. "Meet me there, Hailey?" She nodded.

"I'll meet the rest of you guys back there. I want to see

how he is, too," I cried, "And Santo's, keep a watch on Tessa for me. Yell if Rasvampin tries anything while I'm leaving. I'm gonna circle around. Would you guys mind watching my back till I get there?" I asked. Jack and Hailey nodded, too weary to speak.

Chapter Thirty

After scanning the area to avoid as many demonic obstacles as possible, I waited until the moment his vileness, the Demon Destroyer's attention, was drawn elsewhere. Then I let go of Santo's hand and headed out in the opposite direction of Jack's van. Using every cover I could find, I made my way to the far side of the road and crept behind the cars until I came to it.

Christian lay slumped against Hailey, his forehead against her shoulder. As I sat down across from him, Jack and Hailey opened their eyes. I reached over, and Jack and I helped Hailey stretch Christian out on the seat. His cast hung off the end and banged onto the floor, but he never opened his eyes. I grabbed a sweatshirt from the back and placed it under his head. Just as I did, Christian jerked and had a spasm, groaning in pain, and then was quiet.

"He's not OK," Hailey said. I noticed her hands trembling. Jack pressed his ear to Christian's chest, listening. When he looked up at me, his eyes were troubled. My mind went into rescue mode.

"There must be a way. There has to be a way. He's been

infected with that demonic ...I don't know...poison extract. I know it's not really venom, but it's affecting him that way. There must be something... What can we do?" I turned around twice where I stood. At the moment, it was my equivalent of pacing.

Santos opened the door, breathing hard. "Wow, the whip. It almost got me, but the angels, they protect me. It was close," he said, coming in and rounding on Christian. He knelt by Jack. "Is he going to be all right?"

"We have to find some way to help him. Didn't Darius say that the mantle gives the *Link* amazing healing powers right after it's assimilated? That it's very volatile right at first but then it settles down?" I asked excitedly.

"You're right," Hailey said, grabbing my hands. "She said it only lasts a couple hours or so...but that should be enough time." Christian jerked and another spasm wracked his body. Santos, who'd been looking out the window, stared at him and then at us.

"He is jerking at the very same time Rasvampin is using that snake whip." Santos said, looking out the window and then back at us again. "Watch."

"Santos? Where is Tessa?" I asked, suddenly alarmed.

"She's OK. I left her with the angels. She says she'll wait for us, but we need to go in the house with her to get Nathan. The time, it is getting close. But Rasvampin, he's not letting many people walk by without going after them. Especially us. He knows us...we'll have to be careful." Christian began writhing, and we automatically looked out the window and watched Rasvampin's whip unfurling, then snapping on another victim. This one fell to her knees and began to vomit at the same time Christian groaned and went into another spasm.

"Listen. I think I'm supposed to do something... I think I

need to go back and meet Rasvampin alone... challenge him." I said.

"What—now?" Jack looked at me; his face even paler than it was earlier. "No, I don't think that's a good idea," he said, shaking his head.

"But we've got to get the mantle to Nathan! And we can't waste any more time— Christian's life is at risk. Let's face it. There are even more lives at stake than his. This war wouldn't be over just one person's life."

It was easy to see how angry Jack was, but he closed his eyes, got up, and stepped over facing the door. When he turned his face was a mask. But I knew him well enough by now to realize he'd just mastered his emotions—rather than simply controlling his features—and couldn't help wondering how long *that* might take me to get good at... "All right," he said, evenly.

I decided to fess up. "The only problem is, I'm scared," I said, realizing I didn't have a clue as to what God expected me to do.

"Did the information in the leather satchel give you any clues—help you at all with this?" Hailey asked.

"I don't know, maybe..."

Jack took my shoulders. "You don't have to do this..."

"Yes I..."

"Wait, let me finish. You don't have to do this ...by yourself..."

"But Hamaliel told you..."

His sort-of-smile began to pull at his mouth, "Let me finish," he said. "If you'll go in your weakness, God will meet you. He'll perfect in you the things where you feel unworthy. He doesn't wait until we're perfect or *ready*. It's about... Well, you know what it's about," he said, not looking at me as much as looking into me.

Suddenly, I did know. Suddenly, I had the answer. "It's about faith. It's always been about faith."

Jack kneeled down in front of me. I looked around embarrassed until I realized there was no room for Santos and him to sit. I quickly sat down with Hailey next to me, and Santos knelt in front of her.

"I think Santos is onto something with the whip affecting Christian. Let God work through you to disarm him. It's his weapon. At least try for the fangs. They're what's filled with poison. You're good with your blade, no one's better. But don't let him get to you...no matter what. Come back here; get back ...to us," he finished, looking steadily into my eyes.

I nodded. "Once I engage Rasvampin, one by one, you must meet up with Tessa and get inside the house," I said, looking back at him. "I'll meet you there."

We four took hands, but I couldn't help opening my eyes just once more. He was looking at me, too. I know he saw the tears in mine before I scrunched them shut, but I didn't care. He was...he was... well, it's hard to describe what he was to me at that moment.

Words began flowing into my heart. Amazing words! Words of praise began filling that desperate place of uncertainty and fear with hope, and peace and even joy... *"I will praise the LORD at all times. I will constantly speak his praises..."* *"I will boast only in the LORD; let all who are helpless take heart. Come, let us tell of the LORD's greatness; let us exalt his name together..."* *"I prayed to the LORD, and he answered me. He freed me from all my fears. Those who look to him for help will be radiant with joy; no shadow of shame will darken their faces. In my desperation I prayed, and the LORD listened; He saved me from all my troubles. For the angel of the LORD is a guard. He surrounds and defends all who fear him..."*

I was there, standing alone in the blazing circle. I had no

one to lead me out this time except my faith in something *unseen*: the thing that held me together: The cross of Christ. I stepped out, and there I was, standing smack dab in the middle of a very bad situation—with Rasvampin towering over me, not one hundred feet away. Now I'd heard the story of David and Goliath my whole life, and I had the distinct feeling that this had to have been a bit like the scene David encountered. The only difference was, I was no David; I'd gathered no stones, and for all my talk of faith, and the truly wonderful emotions that only moments before had been flowing into me, I was feeling fairly screwed. Rasvampin however, looked very comfortable with his role as the giant, standing with his whip writhing at his calf, and sneering with a mixture of dark pleasure and profound distaste in his hateful eyes. I felt my insides freeze as he watched me. He snapped the coiling whip into his hand, and I had no idea how I'd ever thought I could confront him alone.

"I am tempted to simply kill you where you stand...*you pathetic excuse for an adversary.*" His voice was a whispered hiss, but nonetheless, boomed within me and all about me. "Still, you are a puzzle, and I cannot help wondering why, of all those who were, and who might have been chosen—why were *you?*" I swallowed and tried to speak, but fear and doubt clogged my throat. That very question had been hiding in the recesses of my mind for so long, it was almost a relief to hear it spoken out loud. ...*Almost.*

"And you alone have no gifts from God...you squandered the one given to you at birth and chose rebellion and defiance in its place—both qualities I highly esteem—but not something I would think my adversary likely to choose in a champion," he continued, not realizing that what was left of those very attributes were rising up in me as he spoke.

"Stoppp... rrright there!" I managed to half sputter, half yell, putting my hand up, fingers spread like a grade school crossing monitor. Too late for correcting that image, I resisted the impulse to lower my arm, but I did put my fingers together. It worked, and Rasvampin stopped. He was either stunned by the audacity or dismayed by the stupidity. I assume both, but he stood for a fraction of a second looking almost surprised.

"Well, at least before I kill you, why don't you tell me how you, of all people, would dare confront me," he jeered, continuing to hold his viper whip at the ready.

"I've...I've come to challenge you!" I shouted, raising my sword in defense of what was sure to come hissing my way. Rasvampin looked at me for a moment and then put his head back and roared his laughter. It wasn't pretty.

"There is nothing, and I mean nothing on this earth, and I have been around for so very long, that you could ever challenge me in and win. You are just wasting time..." His whip hissed as it coiled in his hand, and I felt myself begin to shimmer.

"You're right!" I shouted, attempting to hold onto a thin line of bravado, "...Not about the time part, and there isn't anything I could challenge you in, at least not on my own... but I have faith..." He continued his cold stare, and I knew I had only seconds... "Are you afraid?" I asked quickly, letting my belligerent side take the reins. "Well, I guess I understand," I continued, "After all, big doesn't mean clever. Shoot, look at those guys," I said, pointing with my sword to the few Maltorphs still standing near us. "Big, strong, but not a lot in the 'ole brain department."

"Of course, but you're not even smart enough to know what, or whom you toy with," he growled, grimacing a smile. "However, I'm certain you're not stupid enough to compare *me* to a Maltorph," he continued, his eyes turning a spooky pale. And I knew I'd hit the target of his pride.

I swallowed hard. "Um, well, no, of course not. But

maybe you're ...scared?" I ventured, "Scared you're not as smart as this little human girl? I mean, of course you're not a Maltorph. But turning down a challenge, from the likes of me, well, it's not exactly what one thinks of when they hear the term 'Demon Destroyer,' either," I said, smiling insincerely.

He tried to smile, but it was *so* much more than insincere. "And you think I'm scared of *you*?" He sneered. My mouth was so dry it felt like I'd eaten the dust of ten Maltorphs.

"Uh huh."

"*You* want to challenge *me*?"

"Ye...yes."

"You do understand that I let you live—all of you—only for my own purposes. Why, in the name of the slayer of souls, would I bother with your wishes?" He seethed.

My mind went blank. I mean, why would he? "B..b..because there's something you want from me?"

He examined me for many long years. It was really only a fraction of a second, but it felt like forever. Finally, his eyes narrowed, "Your soul?" And I was almost sure the guttural grunt he emitted was a laugh.

"Um, not mine to give, someone beat you to it." I tried to wet my lips, but my tongue was parched.

He grimaced again, and I'm pretty sure it was his version of "attractive." Then he said, "I wait for the angel—who brings to—the *Link*—the mantle at the appointed hour," he said softly; and it was still loud enough to echo threateningly.

"Sorry, I don't have the mantle, and obviously, I'm not the *Link*."

"Yes, *that* at least is obvious. *Tell me which one of you is...*"

"Ah...the angel... ah...wouldn't tell us. We have to wait. ... But, hey, just *what* makes it *so* obvious it's not me?" I asked, kind of bugged.

He made a grunting sound. "Among so many other things, you are *much* too vain."

I lowered my head, "You should know," I said under my breath.

He eyed me menacingly. "Also, I'll know when you lie." He added. "Tell me. What is the angel's name? The one who you met, and gave you permission to act like any of you, besides the *Link*, matters at all in this battle between a great angelic being and—myself? I need to...*I wish to* know my opponent's name," he said, observing me carefully, his sinister eyes now red.

"I... d...don't know his..."

"YES! YOU DO!" The whip lashed out, hissing so close to my face I was knocked sideways. I was stunned at how quickly it had reached me from that distance.

"ALL RIGHT!" I yelled back at him, righting myself. I didn't know if I was scared or mad. Suddenly, the two emotions felt strangely intertwined. "I'll tell you if you win," I said, glaring at him. He appraised me coolly as hate emanated from his pores.

"And what is it you want from me?" He asked.

"The fangs out of your whip," I said, heat penetrating my entire body, even though I no longer inhabited the physical form.

"Ah, I see. So that's my part. All right. And if I win, you will tell me my opponent's name, the angel's name, and...as a parting gift, a reward, so to speak, you will also receive the fangs *in* my whip."

"The fangs *in* your whip?" I repeated, suddenly afraid I was about to lose my grip and end up back in the van. I stood in shock, and barely made sense of the words his booming voice blared in my direction.

"What do you have the audacity to challenge me in? The newest decadent styles of the formerly hedonistic, self-indulgent-but-recently-converted, Christian cheerleader types who still wish to wear debauched fashion trends while quoting the Bible?" His smile was amused and disdainful at the same time.

"Nice." I said under my breath. He really knew how to tick a girl off. We stared at each other for a moment. "I wouldn't start spouting off about fashion if I were you..." I started, but the look in his eyes was enough to stop me. I didn't need him to begin fingering his whip again... "OK, OK," I said, and the words came out before I knew what I was saying. "How about words, you know... books, literature." Three smooth stones, I thought. Dear God, help me unlock the cupboard...I mean the whatever...the nook... oh dear Lord, help me... Rasvampin was quiet, too quiet, smiling, ...sort of.

He then began a low laugh that sounded a lot like growling. "The last I heard, a *very* short while ago, was that you couldn't remember anything from your early life." He leered at my startled look. "Surely you know about the prince of the air? You can't speak these things without our hearing! And you should know this, although I'm afraid it's too late for you now, but I'm as well-versed in literature as I am in lies. But tell me this, since last I heard, have you been able to unlock the memories of your past?"

"No." I said. He held my stare; and I could tell my answer pleased him because his ugly smirk held such smug satisfaction.

"I have lived thousands of years—and you have no memory. Yet you have the audacity—the *gall*—to challenge me!" I stared at him. "ANSWER ME!"

"No," I said, "I'm here because I believe...in my weakness, He will be strong."

He smiled; it was even more grotesque than before. "Well, *'faith'* it is then."

"Um. Excuse me, but what are the rules?"

"Rules?" He asked, sneering. I was standing in front of a Demon Destroyer. What was I thinking? Was I insane? Too late, the answer was obviously, *yes*. "Well, OK. How about, you recite something...and I'll try and tell you the title and author..." I ventured.

"Ah, yes, but then you must also recite back a rebuttal from the same volume," he said slowly, "best two out of three. I don't have all night. I have an angel ...and *so many* people to destroy."

Again, I felt myself shimmering and losing hold of my spiritual form. In my mind, I remembered Christian lying in pain, and Jack speaking into me. "Lord, I know I've been saved through faith," I said aloud, and I saw Rasvampin control a cringe. Suddenly, a scripture coursed through my veins, and I felt my strength returning, *"Be strong! Be courageous! Do not be afraid of them! ...of HIM! For the Lord your God will be with you. He will neither fail you nor forsake you!"* I shouted.

"I BEGIN! *YOU* ARE SILENT!" Rasvampin roared, and I knew he hated the Word. It was as debilitating to him as it was revitalizing to me. "Here is my selection," he continued. Standing with his clawed hand on his chest and in a booming voice, he recited:

"but to fight... ('tis necessary to find the skulkers; and to eat), 'tis necessary to—talk of the devil and he will come;"

I waited, but he didn't say anything else. I looked at him as if he were out of his mind. "Oh, come on! That's hardly a recitation! What? You pick the one line out of some random book that has the word 'devil' in it?" I fumed.

"I assure you that the book is far from random. You have no memory! You've simply forgotten! It's sad, really, but I'll even give you more," he said, smiling in his horrible way. And I knew he loved hearing the sound of his own voice reciting. Throwing back his head, he continued:

> "...I should think myself *wicked, unto rebellion against His will,* was I to burrow with such warnings in the air! Even the weak soul who passes his days in singing is stirred by the cry, and, as he says, is 'ready to go forth to the battle' *If 'twere only a battle,* it would be a thing understood by us all, and easily managed. But I have heard that when such *shrieks* are atween heaven and 'arth, it betokens *another sort of warfare!*"

He was so clever, I thought, using passages to highlight his God-*forsaken* agenda, and then giving certain words his own emphasis. Well, fine, two could play at that, because he'd just given it away. ...or caused it to slip under the door. I smiled. Taking my sword, I swiveled it in the air until it sang. Setting its tip down in front of me with a flourish, I said, aloud, "*I put my hope in the LORD. He is my help and my shield. In Him my heart rejoices, for I trust in his holy name. Let your unfailing love surround me, LORD, for my hope is in you alone.*' Psalms 33:20-22." I said smiling and began to proceed with my rebuttal.

"WAIT!" Rasvampin thundered, "You will not speak or use verse from that text in this competition or you forfeit!!" I looked at him, and this time my eyes narrowed. Interestingly, he couldn't tell the difference between his fear and anger either. And boy, oh boy, scripture really chapped his hideous hide.

"All right, but I'd think you'd have mentioned that tid-bit in the rules if you were so adamant about it," I said, shaking my head, providing me the perfect expressive launch for my response to his recitation.

"'If all our reasons for fear, my friend, are confined to such as proceed from supernatural causes, we have but *little occasion* to be alarmed,' continued the undisturbed Cora. 'Are you certain that our enemies have not invented some new and ingenious method to *strike us with terror*, so that their conquest may become easier?'"

"And these would be from chapter seven of *The Last of the Mohicans* by James Fennimore Cooper." I said, bowing, which I'll admit was stupid. Once again, I heard the hiss next to my face. The whip snapped back into his hand before I'd even had time to look up. I'd have to be more careful—that's for sure... "Now...uh...don't be a sore loser..." I said. "We still have another round..."

"I didn't lose. You should have gotten that on the first try. I gave that to you..." He said, growling contemptuously. "Besides, I thought you'd lost your memory! Are you cheating?" He asked, expanding in size with his anger.

"You know I didn't lie. I am depending on my God!" I said, and his sneer assumed an even deeper degree of disdain before he began again.

> "In thrilling regions of thick-ribbed ice,
> To be imprisoned in the viewless winds,
> And blown with restless violence round about
> The pendent world; or to be worse than worst
> Of those that lawless and uncertain thoughts
> Imagine howling! 'tis too horrible!"

Rasvampin's voice snarled out the lines. I stood transfixed by the image. I knew the sound of the verse. It was Shakespeare. But help me, dear God, what was it? Would my father have made me read Shakespeare to Him? So far, I'd studied *Hamlet* and *Romeo and Juliet* in school, and had quickly perused *Taming of the Shrew* and *The Merchant of Venice*. And let's face it. I hadn't *really* studied… Still, I didn't think that verse was taken from any of these, but it could have been… Dear Lord.

I played for time. "Wow. That's quite a place. Been there often?" He raised his head, his eyes again turning pale with cruelty. *What was wrong with me?* "OK… It's Shakespeare. William. A play obviously, but I'm not sure…"

"YOU LOSE!" He roared.

"Wait! I still have another chance. It's two out of three. I've lost one, and so have you," I said quickly.

"I *didn't* LOSE!"

"Well, neither did I! Not the first one, anyway." I amended. Clearly, I'd lost this round. I could see Rasvampin's eyes turning less and less concerned with winning and losing. He became more and more interested in getting rid of me for good. There would be no next round. Time was so distorted between the dimensions that I wondered if everyone had made it into the house with Tessa and found Nathan yet.

"Next round, winner takes all!" I said, quickly.

He eyed me malevolently with his hypnotic eyes, but I wasn't so enthralled by him that I couldn't see his trusty snake-whip slowly coiling. It readied itself to strike. Win or lose, I'd have to be ready to disappear. And then, in my mind, I imagined the whip heading toward me, its mouth open, and its fangs bared, just as it had a half dozen times already this night. It had always struck from a certain height downward, and it always swerved either left or right away from our swords, never up or down.

If I moved sideways at the last possible moment, and struck up, not down, I might be able to hit it. I might be able to graze it, anyway. It would be lightning fast at this distance. If I missed, it would be on me. I wouldn't be able to transfer back to the van fast enough. But I had to try. *I had to have faith.* After all, God knew me before I was born, and He knew me in my mother's womb. He knew I was, well, a performer of sorts, and I could make Rasvampin believe I wasn't paying attention. He further knew that I was into my own performance. All these thoughts sped like quicksilver through me. Still, Rasvampin had already begun. His usually booming voice had become eerily dark and chilling:

"...With the wan moon overhead, There stood, as in an awful dream, The army of the dead.Encamped beside Life's rushing stream, In Fancy's misty light, gigantic shapes and shadows gleam portentous through the night.No other voice nor sound is there, in the army of the grave. No other challenge breaks the air, but the rushing of life's wave.Down the broad Vale of Tears afar *Men's spectral faith is fled.* Fear shineth as a morning star, for their ghastly fate is death."

I stood stock-still. His words appeared in my mind—passages—but something seemed off. There was no possible way I could know what this was, and yet, the words were, words were... "Wordsworth, wait. Wads...worth. Henry Wadsworth Longfellow! *The Beleaguered City!*" I cried, "But you screwed it up a little bit, I think. Did you leave something out?" I asked, pretending not to notice Rasvampin's building wrath. "Oh, my turn, right? OK, Here goes, and check me if I'm wrong...because, as you know, I'm a little sketchy in the memory department ..." Holding one hand dramatically over my heart, I tilted my head to the side in such a reverent way that the only thing I could see was Rasvampin's hand readying his vile whip. My other hand was holding my sword, which rested easily at my side. I hoped Rasvampin couldn't hear the tension whining in its steel as I began:

"And when the solemn and deep church-bell Entreats the soul to pray, The midnight phantoms feel the spell, The shadows sweep away..."

I didn't get any further. The moment I saw his fingers twitch, I knew. But I waited only a fraction longer, and then in one action, I moved sideways and sliced with all my strength upwards. The surreal hissing stopped as I watched venom spew wildly onto the ground. The head of the snake-whip flailed toward me, knocking me over, but the amazing bodily lightness of this realm came to my aid. I flew to my feet, ducking another erratic swing of the snake's skull. The viper was badly wounded and losing venom. Because of its twisting, I couldn't see well enough to know if I'd taken off both fangs, but I had to have severed at least one. Rasvampin was roaring, trying to control his whip so he could kill me— and then kill me again—and then maybe again. I decided it was time to go. I shouted as I began to shimmer,

"Down the broad Vale of Tears afar the spectral camp is fled; *Faith shineth as a morning star,* our ghastly fears are dead!"

Rasvampin stopped his roaring and was staring at me, his face contorted. And I don't know what got into me, but I yelled, "Hamaliel sent us! But don't bother waiting up for him!" His stare changed into a look both furious and disbelieving. And then I was in the van—and probably not a moment too soon. Santos was still there, holding hands with me. He stared at me like I'd lost what little sense had ever been mine in the first place. Of course, I understood why, but asked anyway, "What?""Really? You gonna cut the teeth off his whip, and then you gonna give him more reason to want to kill you? This isn't over yet. And he's still got that whip, ya know." I looked out and saw Rasvampin storming up and down the entire area, cracking his flailing whip while hitting people haphazardly. The effect of the weapon, even somewhat neutralized, was still wreaking havoc. Just then, Christian stirred."Christian!" We both called out together. He tried sitting up, but lay back down again, and we knelt beside him.

"How do you feel, man?" Santos asked. "We been real worried."

"Not...so good. What happened? Wait. Was I in a football...game? Are my brothers...here?" He asked, his eyes still unfocused. I couldn't help smiling.

"No, man. You been fighting evil. And you saved Cassie. You were awesome!"

"Cassie? OK Cool... She's coo..." he didn't finish. Closing his eyes, he slept, but it was different. He seemed to be out of pain, and there were no more spasms.

"It worked," I said, leaning my head on Santos—grateful beyond measure.

"We all watched, and you did good. *Real good*. Except for the last part," he added with a worried look on his face.

"I know. It's just that Rasvampin's *such* a cheater." I added rather lamely.

"Oh, now that's a big surprise," Santos said, shaking his head... "Will you try and remember the other things he is? Like a liar, a stealer, and a killer—especially try and remember the last one..."

Chapter Thirty-One

Santos and I slipped out of the van holding hands and crept a long way up the road before cutting over toward the house. I looked at my watch, and was shocked to find it was only 10:45. It felt like we'd been at this demon-fest *a lot* longer. It was then I realized, that without a doubt, this time warp stuff could work for you, *and* against you.

Some of the cars had already began thinning out but considering how many fights were springing up; I wasn't too surprised. But there were also new cars of kids arriving late. Evidently word had gotten out, and I knew it couldn't bode well, considering the type of personalities the news of a rowdy party would draw. We were still a distance from the house when I said, "Thanks, Santos. I appreciate you're coming with me and staying to wait for me. I hate not being able to see what's out here."

"No problem, Cassita. I know what you mean. But I don't think either one of us is going to want to see what's in the house."

"Yea, well, that's if we can even get in. Did the others get in OK?"

"No problem. They had to kill a few Maltorphs, but not too many. Rasvampin saw Jack go in just when you guys finished. He was real mad. But he was mad anyways. I don't know if we'll get in or not. But the others are there. That's what's important." he said.

"How long ago was that?" I asked, still surprised by the time. Santos looked at his watch.

"Let's see—almost four minutes ago? Wow, time is crazy. Seems longer. OK, stand here while I look around the corner. Yea he's over there. OK, you see him?"

I took hold and peeked around the corner, too. "Yes, but he's not too close to the door. He's far enough to the other side that I think we can make it."

"OK," Santos took a deep breath. "We stay together. Walk fast, but don't run. If he goes after us, we don't split up. Call for angels, OK?"

"You bet."

We started for the door at a quick pace. Santos looked everywhere at once, talking to himself the whole way, *"I don' like that house, they'll be doing drugs...the demons...really bad ones...different than the others..."*

"He's seen us, Santos," I said. We'd nearly reached the door, and Rasvampin had spotted me. He was watching us, and it seemed a certain look of satisfaction came into his evil eyes. It was enough to give me pause. But that's all I did, pause. Meeting his malicious gaze one last time, I drug a momentarily hypnotized Santos over the threshold and into the house's darkened interior. We stood for a moment and looked around.

Of course, the first thing that struck me was the music. It was a good thing Rachel's house was set out on acreage and was away from neighbors. Had anyone lived next door, the sheer volume of the music would, in very short order, have caused irreparable damage to anyone with old ear canals. But I had to admit that the vibration of the bass went through my body pounding in my blood. It felt good and was itself intoxicating. For an instant, I recognized the pull—the attraction of the dark pulsating room—filled with people seeking physical gratification.

I closed my eyes for a moment, allowing my pupils to adjust to the darkness. When I opened them, I couldn't believe how many people were packed into each room. A strobe light distorted the twisting bodies of the dancers. It was a second before I realized that not everyone I saw was human. Of course, there were Siphons of various breeds, both ugly and sickening, but we'd gotten almost accustomed to their hideous, evil, sucking presence. And there weren't that many, considering the quantity we'd dispatched at the school. Although, I was looking at a different creature on the dance floor tonight. What made their presence so difficult to determine was the nature of these entities. At first, I wasn't sure they were demons—but then I realized, they had to be. They were so dark, and as I looked closer, there was something about their solidity that made them almost more frightening then Rasvampin. These beings were the shadow images of the person they attached themselves to only... entirely black, no essence of color...no light at all. They were empty. They were dark holes...

I sensed, rather than saw, the deep "hooks" connecting them to their human forms, and saw how very hungry, insatiably hungry they were. I felt Santos' hand tightening on mine. "Let's get out of here. These are the ones I was talking about," he shouted so I could hear over the din.

"They remind me of a something ...too terrifying to remember," I yelled back, not kidding even a little. I hoped that none of them looked over at us, even for a fraction of a second. If they did, we could be lost forever in what had to be the endless spiraling hole of their emptiness. "This must be Satan's favorite design," I said, ready to take Santos up on his idea of leaving. Suddenly, facing Rasvampin seemed less terrifying. Then I saw Tessa. And next to her, Hailey...and there was Jack. I pointed toward them, and Santos sighed.

As we walked over, I focused only on their faces, and I assumed Santos did the same. Their expressions lit up when they saw us, and we embraced each other. Tessa pointed to Nathan. He sat with his back against a wall. Alyssa on his lap, leaning against him while his hands moved languidly over her body. Suddenly she rose, and taking Nathan's hand, Alyssa pulled him with her over to a table. She walked slowly and lazily, as though she'd already taken something, but the two stood in front of the tabletop looking down at lines of powder. A few dark formless spirits lurked behind them... silent, vacant, and cold. They waited for someone to decide to move far enough into their world so they'd be able to attach.

"See that stuff?" Santos yelled barely loud enough, "The lines of white powder?"

"Yea. What is it?" Jack shouted.

"It's the purest form of Ecstasy. That's what Rasvampin sold to my friends. My homies, they all love it. They say it's a great high, man. It's supposed to be the best," Santos answered.

"And look at all the nice friends who want to come along for the ride," I yelled, still watching the black holes wavering behind Alyssa and Nathan. "If your friends could see this, they might be *a little less*...ecstatic." I shouted, wondering if one of us... *Jack*... would have to tackle Nathan. Outside, the incoming storm was brewing. Wind had begun lashing the tree limbs against the windowpanes, and every very few seconds the sky lit up with lightening in bright electrical zigzags. There was no way to hear the thunder however, not over this soundtrack. And there was no way to tell what Rasvampin was planning. I was becoming more and more nervous.

Alyssa bent over and picked up a rolled dollar bill from the table. She began inhaling a line of powder as Nathan watched pensively. One of the vacant shadows slipped so quickly around her waist that I didn't see it happen. It took her form and began sucking her neck. A cold shiver ran through me at the same moment Alyssa shivered in the Ecstasy rush. Emotions washed over Nathan's features as he stood watching her. He'd always hated drugs—had never taken them before, and I wondered just how much things had changed. Suddenly, he turned away from Alyssa—and saw me. Our eyes met—mine were pleading. Alyssa saw me, too. She wandered over and wrapped her arms around my neck, pressing her body against me. And if that wasn't bad enough, she'd brought along the "well" of slinking hunger on her back. It was more than yuck; it was scary. I couldn't help cringing after being so close to it—and I wasn't particularly drawn to Alyssa either. Surprisingly, the form began dragging her backwards away from me, thankfully taking Alyssa with it.

Tessa touched my sleeve. "We'd better hurry," she mouthed. Nathan stared at us, looking unsure. We five stared back, saying nothing. It was now or never. Rasvampin hadn't let Santos and me into the house because he'd wanted us to enjoy the party. Dread began to tickle the back of my brain. We were in trouble, and I knew it. Nathan was either in or out, but if he wasn't willing to accept the mantle, we'd have to find a way to protect it until we could get it back to Hamaliel. We would have to defend it until another who could fulfil the destiny could be found. And getting it out of here wasn't going to be easy. But either way, as Darius so succinctly put it, Rasvampin had to be "taken out."

Nathan's hand went unconsciously to his throat, massaging the snake-whip's invisible wound. Alyssa attached herself to him, kissing his neck and rubbing herself along the length of his body. He pushed her away. She turned and found someone else. Walking over, he stopped in front of us. "All right. What am I supposed to do?" He called, fear shadowing his eyes.

Jack stepped up. "Nathan." I was surprised at the underlying kindness I heard in Jack's voice. "You've already accepted Jesus as your Lord, but your 'will' has never been given to Him." I saw Nathan stiffen. "The things of the world aren't more real than things of the spirit. In fact, they aren't as real, but if you want the world, it's yours...for now. But you can't have God, too," Jack shouted, meeting Nathan's stare without blinking. Nathan looked away.

"Well, after tonight, I've kind of I've lost my taste for the things of the world," he yelled, looking back at Jack. Santos took Nathan's arm, and it was a moment before his face registered the shock of seeing all the hungry black holes attached to our friends.

"Yes, that's how we are all feeling. Glad to have you back, man." Santos shouted.

"Are you willing to stand for the Lord your God? You'll be tested." Jack yelled.

"I don't know. But I'll try. I'll do my best," he shouted back, still shaken. Jack never took his eyes off him.

"All right then—Tessa—give him the mantle." Tessa smiled and reached under the layers of her shirts. Her smile faded as her small fingers began frantically patting her inside pockets.

"It's not here, how can that be? I just felt it a few moments ago. It was so warm...I knew it was time..." she shouted, looking up at us.

"Tessa, look at your fingers," I yelled, staring in surprise.

They glowed, brightly, the tips luminescent in the darkened room, and then began to fade. "Tessa!" I yelled, "You're the *Link!*" She looked up at me, her eyes steady, but fear magnified none-the-less. The mantle had been assimilated.

Taking Tessa by the shoulder and smiling at her, Jack yelled to the rest of us, "All right! Let's get out of here," She looked up at us and nodded, and somehow, I knew she'd be OK.

"Everyone needs to touch each other in order to see the demons," Jack continued, explaining it to Nathan. "So, let's head for the van. Most of the Maltorphs should be gone by now, but there may be a stray one or two the angels have missed. The real problem are the people that were hit. Things are out of hand out there, and someone may already have called the police. Therefore, we should get away from here as fast as we can," he shouted. Our line began moving.

"Jack?" I yelled, following him with my hand on his shoulder and grasping Nathan's hand with my other one. "Have you forgotten about Rasvampin?" Suddenly, there was a crack of thunder, and it was loud enough to be heard over the music. I knew that could only mean one thing, and it wasn't bad weather. A red blazing light suddenly surrounded us, and the room instantly went silent. In a way it brought relief, but everyone around us had disappeared. Where there had once been a raging party, now there only stood an empty house. The six of us huddled together, too startled to speak. And even this was not comforting.

The once warm pulsating room was now cold. Wind still howled outside, and branches scratched the dark panes of glass. However, the only light came from a red glow which didn't seem to have a source. It only gave the room a very spooky atmosphere.

"It's a different dimension," Tessa said quietly, evidently grasping this fact much more quickly than the rest of us. The most I'd been able to conclude was that it probably wasn't a hallucination. After all, there were too many of us. Given two more seconds, I'd probably have nailed the "different dimension" thing. …But maybe not.

Once again, we heard the crack of thunder, but this time I knew. It wasn't thunder we were hearing; it was the crack of Rasvampin's whip. Still, he was nowhere to be seen. The sound came from somewhere deeper in the house, but we stood huddled together unmoving. Meanwhile, the house began creaking and groaning under the onslaught of the windstorm outside. Moving along the walls, dark images with ghoulish mouths and empty eyes quietly moaned and made whispering sounds but made no move toward us.

"I feel like we're in a *real* haunted house," Hailey said, her eyes wide with fear.

"I think he's trying to scare us," Jack stated. His face was stern, and I wondered if that was a reaction to his fear, or just plain anger—something I'd thought a lot about today.

Nathan squeezed my hand. "What's going on?" He asked. Suddenly, without warning, a hatchet flew and landed in a door post next to Santos' face. He yelled and fell to the side, letting go of Tessa and Hailey's hand. Slowly, he reached out and touched the weapon. It was solidly embedded in the wood, and he quickly dropped his hand.

Interestingly, nothing changed when the rest of us were no longer in contact with Santos. So, we released each other's hands, although I still held onto Nathan's, and we began walking toward the door leading outside. Disconcertingly, it kept receding further and further into the distance. Suddenly a floating figure of a smiling child with gore and blood for eyes moved into view. She stretched out a ghostly pale arm and we could see she held a long-bloodstained knife. Laughing a giddy, little laugh, she rushed blindly toward us. Hailey and I screamed, crouching near the floor in panic. The manic child disappeared through a wall.

Tessa looked around almost coolly. "He's really scraping the bottom of the barrel. He thinks he can disarm us with fear." She stated, scornfully.

"Yes, well, I can actually see the logic in that plan," I said, getting up and trying to dust off my pants. I hadn't realized that knees knocked together if you got scared enough. I'd always thought people made that up.

"OK, listen. This isn't real. Not unless you believe it," Tessa said. "Watch." She went over to the hatchet and her hand passed right through it. Santos followed her and pulled it out of the mantle.

"It looks pretty real to me," he replied.

"Santos, it isn't. You were scared by it," Jack said, walking over to him. "I'm telling you; it's your fear. Let go of it." Santos kept his eyes fastened on Jack and released the hatchet. It never fell to the floor, but simply vanished from sight. "OK, keep walking," Jack finished.

The crack of a whip came again, but this time behind us. We spun around, and Rasvampin stood at the end of the room. He was now at least fifty feet away. The ceilings were now at least twelve feet high, and he towered over us, filling the end of room. At this point, I realized he'd appeared the same size when he was outside at a hundred feet away. And at two hundred...

He began his low growl.

"Hamaliel. He played his game... very well ...shamefully, but quite well. So, he managed to hide the mantle...but only because he was too *cowardly*, too *gutless*, and too *frightened*, to meet me! Instead, he sends..." his face twisted in disgust, "you, you..." He spit the words out at us, "creatures of less value than the offal of dogs... *to challenge me?* And now, I sense the mantle has been integrated. Very well..." Then as if to himself, he raged, "Of course, I couldn't have guessed! Clever, clever…

"However, this war is far from over. I know one of you is the *Link*. I may not get the mantle of power, but then neither shall this world; not this time. I feel the presence of it. My skin aches with its nearness, and I ache with the need to destroy…"

When I'd faced the Demon Destroyer alone, I realized the fear he created in me was so much greater than when the seven of us stood together. Together we had power, and I was able to discern that, as angry and evil as he was, Rasvampin's underlying love was also for the spectacle of this moment. Evil seethed beneath a surface of swagger. He moved slowly, back, and forth, whip furling and unfurling in his hand. He even had on the ridiculous cape again. It swirled at his boots, which I noticed were intricately buckled. *Hmm, clever design, but too funky and over the top. He really needed help… Well, obviously he needed help!* And mentally I slapped myself. I needed to pay attention. I couldn't believe I'd unconsciously switched to fashion mode.

"However," he was saying, "along with the silver lining comes the dark day, and although it may have seemed clever of Hamaliel to place the mantle where I'd never guess—with the likes of you—unbelievable! *Children* were chosen to protect the mantle! Ha! Well, with that decision comes the reckoning. Because now you *children* are *all* that stand between me and the *Link*." He gave what I suppose was his smile, showing dark pointed teeth, and I shivered. "Unfortunately, there are rules in this realm. Otherwise, I wouldn't hesitate to kill all of you—outright—and with great pleasure," he said, looking at me. "However, the great Hamaliel probably didn't tell you one rather important item of information. And it's one rule about this realm that gives me such pleasure. If I break just one Guardian, the rest of you are also *mine*." He said, trying again to frighten us while definitely frightening me. "I'm guessing Hamaliel didn't think you were quite up to having *that* part shared with you," he said, his foul smirk on his face.

And I didn't know about anybody else, but that bit of information was very unnerving. The *"all* for *one"* seemed a little...unfair in these circumstances. Besides that, I knew from experience, that if Rasvampin felt he had to abide by the "no killing" us until he got to the "one of us" rule, the consequences of him breaking it had to be pretty severe. Personally, however, I wasn't counting on that holding him in check. I mean, what were his consequences, going to Hell?

He cracked his whip and lightening lit the sky outside, flooding through the windows in an eerie blue burst. "I think I shall begin!" He stood eyeing us, his gaze shifting and searching. "Let's see, let's start with... you!" He said, swinging and pointing at Hailey.

She stood transfixed; her eyes held captive by Rasvampin's cruel stare. "I'll make this easy for you. I don't feel the mantle upon you as I'd hoped. You seemed the most likely, as you were the most *unlikely*. So, all you must do is place one knee upon the floor. No declaration of allegiance. No need to sign a paper and sell your soul. It is so simple. Merely place your knee upon the floor, and everything that I promise you, will be so."

"Don't listen to him, Hailey," Santos urged. Hailey looked around frantically but didn't meet our eyes.

"We've vanished to her; she can't see us anymore. She may not even think she's still in this room," Tessa explained, quietly. "How does your sister know all this stuff?" Nathan whispered in my ear. I only had time to shrug. The truth is, I didn't have any better answer to that than how she knew when a coefficient of a logarithm could be turned into an exponent. I mean *please*, she was a genius.

Rasvampin's voice became soothing, or at least his version of it. "Hailey, I will give you beauty. Great beauty. You will never worry about food, or your figure again. Men will look upon you with longing in their eyes. Women, girls, your so-called-friend Cassie, will never laugh behind your back again. They will envy you. They will want you with them, just to bask in your beauty."

"Get behind me, Satan!" Hailey yelled, frantically looking around and finding herself alone and probably in the dark.

"Do you really think you need to talk to me like that, Hailey? I'm giving you a chance, right here, right now. And it's a chance for a better life. Those times your stepfather knocked on your bedroom door, and all the times he beat you when you resisted him. I can make you forget—and I can make him pay. You won't wake up in the night afraid anymore. You will sleep like a baby," Rasvampin cooed.

With each word, Hailey flinched as from a blow. Her head lowered with each sentence until it was bowed, and she began crying. He was attacking her at a level deeper than her logical mind was functioning. Only her spirit could determine her answer. She began to waver, tears running down her face, and I wanted to hold her swaying body, but I knew she wouldn't even feel my touch. I wept with her, and there were tears on Tessa's face and in Santos' eyes. We began calling out to her, knowing she couldn't hear us, but needing to voice our support.

"...There is surely a future hope for you, and your hope will not be cut off..." "Arise, shine; for your light has come! And the glory of the Lord is upon you..." "... He will not let you stumble and fall; the one who watches over you will not sleep..."

As we were calling out, Rasvampin continued coercing her. "One knee, Hailey; that's all I'm asking. Come now, your whole life will be different. You will be happy. You will have so much fun! Come, Hailey. One knee touching the floor. I'm not asking too much, am I? Not considering everything I'll give you..."

Suddenly, Hailey's head shot up, and she wiped the tears from her face. "What am I doing?" She asked herself angrily, and then shouted, "Go away and leave me alone. I don't want *you* to change my life! Don't you know? *My light affliction, which is but for a moment, is working for me a far more exceeding and eternal weight of glory,*" and the five of us watching began to yell and holler, reciting along with her, *"... while we do not look at the things which are seen, but at the things which are not seen. For the things which are not seen are eternal!"*

There was another flash of light and Hailey turned to us, with us again, and we fell into her arms. But Santos stood like a statue, as though in a trance.

"OK, looks like he's got Santos now. What are we going to do? Let him bully each one of us?" Jack asked.

Santos stood, a look of stark fright on his face. "Ah, wrong again. Well, all right, but you don't need to be afraid of me, Raphael. You won't need to be afraid of anybody or anything ever again. I know how you want to find your place in this world, and I can make it happen. People will nod their heads with respect when you pass. In time, you will become a powerful man. You will always have everything you need, and everything you've ever wanted," Rasvampin promised.

"Where am I?" Santos asked, and we knew he'd forgotten what had happened to Hailey just moments before. He was alone with the demon of his worst fears and deepest longings.

"Your friends have left you. You didn't fit in. After all, they're all white. But I'll make you so powerful no white person will dare defy your will. Power is what makes the world go 'round. All I'm asking, is for you to drop one knee to the ground, for one second."

"All right, he's gone far enough. If I had my sword, I'd... I'd...slice him!" I shouted, secure in my knowledge Rasvampin couldn't hear us. At that moment he lifted his malevolent eyes to mine, sending a shock through me, and I almost wet myself.

Returning his gaze to Santos, Rasvampin paused. He waited, as he stared steadily into Santos' eyes, watching as his knees became loose, and said, "I will give you all that you have ever wanted. Your mother will never have to clean another toilet..."

That's as far as he got. Santos heard the word, "mother," and his face changed as though he'd heard her call his name. "My mother...*my mother*, she used to pray over me at night. It was Psalms 97:10. Listen up, Rasvampin. I'm not afraid of you; and I'm not afraid of who I am. '...*Let those who love the Lord hate evil, for He guards the lives of his faithful ones and delivers them from the hand of the wicked...*'" Of course, we'd all begun cheering wildly, but Santos wasn't done. "I don't need your promises, man, and I don't need to be kneeling to the likes of you..." he continued bravely, if foolishly, when, with a clap of thunder, Santos blinked. He was back.

We looked around. At first it looked like we were all still with each other, but then I remembered Nathan. I turned around to see him standing further off in the room toward Rasvampin, staring.

"Jack, he's not strong enough yet! What are we going to do?" I asked frantically.

"We're going after him," Jack stated.

"How?" We all seemed to ask at once.

"There must be a way. Why should Rasvampin be in charge? I think we're giving him power he doesn't really have!" Jack asserted.

"Jack's right," Tessa agreed. "Let's take hands and start praying."

"Yea, and if he can have his whip—one eyed and toothless, I might add—then there's no reason we can't have our swords!" I said. I couldn't believe how quickly we five were able to achieve focus in that weird place. We didn't even end up in a different circle. Within moments, I simply found myself holding my sword. Miraculously, my fear, all my earlier anxiety and trepidation, had vanished. "Leave him alone, Rasvampin! We've just ... *put on the armor of God!*" I yelled, as we began moving toward him.

Chapter Thirty-Two

Rasvampin spoke to Nathan in a firm voice, not using the same wiles he used on the others. He must have sensed Nathan wouldn't need the same kind of coercion. "What? It isn't you either! No matter because I will give you the presidency of the United States. You will be the most powerful man in the entire world. You know you want it, and you know I can get it for you. Don't be a fool." Nathan's upper lip was beaded in sweat, but his back was ramrod stiff.

"No," was all he answered. As I advanced on Rasvampin, he raised his whip, slashing it down on me and throwing me across the room. The jagged edges of the whip's shorn fangs snapped only inches from my face. The viper's jaws would have continued after me, but Jack was attacking Rasvampin from the other side.

Lying on my back, I watched as Jack came to my aid and was whiplashed sideways, thrown headfirst into the corner. A lash mark burned onto his shirt. Both of us lay helplessly watching as Hailey and Santos were each thrown one direction, their swords sent flying in another. Only Tessa stood, strangely hidden in the shadows, praying. She was facing Rasvampin and was only a few feet from Nathan. To my relief, however, he ignored her completely, and turned his attention back to his target, as though she didn't exist.

"No? *You,* say '*no,*' to *me?* Well, maybe I didn't make myself clear. If you don't kneel, I will kill you. But, if you do, and with only one knee, not only will I make sure your dreams of becoming President come true, but I'll also make sure you have *Cassie.*"

I heard my name and gasped. Nathan faltered. He looked up into Rasvampin's eyes, clarity coming into his own. I saw him mouth my name. "You'll make sure I'm President, *and* I can have Cassie?" He asked, his voice low, his eyes intense.

"Nathan!" I screamed, "He can't promise you *anything,* Nathan!" I got up and began running towards him, but once again, I was thrown to the other side of the room. "OK, that's it." I got to my feet and dusted myself off. Rasvampin had put all his power into his version of a mantle, too. Darius had said so, and it had to be invested in that corny whip of his. Granted, the ugly little accessory was effective— but so what? It could be damaged; we'd proven that. Now, we just needed to get at it. Rasvampin had his eyes glued to Nathan who stood wavering, one knee already partly bent. I ran over to Jack.

"Jack, we need more faith. Faith in *God's* Word..." Rasvampin looked up.

"You're right," Jack said, and together we began speaking scriptures out loud. Santos looked over, and started, and then Hailey joined in. Our swords began to hum and sing.

"Rasvampin has put all has faith in his own power, and it's all wrapped up in that whip," I called, interrupting our recitations.

"All right, then let's all go in at the same time—whoever has a shot—take it! Chop it up if you can!" Jack yelled.

Rasvampin looked up again, alarm showing on his hideous features for the very first time. We all ran toward him together, and as his whip sailed hissing through the air, we sang our scriptures out. Our blades swung at its twisting, slithering length.

I don't know who severed it first, but I know I got a good slice before finding myself knocked over; four foot of the tip lay next to me hissing and writhing.

I looked up and saw Rasvampin, smaller now, down on his knees holding only a short stubbed off crop in his hand. Long chunks of the whip lay withering on the floor around him, and a look of fury contorted his already hideous face. Jack was behind him where he'd landed, spinning on one knee. He'd chopped a sizable chunk of the whip onto the floor beside him. It was then the demon saw Tessa. She stood with her head bent, her hands pressed to her sides, and her eyes wide and staring. All the while, she was reciting scripture. Gasping, Rasvampin lunged towards her. All I could do was scream.

He caught Tessa in his one free, claw-like hand, while the other clung to the end of what was left of the whip stub. Tessa was caught and stared with horror into the eyes of horror itself. "You! It was *you* all along?" He bellowed his voice filled with rancor and disbelief.

Nathan, hanging on, trying to resist Rasvampin's trap. He stood straining against his own buckled knees, but when he heard my scream, he came to himself. Seeing Rasvampin clutching Tessa, he looked over at Santos. Nathan was without a sword, but Santos threw him his own. Nathan caught it in both hands, and in one smooth movement, turned and swung down. He caught Rasvampin between the shoulder blades. At the same time, Jack saw the stub of whip clenched in Rasvampin's hand and slashed at it, sending it skidding to the other side of the room. The Demon Destroyer threw back his head and roared. He let go of Tessa and stood, trying to come towards me. His face enraged, he only stumbled forward and went down. Jack walked over to him with his sword gleaming. "Cassie, I think you need to do the honors."

The demon, rising to his knees, looked at me as I came towards him. He was malevolent, and evil, but also, I sensed, filled with shock and shame to be so undone by a bunch of humans—kids no less. My emotions swirled. "Rasvampin..." I began.

"I'll be back, and I'll find you, and I'll defeat you... all of you!" he cried.

I looked at him for a long moment. He'd put us through... hell. Still, I sure knew how grateful I was to be forgiven. "Here's the thing," I said, "I should hate you. In fact, I'm supposed to be the one to kill you," At this, Rasvampin gave an exultant smirk, filled with revulsion. I ignored it. "But you see this sword? It's the Word, the Word of God. I was saved from exactly what you consist of: nothing, nothingness. Now, I've been thinking. If each one of us were to pray for you and ask the Lord to forgive you for all that you've done to us...in other words, if we were to surround you with love right now —instead of hate—well, even *you* would have a chance. I believe that." Rasvampin's countenance, which earlier had shown alarm, was suddenly transformed into sheer terror.

I saw his fear and knew how he felt. "Don't worry. At first you think you have to give up everything you want and everything you think you need in order to be happy. Although, I guarantee that *you* are *not* happy. In fact, you can't *really* exist except in God. So, you honestly have nothing to lose. And we won't get weird and lay hands on you or anything. I, for one, *am not* touching you. Now, I know it's strange, considering your allegiance has always been to Satan. Still, we're asking you to let God come into your, well...

nothingness; but if you don't, the decision you make will be eternal." I noticed everyone looking at me with their mouths hanging open. Only Jack was smiling, but it was his sort-of-smile, which of course, didn't count. I never knew what the heck that meant. "Right?" I asked, looking around.

"Oh, yea, sure..." Nathan said, very unconvincingly. But really, I reasoned, what did he know? He'd probably have chosen a similar path himself if we hadn't gone to such great lengths to get him to see the truth. Tessa, Santos, and Hailey nodded in agreement, but their shocked expressions never changed. I chalked it up to exhaustion.

Rasvampin remained silent, his mouth twisted, his eyes still filled with alarm. I recognized this might not work—but really, what did we, or he, have to lose? If something didn't change him, change his very make-up, or change what held him together, and I was forced to destroy him, he'd be gone—kaput. He wouldn't get another chance, well, in Hell, to put it bluntly. It was now or never, and when would he ever have a better opportunity? And maybe, just maybe, down deep, like me, he wanted something more than nothing... more than himself. "Let's start. Tessa, would you begin?" I asked, holding my sword, it's blade flat in front of me, and closing my eyes. Tessa held her little hands toward the Demon Destroyer and began praying. I peeked out and watched as Rasvampin immediately began roaring, seething, and I took this as a sign. Of something...I just wasn't sure...what.

We all began saying our scriptures under our breath, and with all my heart, I asked the Lord to redeem this horrible creature, because after all, those who have been forgiven much, love much. And that meant he'd love... well, let's face it, he ought to be the most loving. My prayers were interrupted by the sound of an explosion. Not like dynamite, but a lot louder than an exploding Maltorph.

It seemed I was the only one shocked to find nothing was

left of the lethal Rasvampin except a lot of soft powder smelling like... sulfur. I was very glad I'd held my sword between my body and those noxious particulates. I stood looking at the pile. He'd been *so* terrible. I supposed it was too much to hope his un-soul... no...I reasoned; he was probably just too evil. Then there was his fashion sense; *really*, it was unforgivable.

I was so tired. I think that's why I started laughing; it had to be. There really wasn't anything funny about what happened. I turned to find everyone standing in a circle, staring at me, and looking a bit surprised. They were just as tired, and then they all started laughing too. We were sort of hysterical, really.

And then, slowly, we met in the center of the room. We fell into each other's arms; and even though I tried to control myself, I began crying. Tessa, thankfully, joined in, and then, of course, Hailey let loose, too. The guys continued to chuckle, but even they settled down some; it was the music that finally brought us to ourselves. Blaring, the bass reverberating through my body once again. We let go of each other and looked around. I wiped my face.

"Let's get out of here," Jack said.

I stared at my watch. That eternity had lasted all of six minutes. Nathan looked around stunned. I was glad I wasn't touching Santos at the time; therefore, I didn't have to see the vacant-black hole-attached-things that danced in the room. I looked over at Santos and his head was bent, looking only at his feet. Poor guy—I thought—heck of a creepy gift. As we made our way to the door, Alyssa came up still wasted, which, considering the time-warp, was understandable yet... even so... regrettable. Be that as it may, she hooked her arm around Nathan's waist. "Come on, lover, don't go home," she whined. "I'll give you anything you want. In fact, I feel like giving you everything!" she smiled stupidly. Nathan managed to dislodge Alyssa and get out the door with us.

Jack was standing with Santos on the porch scanning for any surviving Maltorphs. I touched Santos' arm and saw that they were gone, but the chaos they'd created was still in full swing. Beer cans lay strewn on the grass. Two groups of kids faced off against each other. Why they'd chosen sides was uncertain, other than an uncontrollable need to fight had been invisibly carved into them by rusty demonic blades.

Jack looked over and caught my eye. He tried to tell me something, but I couldn't figure out what it was. I smiled, and he returned his inscrutable smile. Ooh, it was infuriating. Nathan walked up behind me, putting his arm around my waist, but it must have felt awkward, because he squeezed me, continued, and stood next to Jack.

"Let's steer clear of the lawn. It looks like there's a fight about to happen," Jack directed. I took Tessa's hand. The six of us made our way to the far edge of the lawn and then down to the road. We were walking along the road when Hailey saw them. She was holding Santos' hand, and I liked to think it wasn't just so she could see demon activity. Suddenly, the streetlights shone on a car coming toward us driving very slowly. As the doors opened, she saw the back of a Maltorph's head extending out the top of the car. She stopped and pointed, no words coming from her mouth.

Jack and Nathan were ahead of us crossing the street toward the van. A boy leaned out of the car, and Santos, recognizing him, called his name. The boy hesitated for a second, but Santos saw a flash of metal and an arm pointed toward Nathan's receding back. Santos yelled again, and running, tackled Nathan just as the gunshot tore through the night. The kids on the front lawn began yelling and screaming, their need for violence finally finding an adequate expression.

The rest of us ran to where Santos had fallen, blood spewing from somewhere on his body, as the sound of the car's tires squealing off.

Nathan scrambled away; his face again contorted with fear. When he turned, he saw Santos, and in anguish yelled, "No!" He turned back, and quickly kneeled alongside his friend. "Where were you hit? Santos, where are you hit!" He yelled. Santos opened his eyes.

"Not sure...I think ...they got... my arm, man," he answered with a groan. We were all frantically searching for something clean to staunch the wound. "Call 911!" I heard several people yell, and the house began to empty. Drugs disappeared, and the backyard dumpster began filling with empty beer cans and bottles.

"Are you all right, Raphael?" Hailey asked, her voice breaking.

"Yea, but my arm, it's starting to sting bad," he said, his voice barely more than a whisper.

Tessa kneeled near his head. "Let's see. Lifting two multi-colored garments and exposing yet another, she reached into an interior pocket and pulled out a large white handkerchief. It glowed, strangely luminescent in the night. "Here," she said, "I'd been wrapping the chain in this."

Jack took it and tore it into four wide strips, knotted it and handed it to Hailey. She looked up at him with gratitude, and tightly, but carefully, wrapped the bleeding wound. It was then I did the most amazing thing.

"Let's pray," I said, totally shocked when the words came out of my mouth. I mean, there we sat, smack dab in the middle of a bunch of onlookers, some I'm sure who knew me. All were coming from the biggest—and obviously, by very perverted standards—*but still*— coolest high school party of the year and maybe decade, and still I wanted to hold hands and pray. But when the rubber meets the road, it's a dang good thing to have some tread, and well, I was finding out I did.

The four of us began praying, Tessa, Hailey, Jack, and me, and then I saw Nathan place his hand on Santos. He started praying, too. After a few minutes I noticed one more pair. They were old, and wrinkled, and they poked out of tattered sleeves. I looked up into the merry twinkle of Darius.

It seemed so out of place that look of cheer. My mouth opened to say something, but she winked, and nothing came out. I was instantly enveloped in a sense of peace. A distant wailing caught my attention, and I looked down at Santos. "Are you doing OK?" I asked.

"Yea, I feel warm," he answered. Hailey caressed the side of his face with her fingers. The ambulance arrived seconds later, and Santos was able to stand and get in with only a hand up. And he asked Hailey to go with him.

The rest of us, including Darius followed in the van. When we opened the door, Christian was sitting up, looking much more like himself. "What's all the commotion about?" he asked, as we piled in. "I started to get out and see..." He caught sight of Darius and stopped.

"Ah, this must be the valiant, and remarkable young warrior all the heavenly realm is still buzzing about! I am so pleased to finally meet you! It's Christian, isn't it?" Darius said, clapping her hands together, her face wreathed in smiles. "How aptly named you are, but then your mother, ah yes, she had already discerned many things about you!"

"What...really?"

"Hey, Darius," Jack called from the front, "Don't be telling him stuff that will give him any bigger head than he already has!" he said, laughing with Nathan who rode beside him.

Christian smiled. "Ha, ha," he said, turning in the seat toward Jack. But he quickly turned back. "It's really nice to meet you, Darius. I've been hoping I would," he said to her in a voice not quite back to normal.

"Believe me, the pleasure, as well as, the honor, is mine."

I'd never seen Christian blush, but he turned red. I almost started laughing, but managed to stop. I decided Darius was right; it *was* an honor to meet him. However, I knew that even though this was a private admission—sooner or later I'd probably kick myself for even thinking it.

Darius turned toward Tessa, and her face became radiant. "My Heaven—what an extraordinary night. It will be some time before *you* feel quite yourself again." Tessa lowered her eyes and smiled wearily. "Ah yes, my dear, I know. But Tessa, there is something more required of you before this day is over. In fact, before the hour is through, I'm afraid." Even though Tessa's small face was pinched and fatigued, she silently nodded.

"It is because of your strength and character, and, at least in part, your willingness. Even when you are so weary, you were still chosen as the *link*." Darius said smiling, "Which, I must tell you, is not what you are any longer. Now you are simply Theresa, that is, Tessa, Connor. But the mantle you've been given, will, in time, come into fruition and aid you in your quest to serve the Lord."

"And tonight?" Tessa asked.

"Ah yes, tonight! Tonight, the mantle's power is available for a short time in its pure form. Much of it was used when you destroyed a major demon, and what a great work was accomplished! So many lives have been saved this day...so many lives. Rasvampin was not named a 'Destroyer' lightly."

Darius smiled as if to herself, and I saw something I'd never seen before, a look behind the twinkle of her eyes that made only a part of her seem old, while another glinted young, and hard and strong like steel. The instant was gone, and she was back. Smiling, she continued; "Rasvampin would never guess that children could find his weakness. That hope for his 'demon self' and forgiveness, that prayer for his 'un-soul,' could destroy him. Anything else would simply send him back to Hell; and there, he would mount another attack, at another time."

"So, someone *prayed* for him?" Christian asked incredulously. Everyone nodded, laughing. Only I looked out at the passing scenery, embarrassed. "Wait, let me guess..." he said. And I glanced over to find him smiling at me like a loon.

"Darius, I don't know if Christian just looks goofy right now because of that silly grin on his face, or if it's because of Rasvampin's whip. Although, he really doesn't look ...quite right ...at all," I said, honestly. Christian bent his head sideways and gave me what was supposed to be a smirk, but he couldn't pull it off, and now I was really concerned.

"Well, Cassie, that brings me back to my point. Although Christian's wounds are spiritual, they are very severe, indeed. Tonight, his bravery went beyond the enemy's ability to fathom in one so young," Darius smiled, turning her bright twinkling eyes on Christian's now sober face. Turning toward Tessa, she continued. "But they don't know how many years this young man has trained—righteous, deserving—yet he was held in reserve. So, when his time arrived—" She turned back to Christian, "you would hold nothing back—and tonight you gave all—and even more. The Father is well-pleased... Oh good and faithful servant."

Christian who had no emotional reserves, tried very hard to maintain his composure, but gave in and folded one arm over his eyes and wept. Darius looked at Tessa. "Place your hands up, palms toward him, and begin praying silently whatever prayer comes to your mind. The power of the Lord is placed upon you through this. Your mantle will heal his spiritual wounds. We sat silently as Tessa prayed until we reached the hospital.

Chapter Thirty-Three

"You're a lucky boy," the doctor informed Santos while the rest of us stood around the end of the padded steel table where he sat. He'd already been given a tetanus shot, and the nurse finished wrapping his arm in a white bandage. "They missed your brachial artery by centimeters and your heart by inches," the doctor continued, "As it is, there should have been more blood loss, but I understand this young lady bandaged you," He said, looking over at Hailey's reddening face. "You did an excellent job staunching the blood flow. You should consider becoming a nurse," he said.

"Or a doctor," I added.

He smiled at me. "Or a doctor." He cleared his throat. "I want to look at this in the next few days, but I don't see any reason to think there will be a problem. Like I said, you're one lucky boy." He started to walk out but turned back. "What happened, anyway?"

"He saved my life, that's what happened," Nathan said, going over and shaking hands with the doctor. "Thanks for taking care of him. Then walking back to Santos, Nathan said, "Thanks, man, I owe you."

"You don't owe me anything," Santos said smiling, "That's what it's all about, man." Nathan looked away. "What's the matter?" Santos asked.

"Ah, nothing. I'm a slow learner, but I think I'm finally catching on," he said, looking over at Jack. Jack nodded and smiled, but then kept talking to Tessa like he wasn't paying any attention. *Guys*, I thought, *would it kill them to hug?*

Jack and Nathan aside, my attention was constantly drawn to Darius who'd stayed with us. She had the most amazing calm about her, and it helped me just to look at her. Finally, she decided to speak. The doctor had gone, explaining he still needed to fill out a police report, and instructing Santos to wait until a detective got a statement from him before going home.

"Your mother and father are on their way," Darius told Santos, beaming her smile upon him. Then she looked at the rest of us. "I want to tell you all something. Amazing events occurred this night. Things beyond even our expectations! We hoped! And oh, had great faith, but to have this end so well!" She looked at Nathan. "To have you with us..."

"What?" I asked, startled. "Wasn't Nathan supposed to be *with* us?"

Darius smiled at me. "Actually, Nathan was in less physical danger than the rest of you," she said. "But there was very real danger for each of you Guardians, and we despaired for Nathan's spiritual decision right to the end. The outcome was so much more than many had predicted..."

"Why, Darius? Why did things change?" Hailey asked.

"Because of the choices all of you made. Christian, willing to give himself so bravely for Cassie, was hoped for— but could he—would he? When he did, it was miraculous! But Cassie's decision to face Rasvampin? To challenge him?

Only her courage, and Jack's wisdom, could lead her there. Oh, the fate that turned with *that* decision. Surely, at least one of you, would have been impaled by the whip's fangs in the realm of that room tonight." I swallowed, remembering how close they had come to me.

"And Nathan," she said turning to him, "you *are* with us. Had you resisted and gone the way of the world, another would have taken the bullet tonight. It would not have passed through Santos' arm—the timing so different, you see—but into Jack. ...Shot in the back." I saw Nathan's head jerk up and his eyes focus on Darius. I felt my own heart lurch.

"What?"

"This was a scenario played out before us—and all heaven wept! The great warrior struck down by the Demon Destroyer's instructions to his remaining slave Maltorph. And yet, the greater grief was for you, dear boy." Nathan met Jack's eyes for a moment, and I couldn't tell what passed between them. Both their eyes were so intense; their faces completely still. "I could go on, and on," Darius continued. "This was not a game. The conclusions were never sure. But Rasvampin is gone. A victory no one in Hell, not Satan himself, foresaw! And Heaven! Such rejoicing! Oh, there were so many angels out in the upper realms I was nearly blinded!" She said, beaming. She stopped for a moment and then said quietly, "Now, you all need to get some rest; and Raphael, you and Christian must heal up."

Everyone was quiet, but the room seemed full of something unsaid. Finally, Santos looked up. "We're not done, are we?" He asked, his voice weary.

"Oh, my dear boy—I wish I could say you were. I wish I could say it was over. But I think you know it is not. Hell is quite undone—there is revenge in the wind." Darius looked off for an instant and then was back, bright eyed. "But this is not to be worried about now!" She smiled again at Nathan.

"And I am so glad you are with us—and I believe you will find, you are in need of us, too." I realized Darius meant this in more ways than he realized, but Nathan nodded and looked toward the floor. I could tell he wasn't completely sure about anything now. Oh, I knew what being a charter member of that club felt like.

Well, I couldn't be sure about the others, but the little bit of news about more hell on earth, came as a blow to me. Suddenly, I was feeling a bit strange about the way things had ended. It was like we were all going to be milling around the lobby of life during intermission to, *"Hell on Wheels: Part II of the Rasvampin Horror Show."* But right now, I was too tired to argue or throw a fit. I'd take an intermission. Jack looked over at me and said, "Come on, let's get everybody home. We all need rest." Hailey looked over and told Santos she'd call him in the morning. I went over and hugged him, and Tessa followed. I think that gave Hailey nerve because she backtracked and hugged him, too.

Darius would not let us take her home and said she had transportation. I decided I didn't want to know anything about how Darius got where she got, or knew where to go, and when, or why...or whatever else. Enough is enough.

We took Nathan back to his sports car, which luckily, he'd parked far enough away so we didn't have to see the scene of the party again. He didn't offer me a ride home, with exhaustion, fear of rejection, or a final acceptance of reality coming into play. Even though I hoped for numbers one and three, he said he'd call me.

Jack, Tessa, Hailey, and I drove almost in silence. Christian's loud, low guttural snoring was the only sound to fill the van. We dropped Hailey and Tessa off first. Hailey hugged us goodnight. Tessa kissed Jack and me, and I'm not sure she was awake when she did it. She got out like a robot and walked inside with Hailey holding her arm. I was glad they'd decided to bunk together tonight, assured that someone would help Tessa find her bed. Then I had to go home with Jack to help him unload Christian. No matter what we did it was impossible to wake the big lug up—so we had to carry him. I was beginning to wonder how long I'd feel compelled to be nice. It wasn't all that easy when a glass of cold water would have simplified this issue. Actually; it wasn't that bad. All I had to do was hold his cast up off the ground to keep it from banging around, with Jack dragging him from under his arms. But it was all the way to his room, and unbelievably, he never woke up. He was *that* tired. I kissed his mangy forehead and quietly, not that it mattered to him, I shut the door. Mrs. Graham stood at the bottom of the stairs. "Is he, all right?"

"He's just asleep. You'd have been proud of him, Mom. Lived up to his name tonight." Jack said.

She looked at her son for several seconds, and then turned her gaze on me. Satisfied, she said, "That doesn't surprise me. Turn the front light out after you walk Cassie home. Good night, Cassie. God bless you, child."

"Good night, Mrs. Graham," I said, "God bless you, and sleep well." She smiled, and turning, went back upstairs.

Jack silently walked me home under the night sky and up the stairs onto the porch. For the first time since we'd moved to Pinedale, the lights inside my house were off after ten thirty. My mom had gone to bed, and she wasn't up scouring the house... vainly searching for something she'd lost and couldn't find.

I sat down on the chaise and looked out at the trees, and without saying a word, Jack sat next to me. Feeling his eyes on me, I turned. "You did real good tonight, Cassie," he said softly.

"Thanks. You were so amazing. And Santos, and Hail..." I didn't finish because his mouth was on mine, kissing me, and it was better than anything I'd ever even dreamed ... because it was real.

"Ah ...you... know...we still have a job to do and I'm not sure Hamaliel ...would approve of this kind of hanky-panky by two of his elite demon warriors," I managed to breath onto his lips.

"This isn't hanky-panky. Don't you even know the real thing when it finally shows up, Connor? Does everything have to be explained to you a hundred times?" He asked, that sort-of smile of his lingering on his mouth. For some reason, I liked it more just now.

"Yes, well, I'm afraid Tessa got all the genius stuff, remember? So, I guess you're just going to have to go over it a few more times for me," I said, pulling his lips to mine again.

The very near future was most certainly going to be filled with demons and danger and the wicked cry of evil in the night. As we sat together holding hands and feeling that deep-down peace that comes when things are finally right, the only sound to be heard was the beginning patter of rain. The dry spell had come to an end.

Dear reader, thank you for taking the time to read, *The Guardians*. I hope you liked it.

Reviews help other readers discover my books and keep me writing. Please consider leaving an honest review on Goodreads, Amazon, or your favorite review site. It's the easiest way you can support my continued writing efforts.

Thank you and all my best,
S. Lee Holland

Book Club Questions

- What did you like best about the book?
- What did you like least about it?
- What other books did this remind you of?
- Which characters were your favorites?
- Which characters didn't you enjoy?
- What feelings did this book evoke for you?
- What do you think the author's purpose was in writing this book? What ideas was she trying to get across?
- How original or unique was this book?
- Did this book seem realistic?
- How well do you think the author built the world in the book?
- Did the characters seem believable to you? Did they remind you of anyone?
- Did the book's pace seem too fast/too slow/just right?
- How original and unique was this book?
- Had you heard about the book before starting it? Do you think it was overhyped or should be celebrated more?

Acknowledgments

I'd like to thank those who along the way read the book and encouraged me: my sister, Lynne Schwarm, friends Deb Hernandez and Michelle Bower, my compatriot Don Ham, who was a part of my own high school experience, my wonderful sons Corban and Tyler, and most importantly, the man who has stood beside me through this journey and fifty years' worth of many extraordinary adventures, my beloved husband, Carty.

I would also like to thank Zamiz Press for their commitment to making a better book. Thank you to Marie White, Eliza, Nathan and all those involved for their advice, encouragement and insights, which have been immensely helpful.

About the Author

S. Lee Holland has always been a prodigious reader and writer of stories. But even before this, her relationship with God came before all else. Books have always given S. Lee great happiness, and she hoped one day to give back some of that experience to others. After raising four children, she returned to school and graduated with honors in English Literature from Cal Poly San Luis Obispo. In her debut novel, The Guardians, she delves into the subject of a high school girl's struggle with belief and identity in the midst of supernatural adventure and the joy that comes from standing in faith.

S. Lee Holland has always wielded a mighty pen. From her youth, books served as a wellspring of joy for Holland,

and it was her fervent hope that one day she might kindle a similar flame in the hearts of others. Holland has taken up her pen in her debut novel *The Guardians*.

You can connect with Sharon at https://kieuz-freary-kwouds.yolasite.com.